BLOODLINES

BOOK ONE OF THE GUARDIAN OF EMPIRE CITY SERIES

PETER HARTOG

To Ms. Long, who encouraged my imagination.

To Doug, whose still waters always run deep.

To my dad, my biggest cheerleader, and the man who taught me character is about action, and not words.

To Traci, who is my rock, and the boys, who are my world.

And to my mom, for buying me books, and everything else that matters.

CONTENTS

CHAPTER 1

*N*o matter what century you live in, the world will always be filled with assholes.

"Watch the threads, man!" my prisoner cried as I led him roughly toward the booking officer's workstation. The suit's hands were cuffed behind his back. I put my hand on his shoulder and drove him face-first into the top of the metal desk.

Hard.

"Oops, my bad," I said, then grabbed his shoulder again and shoved him into the chair.

"I'll have your badge, asshole!" he sputtered.

See what I mean? Blood from a split lip decorated his starched dress shirt in pretty crimson splotches.

"Yeah, you and everyone else," I muttered, then nodded at the booking officer, who gave me an aggrieved look before manipulating the virtual controls of his workstation.

Holo-windows clung to the air above the workstation, translucent bubbles full of text and images. The glimmering ghosts contained the personal data of James Reynolds, including enclave ID, home address, and known associates.

"Now, nice Sergeant Collins here is going to ask you some

questions," I instructed. "Cooperate and make this quick, or I'll dump your sorry ass Upstairs. I hear the crazies love Wall Street boys. A pretty e-trader like you will fit right in."

It wasn't an idle threat. "Upstairs" referred to the holding cells on the floor above where all the violent offenders cooked before being sent offsite to less pleasant accommodations. Downstairs catered to a tamer crowd—drunks, *goldjoy* addicts, and anyone not sent Upstairs. I'd dubbed the rest of the 98th Precinct's Central Investigation and Resources Division "Purgatory" the day after I'd arrived here six years ago.

"I know my rights, Holliday," he stiffened. "You wouldn't dare."

"Try me," I growled.

The name's Thomas Henry Holliday. Sometimes I worked the homicide table for the Empire City Police Department. Most days, though, I was chained to a desk filing everyone else's paperwork.

What few friends I had called me "Doc." While I liked to think that I'd earned the tough guy sobriquet after the famous gunslinger, the truth is I had a PhD in classical literature from Empire City University.

Oh, and a Master's in gourmet cooking. I was a pro at boiling water.

But I still had plenty of bite to go with my bark. You see, I used to be one of the three best homicide detectives in Empire City. Used to be.

"Holliday!" Lieutenant Joan Flanagan bellowed from across the room.

God, I hated mornings. Especially Mondays. And, in my experience, nothing good ever happened on a Monday.

Guess which day it was?

"In a minute," I yelled back.

The bullpen was busy today. And loud. I had already developed a nice headache from spending the past five sleepless nights interviewing witnesses, collecting evidence and running down the

2

leads. By the third day, it had escalated into a full-blown pounding.

"Your desk in ten," Flanagan ordered.

"Whatever," I sighed.

"I want my lawyer," Reynolds whined. A sullen red weal had formed on his face from where it had met the table. "I want my call. I want—"

I'd had enough.

"Listen up, pal." I leaned in close. "I've got you on Murder One for the job you pulled on Frederick Murray last Thursday. Remember him, your co-worker whose drink you spiked with 'joy at D'Antoni's Rooftop Bar? Then he 'accidentally' fell ten stories to splatter his brains all over the clean pavement? Did you know he had a three-year-old daughter named Molly? Thanks to you, someone else will have to walk Molly down the aisle. So shut the fuck up, you sack of shit. Your life is officially over."

"I don't give a fuck about them," he sneered. "Or you."

Something in his voice gave me pause. A familiar tingling formed around my eyes, then raced down my back. My hands trembled. I clenched them into fists in the vain hope that would halt the tremors, but my breathing quickened in time with my racing heartbeat. The precinct's clamor dropped to a dull roar, as if I stood behind a closed door in another room. I concentrated on the cocky e-trader in his designer suit and slick hair, my eyes burning with a white fire only I could see.

Suddenly, true dread dripped into my bones.

Reynolds' features bled away, his face growing sallow and sunken. Withered, dry tissue covered his body, as if his skin was wrinkled parchment. Gone was the arrogant businessman, replaced by a helpless scarecrow, all scrawny arms and legs. A twisted shade had wound itself around the cadaver that had once been a man, trapping Reynolds in its intimate embrace. Small motes of living light seeped from the e-trader's flesh in a glittering shower. Each fragment was plucked from the air by the creature's shadowy fingers, then devoured as if it was the finest of delicacies.

My mind reeled at the sight. The parasite was grafted to the man in ways I couldn't begin to imagine. I experienced Reynolds' agony as something tangible and real. Paralyzed by horror and fear, I was transfixed by this tableau of a helpless, soulless man, and the thing born from nightmares that fed on him.

The shade regarded me with dark, endless eyes. It uttered an empty shriek, but I heard nothing.

And then the vision was gone.

Reality returned in a blinding rush. I jerked backward and jostled the empty desk behind me, bashing my hip. Jolts of pain coursed down my leg. I caught myself before I toppled over.

"When I'm finished with you, you'll wish you'd never been born," Reynolds shouted as two uniforms led him away to be printed and imaged. "You hear me, Holliday? YOU HEAR ME?"

I stared ahead, not registering anything. I felt wasted, as if I'd run a marathon in late summer while wearing winter clothes.

"That it?" Collins asked without looking at me. He'd been busy collating the data that he had collected from Reynolds. I blinked, quickly regaining focus, then looked around. No one else had noticed my reaction.

"Um, yeah," I said. "Yeah, thanks Mike."

I stumbled drunkenly across the floor toward my desk. Crashing into my chair, I waved a weary hand in front of my workstation to clear most of the holo-windows of filings and reports everyone else had dumped on me from the previous week. I worked a breathing exercise I'd mastered to get my shit together. My heart rate steadied, but the image of the awful thing I'd just witnessed screamed at me whenever I closed my eyes. I'd have to live with it, along with the long catalogue of other strange and horrible things that I'd encountered over the years.

I grabbed my mug and gulped half its contents, then grimaced. It was disgusting, but cold coffee was better than no coffee. The coffee slowly worked its potent spell on my body as the sludge pretending to be my brain slipped into second gear.

A lone window floated above my workstation detailing an article posted last night by a beat reporter for *The Daily Dose*. The *Dose* was an online rag full of sensationalized stories, from celebrity bed-buddies to government conspiracies. I ran through the article, using the distraction to bury my macabre encounter with Reynolds and his dark passenger to the remotest corners of my mind.

"Jesus Christ, Holliday," Flanagan interrupted, stomping toward me. "You look like shit."

The squat, carrot-topped officer hovered over my virtual workstation like the harbinger of halitosis. The fat fuck reeked of old gin, stale sex and dirty socks. I glanced up at her, my haggard face warm from the glow of flickering data flowing across my holo-screen.

"Gee, Jo, thanks for caring." I graced her with a wan smile.

"Yeah, right," the lieutenant grunted. She stepped closer to squint at my screen. "Vampire in Lower Manhattan, news at eleven." Flanagan chuckled in derision. "You actually read this horse shit?"

"Reading this 'horse shit' breaks up the monotony of my day," I replied, asserting a false bravado. Dealing with the lieutenant always brought out the best in me, which wasn't saying much.

She fixed me with a gimlet glare. "Glad to know you're so busy."

I held up a placating hand and placed the other on the wrinkled lapel of my faded brown blazer.

"As a proud member of the 98th, it is my sworn duty to protect the lives and property of our fellow citizens, and impartially enforce the law." I indicated the news story with my chin. "Besides, the vic lived nearby, in Bay Ridge."

"So?" Flanagan shrugged, her expression shifting from dour and annoyed, to dour and grim.

Flanagan gave me shit most days, but we're supposed to be people first and cops second. Sometimes I wondered which one I was.

"So," I continued, drawing out the word. "The stiff was found last night in an alley down in the Financial District. Her throat had been shredded. But here's the interesting part. According to the EMTs, there wasn't any blood. Crazy, right? I mean, no blood? How does that happen?"

Flanagan's pasty complexion grew two shades lighter. Sweat formed on her brow, and one of her eyes twitched. Not exactly the reaction I'd expect from a veteran cop who'd probably seen worse back in her glory days.

"And so now you believe some goddamn tabloid?" She recovered, clearing her throat nervously as she scanned the bustling floor. "Nice detective work, Holliday. Real professional. Is that how you close all of your cases? If it's in the Dose, it's the gospel? Let me give you a piece of advice, free of charge. Let. It. Go. It's not our jurisdiction. Besides, your old pals from downtown will handle it. Am I clear?"

"Crystal."

"And file those reports," Flanagan grumbled as she wandered off to berate another detective on the floor. "They were due *last* Monday."

I took a fortifying breath, then shunted the article aside in favor of the mountain of e-paperwork that awaited me. Dozens of holo-windows repopulated the screen. My own collar would have to wait until I'd finished with these, otherwise I'd see more of Flanagan, something I tried to avoid as often as I could.

"EVI, halt streaming and fade to black, please," I instructed. The holo-screen went dark. "Play *Sonata Pathetique,* first movement, low volume, and bring up my calendar."

Empire City's law enforcement, social services and emergency services worked within a centralized network administered by an AI called Engineered Virtual Intellect. Through the implants all

ECPD personnel carried in our skulls, I accessed a vast cloud of detailed information, manipulating the data in the literal blink of my eye.

EVI controlled everything, right down to the lunch menu. To some, it was scary, but the machines hadn't taken over just yet.

I had no idea what they were waiting for.

The tech boys had given the AI a soft, feminine voice because they were a bunch of frustrated nerds who needed more holo-porn.

"You're welcome, Detective Holliday," EVI replied coolly in my ear.

The soft melody in C-minor floated through my brain's audio center. A grid materialized in the top right corner of my main holo-screen outlining the month of October. Other than today, a single cube next week containing the image of a grinning jack-o'-lantern stood out from an otherwise empty calendar.

I sighed, then downed the rest of my coffee. With my headache fizzled, I got to work.

An hour later, I wandered to the break room for a fresh cup of java, navigating the frenetic floor as officers escorted handcuffed perps decrying the system or pleading their innocence. A handful of officers nodded as I passed, but most ignored me.

Armed with a full mug, I loped back to my little slice of heaven. Three prostitutes, each cuffed to a different chair, blew me lewd kisses with their free hands. My tired grin broadened as one offered up a few interesting suggestions on what we could do later if I happened to find the keycode to her cuffs. I chuckled, shook my head and walked away.

At least someone wanted me.

To be honest, I'm not what you'd call pretty. Disheveled and careworn, I sported a broken nose and deep, dark circles under my baby blues. Measuring around six feet, I was wiry, but made of thin-corded muscle. As the old saying went, mine was a face for radio.

My scratched and crooked desk rested in a nook, obstructed by the blunted corner of a faded and cracked plaster wall. I sat alone, ostensibly due to a lack of space to accommodate a partner, which was convenient since I'd never been assigned one. I'm like your annoying Uncle Frank who no one wanted to get stuck with at the family reunion. Except for the occasional table scrap Flanagan tossed my way, my case load was non-existent.

As I turned the corner, I came up short, spilling hot coffee on my hand.

"Morning," the man occupying my chair said with a cheerful drawl. Shrewd brown eyes regarded me.

I flicked my wet hand in annoyance, then set the mug down with care.

"Not a bad job with that fuckwad, Holliday," he continued placidly. "Open-and-shut. Still, anyone given a shit case like that would have to be a complete idiot to fuck it up."

He was my age, somewhere between late thirties and early forties. Sharp features framed high cheekbones, a hawk nose and grizzled mustache with goatee. A small silver hoop hung from his left ear. Dressed in street clothes beneath an ill-fitting leather jacket, he resembled one of Sam Gaffney's narcs. Cigarette smoke clung to him like a second skin. Faded white scars crisscrossed the knuckles of both hands, and old calluses decorated the tips of his fingers. The man was no stranger to a fight.

"Who are you?" I asked, eyes narrowing.

"Deacon Kole." He didn't extend a hand. "You boys in Empire City sure do like your e-paperwork. Damn, son, it's a wonder y'all get anything done 'round here."

I frowned. He seemed at ease, but I'd catch his eyes straying past my shoulder. It was something born from habit, a practiced paranoia all cops learn early in their careers. That's when I made him.

"You're a *Protector*," I said. "What do you want?"

The Confederate States of Birmingham was the seat of religious extremism and intolerance on this side of the world. The Deep South survivors of the worldwide terrorist nukes and the pandemics that had followed rallied around churches, using faith as the driving force for unity. Their enclave ruthlessly excised differing beliefs, adhering to a rigid morality. Decades later, the lunatics in the CSB still believed the Rapture had happened, and Armageddon wasn't far behind.

As for the Protectors, they were Birmingham's twisted version of cops. From everything I'd heard, they were first-class nut-jobs, acting as judge, jury and executioner.

To say this guy's presence was unusual was like saying the sun rose in the west.

The look he gave me was cool, the expression shifting to something more calculating. It was the kind reserved for idiots and unpleasant meals.

"Former Protector," Deacon corrected, offering me a humorless smile. "The Church and I had a come-to-Jesus meeting a while back. We decided to part ways."

"You didn't answer my question," I pointed out.

Deacon's smile widened, never reaching his eyes. He was taking my measure, and it annoyed the shit out of me.

"How'd you know it was the e-trader?" he asked.

"What?" I frowned.

"Your collar," he said. "How'd you know it was him?"

The tingling sensation from before returned, rippling along the back of my neck, as if I were standing near a live current. However, my eyes felt normal.

"I interviewed Murray's assistant, Glenn Abernathy," I said slowly, wondering where this was leading. "There was a fresh bouquet of white lilies in a vase on his desk the first day I came by the office. No card attached, and he wasn't wearing a ring. When I met with the suspect, his office held several images showing where he'd traveled, and most of those accompanied by young, attractive men. Then I noticed one shot of him standing next to an older woman in a garden filled with lilies. Turns out Reynolds' mom grew them at her home."

Deacon leaned back in my chair, hands clasped behind his head. He propped his soaked boots on my desk with a thump. Rainwater collected underneath.

"You mind?" I glared at the boots. He didn't move. "Fine. The 'joy in Murray's system was out of character, although he could've hidden the habit. Add in Abernathy, the lilies, and Reynolds' lifestyle, as well as a limited suspect pool. It didn't take much to figure out Reynolds' relationship with Abernathy gave him the access he needed to steal Murray's key accounts. As for D'Antoni's, it had plenty of distractions making it easy for Reynolds to spike Murray's drink and then let the drug do the rest. Motive and opportunity. We done here?"

"Very logical, Holliday," Deacon spoke quietly. "But that's bullshit, and we both know it."

"Listen, pal," I shot back. "I've got fifteen years as both a beat cop and homicide detective in the ECPD. I investigate and ask questions, because that's how it's done. I pay attention, follow the leads, review the evidence and reports, and sometimes I get lucky and catch the bad guy."

"No shit, Sherlock," Deacon scoffed. "Just like every other dipshit here. But you ain't like everyone else. They don't know it. But I do."

"I don't have time for this," I declared. "Get out of my chair, get away from desk, and leave me the fuck alone. I'm busy."

I folded my arms and gave him my best glower. It was like trying to melt spell-forged steel with a candle.

"No need to get so riled up, Holliday," Deacon replied mildly while rifling through the text on my screen. The details of the *Dose* article reappeared, scrolling along like some abstract painting. He flicked the holo-window away with a lazy wave of his hand, then turned to regard me.

"What did you see back there?" he asked.

"Excuse me?" My face flushed with anger.

"You heard me." Deacon's intense dark eyes bored holes into mine. "What did you *see*?"

"Who the fuck *are* you?"

A cold lump settled in my stomach. I glanced over my shoulder, wondering if anyone on the floor had noticed our exchange.

"They're all busy, and don't give a shit about you," Deacon said. "Don't fuck up this opportunity, son. It's the best chance you're gonna have to get out of this shithole."

CHAPTER 2

"I've read your file, Holliday," he stated with a hard stare. "You were hot shit before Internal Affairs tore you a new hole seven years ago. But they never did pin anything on you, did they? Then came the booze and drugs. Or were you already fucked up by then?"

My face went slack, and I stared at the chipped paint on the wall behind Deacon. Bitter images of the past flooded my mind, from a time when I took care of my appearance, the clothes I wore, and the people I once called friends. Don't get me wrong, I was also young and stupid and no one's angel. I'd just pissed off the right people at the wrong time. And I hadn't been the only one. A lot of other cops had lost their shields after that shit show. IAD and the DA's office had been thorough. Mostly.

"Don't really matter." Deacon shrugged. "You checked into rehab, put your life on hold while you got your shit together. Toed the line and followed department policy. When you got out, you'd been exonerated and reinstated, even kept your shield, which is a fucking miracle by itself. But the backlash to the department sent you packing, which is how you wound up here. Lucky you."

"Ancient history, pal," I replied, folding my arms.

ECPD had been embarrassed by the investigation. Despite my reinstatement, something had to be done to salvage their precious public image. Mayor Harold Samson wanted heads rolled, so I was elected one of their fall guys.

At the time, it seemed a proper penance. The slings and arrows of outrageous fortune buried Hamlet. They nearly buried me.

"But that ain't the whole story."

The hair on the back of my neck stood on end. A faint buzzing rattled my ears. My body trembled, but not from any chill. Sweat formed on my brow.

My chest tightened as I experienced a very old and familiar agony. Deacon observed me with hooded eyes.

"You want to tell me what happened?"

"You seem to already know."

"Humor me." Deacon's voice was iron and stone.

"Fine." I wiped my nose, then ran a jerky hand through my hair several times. I paused, my lips struggling to form the words. Deacon sat motionless, a grim specter awaiting judgment. "She... Kate...she'd broken the bathroom mirror. Punched it, because her knuckles were cut. I found empty goldjoy syringes by the tub. She'd taken three full hits. And she just lay in that tub, in that bloody water. I couldn't wake her. I tried, but she wouldn't wake up. And the blood...the blood was everywhere. She'd slashed her wrists with the glass. I was too late. There was nothing I could do. But I couldn't let her die alone. I couldn't. The glass covered the floor. I picked up a piece of it, and I..."

Everything came out in a rush. I couldn't stop myself, somehow compelled by Deacon Kole. I stood there lost to the memory of that night, reliving each awful moment. But I couldn't finish it, either. Despite whatever power the former Protector held over me just then, the memory hurt too much. I hurt too much.

"Kate Foster was pronounced dead at the scene," Deacon said after a moment, his voice cool and calm. Whatever compulsion I'd been experiencing had disappeared. "Lucky for you one of the facility's attendants had come by to check on her. He called it in, and between the onsite medical staff and the EMTs, they kept you alive long enough to get you to the hospital."

I rubbed my arms, noting the worn and frayed cuffs. I pulled back one to stare at the jagged marks on my wrist, consumed by a terrible loss.

And Kate.

In five minutes, this stranger laid bare a part of me that I'd buried for years. Nobody at the 98th cared about me. I was the pariah who was damn good at filing their paperwork. My past was old news. Faded, but not forgotten. However, no one here knew what had transpired the day Kate died.

No one except Deacon Kole.

"How do you know all of this?" I hissed, my mind awash with memory and pain.

"Because it's my job."

"I-I don't understand."

"Wake the fuck up, Holliday." Deacon leaned closer, pressing his fingers against my desk.

"What's happening?"

"Look at me," the Confederate commanded. I met his hard gaze. "When you met James Reynolds at his office, from that very moment, you knew he'd murdered Murray. How did you know?"

I stood still, afraid that if I moved, every little secret I'd kept over the years would spill out in a mad rush.

"How did you know?"

"Because—"

"Because you looked upon his soul," Deacon supplied.

"No," I replied, resigned and bitter. "Because I saw he didn't have one."

Deacon studied me with a passionless expression on his worn face.

"I ain't never met a dead man walking before," he said quietly.

"Well, not like you, but I reckon there's a first time for everything." The Confederate stood up and maneuvered around my desk. "Interview's over. Let's take a walk."

"What?" I asked, shoulders bunched as tension ate at my every nerve.

Without answering, he moved from my chair, turned the corner and strode down a side hallway off the main floor. I followed, shambling like a zombie from a bad horror holo-movie. A few strange looks came my way, but I ignored them.

A shadowed hallway greeted our approach, a section of empty offices designated for a new racketeering unit that never panned out. He proceeded toward a square of light at the far end, then stepped into the shadow of an open doorway.

I hesitated, glancing over my shoulder.

"He ain't waitin' all day, Holliday," the former Protector called out before stepping inside.

Doubt crowded my mind. Behind me, the dull roar of the 98th beckoned, a familiar buzzing that spoke of dead ends and old routines. I sucked in a breath, then crossed the distance and into the office. Deacon closed the door behind me, and leaned against it, arms crossed. Stark white paint covered the walls, with boring slate gray carpet on the floor—the cheap, durable kind. The office included an empty workstation and two chairs, but no holo-tech.

A white-haired man wearing a charcoal suit and navy dress shirt unbuttoned at the top sat behind the desk. He was past sixty, clean-shaven with deep shadows beneath intelligent, wintry eyes, and sunken cheeks. A plain gold wedding band encircled one finger. His gnarled hands rested atop a thin yellow folder, a classic nod to the old paper-pushers from a bygone age.

Curiosity overcame the emotional muck slogging my brain. My heart rate settled to something short of cardiac arrest. The hint of fresh coffee and cigarettes hung in the air, though neither was present.

"Bill Mahoney," I said, registering surprise. "What are you doing back in town? I thought you were retired."

"Technically, I still am," he replied, studying me for a moment.

His was a grandfather's voice, gravelly from hard years of smoking and drinking.

The older man gestured for me to sit.

Captain William "Bill" Mahoney was a legend. He had handled all ECPD's high-profile cases. The man got shit done. Entire classes were taught at the Academy devoted to his old case files. I would've sat through all of them twice if my instructors had let me.

Mahoney's final case was the "Midnight Murders," a run of brutal serial killings that involved young women. All the victims had been sexually assaulted before their throats were slit. Medical examiners determined their time of death was around midnight, hence the name. Bill spent two years working the case.

The last victim was an ECU student named Cheryl Dwyer. During a random goldjoy bust, the narcs found her body stashed inside the basement of a vacant house in Bedford Stuy. Once Dwyer was identified, Mahoney and his team went to her home in Queens. There they discovered she had an unopened birthday present sent from her English Lit professor, Mark Madsen. On a hunch, Bill dug deeper into Madsen, and then the pieces fell into place.

Madsen had led a cult of whack-job fanatics who worshipped the professor like he was the Prince of Darkness. Dwyer had been a cultist for a short time but wanted out. Madsen didn't take it well and made her an example to the others.

Mahoney arrested Madsen before a full classroom. Social media exploded with videos of a furious Madsen stabbing an officer with an antique dagger. Forensics found traces of Dwyer's DNA on the blade, and that was that. Later that year, Madsen was electrocuted on live holo-vision. Before he died, he vowed vengeance on Bill and his family.

Three months later, Mahoney came home to find his wife and son murdered in the same manner. The subsequent investigation came up with nothing. They presumed the murderer was a protégé the ECPD had missed. Eventually, the case was closed. No suspects, and no arrests.

But Bill couldn't let it go. He continued his own private investigation, and a lot of folks downtown thought he'd lost more than his family that night. Eventually, he turned in his sidearm and badge, packed his bags, and left Empire City faster than you can say "Fuck this, I'm outta here."

That was more than ten years ago. Speculation was, he'd traveled east to get as far from here as possible. But I'd always wondered. Forensics never discovered how Madsen had removed the evidence from every crime scene. And top that off with Mahoney's family murdered from beyond the grave, in the exact same manner?

My money was on magic, and not the good kind.

I knew better than most. A shard of broken glass had taught me that.

Madsen had performed sorcery, the same foul magic the ancient poets scribed about. Mahoney couldn't prove it, but Madsen had manipulated the Nexus Point energy in ways that baffled the imagination. To me, magic was the only answer that made any sense.

None of that, however, explained why the captain was here, or what he wanted with me.

"And you're late." Mahoney drank in Deacon with a hard look. "What the hell happened to you?"

"Got sidetracked," Deacon huffed.

Mahoney's brow rose, sparing a pointed glance toward the leather jacket Deacon wore.

"Had to teach a banger a lesson on my way over here," the former Protector chuckled, admiring how his arms protruded from the shorter sleeves. "My umbrella broke over the fucker's head, so I took his jacket."

"You know, there's this wonderful invention called public transportation," the older man sighed. "Gets you places without walking all over creation. And they're enclosed, so that way you stay dry and comfortable, and still get to your appointments on time."

"Yeah, and then the woman that banger assaulted would be dead," Deacon shot back. "Y'all can keep your fucking transit *pods.*"

He removed the jacket and dumped it to the floor, favoring his right side. Underneath, Deacon wore a plain black t-shirt, torn in places and covered with grimy splotches. His arms were lean and muscled, with faded tattoos along his upper arms, although I couldn't make out what they were. An ugly bruise covered the underside of his right forearm, along with a few cuts and dried blood. A fine silver chain hung at his neck. As he stuffed it beneath his shirt, I spied a silver lemniscate charm attached.

Strange it wasn't a cross or a patron saint. Confederates weren't known for quitting the faith. Had Deacon managed to leave behind more than just his job? I couldn't imagine the Church of the Tribulation taking that snub well. Birmingham's intolerance of everyone other than their own usually ended in stakes and fire.

Mahoney produced a pair of tortoise shell frames from an inner pocket and settled them on his nose. He opened the folder and sifted through a variety of documents, many of them bearing the official seal of the mayor's office. He reviewed the papers, withdrew a single page, and returned the rest.

"Tom, I'm heading up a newly-formed Special Crimes Unit, and I'd like you to be a part of it," Mahoney said without preamble, removing the glasses and placing them atop the file. "You'll have jurisdiction over the entire enclave. The purpose of this taskforce is to solve the unsolvable and inexplicable by any means necessary."

"Okay, I'll bite," I said, my emotions settling as the gears ground in my head. "What's the catch?"

"You say anything to him?" Mahoney addressed Deacon.

"Didn't want to steal your thunder," the Confederate replied.

"Right," Mahoney said, eyes glittering, then turned back to me. "The catch is you won't be official ECPD anymore, although you'll still have your chip and full access to EVI. You'll lose your seniority, all your benefits, vacation time. Everything."

I raised my eyebrows, but the captain continued before I could interrupt.

"As far as everyone else at the 98th is concerned, you've been transferred somewhere else doing none of their goddamn business. In the beginning, only the mayor, DA, and a consultant will know your purpose. You'll report to me, and me only, acting under my authority."

"Okay, but this sounds more like a job for the ECBI," I pointed out. "Won't we be stepping on their toes?"

"No." Mahoney grimaced as if he'd just swallowed day-old puke. "I've already been down that road. They aren't equipped to deal with the things that I want Special Crimes to handle."

"Such as what, exactly?" I asked.

"Things that require more than a badge, a pair of handcuffs and a warrant," Mahoney replied, fierce heat coating his words. "Things that laugh at the law, thinking they are above, or beyond it. Things that don't give a damn about you or me."

"You mean things like Mark Madsen," I said.

He exhaled like a balloon with a slow leak.

"Something like that."

"Fair enough," I conceded, "but there must be dozens of guys that are more qualified. Why me?"

Mahoney exchanged a look with Deacon.

"Thirty-one, actually," the former Protector drawled. "Took me two years to narrow the list down to five. The other four were too fucking incompetent."

"And I'm not?" I leaned back in the chair. "Tell that to Joan Flanagan."

"For the last six years, you've done a helluva job burying yourself in this shithole," Deacon stated. "In that time, you've worked twelve cases, and every single one ended with an arrest and conviction. Nobody's that good, yet here you are."

"Maybe I'm just lucky," I quipped.

"Cut the crap, Holliday," Mahoney snapped. "That doesn't happen by chance unless there's something else at play."

"Captain, you've been out of Empire City for years," I countered. "And now, suddenly, you're back and offer me a job, someone you barely know, but have obviously researched. And I'm supposed to just accept it?"

"He's got a point, Bill," Deacon chuckled.

Mahoney caught himself as if about to say something, then fell back in the chair. He looked older, as if the world had beaten the shit out of him, and then came back to kick him some more.

"Tom, we need you," he sighed. "Empire City needs you. If you've read the latest feeds, then you know what I'm talking about."

Out of the corner of my eye, I noticed Deacon shift his weight.

"The so-called vampire killing?" I asked, incredulous. "Even if I believed the story, it's not my problem. Downtown Homicide's handling it."

"No, I appropriated it an hour after it was called in," Mahoney said. "The scene is clean. It's SCU's now, and I want you taking point on the investigation. You've got a gift that gives you something, an edge, an ability to see the truth for what it is. You can rationalize all you want about logic, doing the dirty work, following the leads. But there's more to you than meets the eye, and we know it."

"It's more than instinct," Deacon added. "You've got a supernatural perception you've kept hidden from the other fucktards here. I've heard about your gift in other places, but ain't never seen it myself, until I showed up this morning."

"Tom, I know this isn't easy, but I need you to trust me," the captain said. "Something happened to you the night Kate Foster committed suicide. We need to know what."

I chewed on that, weighing the possibilities. Denial would get me nowhere. And it wasn't like they were wrong.

So I decided to go with the truth.

CHAPTER 3

"After...rehab...and Kate," I explained, choosing my words with care, "the world around me possessed a new clarity. I thought I was hallucinating, some aftereffect of the detox process that purged the chemicals from my system. One night, I noticed a woman sitting alone at the bar. As I watched, everything about her changed. Her clothes, her face, even her skin, as if a curtain had been drawn away to expose the truth."

What I said wasn't entirely true. All rehab did was screw my head on straight enough to realize something more profound had happened to me when I used the glass on my wrists. I paused to gauge the reactions of both men. Deacon didn't miss much with that glare of his. He could probably smell a lie like alcohol on my breath. They looked at me expectantly, so I plowed ahead.

"This went beyond simple profiling and gut instinct. I somehow understood that woman's intent and character as if it were laid out in a report. I tasted her addiction, right down to what she was hooked on, why she was there, and where she'd go if she couldn't find it. Her emptiness left me cold. I left because the whole thing reminded me too much of Kate."

I let out a long breath, glancing at my wrists.

"I've done the research," I continued. "New Age religionists call it a third eye, referring to a window that opens up to a higher form of consciousness. I've been calling it the Insight because it feels right."

"A remarkable ability," Mahoney said. "And you've solved cases because of it."

"You've seen my record, sir. But those investigations caused me problems. Sometimes, the Insight just didn't work. I'd feel its presence lurking, but it remained dormant. Other times, the sensory overload was too much. I'd stay in my apartment with the lights off and stare into space while everything replayed over and over in my mind. I couldn't unsee any of it. And the dreams are the worst. I've been sleep-deprived for I couldn't tell you how long. Once I learned some meditation tricks, recovery became quicker, but not easier."

Deacon wore a small smile. My eyes narrowed with suspicion.

"I wasn't joking when I said Reynolds didn't have a soul." I glared at him. "That thing I saw, whatever the hell it was, had eaten it."

"What thing?" Mahoney asked.

"A *fetch*," Deacon answered, his expression remote. "It's a parasite, a shadow creature that feeds on the darkness in a person's soul. Powerful negative emotions attract it. I'd reckon Reynolds did a bunch of dirty shit before he got hired at that firm. Once it latches onto you, it fills your mind with an overwhelming urge to misbehave. And you'll keep on doing what you're told until you're gone.

Takes consecrated weapons to kill them fuckers, too. Holy water, blessed bullets, that sort of shit. The bastards are hard to find, even when you know where to look. By the time you realize one's there, you're already fucked."

I shuddered. Wrestling with your inner demons was one thing. Having real demons using you as their personal soft drink was something else.

"Cheer up, Holliday," Deacon added with a grin. "I've seen all kinds of weird shit down in Birmingham. Far worse than some *fetch*."

"And we're the guys to stop them?" I asked, wondering what was worse than the *fetch*.

"Something like that," Mahoney answered. "You and your Insight would help a lot of people."

"You're right." I fidgeted with my shirt sleeve, staring at the scars on my wrist. "It would. But I think the Insight's also destroying my mind. I can feel it unravel sometimes. Strange visions, nightmares. So, yeah, I've got it handled, for now."

"I appreciate the personal cost, son," Mahoney said not unkindly. "I've been there, and I've spent years working my way back. But Empire City needs you, Tom. We need you. You can remain at the 98th, wasting away your career, or you can take a chance and make a difference. The choice is yours."

A heavy silence fell between us, broken by the faint buzzing of the ceiling lights.

How many times had I wondered this very thing? I contemplated my life before rehab, about a time when an idealistic and hungry version of me was more interested in furthering my career than doing the right thing. After I'd been promoted to detective third grade, I rarely considered the message behind the oath I'd sworn or the badge I wore. I didn't care about the families I helped, or what their lives were like, or the damage caused by the criminals who hurt them. Innocence and guilt were just different sides of the same coin. Once those scumbags I bagged got processed, my responsibility ended. It had all been about the thrill of the hunt, and the glory that followed.

When the corruption scandal came down on the department, my life turned inside out, and everything changed. Colleagues and so-called friends disowned me. My supporters were few and far between. My dad was no help, and both my mother and grandfather were long gone. Other than Abner and Leyla, very few people gave me the time of day. I never felt as alone as I did during those months. And then I met Kate at Wallingbrooke Rehabilitation and Recovery Center, but we know how that ended. I was a professional failure, adept at how little I cared about anything since then. And I'd been drifting through life ever since.

"The only thing necessary for the triumph of evil is for good men to do nothing," Deacon murmured.

I let out a deep breath, unaware of how long I'd been holding it.

"Sir, there's a lot of fucked-up people out there, and most of them aren't even criminals." A sad smile played across my lips. "What's a little more psychic scarring going to do to a guy like me? If it means catching the bad guy, I'll do it every time. It's why I became a cop in the first place."

For some reason, saying that made me feel better. I couldn't tell you why, other than a renewed purpose now replaced the unease from earlier. I might be damaged goods, and I'm not proud of the things I've done, but this felt right.

It felt real.

It felt good.

"So, I get to play a real homicide detective again with the under-the-table blessing of the mayor and the DA's office, but they have plausible deniability for anytime I fuck up," I mused. "When do I start?"

A silver shield slid across the desk to rest in front of me. The sigil of Empire City was imprinted on it—the scales of justice held between two toga-clad women, one blindfolded, and the other bearing a curved sword pointed down. It gleamed with possibilities.

I picked up the badge. A strange chill ran through my fingers and down my spine.

"No number?" I remarked, turning it over in my hand.

Mahoney smiled. "You're off the 'official' books, remember?"

"People will believe it?" I scratched my chin, regarding the badge dubiously. "What if someone calls it in?"

"Let them," he replied, and leaned back in the chair, his smile widening.

"You're the boss." I shook my head in bemusement, wondering if I had missed some private joke. "What about my desk? I've still got a shit-ton of e-paperwork to complete for Flanagan. I'm just supposed to leave all that?"

"That's right," Deacon stated, the leather jacket slung over one arm. "As far as everyone at the 98th is concerned, Bill has unretired, and one of his first duties is to come here and shitcan your sorry ass."

"I thought I was being transferred?" I asked.

"Transferred, shitcanned," Deacon shrugged.

I rose from the chair.

"I guess I should go get my stuff."

"Not so fast, Detective." Mahoney held up a hand. "There's a couple more things you need to know."

"Such as?"

"Sometime in the next hour, IT will run a system-wide diagnostic," he explained. "When that happens, EVI will be updated with your new credentials, including all appropriate licenses and paperwork for your badge and your new sidearm. I also made some calls. The autopsy was performed earlier this morning. The Chief Medical Examiner is waiting on your arrival. At your desk is a bag. Don't open it until you leave here. Inside is the dossier and personal effects for Vanessa Mallery, the victim. I retrieved them from Evidence before I came here. There's also a couple of earpieces dedicated to a local private communication line in case you don't want to use EVI."

He looked at Deacon and said, "Am I forgetting anything?"

"His new peashooter," Deacon answered. "You'll be turning in your old badge and weapon before you leave. I reckon you'd prefer carrying in case something tries to eat you."

"Man, you sure are full of sunshine and rainbows, aren't you?"

Deacon returned my smile with a wolfish one of his own, an expression that never reached his eyes.

"You have no idea."

"Is that it?" I asked.

"For now," Mahoney said. He stood up and straightened his jacket. "There's a dead girl in the morgue, her throat torn out, and no trace of blood in her body."

He locked eyes with mine.

"Get going."

Back at my desk, I scooped up my coffee mug and paused to give the empty space a quick once-over. Six years I labored here. Staring at it, I felt nothing. No attachments. No regrets. I was finally leaving Purgatory on my way to, well, somewhere else.

"*Some rise by sin, and some by virtue fail,*" I said.

"Come again?" Deacon asked.

A black leather jacket lay atop a duffel bag on the floor. He donned it with a small, satisfied smile.

"*Measure for Measure,*" I replied easily. "Shakespeare. He's one of the poets of my soul."

"Right."

I grinned.

"EVI, please reserve a pod for me," I thought via the implant. "Time to visit the morgue."

I stopped by Flanagan's office, but she wasn't there. Several active holo-windows floated around her workstation – requisition requests to Supplies, a loss prevention survey detailing EVI's power consumption, a department-wide report from Gaffney on another failed goldjoy raid, and one from HQ about my abrupt transition from the 98th. Flanagan was probably on the floor celebrating my departure. I dropped my old badge and sidearm on her desk with a satisfying thump.

No one acknowledged me on my way out the front door,

which was just as well. I hated long goodbyes, and I'm sure they did too.

A moderate walk down a different corridor from the main floor led to an elevator. Up ten floors later, we were at the entrance to the ECPD Transportation Hub, an enormous multi-storied terminus housing dozens of pods for personnel, supply and prisoner transportation. Hanging platforms connected by steel and cable were arrayed in tiers around a central dispatch center. The whole thing was lit up like a Christmas tree.

Everywhere, the sounds of industry filled the air. Robot-controlled hydraulic lifts hauled massive metal crates, while the electromagnetic plates beneath dozens of pods buzzed and stirred. Machinery moved or screeched to a halt, while whistles and shouts from sweaty EC Department of Transportation workers directed the flow. There was a sudden tension in the air, and a supply pod whooshed past us, exiting the Hub along its wide track in a windy rush. It was both art and science, a frenetic anthill made of steel and motion, and whose worker drones were orchestrated by Queen EVI's virtuoso virtual command.

After a quick thumbprint scan to an attendant's pad for final authorization, we moved up to the second-floor platform. A dozen parked round-shaped transports resembling a centipede's body segment idled, each bearing the silver ECPD shield and a black unit number. Each pod could connect to another via magnetic couplers, up to a maximum of twelve. I spied ours and led Deacon toward it.

Soft light filled the interior as we entered through the main hatchway. The transport boasted an infirmary, fire suppression, a small armory, and most importantly, a beverage dispenser. It contained enough space for two operators and six other passengers, although EVI did most of the heavy lifting. The pod was fabricated from the same spell-forged alloy that comprised most of the skyscrapers located downtown, as well as the massive exterior walls protecting the enclave. I'd heard the pod's exoskeleton was strong enough to withstand heavy armament but had never tested it.

You see, Empire City's a big place in a very small world.

We are one of fifty-two enclaves that house all that remains of the billions who once overpopulated Planet Earth. This, thanks to several coordinated, worldwide terrorist cyber-attacks, a bunch of nuclear catastrophes, and the pandemics that followed long before I was born. We've spent decades putting Humpty Dumpty back together again, with mixed and strange results. The world had become a very different place.

The nuclear detonations weakened the fabric of reality and activated naturally occurring energy housed in stable nodes called Nexus Points throughout the world. They'd been present all along but were phase-shifted before the nukes exploded so we couldn't see them. The concentrated energy they contained exhibited unquantifiable effects unlike anything our scientists and engineers had ever seen before. The energy provided cleaner and more reliable alternatives to electricity, gas, and coal, since there wasn't much left of the latter after the world went to hell. Nowadays, Nexus energy powers our machines, heats our showers, turns our lights on, you name it.

Scientists have since thrown out theories such as "spatial accumulations synthesized into a purer form" and "coalescence of multi-tiered quantum anomalies." They figured that'd hide the fact they knew as much about Nexus energy as the next guy.

Most folks called it magic, because the word just fit.

And a select few, like Mark Madsen and myself, were somehow attuned to the energy's frequency, allowing us to manipulate it in different and unique ways.

EVI's voice issued from the onboard speakers instructing us to buckle up. The hatch door closed, and off we went with a powerful thrust of electromagnetic propulsion.

I considered the *Dose* article I'd read. Vanessa Mallery's body had been reportedly drained of blood. Two eyewitnesses claimed a vampire did it.

That last part had to be sensationalized media bullshit.

Right?

Images of the *fetch* danced in my vision, and I shivered. Mahoney was right. Downtown Homicide or the ECBI weren't equipped to deal with a crime like this.

Hopefully, I was.

CHAPTER 4

*D*eacon sat across from me in the co-pilot's chair. He stared out the rain-streaked window as buildings, streets and other vehicles bled past. I followed his gaze.

If the Transportation Hub was an anthill, then the island of Manhattan was a neon beehive. Gaudy blinking lights from hundreds of transmission towers and beacons competed with gigantic, multi-storied, high-definition holo-advertisements. Transit and municipal pods, far more efficient and durable than the old subway system, rode along massive winding tracks called Pathways, or 'ways for short, that twisted and curved throughout the enclave, sometimes to dizzying heights. Below the 'ways, ground automobiles and other transports rumbled along the grid of the original city. In the daylight buildings gleamed and windows sparkled, intense and bright. Traffic above and below flowed like blood through the arteries of some enormous mythological beast.

A lot of things hadn't changed since the nukes. At the heart of Empire City were the Five Boroughs. Many streets and neighborhoods still retained the character that epitomized New York City before things went to hell. This continuity kept those of us living here connected to the days when the United States was still fifty states. My hometown was self-sustaining, and boasted agriculture, fishing, hydroponics, animal cloning and vertical farming, plus all manner of synthetic foods. A democracy with elected officials, Empire City followed our own modified Constitution. Digital credits replaced most money, accepted as the worldwide coin of the realm, although gold and silver retained their value. There was commerce aplenty, and trade with the other enclaves, virtual entertainments, public services, hospitals, e-Sports, politicians, and trash collection.

I unzipped the duffel bag and withdrew several items—a new shoulder rig that was larger than my old one, a couple of earpieces, another paper file bearing the victim's name, three bulging evidence bags, and a metal briefcase.

The briefcase intrigued me, so I popped it open first. Inside lay a large handgun, with a short double barrel and wide handle to accommodate bigger ammunition clips. It was designed for dual-action, cycling between semi-automatic and pump-action modes of fire. Nestled beside it was a single ammunition clip. The bullets were arranged by size and color.

"Peashooter my ass," I muttered. "What did Mahoney think we were going up against? Tanks?"

Deacon didn't respond.

The gun was one of the Superior Military Armament Retaliatory Tool prototypes. I had read several articles from the R&D Department touting the latest in next generation critical response technology but had never actually seen one. The gun was linked to the user's DNA so only the bonded person could operate it. There was voice and chip command to load specific rounds, depending on what was available in the clip. I withdrew the weapon from the case and held it up for a moment to admire its lines and sleek design. It was lighter than I expected.

A sudden burning sensation seared my palm. I yelped, nearly dropping the damn thing on my foot.

"Attunement complete," the SMART gun's tinny robotic voice stated in my ear. "Access for Detective Thomas Henry Holliday, Special Crimes Unit, confirmed. Await instructions."

"Uh, safety on," I said aloud. "Remain on standby."

"Confirmed."

"What kind of ammunition do the clips contain?" I asked.

"Each clip contains standard and armor-piercing rounds. Voice or neural command for active round. Safety engaged."

Demonstrations of the different options cycled across my vision center.

Nice work, R&D Guys, I thought to myself. *That's some heavy-duty shit.* Special Crimes was looking up!

A clip was preloaded into the weapon. I took off my blazer, wrapped the rig around my right shoulder, and slid the gun into the holster. It was bulky, so anyone with half a brain would know I was packing something serious. Still, a little intimidation couldn't hurt. Unless I was surrounded by trigger-happy unfriendlies, in which case I'd better be quicker on the draw.

I was Doc Holliday after all, PhD notwithstanding.

Chuckling, I closed the briefcase, then fit an earpiece into my right ear. I picked up the file and settled into a passenger seat. After scanning its contents, I had EVI replay for me the body cam footage from the officers at the scene. I studied it intently, but the footage was grainy due to the late hour, the rain and mist, and the officers' flashlights.

I dismissed the imagery, then popped open a slide table from a compartment along the pod's wall and poured out the victim's purse and personal effects from the evidence bags. Attached to the table was a rubber glove dispenser, as well as an ePad and a small flashlight device with a cord. I yanked the flashlight from its holder, turned a switch, and splashed violet-white light carefully over the items for several minutes, noting the readout results.

Once finished, I withdrew a thin metal pointer I kept in my shirt pocket and separated the items into smaller piles. I had EVI collate the data for future reference. Our neural connection allowed her to see and hear everything I did, recording the information to the master cloud managed by ECPD HQ. Going forward, I could access everything via imported impulses, although I'd never tried it when my eyes were fueled by the Insight. I doubted EVI could perceive the world in the same manner, but I had no interest in finding out.

"EVI, please contact the decedent's phone carrier to get a list of her activity for the past three months," I instructed aloud.

I knew the diagnostic would happen soon, so I wanted EVI to store as much information as possible in the meantime. As if on cue, she announced the start of the diagnostic.

EVI had been a constant companion ever since I received the implant when I joined ECPD. Think of it as if you're always suffering from hay fever. No amount of decongestant ever helped. I basked in the glorious relief of being alone in my skull for the first time in years.

Vanessa's crushed phone sat apart from the other piles. It appeared to have been placed in a vice, the display ruined and the command keys useless. I popped open the sleeve containing the tiny Nexus battery and memory chip. Both had been destroyed. The phone was the only damaged item in the lot. The rest consisted of beauty products, a handkerchief, enclave ID, Metro pod card, an ID badge for Hughes Advertising Agency, an electronic passkey to a house or apartment, two credit cards and a prescription bottle for sleeping pills.

I made a mental note to have EVI research and store the online receipts for all her cards, as well as track her Metro usage. For now, I focused on the damaged phone.

"Squashed like a proto-cola can," I mused curiously, tapping the pointer against the table a few times.

"Random killing?" Deacon asked, swiveling his chair toward me.

"Murders are usually perpetrated by someone they know, or

are acquainted with in some way," I responded while studying the pill bottle. It had been prescribed by a Doctor Tamara Ettelman.

"Start of a serial killing then?" Deacon said ominously.

My brow furrowed at that. I sat up straight to let that thought wander merrily through the darker parts of my mind.

"Maybe," I said. "We won't know until there's another victim. I haven't heard of anything resembling this coming over any of our internal feeds. A murder like this feels personal, though. Her throat was ripped out, and whoever did this had the presence of mind to destroy her phone, too."

"I've read the official report," the Confederate said. "Officers at the scene said the killer leapt thirty feet straight up to a fire escape, then disappeared. I reckon something with that kind of strength could crush a phone in its hand."

"Sounds like cybernetic implants to me," I countered. "I've encountered a few individuals jacked up on illegal implants before. They have three times our strength, and ten times the bat-shit crazy. The officers' body cam imagery didn't show much, but did record the killer jumping up and grabbing the fire escape. Unfortunately, they didn't get enough to make out a face."

"EMT report stated no blood in or on the victim," Deacon shook his head. "You ever heard of an implant-junkie capable of doing that? Besides, where'd our killer store the blood? No, this is something else."

"What, you mean like an actual flesh-and-blood vampire?" I asked lightly. "That's just what this enclave needs, some nutcase dressed up like Dracula right before Halloween running around murdering people. Forget it. I'm no Van Helsing."

"You saw that *fetch*," Deacon said solemnly. "You can believe that a creature like that exists, yet you can't accept Vanessa Mallery's killer could be a vampire? That's what SCU is all about, Holliday. Taking down the things that go bump in the night."

"What's in it for you, anyway?" I asked, changing the subject.

Deacon's grin widened as he leaned back, clasping both hands behind his head.

"I told you, I don't work for the Church no more."

"Have it your way." I shrugged and placed the phone on the table. I returned to my dissection of Vanessa's effects.

"What do we know about the victim?" Deacon asked.

"Female, Caucasian, twenty-five, single, five-foot-ten, red hair," I rattled off absently while examining the beauty products. "Lived in Bay Ridge, Brooklyn. No criminal record. She graduated from ECU a year ago, double-majoring in psychology and business management, and worked as a demographic data analyst for Hughes Advertising Agency for the last nine months. Her parents died right after her birth, leaving her a trust fund administered by her aunt, a Jennifer Watson. The aunt lives in New Hollywood but has been on a tour of the European Bloc for the past month. Apparently, Aunt Jenny hasn't returned ECPD's calls yet. When EVI's back online, I'll ask her to take a deeper dive into Vanessa's background."

"No prints?" Deacon grunted.

"You see that over there?" I pointed at the flashlight device I'd used earlier. "It's called a p-scanner. Replaces fingerprint powder, among other things. I scanned every item here. Vanessa's prints were the only ones to be found. Whoever crushed the phone was wearing gloves, or something that didn't leave prints. I know Mahoney said the scene was clean, but the file didn't have anything from CSI either, which is strange. They should've done their initial sweep by now. I'll check with EVI about that, too. The medical examiner will let us know if there are any foreign materials, clothing fibers, fluids or skin debris to be found."

"What about the witnesses?" Deacon asked.

"Tony Marrazzo and Julie DeGrassi." I picked up the report and flipped through its pages. It was strange reading from paper rather than via EVI, but I enjoyed the retro feel of it. "He's a sales exec at Wrigley-Boes Pharmaceuticals. She's an executive assistant at Wieskampf-Bottleby-Jones Investment Firm. They were partying in the alleyway when they heard screams, then came across the killer. We'll hit the morgue first since it's closer, then visit the scene and interview the witnesses after."

I felt the sudden rush of sinus pressure again and gripped the side of the table to stabilize myself.

"EVI's back." I ground my teeth in discomfort.

I accessed my personnel file first. EVI confirmed my reassignment from the 98th as well as my status with Special Crimes (although I didn't see a pay grade), new badge (even though my badge was blank), and associated permit for the SMART gun (which looked legit).

"Arriving at the Empire City Office of Medical Examiners," EVI announced over the speaker. "Outside temperature is forty-four degrees, with a slight drizzling rain, and winds out of the south."

Well, I supposed I was officially official. It was time to kick the tires.

The pod decelerated to a fine crawl, then stopped. Deacon stood by the hatchway as I scooped up Vanessa's personal effects and returned them to the evidence bags.

"I have informed Doctor Stentstrom of your arrival," EVI stated.

"Thanks, sweetie," I replied with a smile.

Deacon arched an eyebrow.

"She's the next best thing to a real girlfriend, minus the sex of course," I explained congenially, and gave the interior hull a fond pat. "She's loving, nurturing, helpful, and courteous; she never argues or raises her voice, and she'll never break up with you. She's nearly the perfect woman."

"Thank you, Detective Holliday," EVI said, and for a moment I imagined hearing satisfaction in her voice.

Deacon shook his head and disembarked the pod.

The office building was a bland, squat affair made of old brick and time. It sat between an even uglier windowless building and an empty street corner. Its front consisted of two exterior windows and a single glass door reinforced with steel. I pushed through the door and strode inside.

We paused at the front desk to check in with the bored clerk, a young man with too much acne and not enough hygiene. He gave us both a dour look, then swept disinterested eyes over my badge. The clerk spoke in a low voice, paused, and handed Deacon a badge with the word "VISITOR" printed in bright red lettering.

"You'll need to wear this while inside the building," the clerk instructed Deacon. "Sub-level two, examination room three."

I thanked him, and we proceeded to the elevator. A quick ride down brought us to a sterile hallway marred by a single metal trash can standing sentinel to the right of the elevator door. Deacon tossed his badge into the trash can with a satisfied grunt. The hallway ended at a blank wall. Four doors were spaced evenly, two to a side, with the room number etched on a small flat piece of metal at eye level. The air was cool and crisp, and as we strode down the hall I caught the faint strains of classical music.

"Mozart," I mused aloud. "I thought he liked baroque?"

Deacon gave me an aggrieved look.

I grinned, tried the handle of the heavy door, and pushed.

Willowy music greeted our arrival, as the plaintive sounds of the Dissonance Quartet floated round the large examination room. Opposite the entry were twelve square metal vault doors in neat rows of three to house the recently departed. The lighting was bright and sharp, and I noticed three unoccupied metal gurneys off to my left. To the right was a large workstation, flat and elegant, with multiple ghostly screens floating above it. A very spare man with stringy hair in a partial comb-over sat at the desk. He wore a white lab coat and stared bug-eyed at the displays. His left hand waved synchronically in the air as he hummed in time with the music.

He looked up with a crooked smile.

"Ah, Detective Holliday!" he said. The music dropped to a dull patter. "I haven't seen you in ages!"

"Doctor Stentstrom," I smiled, and gripped his hand in greeting. His palm was soft and smooth. "You haven't changed a bit."

"Formaldehyde," he whispered conspiratorially, giving Deacon a sly wink. "Best batch I've ever made! Fuck big pharma and their anti-aging creams!"

"Um, yeah," I replied, my smile faltering.

I introduced Deacon, who glared at the smaller man as if to dare him to try and shake his hand. The medical examiner sniffed and thought better of it.

Gilbert Stentstrom was the poster child for mad scientists. He had the look down, between the thin eyebrows, lantern eyes, sharp nose, and strong sense of crazy oozing off him like bad cologne. Stentstrom could talk your ear off about human physiology, music, the latest fashion trends, origami, and cooking. And I had never known anyone with such a passion for standard poodles. I think he bred them in a secret underground laboratory. His dogs often placed high in the annual Empire City Kennel Club Classic.

Stentstrom was one of the good guys. I had met him during a field trip to the morgue in my first year at the academy. He'd given me a crash course in human anatomy one gooey organ at a time.

"Protector, eh?" he said, eyeing Deacon speculatively. "You're a long way from Birmingham."

"Yeah, I hear that a lot," Deacon drawled.

"Indeed," Stentstrom chuckled, then rubbed his hands eagerly together. "So, who wants to see a dead body?"

CHAPTER 5

*S*tentstrom directed us to the rubber glove dispenser while he opened one of the metal doors. He pulled out the slab bearing Vanessa Mallery's body.

The dead never bothered me much, and it wasn't the cop thing. I wasn't sure if it was the absolute stillness, or the sheer absence of life. Whatever spark they held was gone. In death, they're mannequins, empty shells, caricatures of what once was, and now will never be.

Ever since I was a kid, I had this relationship with death that set me apart from other kids in the neighborhood. I grew up in Little Odessa, more commonly known as Brighton Beach. Mom had been a second-generation Jewish immigrant from the Minsk enclave. She was murdered when I was ten. Home invasion. I wasn't home at the time, but I've read the report and stared at the images more times than I can count. As for my dad, he's Irish Catholic, and piss-drunk most days. Picture-perfect family, right?

We used to live in one of several low-income housing projects along Brighton 6th Street. The *bratva* controlled everything, so there was always something illicit happening in the neighborhood. Drug trafficking, prostitution, fraud and scams, you name it. The Russians liked to get violent, and when that happened, someone ended up dead.

When I was thirteen, I found my first body beneath a pile of trash at the playground. Valarie Aronov. Multiple stab wounds to the chest, but Valarie's face was unblemished, brown eyes wide and staring. I felt the horror that clung to the body, her mouth opened in a silent scream of suffering and pain. I knelt beside Valarie, took her hand, and offered up a prayer to whoever was listening. The police arrived a few minutes later. A nice officer asked me some questions, then took me home. It wouldn't be the last time I'd ride in the back of a police pod. My teenage years were colorful, too.

McMahon was his name, come to think of it. Officer John McMahon. I never saw him again, but heard he was killed while off-duty a few years later. *Bratva* again. Bastards.

The cops never found Valarie's killer, but I had a pretty damn good idea who did it. What happened to her and my mom inspired me to become a cop. I decided then and there someone had to stop the bad guys from hurting innocent people.

Seeing Vanessa lying cold and dead on that slab dredged up a slew of unpleasant emotions. Suddenly, I was thirteen again, holding the hand of Valarie Aronov. With great effort, I asserted my composure and concentrated on the corpse before anyone noticed.

Vanessa had been attractive, with long, straight red hair flowing past her shoulders. She was physically fit judging by the toned musculature along her arms and legs. High, firm breasts rode above a flat stomach. Her eyes were closed.

I wondered idly if they were brown.

Stentstrom's Y-shaped stitching was neat and tight along both collar bones and down her chest. However, the gaping tear that marred nearly two inches of her neck was gruesome.

"Ghastly, isn't it?" Stentstrom whispered, his eyes fixated on the body in rapt fascination.

Deacon stood apart with arms folded while he stared at the body. He looked uneasy.

"What do we know?" I asked, bending down to examine the wound.

"As you can see, the entrance wound consists of a two to two-and-a-half-inch diameter, horizontally-oriented slash," he explained clinically. "There are no traces of any foreign substance or material. Maximal depth of penetration is three to three-and-a-half inches deep."

Stentstrom sidled over to me and pointed two fingers at the unusually pale neck muscles protruding through the gash.

"The wound track was through the skin, the subcutaneous tissue, intercostal musculature, and through the right carotid artery. Normally, there are approximately two hundred to three hundred milliliters of predominantly liquid blood. However, there was no trace of blood within any organs or on the body anywhere, so actual time of death and lividity could not be readily determined."

I stole a glance at Deacon. He hadn't moved.

"In addition, there was no evidence of sexual abuse," Stentstrom pointed out. "In fact, Miss Mallery never participated in any sexual activity, in the Biblical sense that is."

He stared longingly at the corpse, titillated by his own revelation. I shuddered.

"I also did not find hair, tissue or clothing fragments on her person, under her fingernails, or anywhere else that were foreign, or out of place, excluding extraneous and common detritus from the alleyway in which she was found."

Stentstrom withdrew the white sheet covering the rest of her body. I sucked in a sharp breath.

"Other injuries of note are fractures to five digits of the right hand, fractures of radiocarpal joint of right hand, broken radio-carpal joint and torn palmar, dorsal radiocarpal, ulnar, and radial collateral ligaments of left hand."

"Her hands were crushed," Deacon murmured.

"Someone or something of superior-than-human strength gripped both of her hands and squeezed sufficiently to cause that level of trauma," Stentstrom bubbled with enthusiasm.

I frowned.

"When you say no trace of blood, that's because she bled out, right?" I asked.

"No, Detective Holliday," he stated, staring at me unblinking and full of intensity. "My examination of Miss Mallery's body showed there was no trace of blood, red and white blood cells, or any blood-related material of a molecular nature on, or within, her body anywhere. Hence, lividity and rigor mortis did not occur, because the factors were not present."

"Then why isn't her corpse a dried-out husk?" I asked, incredulous. "Don't the dead cells remain for a while before decomposition? She looks perfectly...normal, I guess, the way a corpse should look a day after death."

"The matter of a complete absence of blood in this human body is, by itself, a medical impossibility," Stentstrom enthused. "There are always trace elements remaining. I extracted several tissue samples from a variety of organs. Under the microscope, all of them showed an absence of blood down to a cellular level."

He rubbed his hands together, ardent bulbous eyes about to pop out of his skull.

"Without the presence of blood and associated nutrients the cells carry, tissue, organs, external epidermis, body hair, fingernail, and toenails eventually die. She should not look like a well-preserved corpse, and I have no *scientific* explanation for it!"

"But you got a suspicion, Doc," Deacon stated, giving me a pointed look.

"I do, Mr. Kole," he replied, narrowing his eyes. He raised the finger of his right hand with a flourish. "Gentlemen, the only explanation congruent with the evidence is vampirism!"

I expected to hear the eerie chords of an organ flare up

followed by a lightning flash and boom of thunder. The only other thing missing was maniacal laughter, and some caped figure lurking in the shadows.

"You've got to be kidding," I scoffed. "You, the medical examiner, the objectivist, a man of science with decades of learning, are saying a vampire killed this girl?"

"No, the severe trauma to her neck killed Miss Mallery," Stentstrom explained patiently as if I was a five-year-old. "Vampirism in nature is quite real, gentlemen. Bats, lampreys, moths, and other insects, for example. And lest we not forget how difficult it is for blood to be digested and processed, let alone be the sole substance for something to subsist upon.

"Consider the variables involved. When the skin is perforated, blood flows, and becomes extant on the wound. From the reports provided by the attending officers at the scene, there was no spray against the alley walls or on the ground. Neither her clothes, nor her body, held any traces of blood. The moment her blood was released, it was not allowed to splatter, or otherwise escape.

"The entry wound is consistent with a severe laceration." He traced his fingers along the gaping mess. "The affected area was so thoroughly damaged that it could have hidden an original entry wound. A vampire could have inserted its fangs, fed, and then torn out the flesh once satiated."

I exchanged an exasperated look with Deacon.

"She could've been brought to the alley," the Confederate offered. "Vanessa could've already been dead."

"That is an intriguing possibility, Mr. Kole," Stentstrom replied. "However, the eyewitnesses claim the assailant had fangs. They also said her blood dissolved into its skin. How did it get there in the first place, and with Miss Mallery's body in tow? I cannot imagine it carried her on the Metro in plain view of anyone. And it does not explain how every trace of her blood was removed. I do not know anything in nature capable of doing that."

Nodding, I crossed my arms, my mouth set in a grim line.

44

"Thank you, Doctor." I removed my gloves, then shook Stentstrom's hand.

"Not so fast, Detective," he said, a strange catch to his voice. "There's one other thing. Other than the wound, Miss Mallery is perfect."

"What's that supposed to mean?"

"I did not detect a single blemish on her," he gestured with a slow wave of his hand. "No scars, no previously broken bones or prior trauma, no moles or other birthmarks of any kind. In fact, she was in perfect health before she died."

"So?" Deacon stated. "There're plenty of people who ain't never suffered an injury in their lives."

"Quite true, Mr. Kole," the medical examiner smiled. "But human skin sustains damage simply from being in sunlight. Freckles, spots, any sort of discoloration on the flesh would become apparent at some point. That is not the case here."

"What does it mean?" I asked, staring at the victim's red hair.

"I have no idea!" he replied with glee. "But I plan on finding out!"

I nodded. "Well, as soon as you do, please contact me immediately."

"Of course, Detective," he said, but his wide eyes remained fixated on the corpse.

Back in the pod, I instructed EVI to transport us to Water Street, and the murder scene. The pod lurched into motion, cutting a smooth arc along the 'way as it rose above the streets heading toward Lower Manhattan. The fog obscured much at this height, although I knew the East River was off to our left. The pod accelerated quickly, skirting the edge of East Village heading toward the crime scene.

"What'd your Insight tell you?" Deacon asked.

I collapsed in one of the passenger chairs and let out a slow breath.

"It doesn't work on corpses." I rested both hands in my lap to study them. My fingernails needed clipping. "There's no life to observe."

That was a bald-faced lie, but I had no interest in explaining that to Deacon. It felt juvenile, but I liked keeping secrets too.

"Besides, Stentstrom loves a mystery. He'll take several more looks at the body in case he missed anything."

I moved to the far end of the pod and activated the beverage dispenser.

"Coffee?" I offered, but he declined.

My mug filled with a dark brown stream of steaming liquid ambrosia. I plucked it from the dispenser and returned to my chair. Deacon withdrew a small battered metal case from his jeans pocket.

"Hand-rolled, and specially-grown in Birmingham," he said pleasantly, passing me a cigarette. "The way God intended."

It looked unfiltered and nasty.

"No thanks," I shuddered, handing it back.

"Suit yourself," he replied, then ignited it from a small, hand-held lighter.

"Smoking is not permitted in this vehicle," EVI proclaimed.

Deacon made a rude gesture and continued puffing happily. The pod's interior billowed with acrid smoke.

During our ride, EVI informed me that the victim's holo-phone carrier had sustained a cyberattack the night before. I frowned at that. The timing was damned inconvenient. These days cyberattacks weren't uncommon. As the trappings of modern life became more dependent on technology, so did the danger of being too reliant on it. Consequently, cyberterrorists and hackers became bolder and more sophisticated. In a world that ran on holo-tech and clouds, cyber-terrorism and counter cyber-terrorism had become an Olympic sport. Still, a data breach meant getting Mallery's phone records anytime soon was remote.

"EVI, tell them it's part of a homicide investigation, and to get me that information ASAP."

"Of course, Detective. Vanessa Mallery's medical and dental history, education, family, known associates and associations are now available for your review. I also have the composite from the sketch artist based on the eyewitnesses' description."

"Okay, give it me."

For the next twenty minutes I examined the information EVI provided, the images flashing before my eyes as if I were seeing them on an actual holo-screen. The composite was a vague blob that could've been anyone. I glanced over to Deacon who was on his phone, but I focused my attention on the virtual flow, and couldn't hear his conversation.

I chewed on the information for a while, sipping at my coffee in silence.

"EVI, where's the preliminary forensics report from CSI?"

"Captain Mahoney did not authorize the Crime Scene Investigation team to investigate the scene. The task force to which you have been assigned, called Special Crimes Unit, or SCU, relies on the forensic expertise of its own members to complete that assignment."

"Why?"

"Per Captain Mahoney's orders, the task force shall rely on its own forensic expertise," she repeated.

"Sonofabitch," I grunted.

"What's that?" Deacon asked.

"No CSI guys?" I glared at him.

Deacon's grin infuriated me.

"Think of it this way, Holliday. If there ain't nobody in your department knows what we're doing, the less red tape gets in the way."

"Bullshit. I told the two of you I used the Insight judiciously because of its effects."

"I ain't telling you to use it. That's on you. Bill didn't say it, but SCU's under a tight budget. Between the earpieces, badge, and gun, that's all he can afford right now."

"So how the fuck am I supposed to get paid? Believe it or not, I've got bills, and they don't get paid by themselves."

He chuckled, dashing the cigarette on the control console. The dead butt lay next to a circular black ash mark.

"Beats the fuck out of me." Deacon lit another one, took a long drag, then blew out a cloud of white.

"Great," I grumbled. "Who were you talking with just now?"

"Our consultant. She's meeting us at the crime scene."

"What's her name?" I was skeptical. I'd never worked with a consultant before, and the thought of babysitting one coupled with the data breach and lack of funding really pissed me off.

"Doctor Besim Saranda," he said simply, as if her name was explanation enough.

"Never heard of her," I replied. "What kind of doctor is she?"

"Biology," Deacon smiled.

I stared.

"Biology. You're kidding, right?"

Deacon chuckled.

"She's also a popular musician," he continued amiably. "Sings that coffeehouse, Eurotrash-horseshit that's so popular with college kids. You might like it, though."

"And she's meeting us at the crime scene," I repeated, holding out for a better explanation.

"Yep."

"And you don't see anything wrong with this?"

"Nope."

"Okay, then." I rubbed my jaw. "I'll skip the usual questions and just ask this: what does she bring to the table?"

"She's got a unique perspective."

"Arriving at Water Street," EVI announced. "Outside temperature is forty-one degrees, with rain and winds out of the south-to-southeast. Umbrellas have been provided for your use, Detective."

A small panel near the hatchway slid open revealing several umbrella handles. As the pod came to a halt, I grabbed one and headed out. A brisk breeze swept us, catching the top of my umbrella as it attempted to carry it, and me, away. Fine mist veiled the buildings above the third floor, painting an impression that the world ended at its edge.

Massive skyscrapers loomed to either side like silent steel monoliths, faceless and implacable. Despite the rain, a steady flow of foot and vehicle traffic trundled along. The asphalt jungle's cacophony bellowed and squawked, hissed and spat. It was background noise to me, a vibrant reminder of the ebb and flow of life in the big city.

The alleyway was shrouded in layers of yellow police holotape. A miserable, waterlogged officer stood in the lee of a building. I slipped my new SCU badge onto my belt.

"Detective Tom Holliday," I said, walking up. "This is Deacon Kole. We're with Special Crimes."

The officer was a solid-looking kid who introduced himself as Grissom. He glanced between the two of us, then shivered beneath his poncho. He appeared to have the makings of a bad cold.

"Yessir. Been told to expect you. Your, uh, consultant is already here."

The kid glanced toward the alley, an inscrutable look on his face.

"Why don't you grab a cup of coffee and dry off for a bit?" I suggested. "We'll be here for a while."

Grissom nodded his thanks and stomped down the block in search of shelter.

Deacon and I strode down the alleyway. It was one of those long breezeways between buildings, wide enough for foot traffic, but not enough for vehicles. Large puddles dotted the ground in places. Small piles of trash littered spots here and there. It stank, but no more than usual. Both sound and the breeze died to a dull roar once we were buffered by the buildings.

About midway along I saw a slim figure kneeling on the ground. At our approach, she stood and turned to greet us.

The first thing I noticed was her height. She was well over six feet tall.

The second, her complete disregard for the elements.

And the third, she was a Vellan.

CHAPTER 6

*A*nother side effect of the nukes had to do with spatial frequencies shifting on Earth that created the doorway the Vellans used to pass from their universe to ours. Apparently, there are an infinite number of these parallel dimensions, too.

Yeah, I don't get it, either.

Anyway, they'd also suffered from wars that had devastated their world. To avoid extinction, the Vellans came here. Our Earth was chosen because they'd discovered our reactivated Nexus nodes. Turns out their tech runs on the same energy, tapping into the Nexus nodes and converting the magical energy into recyclable fuel. The Vellans provided to all the enclaves the blueprints to build these machines, in exchange for peaceful asylum on our world. They also taught us how to fabricate spell-forged steel, a blended compound infused with magic to create an alloy far stronger and more durable than any man-made metal.

Once everyone overcame the initial shock of meeting interdimensional aliens, we stowed the guns—within easy reach—and it was business as usual. Relations with the newcomers improved to the cautious friendship of this particular meeting. Unfortunately, bigotry and ignorance remained two of humanity's least favorable traits. Difference, be it skin color, religion, or pointed ears still scared stupid people, and there were a few enclaves who wouldn't allow the Vellans inside their borders without an armed escort. One guess which of the American enclaves fell into that category.

In a short amount of time, the Vellans learned all of our languages, and spent decades acclimating to our world. Although geneticists determined early on the two races couldn't reproduce, that didn't stop us from getting better acquainted. I'm told sex with a Vellan is quite the sensory experience, if you can stay conscious for it.

However, none of that explained why there was one at my crime scene.

She towered over me. Almond-shaped, gray eyes, wider than a human's, framed an oval face with delicate features and a thin mouth. A colorful bandana clung to her head from the constant rain. She wore an unbuttoned black longshoreman's coat over a blue peasant top and ruffled patterned skirt that reached her ankles. Open-toed sandals covered feet whose toes were adorned with small silver and gold rings. Her toenails and fingernails alternated between red and orange polish.

I was hard-pressed to call the Vellan attractive, but she wasn't ugly either. And then there was the makeup. Her face was covered in it, as if caked on by some stoned bricklayer. It sloughed off her face in viscous, colored rivulets. Even her hair was dyed a dark color, the ink staining a ring around her scalp where the bandana ended.

Now *that* was interesting. Every cop studied Vellan culture back at the Academy to better understand our interdimensional friends. It helped with any disputes involving them, although I'd never heard of a Vellan breaking any of our laws.

Theirs was a caste system, a hereditary lifestyle that included occupation, social status, economic wealth, you name it. Hair color was one key component of determining societal rank, and they were forbidden to alter its natural pigmentation.

Was she trying to hide the fact that she was Vellan?

Oh, no, that wasn't weird.

"Detective Holliday." She approached me, extending her hand in greeting. It was a very human expression. "I am Besim Saranda. It is a pleasure to meet you."

Despite a thick accent, her voice was musical, every word trembling with elements of tone and rhythm.

I gripped her larger hand in response. The handshake was firm, and I was surprised at her strength. She examined me dispassionately as if I were one of Stentstrom's tissue samples. I shot a furtive glance at Deacon. He squatted beneath the large canopy ECPD had set up last night to study the ground.

"Doctor Saranda," I acknowledged.

"Please, call me Besim." She offered me a demure smile, the ghastly expression resembling melted wax. "Rarely do I employ the title."

I eyed her disheveled appearance and offered her my umbrella.

"No thank you, Detective," she replied, gesturing with a smile. "I enjoy the water. It cleanses both body and mind."

"Uh, sure."

Deacon chuckled. He stepped around the crime scene as if it were a mine field.

"I have already examined the ground, and the walls to either side," the Vellan said with mild reproach, joining Deacon beneath the canopy. "Their policemen are correct. There is no trace of blood."

"Yeah," Deacon grunted. "But you ain't got the first fucking clue what you're looking for."

The Vellan frowned but didn't respond. Instead, she produced a thick handkerchief from one of the heavy coat's inner pockets. She wiped at her neck, cheeks and brow with fastidious care, the movements precise and economical. The wreckage of her made-up face transformed into something less freakish and more, well, alien. Her face bore no wrinkles, almost piquant, like a fox. Across her forehead, down her cheeks, and along the sides of her neck were elegant markings, her familial tattoos, reverent inscriptions denoting her lineage and standing among Vellan society. It was their version of a fingerprint, a kind of artistic genetic code.

It was bad juju to cover them up too.

First the hair, and now the tattoos.

Curiouser and curiouser, eh, Alice?

"The wound described in the report, as well as the images provided, indicate a blood spray of a certain volume, angle and distance," the Vellan said, her tone cool. "I find it remarkable that no such spray occurred, nor any presence of blood on the ground."

"That's why they call it a 'mystery,'" Deacon replied easily. "If everything in life were that simple, y'all wouldn't need cops."

"Such is my point. I do not believe—" she began.

"Whoa, people." I held up both hands. "This is *my* crime scene, and, no disrespect ma'am, you aren't ECPD. So, before I let you contaminate things any further, I need to see your credentials."

Besim held my gaze but didn't blink. She folded the handkerchief into a neat square and returned it to the coat's inner pocket. Then she produced a silver shield akin to the one I had on my belt, offering it to me. I stared at it hard.

"Will this suffice, Detective?" she asked mildly, one sculpted eyebrow quirking higher than the other.

Well, of course she has a fucking badge.

"I am assisting William with this investigation," she continued, unperturbed. "He felt my knowledge would be of use to you. It was my understanding he made you aware of this arrangement at your meeting earlier today."

"Well, *William* neglected to mention a few things." I glared at Deacon, who ignored me.

"Then I must apologize to you, Detective Holliday." She stiffened, a troubled frown creasing her face. "It was not my intent to insult or intrude. If I have caused—"

"Are you two done yet?" Deacon demanded. He peered up one wall. "This fucking rain is really pissing me off."

Stepping under the canopy, I knelt near the holo-outline. I opened my bulky metal case to remove a larger version of the p-scanner. Dropping the umbrella, I waved the business end of the scanner over the ground in a slow arc, noting the readout. I spent several minutes maneuvering the device in wider arcs from the outline, outside of the canopy, along both walls for several feet, and then further along the alleyway in both directions. The alleyway extended the length of the two buildings, spilling out onto another street across from which was a Metro station.

I returned to find the others at the opposite end of the alleyway admiring a small security camera attached to one wall.

"The scanner is no replacement for CSI, but for what it's worth, it confirmed no trace of blood," I said. "And the rain obliterated any quality footprints."

Something else occurred to me.

"An anonymous caller alerted ECPD. But with weather like we've had the past few days, how could anyone see anything? Uniforms arrived in time and almost nabbed our killer. I know our response time is fast, but that's impressive even for the guys downtown."

"Somebody must've heard something," Deacon said, frowning at the camera. "Bill's got officers canvassing the tenants of the bank and apartments. Maybe it was one of them."

"Maybe," I answered, unconvinced.

I surveyed the walls, noting the presence of the closest windows with the best vantage point. Then I glanced at the camera. There was scoring around its housing, but I couldn't tell if it was rust, or something else.

"I'm going to check the other end to see if there's a twin to this one," I said.

I trotted back and found another with the same discoloration. That couldn't be a coincidence.

"It's the same," I said as I walked up to them, and pointed at the device. "See that? It looks fresh, like a lightning strike. It didn't storm last night. Something fried the circuits in both boxes. I need to see the bank's security footage."

We walked around the corner to find Grissom with a cup in hand, drenched and more miserable than before. We exchanged a few words, then made our way to the bank's entrance. I felt bad for the kid. The rain wasn't letting up. Hopefully, someone would relieve him soon.

The three of us were quite the sight strolling into Empire City Savings and Loan. Several customers gawked openly, and a few gave us a wide berth as they exited the building. I didn't blame them. Bedraggled as we were, I expected the bank's security to escort us out before I could show them my badge.

We were midway across the lobby when Besim was manhandled by a short, middle-aged woman in a dark business suit. The two embraced, somehow managing it without looking too awkward. As they disengaged, the woman fawned over the Vellan.

"Doctor Saranda!" she gushed. "What a delightful surprise!"

Besim smiled, her face transforming from cold and aloof to beatific in the blink of an eye. Color appeared in her cheeks, and her economical mannerisms became languid and relaxed. Even her mismatched clothing somehow seemed to match, as if her fashion sense was in tune with her sudden mood change.

"Darlene!" Besim crooned. "It has been too long. You look fantastic! How is Edward?"

The two wandered away, chattering happily with their arms linked.

I stood there blinking several times.

"What just happened?" I asked.

The two settled into Darlene's office, carrying on like old sorority sisters. Their laughter flittered out in tinkling bursts. The banker stood up to close her door.

"Saranda's got a lot of friends," Deacon replied, amused by my reaction. "She don't look it, but between her music and other business interests, she's loaded."

We tracked down the bank's head of security, a portly man in a cheap suit named Bines. After questioning him and several of his technicians, they confirmed that something had overloaded the exterior cameras, including the one in the parking garage they shared with the apartments above the bank. Bines handed me a microdrive with last night's footage, we said our goodbyes, and returned to the main banking floor.

We rescued Besim from the tearful clutches of the banker. After several embraces, a blubbery farewell (on the part of Darlene), and vague promises for get-togethers in the future (also by Darlene), we exited the bank.

"I trust your meeting with the security director went well?" she asked politely. Gone was the lively and ebullient musician, replaced by the demure, analytical doctor.

"It's a start," I replied, but didn't elaborate.

I was annoyed and had no interest in answering any questions from our "consultant."

On the walk back to the pod, a quick check with EVI confirmed Besim's authorization to be on board. I tossed the umbrella onto the floor with a scowl and crashed in a command chair. Rubbing my face a few times with both hands, I turned to Deacon. He gave me the microdrive, then lit up another smoke. Besim sat next to me, hands folded in her lap. Ignoring her, I plugged the drive into the control console.

"Detective, while I process the data, I have completed collating the decedent's pertinent information," EVI informed me.

An instant later, Vanessa Mallery's online history appeared in my eye.

I reviewed it, but nothing leapt out. Vanessa was an active participant within the online community. I presumed her position as an analyst at Hughes Advertising required a high level of social immersion as well. But none of the interest groups were unusual, nor did it appear she was involved in anything controversial.

Vanessa owned a modest savings account, student loans, small amount of credit debt, no liens or criminal record. She paid her taxes, owned a brownstone, but no car. She wasn't outwardly religious or political, nor did she follow any e-Sports. Vanessa enjoyed live acoustical music, followed several artists, and hosted a website devoted to her paintings. Her work consisted of seascapes, and to my untrained eye, she was talented.

There were no excessive purchases or deposits, although she owned a cat. I found several receipts from Pet Depot and Butters Animal Hospital in Bay Ridge. And then there was Armin's Coffee House. Six receipts from there in the past three weeks. Perhaps a connection between the killer and one of those places? My money was on Armin's, because, well, coffee, and the fact the coffee shop was located a couple of Metro stops from the crime scene.

"Anything useful?" Deacon asked. A thick haze shrouded him.

I instructed EVI to increase the pod's air filtration and halted the information stream.

"Vanessa was a boring girl," I said, then recounted what I'd seen. "We'll go to Armin's after we interview the eyewitnesses." I turned my full attention on my unwanted consultant. "And as for you, let's get a few things straight."

She met my hostile stare with a placid one of her own.

"Of course, Detective," Besim said in a matter-of-fact tone before I could continue. "You wish for me to remain out of the way. I am not to handle, or otherwise jeopardize the investigation because of my inexperience. You expect me to maintain a low profile, as much as someone of my…distinctiveness…is able. You will listen to my opinion, but only when asked, and solely out of respect for William, your commanding officer. Have I omitted anything?"

"Yeah." My smile was unpleasant. "Try not to get killed."

Besim inclined her head.

"Review complete," EVI announced.

"Patch it through here, please," I ordered aloud.

The front windshield turned opaque, then lit up with the bank's recorded security feed.

"The images produced insufficient data," EVI said over the pod's speakers as we watched the black-and-white footage. "I did not detect any obfuscation or alteration. Sunday, at 9:58 PM, the cameras in the alleyway were disabled. At 10:23 PM, the cameras in the parking garage were disabled in the same manner. There is a shadow depicted in the parking garage footage. It is of indeterminate size and shape. The flash which followed its appearance before the camera was disabled is a result of an overload to the internal wiring systems of the camera. The cause of the overload is unknown. Do you require anything further?"

I heaved a heavy sigh.

"No, EVI, we're good for now. Thanks."

The windshield became translucent once more.

"Looks like our vampire has spooky powers over technology," I remarked dryly.

Deacon's smile was grim. Somehow, that didn't make me feel any better.

CHAPTER 7

"*A* suggestion, Detective?" Besim asked solicitously, interrupting my thoughts.

"Sure," I grunted.

"The Empire City Savings and Loan security team will remove the damaged cameras, and perform a physical examination of its internal parts," she said. "They will determine the root cause as an external disruption field, similar in scope, but not in magnitude, to an electromagnetic pulse. They will provide such findings to the Empire City police in due course, several days from today. In my opinion, that information will prove useless given the supernatural circumstances surrounding Vanessa Mallery's murder."

"First off, that's not a suggestion," I grumbled. "And B, how the hell do you figure the cameras were shut down by a disruption field?"

"A casual observation, then, based upon my assessment of the damaged cameras in the alleyway." Besim smiled faintly, tilting her head like a bird. "Something external destroyed the camera circuitry. I presumed you had also arrived at the same conclusion, and merely visited with the security director to corroborate your findings."

Deacon flicked some ash, watching the two of us with amused eyes.

Realization dawned on me.

"That's why you didn't accompany us downstairs," I said, bristling with annoyance. "You assumed we'd discover it ourselves."

"I did not wish to intrude upon your investigation." Her smile faded. "It is my place to defer to your investigative experience first, and then reveal my theory in the security of this police pod. Since I do business with Darlene and the bank, I recused myself so as not to be a distraction."

I sucked in a deep breath and held it, trying hard to maintain my composure. "Okay, fine. What's your suggestion?"

"Given the lack of evidence, and the report from the eyewitnesses stating a *vampyr* perpetrated the murder, perhaps it would be wise to consult with an expert on the occult?"

"A what?" I blinked.

"*Vampyr*," she repeated slowly. "In the lexicon I employ, it is an alternative pronunciation of the word used to describe the creature that murdered Vanessa Mallery."

"Let's not jump to conclusions," I retorted. "Besides, we still need to speak with the eyewitnesses. According to the EMT report, both were high on goldjoy. They probably hallucinated half the shit they saw."

The consultant inclined her head again.

"That is also true, but my own study of goldjoy has shown the hallucinations are exacerbated significantly by external stimuli. What is seen is merely an enhanced version of the reality. In this case, what the eyewitnesses saw resembled a *vampyr*, whether it was in fact the creature itself, or someone masquerading as such."

"You've researched goldjoy?" I asked.

"One of my business interests involves consultations with various pharmaceutical entities in both the American enclaves as well as the European Bloc," she explained. "Several of my clients have asked me to replicate goldjoy, but I have been unsuccessful."

"You manufacture narcotics?" I spluttered, staring at Deacon.

He shrugged.

"I am many things, Detective," Besim said primly. "One of them involves the development of patented formulae for the pharmaceutical industry. I have assisted in the manufacture of human health aids and vitamin supplements, among others. Goldjoy resembles these products on a microscopic level. However, it also contains significant differences which I have been unable to reproduce. It was my belief that the goldjoy formula could be altered to remove both its narcotic and addictive effects. I had harbored hopes to develop it into something that would prove beneficial for your people."

"Well, then I guess Rumpelstiltskin is glad you won't be muscling in on his business," I said.

Besim regarded me. "Rumpelstiltskin?"

"The mysterious criminal mastermind behind goldjoy," I grumbled, and moved to the beverage station to refill my mug. "It's the name Narcotics gave him because of the drug's coloration. They've been after him for years. He's like a ghost. No one knows who he is, or what he looks like. He has eyes and ears everywhere, and who knows how many cops on the take."

"That is not very encouraging," Besim replied with a troubled frown.

"The eyewitnesses?" Deacon prompted between puffs.

I had EVI pull up their profiles on the windshield display.

"Well, isn't that convenient?" I remarked dryly. "Tony Marrazzo lives in a unit above the bank."

"I believe the word is serendipitous," Besim supplied.

"Whatever." I read through his profile. "He's a sales exec for Wrigley-Boes Pharmaceuticals. You know anything about them?"

"They are an international operation specializing in fitness, and health and beauty enhancers and supplements," Besim replied. "Their marketing focuses on a more organic approach to healthy lifestyles, claiming their products are all-natural. Several of my clients are competitors."

I nodded, sipping at my coffee.

"Okay EVI, please contact Mr. Marrazzo and let him know we're on our way," I said. "In the meantime, let's go check out the parking garage. Judging by the recording we just watched, it looks like our perp exited through there. Maybe we can backtrack his movements and pick up something."

I downed the rest of my coffee in one gulp and belched in satisfaction.

"I don't know what I would do without this stuff," I proclaimed, raising the empty mug as if it were a championship trophy. Coffee always improved my mood. I was by then only mildly annoyed with our consultant.

"I could recommend a few organic supplements that provide the same stimulus as Protogenesis caffeine without any of its detrimental effects," Besim offered.

"Nah," I said while grabbing an umbrella. The hatchway popped open with a hiss of expelled air. "The detrimental effects are what I'd miss the most."

Besim smiled as she and Deacon exited the pod. At least she had a sense of humor.

We walked half a block to the parking garage. A steady stream of rainwater flowed along the grooved drain and merged with the lazy drizzle outside. The garage was an oblong concrete box with low ceilings and poor lighting. It contained seven levels connecting the bank and the apartments, as well as a partially-broken metal door leading to a very fragrant stairwell.

We came to the first camera wedged into a corner by the exit ramp, providing a commanding view of the lane, various empty parking spaces, and the door. No surprise, the casing bore the same discoloration as those from the alleyway.

"Here, make yourself useful." I handed Deacon the portable scanner.

He grumbled but took the device and waved it in arcs in the space between the door and the end of the exit ramp. A few moments later, he reviewed the findings and shook his head.

"Just the normal shit tracked in by people coming and going," Deacon scowled. "It also found traces of lemon freshener and chemicals common to domestic cleaning products."

"Lemon freshener?" I cast him a sharp look. "Let me see that."

Deacon flicked the butt of his expired cigarette away with a practiced motion, then handed me the scanner.

I punched a few keys and studied the readout. Besim was silent as she observed the intermittent foot traffic outside.

"This scanner picks up fingerprints, footprints, traces of DNA," I explained, my eyes focused on the data. "But it can also separate chemical agents from other compounds. Like lemon freshener."

I placed the scanner on the ground and away from any running water.

"It's far from perfect," I continued, scratching my jaw stubble thoughtfully. "The sensors can be fooled, though, which is why we rely more on CSI, who have better equipment, more experience, and would crawl all over everything with a toothbrush. Thank goodness we don't have CSI to get in our way. I mean, why make this investigation easier?"

"Our murderer didn't leave behind shit, Holliday," Deacon said, ignoring me. "Did the scanner detect the chemical in the alleyway?"

I tapped the holo-screen to retrieve the historical data, then shook my head.

"Perhaps one of the tenants works as a janitor?" Besim suggested. She smiled at an old woman gawking at her. The woman stumbled down the block, muttering under her breath. "Their footgear tracks the chemicals while they are so engaged."

"Which floor is Tony's apartment?" Deacon asked.

"Seventh, apartment seven forty-two," I replied.

I followed up with EVI about her contact with the eyewitness.

"There has been no response. I have made three attempts thus far. Shall I try again?"

"Please do," I instructed, glancing at the others. "No response from Tony. I know both he and Julie were discharged from EC General a few hours after the murder, and then taken to the nearest precinct. He should be home by now."

EVI confirmed a single protective detail had been assigned to the eyewitnesses.

"Where are they now?" I asked aloud. She provided the home address for Julie. "Okay, please contact the officers on duty, and inform them we'll be coming by to interview the eyewitnesses as soon as we're done here."

I addressed my companions...co-workers...friends? Okay, not friends.

"It looks like they're at Julie's," I said. "That still doesn't explain why Tony hasn't answered EVI's call."

Besim turned to leave, but I forestalled her with a furrowed brow and a raised hand.

"What is it, Detective?" she asked, eyebrow raised.

I exchanged a look with Deacon, who nodded his understanding.

"Lemon is an effective cleaning agent, and masks other scents," I explained. "And the murderer is still at large. We can use the scanner to track the lemon traces and see where the trail leads. There's been too much rain outside for it to work, but inside is another story. If it's from a janitor, then we've at least ruled that out. But if it isn't..."

"Not bad, Holliday," Deacon approved, a slight smile creasing his lips.

"Let's not get ahead of ourselves. This could be a complete waste of time." I picked up the scanner and handed it to Besim.

We spent the next half-hour slowly following the lemony-fresh breadcrumbs. The trail led up to the fourth parking level, through an access door, and along a dim and musty hallway. No security cameras were in view. A threadbare, ochre-colored carpet decorated the floor. The interior had the look of an old, frayed hotel, with chipped wooden paneling against the walls, and faded brown doors. The doors included keyholes, unlike the electronic passkeys more modern apartments employed. Midway down the hallway was a small alcove for the elevator. A few doormats here and there indicated occupied units, and the faint sounds from holo-visions burbled behind the doors. Besim led the way to another stairwell at the far end. We trudged up three more flights of stairs, my leg muscles burning with the climb.

Don't get me wrong: I was in decent shape, for a guy my age. I always broke a big sweat walking from my desk to the coffee pot. We're talking at least ten times before noon. I also walked two blocks to the Metro station near my apartment.

And I didn't eat a lot of donuts.

Life is a marathon, people, not a sprint.

I tried not to huff and puff, but when Besim called a halt in front of one door, I let out an audible sigh.

"Just happy we're here," I wheezed, as a sickly smile pasted my face.

Besim moved further down the hall, waving the scanner while glancing at the readout, then returned.

"The trail continues behind this door," she stated. The consultant stared at the wood with that same cold, clinical look she must reserve for administering proctology exams.

I bet she ate her dinner uncooked too, like raw meat and stuff. The bloodier, the better.

Yeah, even my issues need a prescription.

The door was demarcated with a brass unit number attached above one large brass knocker. There was a joke here, but I left it alone.

No intercom or door bell. A thin doormat with the faded word *Welcome* on its surface sat crookedly on the floor.

I did a double take at the unit number.

"This is Tony's apartment," I said.

I eyeballed the hallway before drawing my hand-cannon. It was very quiet.

Besim's eyes widened at the sight of the SMART gun. She stepped away from the door.

"Size does matter," I muttered defensively.

Deacon took up a position at an angle that would keep him hidden to anyone inside opening the door unless they stepped out into the hallway. He wasn't holding a weapon, but he looked at me and nodded once.

I knocked on the door.

"Tony Marrazzo, this is Detective Tom Holliday with the Empire City Pol…err…Special Crimes Unit," I said, employing my authoritative policeman's voice. "We'd like to ask you a few questions."

I waited a few heartbeats, but there was no response. One of the neighbors opened their door, but after a quick glare from me, they disappeared. I knocked again.

"Mr. Marrazzo, this is Detective Holliday with ECSCU. Would you please open the door?"

Nothing.

My heart rate picked up. An old, familiar anxiety weighed down my shoulders. I willed my muscles to relax, then silently counted to five. Years of training and experience allowed me to maintain a clear, level head. If you're in this business long enough, you'll run into someone waving a gun and pointing it at innocent people. I'd shot people before, and as far as I and the law were concerned, they damned well deserved it. That's not to say right now I expected someone to come at me with a weapon, but as a cop, I'm supposed to be prepared for anything.

Besides, I couldn't find Vanessa Mallery's murderer if I got killed on my first day on the job.

"It ain't opening by itself, Holliday," Deacon murmured.

I glared at him but didn't move. Besim cocked her head to one side, listening. I glanced from her back to Deacon.

"There is no one home," she stated quietly. "I do not hear anything beyond the door."

"They could be standing still, or on the far side of the room," I pointed out, my voice low.

"A distinct possibility," Besim said. "However, I hear neither breathing nor a heartbeat, other than present company."

"You don't hear a heartbeat?" I looked to Deacon for help. "Seriously, she can hear that?"

Deacon shrugged as the consultant offered me a patient smile. "I am certain you will learn to trust me in time, Detective Holliday. I understand your reservations, but I hope to prove myself to you."

"Fine," I groused. "But you'd better be right."

After holstering the gun, I donned rubber gloves and removed a cloth roll from my blazer's inner pocket. Inside were several thin metal instruments.

Deacon gave me a sly look.

"We're conducting a murder investigation," I explained in a matter-of-fact tone. "One of our eyewitnesses could be in danger, so now I have probable cause."

"Still illegal," he chuckled.

I ignored him, selected the tools I needed, and stuck them in my mouth while I rolled the cloth back.

My modest lock picking skills were more than a match for the door's basic lock. I heard a faint click-click sound, then turned the knob, slowly pushing inward. To my great relief, no flying bullets, feral cats, or psychotic ex-girlfriends rushed out at me. Instead, I was met by the pleasant scent of lemon. I stepped into the dark foyer. Soft lamplight appeared further ahead. The apartment was a one-bedroom affair with a living and kitchen area, a bathroom and two closets.

It was also immaculate.

From the straightened comforter to the pots and pans hanging from pegs in the kitchen, the apartment reeked of excessive cleanliness. Either Tony employed cleaning fairies, or he was fastidious to the extreme. Even the bottles in the wine rack next to the coffee table looked like they'd been dusted off. The rack was nearly full, except for one spot at the bottom where the pinot was kept. I pulled a bottle at random from its setting.

"Expensive taste," I remarked, then put it back.

I handed Deacon and Besim rubber gloves and watched them move about the apartment, opening cabinets and drawers. Several colorful plastic pamphlets were neatly stacked by the coffee table. They were advertisements for Wrigley-Boes Pharmaceuticals, highlighting their spectrum of vitamins and other health aids. The covers were split in half. One side displayed a scrawny-looking older man wearing a white lab coat surrounded by laboratory equipment. The other depicted a handsome young man holding hands with an equally fit young woman. The caption read "Live the life you've always wanted!"

"Cleaning service is thorough," Deacon observed.

"Yeah," I replied. "Doesn't this seem too neat and clean?"

"Or he pays his cleaning service to be thorough," Deacon countered.

"I don't know," I grumbled. "There's just something wrong about all of this."

"Mr. Marrazzo is no doubt traumatized from the encounter last night," Besim pointed out. "It is natural he would wish to remain as far away from the occurrence as possible. Perhaps his cleaning service is scheduled for this morning? They would have access to his apartment regardless of whether he was home."

What they said made sense, but I couldn't shake the feeling I was missing something. I walked over to the window and peered out at the gray and gloom.

"Holliday, there ain't nothing here," Deacon said. "Should we head up to the roof?"

He was right. There was no point in staying.

Forty minutes and a fruitless search of the roof later, we returned to the pod. The scanner hadn't picked up anything on the roof, not even lemon scent.

It was time to interview the witnesses.

CHAPTER 8

I brooded as we sped toward Julie's apartment. Deacon smoked another cigarette, while Besim stared at the evidence bags resting on the slide table, an unreadable expression on her face.

"I'm going to dig more into Vanessa's background," I said after a while, if only to break the silence. "There has to be somebody in her life who is connected to this. Jilted ex-lover, a co-worker, maybe a pissed off milk man?"

No one responded to that, content to sit and wait. I re-examined the physical evidence, as well as Vanessa's file. Investigating a murder, or any case for that matter, was an exhaustive and tedious process. Most times, you ran into red herrings that lead nowhere fast. Solving these types of crimes required patience and dedication, and a meticulous attention to detail. Even the smallest clues held significant meaning. However, everything I reviewed spun a simple story about a single young woman living in the big city. She must have had friends, a close confidante, somebody with whom she socialized that I could talk to and get an idea of what happened. And there was always the work angle, much like the Murray case.

Yet my instincts told me the truth was far more sinister. Her blood had been drained from her body, which threw normal out the window.

The eyewitnesses would add color and depth to the bigger picture, but how much truth would they provide? They had both been wasted on 'joy. Anything they had seen the previous night would be suspect.

I spent the remainder of the trip nursing my jumbled thoughts, and a cold mug of coffee.

We arrived in a classy neighborhood in Soho. The streets were a lot cleaner here, and the eclectic mix of boutiques and residences made the area a haven for artists, free thinkers and musicians. Julie's apartment building was a renovated warehouse with a covered entrance and a uniformed doorman. Its dark exterior walls gave it an industrial character, and tendrils of ivy clung to the brick.

The rain dripped in fitful spurts with no end in sight. I secured the pod, and as we crossed the narrow street, I planted a foot in a pothole filled with cold rainwater.

"Oh, for fuck's sake!" I exclaimed, shaking my leg. A young couple out for a stroll gave me a dirty look.

It was turning into one of those days.

As we approached the doorman, I ID'd myself and explained our purpose. His nametag read "Phelps." The doorman's eyes widened as he took in Besim and Deacon.

"Yeah, Miss DeGrassi's home with her boyfriend," Phelps said. He was mid-fifties, with a plain face and worker hands. "She in any danger?"

"Not on my watch," I said over my shoulder as we entered the building.

We took the elevator. After a quick exchange with the two officers on duty, we made our way to Julie's apartment. There were only six units on the third floor. The place smelled nice, with lighting from antique, torch-like lamps in sconces along the walls.

Julie greeted us at the door. She was pretty, athletic, and wore just enough makeup that she should give lessons to Besim. Her perfume was light and pleasant, and I couldn't help but smile when she shook my hand. Julie hadn't slept much, judging from the bags under her tired hazel eyes, although her clothes were fresh. Some of that exhaustion evaporated when she caught sight of the Vellan.

"Please come in," she said, casting a sidelong glance at Besim as we walked past.

Julie's apartment was the kitschy kind of cute that annoyed me for some reason. Maybe it's because I'm a horrible interior decorator and have no sense of style or color coordination. Let's face it, lawn furniture in the living room has never been popular, but at least I found it comfortable.

Her place was half again the size of Tony's and included a powder room to the right of the entry door. A few quick steps brought us into a living room with two built-in bookshelves flanking a leather couch and matching loveseat, coffee table and reading chair. The shelves were filled with a variety of bric-a-brac as well as several holo-frames. From the images, Julie liked to travel to the European enclaves. An empty bottle of pinot and two wine glasses were on the coffee table. Red dregs stained the bottom of each glass.

The kitchen ran off the living room to the right, and a closed door on the opposite wall indicated the bedroom. A full wine rack rested against the wall underneath a breakfast bar that included two stools. The walls held a few paintings, mostly abstract oils and geometric shapes that art snobs fawned over.

"Not bad on an executive assistant's salary," I murmured to Deacon.

Sitting dejectedly at one end of the couch was Tony, wearing the same clothes from the night before if the mud-spattered pants and shirt were any indication. His head was held in his right hand, and he didn't look up as we entered the room. A few days' growth covered his face, and he had that slick hairstyle James Reynolds and the other young Wall Street punks wore nowadays, a throwback to the Reaganomics era of the 1980s.

"Can I get you anything?" Julie offered. "Coffee or tea?"

I live by a few simple rules, one of which is when someone offers you coffee, you say yes. Unless that someone is trying to kill you, in which case you accept the coffee under advisement.

I smiled, thanking her. Besim requested tea. Deacon declined, wandering around the apartment to study the paintings and holo-frames with unabashed interest.

"I didn't realize there were any Vellans on the police force," Julie remarked from the kitchen.

"She's on loan from their embassy," I jumped in quickly before Besim could respond. "ECPD is test driving a new cross-cultural initiative. They show us theirs, we show them ours, that sort of thing."

Besim arched an eyebrow but said nothing as she settled into the loveseat.

"That's nice," Julie replied. She asked us how we took our coffee. "You want any, baby?"

"Nah, I'm good," Tony croaked in a rough voice.

He cleared his throat a few times before raising his head to take in the three of us with haunted, bloodshot eyes. I'd seen that expression a million times in my own mirror. Poor guy. He yawned and stood up unsteadily to shake my hand. I made with the introductions, then took the chair opposite him.

"Please state your full name for the record," I said, leaning forward with my elbows resting on my thighs. EVI would catalogue the interview.

"Um, yeah, okay, it's, um, Anthony Lukah Marrazzo," he said. "But you can call me Tony."

"Thank you, Tony." I smiled. "Can you tell us what happened last night?"

The smell of roasting coffee grounds floated into the living room. Tony stared straight ahead, biting his lip. I noticed dried blood where he'd been worrying at it.

"It'll be okay baby, you can tell them," Julie encouraged from the kitchen. "They'll believe you."

I gave him one of my patented reassuring smiles, the kind I reserved for little kids, potted plants, and drunks.

"Yeah, okay." Tony rubbed his forehead a few times. "It was dark, y'know? And me and Julie were, y'know, having a little fun in the alleyway."

Deacon took a position between the kitchen and the bedroom door, studying our witness with fixed intensity. Tony ran a hand through his hair a few times and licked his lips again. I smelled wine on his breath.

"It was around ten o'clock. Then we heard this scream, and then it got cut off with, like, a gurgle. It sounded fucking awful. Like all scared and shit. So me and Julie, we ran down the alleyway to check it out, you know, in case somebody needed help."

I nodded my thanks as Julie came around and handed out steaming mugs. Once finished, she sat beside Tony and linked her arm protectively in his. She leaned her head against his shoulder and closed her eyes.

"I pulled out my phone so we could see," Tony continued, drawing strength from his contact with Julie. His words spilled out faster. "I mean, it was raining and really dark, y'know? So, like a minute or two later, we come across this guy kneeling next to this body, this girl, lying on the ground. I thought maybe she'd fallen or slipped or something. But, like, she wasn't moving, and I heard this slurping sound, like when you're drinking from a can. It was fucked up, man. Really fucked up."

Tony's voice trailed off. He started sobbing.

"It'll be okay, baby," Julie soothed, hugging him close. "Just tell them what you saw."

"I can't," he blubbered.

Julie made comforting sounds as Tony's shoulders shook.

I didn't push. You couldn't in stressful situations like these. In my experience, let the witnesses tell their story in their own time.

Unless you're Deacon.

"Get it together, boy!" Deacon snapped, his voice cracking like a whip. "Quit acting like a fucking crybaby! Tell us what happened."

Tony looked at Deacon as if he'd been slapped.

"We ain't got time for your shit," Deacon glared. "And I don't give two fucks that you're scared. Tell us everything you saw so we can catch the bastard who murdered that girl."

"Yeah, yeah, okay." He nodded rapidly several times, then took a shaky breath. "My phone's light didn't show much. Curly hair, maybe, with pointed ears, and dead eyes. Like, there was no life in them or anything. And two fangs stuck out of his mouth, like a fucking vampire! His mouth and chin were covered in blood. But then it all dissolved *into* his fucking skin! I'm telling you man, it was *fucked up!*"

"What was he wearing?" I probed, ignoring his reaction. "Did you notice any tattoos, or jewelry? Any other distinguishing features? Was he tall or short? Skin color?"

"Um, he was my height, and skinny," Tony replied, rubbing at his temples. "White guy, I think. I didn't see any tats or jewelry. Wore a long coat." He looked up, realizing something. "And a cape. Vampires wear capes, right?"

"Anything else?" I pressed, trying hard not to roll my eyes.

"Look man, I already told the other cops everything I just told you." Tony's hands trembled, but he managed to keep it together. He rubbed his runny nose with a shirt sleeve. "That's all I can remember."

"What about the girl?" Deacon said. "Anything about her?"

Tony shook his head.

"I think her hair was red. And her throat had been...had

been..." He made a gagging noise, then bolted from the couch and into the bathroom.

The sound of his retching soured the hot coffee in my stomach. I put the mug down. Deacon scowled, shaking his head in disgust.

"I'm sorry," Julie apologized, her own eyes moist. "This has been so hard for both of us. And Tony hasn't slept. He can't get last night out of his head."

"I understand, Miss DeGrassi." I forced a smile. "Can you tell us what you saw?"

She stood, picked up my mug, and moved to the kitchen.

"It was like being in a nightmare with that thing, those awful, dead eyes and its fangs," she said, the horror clear in her voice. "And the blood covering its mouth and chin! Tony grabbed my hand, and we ran. Then we heard police sirens and shouting. I guess I was in shock, because I really don't remember much after that other than being taken to the hospital."

Tony began coughing from the bathroom, and Julie excused herself to check on him. I exchanged a quick glance with Deacon.

"Fucking addicts," Deacon hissed in disgust. I narrowed my eyes at him. That comment hit too close to home. "What'd you expect?"

"Yeah, well she seems to be handling it better than Tony," I observed, stowing what I wanted to say to Deacon about addicts. Now wasn't the time to pick a fight.

"Indeed, their recollection of the incident last night must be called into question," Besim stated in a flat tone. "And I do not believe Miss DeGrassi is an addict. Her companion, on the other hand, is most assuredly so."

"Let me guess," I said. "You could smell it on him, but not her."

Besim's lips curled imperceptibly. "Not quite."

I waited for her to elaborate, but just then, Julie led a pale Tony to the bedroom. He slurred an apology, gave Julie an awkward hug, and stumbled inside. Julie pressed her head against the doorframe.

"I'm so sorry," she sobbed. "I don't think Tony can handle any more right now. He really needs to rest. Could you come back tomorrow? Please?"

Besim and I both stood.

"Of course." I handed Julie one of my holo-cards. "I'll be in touch. Please don't hesitate to call me in the meantime."

"Thank you," Julie replied, looking tired and frail. She showed us to the door.

"Thanks for the coffee," I said as the three of us left the apartment.

We returned to the pod.

Murder investigations lead to a lot of dead ends. It's just a factor of the business. If the puzzles were easy, and sometimes they were, we'd catch more bad guys. But most of the time, the pieces were vague shapes, full of shadows and half-truths. Relying on this eyewitness testimony, especially if they had been zoned on 'joy, made the process that much tougher.

"What a fucking waste of fucking time," Deacon growled as he lit a cigarette.

"Oh, I don't know," I replied. "The coffee wasn't half-bad."

"We learned jack shit back there, Holliday," he said, jabbing the fingers holding his cigarette in the direction of Julie's place.

"Maybe," I conceded, failing to hide my own frustration. "They were both lit last night, but they still saw something. I reviewed the facial composite from the sketch artist. No hits in the EC Inter-Enclave ID or the International Facial Holo-Recognition systems."

I flopped into a passenger chair and swiveled from side to side hoping the motion might help me think.

Besim settled herself into a seat, offering me an expectant look.

"You have something you'd like to share with the rest of the class?" I asked.

"Perhaps," Besim began. "However, I am still considering the variables."

"Okay, then what do you have so far?" I planted my feet to halt the chair's movement and gave her my full attention.

"Tony Marrazzo displayed the classic signs of addiction, something I do not need to explain to either of you," Besim stated, looking from Deacon back to me.

"Gee Doctor, thanks, I think," I said, although I wondered why she had included Deacon. "How nice of *William* to share everything about me with you. When will you return the favor?"

"Julie DeGrassi, on the other hand, appears merely distraught," Besim continued, ignoring the question. "I would posit Julie does not partake of recreational narcotics nearly as often as Tony. As was previously established, the crime scene is, how do you humans phrase it, 'in his backyard'? Thus, Tony's preference to convalesce at her apartment, maintaining a healthy distance from the source of his trauma. But I do not believe that to be the only reason. In fact, his reliance on Julie is greater than he knows."

"And you figured this out, how?" I asked.

"I listen, but I also observe," Besim explained. "His voice and speech patterns were interrupted by his anxiety, his need for a 'fix,' and obvious sleep deprivation. Julie, on the other hand, was in command of her faculties the entire time. She acted the proper hostess, as if nothing were amiss. Perhaps it is her method of coping. However, I think Julie was more in control of her circumstances. I must give it more thought before concluding anything further."

I was about to ask another question when the audio center of my brain exploded with screeching feedback. Crying out, I covered my ears with both hands. At the same time, Besim doubled over in pain, also gripping her head. Deacon rushed to her side.

As soon as the noise began it vanished, leaving behind a deafening echo. I blinked several times and stretched my jaw. After a few moments, the echo faded.

"EVI," I rasped, wincing at the sound. "What the hell was that?"

"A power surge at Headquarters occurred as the result of an explosion to several Nexus generators at the adjacent power company," she said between bursts of static.

Images appeared on the windshield display. Thick black smoke and flashes of a raging fire engulfed part of a broad four-story building.

"All implanted personnel were physically affected. The cause of the explosion is unknown. Emergency services have been deployed to assess the damage, including potential casualties. The enclave utility employs four hundred and—"

"I get the picture," I interrupted, flinching a little whenever I moved my head. "What's your status?"

"Disaster recovery systems have also failed," EVI replied. "I will be engaged in an emergency diagnostic with our technicians and will be unavailable for finely-tuned data functions such as data collection and assessment until it is completed. Base functionality, including enclave-wide internal and external communications, and logistical deployment and control of transportation, will remain operable during this time. Detective Holliday, I apologize for any inconvenience."

"That's okay, sweetie." I patted the dashboard. "You hang in there."

"Thank you," EVI replied, ending the communication.

"Well, isn't that just a nice kick in the nuts," I grumbled. "Looks like we're on our own, folks. EVI will be down for a while."

Besim, now recovered, thanked Deacon with a slight pat on his arm. He returned to his seat but shot her a concerned a look.

"You all right?" I asked.

Besim gave me a wan smile. "I will recover, Detective."

"I guess having super hearing powers isn't all it's cracked up to be, eh?" I smiled back.

She laughed, a genuine sound filled with soothing music that made the pain in my ears fade and my smile grow. The laughter transformed her face as it had back at the bank. Her eyes lit up with warmth and color. I caught myself staring, blushed, and looked away.

What the fuck was *that* about?

"What now?" Deacon interrupted, a new cigarette between his fingers.

I cleared my throat, slightly nonplussed, and turned toward the front of the pod. Noting the time displayed in silvered digitized numerals on the display, I realized I was famished. Skipping lunch and living on coffee had its drawbacks. And I'd had enough of my new so-called partners.

"Well, it's been an eventful day." I clapped my hands together, then grimaced. Stupid ears. "And I'm sure you're all just as tired as I am. With that in mind, we'll reconvene at 0700. Meet me at Mortie's Kosher Deli over on East 28th. Trust me, you'll love it."

"Whatever, Holliday." Deacon took a long drag from his smoke. Both he and Besim stood up and moved to the hatchway.

"You're getting out here?" I asked curiously, activating the door. Wet air blasted into the pod interior.

"Don't want you losing beauty sleep carting us around in your fancy pod, Holliday," he replied with a sarcastic smile. "We'll be fine. See you tomorrow."

CHAPTER 9

*E*VI dropped me off at the Metro station two blocks from my place. I left her with instructions to be there at six. With the hatchway closed, the pod set in motion and flowed effortlessly along its 'way before merging with a separate public transportation track. Both paths were part of a latticework of heavy girders and infrastructure rising above the ground, a separate highway with its own traffic rules. Moments later, the ECPD pod connected electromagnetically to the rear of a slower and much longer Metro pod before being swallowed by the rain and fog.

I trudged along the cracked and rubbish-strewn sidewalk, misty rain enveloping me in wet armor. I lived in the "nicer" section of Dyker Heights, once an old, affluent neighborhood, now a festering armpit of drugs, gangs, and lost people. The stately bungalows and ornate homes that had once decorated these streets had all been torn down decades ago. They'd been replaced with shitty, multi-family tenements owned and operated by a conglomeration of real estate moguls who didn't give a rat's ass about the people living in them. As you'd expect, crime ran rampant here, but the rent was dirt cheap, and it was all I could afford. The last report I'd read put Dyker Heights tied for third-worst neighborhood in which to raise a family behind parts of East Harlem and Bedford-Stuyvesant. I couldn't remember who we were tied with, but at least we were in the top three in something.

Dorothy had been right. There really was no place like home.

As I made my way into the hollowed-out lobby of the Renaissance Apartments, I ignored two teenage punks lounging on one of the cushion-less couches. They took turns taking hits from the same goldjoy pipe. Their eyes glittered with gold, lost amid fantasies only they could imagine.

"The stars are so beautiful tonight," one cried, his outstretched hands grasping at phantoms. "Can you see them? Can you see them, Bobby? Fly me to the moon. To the moon, and the stars and into the fucking sun!"

"This 'joy is the shit!" Bobby laughed. "Quit hogging the pipe, Mal! I need me some more of that shit!"

Mal tried to stand before collapsing onto the couch. Bobby leered at me, then rifled through his wasted buddy's clothes, yanking out his enclave ID and waving it around as if he'd won the goddamn lottery. I moved past them without a word.

The elevator was out again, so I took the stairs. Pushing past the door, I was assaulted by the sick smell of piss and other unidentifiable things. Another half-naked junkie lay prone on the stairs. I didn't bother checking for a pulse. Instead, I held my breath, skirted the body and proceeded up three flights of stairs to my floor. A quick walk down an empty hallway brought me to my apartment. Once inside, I secured the triple locks and exhaled sharply. I leaned my head against the inside of the door. Fresh air circulated thanks to the portable air purifier sitting on the floor several paces inside my apartment. I breathed in the air greedily. It was one of only a handful of luxuries I allowed myself, thanks to Abner's constant nagging. I waved a hand over the sensor attached to the wall, activating the reading lamp sitting on a nightstand by my bed.

I kept my place neat and tidy. Everything had an order to it, and I preferred to keep things simple, given how disorderly my life had become over the years. Mine was a one-bedroom efficiency with a tiny kitchenette, a smaller bathroom with standup shower, a broom closet, a fold-out cot, two plastic lawn chairs, and an end table with a portable and very outdated holo-rig currently in rest mode. My wrinkled clothes hung in a neat row along a plastic clothesline I'd installed that stretched between the bathroom door and the window. I doffed my blazer and hooked it to the line with some pins, then unwound my shoulder rig and placed the SMART gun carefully on the end table. Next to it was a broken holo-frame displaying the image of a pretty brunette wearing a pink dress standing next to an old man in a suit. A young, curly-haired boy with big blue eyes sat on a stool between them. Marching into the kitchenette, I activated the coffee maker and retrieved a fresh mug from the single cabinet above the sink, setting it on the counter.

Back at the living area, I waved my hand over the holo-rig. The voice-activation feature had busted years ago, and I hadn't bothered asking Leyla to fix it. Two holo-windows materialized above the device containing unread voice messages, and a shadowy third that held one saved message. I flicked my fingers over the first of two, deactivating the visuals. Tinny audio played quietly from the rig's speakers.

"Tom, it's Abner. I hope the day finds you well! Listen, Tom, I'm worried about Leyla. She's been out every night. And before you say anything, I understand this is what young people are prone to doing but...would you please speak with her? She looks up to you, although I haven't the foggiest as to why. That was a joke, Tom. Anyway, I hope you haven't forgotten about the Steinbeck reading this Saturday morning at the library. Nine o'clock, and don't be late! Take care, and I'll talk to you soon."

A wry smile crinkled my lips. I'd swing by the bookstore Saturday and have a sit-down with Leyla before the reading. It wouldn't help, as the willful girl did what she wanted, but it would mollify Abner. I deleted the message.

"Detective Holliday, this is Rena MacIntosh with the *Daily Dose*. My sources tell me you're involved with the so-called downtown vampire slaying. I'd like to get your take on it. Call me at—"

I cut the message off and deleted it, shaking my head. How Rena had gotten a hold of my number was anyone's guess. I'd never spoken with her or the *Dose* before on any of my previous cases and had no interest in starting now. The media had their uses, but our relationship was like divorced parents with shared custody of the kids and lots of acrimony.

The third remained. I stared at its darkened holo-window. A faint wetness painted the corners of my eyes. My shoulders slumped. The message was indelibly printed in my memory.

"Hey baby, it's me. I really need to talk to you. There's something you need to know. About me. About us. Something…well, anyway, just come by my room when you're done with counseling, okay? I love you, Tom. No matter what happens, I will always love you."

My fingers froze, so tempted to replay it, to savor her sound and drown myself in her voice again. To never, ever let her go.

I licked dry lips. My throat grew raw. The memory of her lying in the tub replayed in my mind. The blood. The glass. The silence. The loneliness. The despair.

The drip from one of nature's greatest creations saved me from wandering down that dark road again. I sighed heavily, then returned to the kitchen to pour myself a much-needed cup of joe. Black, sugar, no cream, deliciousness. After downing the first cup in two swigs, I poured a second before wandering back to settle in one of the lawn chairs. I stretched out my legs and kicked off my wet shoes.

"Helluva day, Holliday," I muttered, sipping coffee.

I didn't own a holo-vision. My job was depressing enough without watching the news or other reality entertainments on the hundreds of channels from which to choose. Besides, I had plenty of worlds to dive into, right at my fingertips. Built-in bookshelves lined every wall of my apartment that didn't include a door or window, and all of them filled with books. I'd subdivided them into sections, from various annotated works of Shakespeare, to the likes of Hemingway, Dickens, Woolf, Tolstoy, Austen, Asimov, Wilkie Collins, Harper Lee, James Joyce, and Rowling. And I'd read them all more than twice. Most had been collected with the help of Abner. We had scoured the enclave searching for these belletristic treasures. With much of the United States desolated by nukes, sickness and famine, a lot had been lost. Abner and I had done our small part in protecting humanity's precious literary past.

A muffled crash followed by two voices raised in anger shattered my brief moment of calm. The Slotnicks in 33b were at it again, their shouting match now an unfortunate nightly ritual. The thin apartment walls barely contained what they said, but I'd grown used to it. However, after today, my patience ran thin. I grimaced, then wiggled my fingers over the holo-rig's control panel activating my music library. With a quick glance at the current selection, Chopin's Piano Concerto Number 1 began, its dark and dramatic opening lending well to my mood while simultaneously drowning out 33b.

Nothing was ever easy. I shrugged, then swallowed more coffee. My hand unconsciously waved to and fro in time to the piano's beautiful rendering. Some of my calm returned, and I thought back to my first meeting with Deacon Kole.

I'd surprised myself with how readily I had opened up to the former Protector. It was almost instinctual. I somehow knew I could trust him. Let's face it. As a cop, I wasn't what you'd call an open book. Hell, I had more walls than New Rikers prison! The job had a way of hardening you. And a corruption scandal wasn't something that generated trust in your fellow man or woman, either. Still, there had been something about the character of his voice, or maybe it was his sheer presence, that had dragged the truth from me about my last night with Kate.

As I considered the subsequent meeting with Deacon and Captain Mahoney, I realized how much I craved being back in the hunt again. I would've said yes to Special Crimes even if Mahoney had ordered me to parade around Manhattan in a clown suit! There was no question the 98th Precinct had sucked the life out of me. I had no future there. I didn't think I had a future anywhere.

"Whereof what's past is prologue; what to come, in yours and my discharge."

Unlike Sebastian in *The Tempest*, I had no interest in a crown. I just wanted to be relevant again. Everything I once had got flushed down the shitter after the corruption probe and my turn in rehab. Like I'd said to Deacon, it was old news. But that didn't stop me from reminiscing. Solving murders changed people's lives, not always for the better, but those cases had given me direction. They'd given me a purpose, something I'd lost along the way. Well, maybe Special Crimes was my ticket back? I'd always believed in second chances. Maybe it was my turn?

Or, maybe, that's what the Insight was all about?

The fickle clairvoyance was an enigma that I'd rolled around in my mind ever since I had started viewing the world in a much different light. It was no secret that every person carried hidden baggage. The Insight allowed me to see all of theirs, right down to the color, brand, and name on their bag tag. It had showed me things I never would have imagined. And the depth of its power frightened me. Only idiots weren't scared of magic. Still, after all the shit I'd been through, I like to think I'd learned my lesson. The Insight could easily be abused. Yet, I'd never felt the urge. Instead, I dreaded the moment when my eyes burned with fire, and everything that followed. And I had little control over any of it.

Oh, I'd considered its origin. Why I wielded the Insight. What made me special. Or cursed, depending on the day. Every answer I'd come up with sounded crazier than the previous one. Before I cut my wrists, I was about as normal as anyone else. But after I woke up in the hospital?

Everything had changed.

Before Deacon and Mahoney, only Abner and Leyla knew about the Insight. I didn't want to freak Father Jack out, so I'd kept him in the dark. The fewer who knew about it, the better off everyone would be.

After encountering the *fetch* and then meeting Deacon, I now felt different. As if this morning was the beginning of something. That the Insight had been waiting for the former Protector's arrival, and by extension, I had as well. It was almost like an intervention, that perhaps I was finally on the right path.

Chopin finished, but the Slotnicks hadn't, so I let the rig randomly choose the next song. Suddenly, heavy rhythmical guitar riffs by the incomparable Jimmy Page followed by John Bonham's powerful percussion billowed throughout my small apartment. My foot beat to the time. Someone pounded the wall. Probably Yuri Slotnick, although Miriam was no slouch. I became vaguely aware of someone yelling at me to turn down the music. Instead, I wiggled my fingers, increased the volume, leaned my head back, and touched the sky.

Sleep overtook me, and for the first time in weeks, the nightmares were held at bay.

CHAPTER 10

*N*o matter what you've read in holo-novels or seen in the movies, homicide investigations were never accomplished on empty stomachs.

Mortie's Kosher Delicatessen and Family Restaurant was located between Avenue U and East 28th Street in Brooklyn. It had been a pillar of the community for as long as I could remember. The handwritten signs adorning the two window fronts promised hot stuff, cold stuff, fresh stuff, homemade stuff, and pickles. The interior was cozy, big enough to accommodate ten tables and booths, and several refrigerated displays.

My grandfather Harry used to take me to see Uncle Mortie on Sundays while my dad slept off his latest hangover. He introduced me to everything a nice half-Jewish kid from Little Odessa could want—noodle kugel with raisins, soup, black-and-white cookies, kreplach, whitefish, bagels, ten different flavors of cream cheese, and dozens of kosher cold cuts. Harry and I would nosh and kibbitz about life, the universe, and everything.

As usual, the place was packed. We sat at a table near the back by the entrance to the bathroom.

"Hey Doc," Myrna called over the roar of the breakfast crowd, weaving her way through the bustling floor toward our table. "You want me to top you off?"

Uncle Mortie's wife carried a coffee pot in one hand and water pitcher in the other, pouring either libation at the request of her customers while carrying on three different conversations. She'd provide long-suffering commiseration and sage motherly advice, and never spilled a drop.

"Please," I yawned, leaning back in my chair.

I was stuffed. Pumpernickel everything bagel with egg salad debris lay scattered across my plate.

Deacon finished devouring his beef brisket, sopping up dark gravy with an egg roll. He made appreciative sounds, surprised a tiny place like this could crank out quality food like that.

Besim stared at a rounded, yellowish-white, doughy dumpling parked in the middle of her plate. Her fork lurked above it, as if frozen in time.

"And you are certain this is edible?" she asked dubiously, her brow furrowed with uncertainty.

"*Bubbalah*, it's a potato knish," Myrna chuckled as she refilled our cups. "We make the best in the enclave! You never seen one before?"

Besim poked at the crusty exterior with her fork, tilting her head as if that angle might give her a better perspective of the food.

"I have not." She pursed her lips, considering the dumpling.

Myrna laughed pleasantly, ambling away.

"Just eat the damn thing," Deacon grumbled between mouthfuls of food.

Besim remained locked in indecision when EVI announced an incoming call from Stentstrom.

"Good morning," I chuckled warmly. "What's up?"

"Ah, Detective, I hope I'm not interrupting anything?" the medical examiner asked.

I heard Beethoven's *Eroica* in the background, his funereal second movement. Although Stentstrom's voice was clear, an echo accompanied it, with each word repeated a half beat later.

"We're at breakfast discussing the case," I replied.

"Very good!" Stentstrom said. "I won't take up too much of your mealtime. I wanted you to know I have completed a full review of Miss Mallery's dental and health records. Her wisdom teeth, for example, grew in perfectly. Miss Mallery's records do not list any instances of poor health, surgeries, or prescriptions other than a sleep aid."

I frowned at that.

"Maybe she never bothered going to the doctor whenever she was sick? That's unusual, but not impossible, right?"

"Taken by itself, it is not impossible," he stated. "However, when combined with my other findings, it *is* improbable. Miss Mallery had all of her immunizations, to be sure. But how many children do you know that have never been sick, or experienced a broken bone? How many who have never needed dental work, or never had a cavity once in their life? Couple that with no birthmarks, freckles or scarring of any kind, and that is *highly* unusual."

"What do you think it means?" I asked, troubled.

"Well it certainly corroborates my observations from the initial examination," Stentstrom chattered excitedly. "As to how or why, I still do not have any *working* theories, and I would rather not conjecture until I have run a few more tests. Unfortunately, I have two more examinations to perform later today, so that research will have to wait. One of them is a real humdinger of a corpse too! A young man was enjoying a noodle bowl at a Chinatown bistro when he was literally eaten from the inside out! Apparently, some of the noodles were infested with carnivorous tapeworms! It sounds absolutely fascinating!"

"Uh, yeah, well you have fun with that," I replied weakly. "Stay in touch."

We disconnected. I recapped the conversation to the others.

"Perhaps the medical and dental records were falsified?" Besim mused.

"Yeah, but why?" Deacon countered. "Everything we know about this girl don't indicate nothing out of the ordinary."

"Maybe that's just it," I pointed out. "Her only family lives in New Hollywood. I'll contact her aunt and see if she can shed some light on her niece. Also, we need to talk to any friends and co-workers. Maybe someone knows her at that coffeehouse too."

"Reckon we can cover more ground if we split up," Deacon suggested. "I'll go to Hughes, while y'all head over to Armin's."

"Okay." I hesitated, looking askance at the Vellan. "Though it'd be better if Besim went with you. I work cases alone, this one being the exception, of course."

"Grow up, Holliday," Deacon chuckled. "We're a team now, so y'all can spend some quality time together."

During the ride to Hughes, I reached out to Vanessa's aunt with no luck, and left her a message to call me back. Why would she ignore ECPD? Was she in trouble? When EVI was back online, I'd have her contact the European Polit Bureau to see if they could track the aunt down.

We dropped Deacon off, then headed to Armin's.

"Do I make you uncomfortable, Detective Holliday?" Besim asked once we were underway.

She took the other command chair, sitting with her back straight, and observed me with dispassionate eyes.

"Not really," I lied, assuming a casual tone. "Like I said before, I'm just used to working alone. I haven't had a partner in a long time."

Besim considered that for a moment. "Yes, but I am not human. I suspect you have interacted with my people in the past, but it has never involved your work."

"I've met several Vellans over the years, even ate dinner with a few, in mixed company. But no, never in a work environment."

I stood up and began pacing the interior of the pod.

"So, yeah, I guess this is a bit strange for me," I continued, the words pouring out of me in a rush. "I'm investigating a murder for some new semi-clandestine unit of the ECPD. A unit, I might add, that may or may not be able to pay me. My professional record has been altered so no one knows what I'm really doing, and I've been given a shiny new badge, and a big gun to play with. Our victim is some girl with a perfect health record, the murderer is supposedly a bloodsucking vampire, and the two eyewitnesses were whacked out on goldjoy, so their memory of what happened is worthless."

I paused by the evidence table.

"And to top it off, I'm saddled with a...civilian," I said, some heat edging my voice. "No offense, Besim. It's just a lot to digest in less than twenty-four hours."

I returned to the chair opposite the consultant.

"Yet you chose to accept the position," Besim pointed out. "You could have refused."

I offered a rueful smile. "Yeah, I'm like that sometimes."

She tilted her head to the side. "Might I ask why?"

"Maybe it's because I saw a chance to turn my life around. Something I hadn't considered since I came out of...since I joined the 98th," I replied in a distant voice, tracing idle patterns with my fingers on the dashboard. "Or maybe it's because there's a dead girl who was murdered, and I have no idea why. And that kind of thing really pisses me off."

"I begin to understand you better, Detective Holliday." Besim nodded. "I had doubts when William informed me of who you were, and your background. Perhaps there is wisdom in his choice after all."

"Gee, thanks. I think."

"Perhaps you should consider my feelings," she said softly.

I noted how still she remained with her hands folded in her lap, a neutral expression covering her face.

"William is a good man," Besim explained. "He sees darkness in

Empire City and has chosen to stand against it. That is why I am here. Among my people, I am of the *Nabira-Shas*, the caste representing business and administration. It means I am more suited to a boardroom than a crime scene. I have never fired a gun or been involved in violence of any kind. I abhor violence, but I understand it is a necessity in your line of work. William approached me, asking for my assistance with the Special Crimes Unit he proposed. I did not want to at first, but he is my friend. I have very few to whom I would attach that word, but I count him among them."

Her eyes glistened with suppressed emotion.

"I met William in Milan six months after he had left Empire City. What I found was a wounded soul, someone who had seen and experienced much pain and injustice. We spent the next year traveling together. While I find your race to be irrational, incorrigible and, at times, quite dangerous, I wanted to show him how the human spirit remains indomitable despite the horrors of your past. He needed to understand not all was lost to shadow, that there was still good in the world. From New London to Roma Indomita, and east into the hinterland of the Russian Conglomerates, we traveled to places where, even after all this time, humans struggle to endure. It changed him, and for the better, of that I am certain. And it changed my perspective of your race to some degree, as well."

She turned from me to stare out the window. The streaming lights from businesses and traffic signals blended with the streaking rain to accentuate her profile's sharp features.

"I have spent my life in search of answers to inscrutable questions," Besim mused. "It was only recently, in the company of humans, that I have come to realize where I might find them. I have cut and colored my hair, hidden my heritage, and blasphemed my culture in this very pursuit. I have chosen to act against my caste and eschew the very foundations of my race by assisting your law enforcement in tracking down this murderer to bring them to justice."

As EVI announced our arrival, Besim turned back to me.

"And, so, I find all of this," she said with a sweeping gesture of her hand, "to be strange indeed."

"Well, then you're in good company, sister," I said with a half-smile.

"May I freshen up before we depart, Detective Holliday?" she asked.

"Knock yourself out."

I watched in annoyed fascination as Besim spent the next ten minutes methodically transforming her face into something less alien. The Vellan replaced her soaked bandana with a fresh one. Her short hair was matted flat, and some of the dye she had used to darken it had bled out in spotty patches. Between the darkened clumps I caught glimpses of auburn and gold, like patches of sunlight after a thunderstorm. With her long, tapered fingers, she raked thin stragglers away from her ears and eyes to establish a semblance of order. Finally, she tied the new bandana into place and examined herself with critical care in the mirror.

"Let's go," I said.

Armin's Coffee House perched on the corner of Front and Peck like a grumpy old owl in the nook of an ancient oak tree. Its storefront was a mishmash of chipped paint and loose bricks, giving it a crooked, disheveled appearance as if it had been rebuilt by a one-eyed stone mason whose hand had been tied behind his back. It anchored a series of two- and three-story buildings occupying most of the block, each separated by a fire wall, and all in equally rough condition. The businesses varied from ethnic eateries to nouveau art. There was even one of those little retail shrines dedicated to the stoned tree-huggers from the People's Republic of Boulder.

As we approached our destination, I spied a multitude of

crude, hand-drawn advertisements festooning most of its windows and the entry door.

I was about to enter Armin's when I realized Besim had paused before one window. She was scanning the flyers with great interest.

"You know any of these?" I asked.

Standing that close to her reinforced our difference in height. I'd never literally been in someone's shadow before. It was disconcerting.

"I am familiar with all of them," Besim gushed with enthusiasm. She pointed at a drawing that was the progeny of a peace sign and three electrocuted cats. "They are known as *Peaceful Intentions*, a three-piece acoustic group from New Chicago. I find their music to be quite soothing."

I nodded, shoving my hands into my pockets while I fought the urge to grab her by the arm and drag her into Armin's. She was tall yet thin, and I was wiry muscle, so it couldn't be *that* hard, right? How heavy could she be? I calculated the math in my head.

"Forgive my indulgence, Detective," Besim said quickly. "You must be anxious to continue the investigation."

"No, it's okay." I waved my hand expansively. "It's just not my scene, that's all. My taste runs real old school, like Mozart, Beethoven, Led Zeppelin, that sort of thing."

She offered me a quizzical look. "I am quite familiar with the first two composers, but who is Led Zeppelin? I have never heard of him. Does he hail from the Scandinavian Fellowship?"

"No," I chuckled. "Zeppelin is classic rock and roll. It's music from the days of my youth, when I was told what it meant to be a man. Maybe I'll have EVI play a song or two later."

She nodded, a bit uncertain, and I held the door open for her as we entered Armin's.

Soft music greeted us, piped in from a sound system not readily visible. The coffee shop's interior was an eclectic mess of mismatched tables, chairs and benches with throw pillows of all shapes and sizes. All the furniture bore gaudy upholstery that was patched and faded with the wrong colors and fabrics as if they'd been repaired by some madman with no taste. The concrete floor was littered with Oriental rugs and Berber carpets arranged with no semblance of order. To our right was a row of stools, along with a rainbow-painted countertop running halfway along the windows overlooking Peck Slip. A few recliners surrounded three small tables to complete the ensemble. Off to our left was a stage constructed from the bones of a Metro pod. The hollowed-out shell included three stools, and a flower-paneled couch.

Pungent aromas filled the air, brewed coffee and tea, as well as stale cigarette and hookah smoke. I glanced up. The ceiling was an open display of rusted ductwork and piping, with dozens of decorative string lights, better suited for the outdoors, hanging low like jungle vines. Two fans oscillated in slow circles, each content to sweep the heavy air in steady, lazy twirls.

What few patrons there were lazed on the furniture. Some sipped from their cups while remotely jacked into their holophones, bebopping their heads in time to music buzzing from their personal collections. No one paid us much attention.

At the far end, opposite the entrance, lurked a waist-high counter, dominated by a five-foot pyramid of stacked colored coffee mugs. Behind the counter space was an open window leading into a kitchen, as well as a closed door covered in more advertisements.

Four glossy menus hung from wires, offering a staggering array of liquid libations. My mouth watered as I ran down the list of potent potables, from the Triple Mocha Pumpkin Spike Polka Latte to Hazelnut Yo Mama's Tea.

It was love at first sight.

A lean young woman in her mid-twenties, with eyebrow and nose piercings and variegated hair, lounged behind the counter. As we stepped up, she welcomed us with a bored smile. Her nametag read "Moonbeam."

"Care for an Exotic Chocolate Caramel Monkey today?" she asked in a breathy voice. "It's our Flavor of the Week."

"I'm not into monkeys right now," I deadpanned, peering at the list of coffees. "But I will take the Not Your Average Joe with extra cream and sugar, please." I turned to Besim. "You want anything?"

Her back was to me while she took in the place. I asked her again, and she declined. Once Moonbeam crafted my order and rang me up, I produced my badge and introduced myself.

Her eyes widened in fear.

"I'm investigating the murder of a young woman," I said. "She may have been a regular."

"Oh, thank God," she said in relief. "I thought you were with the freaking Department of Health again about the rats!"

"No, ma'am," I gave her a long-suffering smile. "Is Armin here?"

"Yeah," Moonbeam replied, rolling her eyes. She hooked her thumb in the direction of the closed door. "He's in his 'sacred space,' down the hall on the left."

I thanked her. Besim was content to leave me to my own devices, so I went to find Armin. The floor was sticky. A quick glance in the kitchen revealed a young man with the butt of a lit cigarette clinging to his lips. He plucked two pieces of burnt toast from the toaster and slapped them onto a plate with some nameless substance that may have been edible once. He gave me a quick nod while wiping his hands on his black t-shirt bearing the caption "If I did it, would you know?" scrawled in white block letters.

Returning the nod, I strode past him to a plain wooden door with a hand-written sign taped to it that read "Meditation in progress. Fuck Off." Incomplete strains of high-pitched acoustical caterwauling echoed from behind the door.

I pounded it with my fist. The sound of the screeching felines faded.

"Read the fucking sign, jackass," a grumpy voice groused.

The ridiculous sounds started up again. I struck the door a second time. The music died. Shuffling feet approached. The door was ripped open by a very short, balding man with thick eyebrows and elephant-sized ears wearing a maroon bathrobe and blue, fuzzy slippers. Cigar smoke hugged him like shit on a pig.

"I told you—" he began.

"Tom Holliday," I interrupted, shoving my badge into his face. "I'd like to ask you a few questions."

CHAPTER 11

*T*he badge stopped him short, pun intended. Armin self-consciously tugged his bathrobe closer to cover up the out-of-control salad on his chest. His beady eyes stared at the badge, then moved up to regard me.

"Yes, hello, Detective," Armin stumbled over his words. "What can I do for you?"

I stepped inside and maintained a brittle smile as we shook hands.

"Please forgive the mess," he said as he windmilled his arms to clear the smoke lingering in his office.

The windowless office was a closet, with enough space to accommodate a desk and two chairs. A lit cigar nestled in an ashtray next to his holo-phone at one end of the desk. The image of *Peaceful Intentions* above the phone explained the noise.

The remaining free space was occupied by plastic containers brimming with old record sleeves. Five were stacked on top of each other in one corner. Several vinyl records were fanned out in alphabetical order on his desk.

Abbey Road, A Hard Day's Night, Let it Be, Love, and *Rubber Soul.*

"Nice collection," I remarked, moving a container from one chair to sit down.

"They're all purchased legally," Armin said quickly.

"I'm sure they are."

"Three hundred and fifty from the sixties and seventies," he explained in a proud, yet peevish voice. "There's a refurbished record player in the back room. Still sounds great!"

I made some bored noncommittal noises while glancing around his office.

"So, what's this about?" he asked, put off by my disinterest. "I'm in the middle of something important here, and I'd like to get back to it."

"I'm investigating the murder of Vanessa Mallery," I said. "She was a frequent customer here. I was hoping you could provide some information about her."

I pulled my phone from my coat pocket, adjusted a setting, and set it on the desk's surface. Vanessa's face appeared above it, taken from her enclave identification. Armin leaned forward, his bushy eyebrows drawn together.

I watched him closely, noting his tells, as his eyes raked across the image. He sported worry lines and wrinkles, and I guessed his age to be around fifty.

"Nope, never seen her before." He leaned back in his chair. "I spend most of my time back here dealing with these so-called 'artists.' Sorry, Detective, but I don't fraternize with the customers. I leave that to my waitstaff. Maybe one of the baristas knew her?"

I nodded, not surprised. Armin struck me as a small-time hustler with little ambition, and not a violent bone in his skinny, bathrobe-clad body.

"Who worked Sunday night?"

"Let's see," Armin tilted his head back and closed his eyes. "It was Bella, Trinity, and Jackass. I usually have three working on live nights."

"Jackass?" I chuckled.

"No, that's just what I call him," he grunted without smiling. "His real name is Jesse, but he's a complete jackass. He's also my nephew."

"You notice anything unusual about Sunday's show? Anyone in the crowd cause trouble?"

"No, it was a good show," Armin recollected. "The kids who come in here are an easygoing crowd. They're interested in having a good time while listening to the best acoustical music in Empire City."

Armin held up a hand.

"Everything's legal," he added quickly. "I run a legitimate business here. No drugs or anything. If I ever saw any of that shit in my establishment, why I'd throw them out on their rear, that's what I'd do. I have a reputation to uphold."

I swept my gaze around the cluttered office, then settled on the little man.

"I'm not interested in contraband *today*," I stated in even tones, locking eyes with him. "I'm trying to track down a killer."

"Sure, sure, because we don't serve killers here either," Armin continued in earnest. "I don't want any trouble."

"I understand that, but if you could—"

I was interrupted by a dull roar from outside. The floor trembled rhythmically.

"What the hell's going on out there?" Armin's head whipped around in confusion. "Nobody's scheduled to play today."

I opened the door and was greeted by dozens of voices raised in harmony. We exchanged a surprised look, then raced down the hallway.

The place was filled to the brim with wall-to-wall customers who swayed and sang. From my vantage point, dozens of people lined up outside the coffeehouse pressing to get through the door.

A singular voice rose above the crowd, modulating with such sweeping nuance that even I was captivated by the sound. It ebbed and flowed throughout the place like delicate thunder. Most of the gathering stood with their eyes closed while they sang along.

"Oh my gawd!" Armin shrieked as if he'd just won the lottery. He pointed wildly at the performer on the stage. "I can't believe it! She's here, *in my place!*"

"Who?" I asked in irritation. "Who's here?"

Armin latched onto my arm and pointed toward the stage.

Besim sat alone on a stool, her large coat pooled on the floor beside her. Back straight and head tilted, her eyes held a faraway cast, witnessing something only she could see. No other musicians were on the stage with her, nor was she holding an instrument.

Because she didn't need any.

Besim began another song, her voice crystalline in its purity, carrying perfect pitch and rhythm, and it was unlike anything I'd ever heard.

Her ethereal melody was soft and strong, replete with emotional depth and range. Although it contained words, the subtle strength of her voice carried powerful images and feelings that washed over and through me. I envisioned the lonely mountaintop of which she sang, a whitecap high above the clouds, untouched by man or beast. I experienced the frost and snow, and I shivered with phantom cold. Her song soared higher still, lost amidst an endless tapestry filled with countless stars until it fell, burying itself within the bowels of the earth. She sang of loss and love, filling shadowed chasms with unquenchable light and turning stark emptiness into shining hope.

A burgeoning audience had surrounded the makeshift stage in a semicircle. Some stood, while others sat on the floor or on the furniture, faces turned toward Besim in rapt attention. It was standing-room only everywhere else. The crowd floated in a sea of silent energy full of anticipation and excitement. We were all connected by one message, one voice. Many had tears in their eyes. I rubbed at the corner of my eye and felt it wet.

Her song drifted into silence, and the moment was gone. Besim hugged herself as she bowed her head, drained by the musical effort.

Thunderous applause rocked the coffeehouse. Armin flew past me and onto the stage, staring wide-eyed at the Vellan towering above him. She raised her head to say a few words to him, a worn smile on her face. He gesticulated wildly, but I couldn't make out what he was saying over the crowd's frenzied chants of "We want more!"

"I *knew* it was her!" Moonbeam babbled at me from behind the counter. "When the two of you came in, and she was like all shy and shit. And then she just sat over there while you pretended to be a cop." She laughed in delight. "You're her manager, right?"

I stared at the young barista, but my mouth wouldn't work.

"I was like 'No, that couldn't be Saranda,'" Moonbeam plowed ahead. "She hasn't been on the scene in, like, months! But then you went back to talk to Armin, and I figured you were working out a live gig or something. And it was, like, not busy or anything, so I went over and introduced myself. Oh my gawd! I still can't believe it! I met Saranda! I can't wait to tell Audrey! She's totally going to flip!"

"How...when...why was she singing?" I asked.

As I struggled to settle my thoughts, thirsty customers surged toward the coffee counter. I staggered to the side.

"I asked!" Moonbeam replied as a broad grin spread across her dimpled face. "I told her how much of a fan I am and, like, how sad I've been that she hasn't dropped any new music in such a long time. I mean, her songs really touch a part of me, like she can 'read the secret places of my heart.' Those lyrics are from *Awakenings*, y'know, the one she just performed? It's, like, her best song ever!"

I rubbed my temples, wondering once again why I had agreed to allow this consultant to accompany me on the investigation.

"But she wouldn't sing," the ebullient Moonbeam continued

in-between prepping customer orders. "And I was like, 'Why not?' And she said she was here with you, and that you had some questions about a girl who was here Sunday night. That's why you wanted to see Armin. So I was like, 'Well Armin is jacking off in his office, so if I answer the questions, would you sing?' And she said *yes*! And then I posted about it!" She swung her head around in wonderment as if it were on a pivot. "Would you look at this crowd! Holy shit!"

"Questions," I muttered, and focused my attention on Moonbeam, shutting out the crowd noise. "What did she ask you?"

"Let me think." Moonbeam paused, folding her arms while tapping her chin with a finger. "First she asked who was working here Sunday night. I don't normally on Sundays, but I told her I took Trinity's shift because she had to study for one of her midterms, and I needed the extra credits. And then Saranda pulled up the girl's image on her phone."

I placed mine on the counter with Vanessa's image displayed above it while the next customer in line mulled over what to order.

"Her?"

"Yeah, I rang her up here." Moonbeam nodded vigorously. "She was definitely my type, tall and pretty, with long red hair."

"Anything else?"

"Nope, that was it," she replied.

"Was she with anyone?"

Moonbeam narrowed her eyes as she tried to remember. "Yeah, some older chick, like maybe it was her aunt or something, but they didn't look alike. She was shorter but, like, in shape, and wore her hair in a ponytail. I really didn't look at her face much, though. She was, like, giving off all kinds of negativity, and I don't need that kind of shit messing with my aura, y'know?"

I could appreciate that.

"Was there anyone else with them? Did anyone try to join them?"

"No, just those two." Moonbeam shook her head.

"Did you notice anything unusual about either woman? Were they agitated? Afraid?"

"Well, the redhead didn't look like she wanted to be here. She kept staring out the window. Didn't drink much, either." Moonbeam gave me a conspiratorial wink. "I kinda checked her out and wanted to see if she was, like, with her friend, or *with* her friend, if you know what I mean. I thought maybe they were on a date, and it wasn't going well."

I glanced over my shoulder to see Besim still locked in conversation with Armin.

"So, which one was it?"

"Definitely not a date," Moonbeam explained with authority. "It seemed more like a business meeting. The redhead was nice, although her friend was an obnoxious bitch. When I took the redhead's order, her friend kept giving me the evil eye, and had that 'kiss my ass I make more credits than you' kind of attitude. I hate that type, y'know? Like the freaking world owes them or something."

"Why do you say that?"

"Because she was pushing the redhead to hurry up and order something so that they could sit down," the barista responded as if it were the most obvious thing in the world. "She kept saying she wanted to get a good seat before the opening act. They sat in the recliners by the window, which isn't a good spot. The acoustics suck, and you're near the door, so there's always someone coming in and out of here. I don't know about you, but that kind of distraction really pisses me off when I'm trying to listen to the music. I mean, it's, like, why—"

"Show me."

Moonbeam pointed at the window facing Peck Slip, opposite the stage where a few recliners and small tables rested. I realized there weren't as many advertisements plastered to the glass on that side, offering a much cleaner view of the street.

"Did you see them leave?" I asked.

Moonbeam shook her head, handing some frothy concoction to a bearded young man dressed in baggy jeans. He glared at me, annoyed I'd taken so much of Moonbeam's time. I flashed the badge, with the words "Fuck off" written plainly on my face. He scowled, took his coffee, and mumbled an apology. Deacon would've been proud.

"No," she replied. "Once the first act was done, I got stuck behind the counter full-time."

"Do you have security cameras in here?" I asked.

"Are you fucking kidding me?" she snorted, rolling her eyes. "We have two, and they're shit. Except for the coffee makers, Armin would rather die than pay to get anything fixed around here. And, like, don't get me started on salary!"

Moonbeam's voice faded as I concentrated on the case. Who was our mystery friend with the ponytail? What was her relationship to Vanessa? Last night wasn't a chance meeting. Did the murderer pick Vanessa up outside Armin's? Did he follow her to the Metro station? Was he already on the mass transit pod when she stepped aboard? And where had Vanessa been going? Her Bay Ridge brownstone was nowhere near the Financial District.

I didn't think there was anything more I would learn from Moonbeam. We needed to catch up with Deacon. I maneuvered through the crowded floor and stepped onto the stage with Armin and Besim.

"...and I'm thinking at least Friday and Saturday night for the next month and a half until Thanksgiving," Armin was saying to Besim.

I coughed loudly, pushing past the little man.

"Time to go," I said in a preemptory tone. Besim nodded and gathered up her coat.

"But we're talking business here," Armin harrumphed in indignation. "Let's go back to my office and we can—"

"Showtime's over," I snapped at him, then steered Besim by the elbow and out the door.

Back in the pod, I instructed EVI to head over to Hughes, then collapsed into one of the command seats. Besim resumed her place with hands folded in her lap and a stoic expression on her face. It was like being observed by a cat.

"Care to explain that one?" I asked casually. "Or was that another distraction?"

I think she blushed, but I couldn't tell because of the miles of makeup covering her cheeks.

"It was not my intention as such," she replied, sounding abashed. "I have not produced any new music in quite some time. I had harbored hope no one would recognize me, given the hour of our visit. I presumed the coffeehouse would be lightly-attended, thus reducing the chances. I was...mistaken. It was a very foolish decision. I regret causing you any consternation."

I was about to bite back with a scathing retort, annoyed at not knowing anything about Besim, why I was saddled with her, and wondering why the universe saw fit to make me a babysitter with a badge. But something clicked inside my head, and not because I had rammed it against an immovable object.

"The *Nabira-Shas* forbids you to pursue the arts or music or anything like that, doesn't it?"

She nodded, head bowed.

"Is that the real reason why you colored your hair?" I asked, genuinely curious. "It's more than just a 'pursuit of inscrutable questions.'"

Besim raised her head to regard me.

"It is one among many, Detective Holliday," she replied softly. "I have lived many cycles, beyond a normal human's lifespan. I have experienced many...things...in my time on your world. I have discovered there is more to...life...than obeying the strictures of any caste."

"Well, then I guess it's a good thing you're in Empire City, and not back home, right?" I said, trying to lighten the mood. "This enclave is built on difference. Back in the day, Ellis Island took in thousands of immigrants from all over the world. The 'land of opportunity.'"

Besim nodded again. "I have read the history of this country. It gladdens me such places exist, despite its violent past."

"Well, we're still a violent race," I said dryly, slouching in the chair. "That hasn't changed in thousands of years."

"Thank you, Detective," Besim smiled.

"For what?" I sat up in surprise.

"For your understanding," she said.

"Well, the next time you're worried about being recognized, please let me know *before* we arrive, okay?" I growled, but without heat. "The more information I have, the happier I'll be."

"Of course," Besim replied. Her expression became business-like. "I shall endeavor to be more forthcoming in the future. What did you learn from the barista?"

I recapped Moonbeam's recollection of Vanessa and Miss Ponytail (because Ponytailed Bitch seemed a bit much, and I was feeling magnanimous) from the night before.

"Perhaps it is her Aunt Jennifer?" Besim suggested.

"I thought of that, but Aunt Jenny's image doesn't jibe with Moonbeam's description," I said, shaking my head.

"Could you not have a sketch artist sit with the barista and obtain a likeness?"

"Moonbeam didn't get a good look at Miss Ponytail," I replied, then quickly added, "But it's a good suggestion."

See? I can be nice sometimes.

"There are many things I do not understand about this case," Besim said, brow furrowed.

"You and me both, sister," I muttered.

I left my chair to pour myself more coffee, offering Besim some in the process, then settled back in my seat.

"We don't have enough information to make any kind of

educated guesses at this point," I stated. "However, there's still Vanessa's place. Hopefully, Deacon picked up something at Hughes to help us see the bigger picture."

Besim held the coffee in both hands before her mouth, as if somehow testing the flavor before it touched her lips.

"Is this always how your investigations are handled?" she asked.

"It's pretty typical," I replied. "I spend a lot of time talking to people, reading the reports from the crime scene team, collating the data, and connecting the dots. It would've been nice to have a crime scene team do some of this bloody legwork for us, but the hands-on approach with witnesses and potential witnesses almost always falls to me."

"William indicated to me the Special Crimes Unit would be short on funding at its inception," Besim said. "It is my understanding he has also, how do you say, 'cashed in a few favors.' Apparently, the mayor and district attorney are skeptical of this unit's efficacy and are unwilling to allocate additional funding until it is proven to be so."

No surprise there. It doesn't matter what century you're in, or how advanced your society might be, so long as there's red tape to deal with they'll fuck you up every time, and twice on Tuesdays.

"Yeah, well that makes three of us, then. We're technically off the books. We still have EVI, although that damn explosion is bad timing. What are the odds? Poor girl." I patted the console fondly.

She glanced at me over the cup of coffee. "Would not using your ability assist in our endeavor?"

I flushed, narrowing my eyes. First Deacon and Mahoney, and now her. I guess I shouldn't be surprised, but it pissed me off all the same.

"Right now, it's not necessary."

"I do not mean to offend, Detective Holliday. But when will it be necessary?"

"When I'm damn well ready to use it, that's when. None of you have any idea what using the Insight does to me. You look at me on a report, analyze my capabilities, and say 'Hey, that's a handy thing to have. He should use it all the time to fight crime and be a superhero!' Well, this doesn't work that way, okay? Some 'gifts' just have their own price."

CHAPTER 12

"**W**aste of time," Deacon declared as we made our soggy way back to the pod. "I interviewed Vanessa's boss and all of her co-workers. Vanessa clocked into work around eight. Ate lunch at her workstation. She was a diligent employee, well-liked, and never took a sick day. She was an artist. Loved animals. Just a bunch of shit we already know."

Deacon's heavy boots plodded through a large puddle, spraying two men in business suits. He returned their glares with an innocent smile.

"Her desk ain't got no personal items 'cause her employer don't allow none," he continued. "They said it 'interferes with the creative process,' whatever the fuck that means. Anyway, our vic never socialized outside the office with co-workers. Just kept to herself. Described her as pleasant, nice, and professional."

As we entered the pod, Deacon noticed the uneasy silence between Besim and me.

"Who pissed in your grits, Holliday?" he asked, eyes narrowed.

I ignored him, instead murmuring instructions to EVI as I sat at the console.

Besim sat behind me, her face a neutral mask. Deacon took the other command chair and lit a cigarette.

"Armin's a dead end?" He studied me, blowing smoke in my face.

I waved the smoke away in irritation and summarized what we'd learned, including Besim's impromptu performance. It irked me still, and I didn't bother hiding my annoyance. The former Protector's demeanor shifted from mild amusement to sharp intensity.

"You found your voice, Saranda?" he asked.

"I did not," she replied with a hint of melancholy.

The two stared at one another, and something unspoken passed between them. I'd never encountered telepathy before, but the hair on the back of my neck stood up all the same. When the moment passed, I sensed the break in whatever connection they had shared.

What the hell was the deal with the three of them, anyway?

I understood Mahoney's motivations—a murdered family, and the stench of the supernatural at the heart of it. He needed to settle the score with the universe, so he chose the scumbags of Empire City as his punching bags, even if that meant doing it from the sidelines. But I still couldn't figure out why these two were with him, despite what Besim had said earlier.

With EVI at half-mast, I couldn't waste resources looking them up, either. I had taken the job to remind myself I could still do it, and because I was tired of being stuck in a rut. But there was something else, an indefinable feeling growing inside of me that I was meant to be a part of Special Crimes. I'd explore that later. For now, the murder investigation was my top priority. Regardless of their respective agendas, I had to get used to the idea of working with these two. The alternative was unemployment, and I wasn't interested in looking for another job anytime soon.

"Vanessa has a friend," Deacon proclaimed, breaking into my thoughts. "Natalie Bonner, from college. Holliday, once you pull your head out of your ass, have EVI bring up Natalie's bio so we can get a look at her."

"All right." I bit back a snarky comment of my own. "EVI, get me whatever you have on Natalie Bonner, and put it on screen."

"Accessing," EVI replied. She sounded like she had just woken up from an all-night bender.

The display darkened as Natalie Bonner's profile materialized before us. Attractive, with long brown hair and matching eyes, a dimple and full mouth. I scanned the information, noting her address and place of employment. I tried to picture Natalie in a ponytail, then recalled Moonbeam describing Vanessa's companion as shorter. Natalie was five-foot-eight, which was two inches less than Vanessa. If Moonbeam thought two inches was a lot, it was possible Natalie might've been with Vanessa Sunday night. I looked forward to speaking with Miss Bonner.

But there was someone else I needed to see first.

"Hey Holliday, Empire City got its own street cameras?" Deacon asked, interrupting my thoughts again.

He was good at doing that.

"Yep," I replied, suppressing a yawn.

I glanced at the time on the display. It was nearing noon. The morning had slipped by, the light creeping toward a murky, rain-filled afternoon.

"Then you got facial recognition programs. Think EVI could take a crack at that?"

I moved to the dispenser and refilled my mug.

"Facial recognition isn't as effective as you might think," I replied after a long swig, burying my irritation in favor of the case. "Sometimes those cameras don't function very well. And then you're talking about hundreds of unfiltered images within several blocks of the crime scene multiplied by the same amount surrounding Armin's, Hughes, Vanessa's place, you name it. Even with EVI collating and analyzing the images at her full capacity, there are just too many variables."

"Such as?" Deacon asked, tapping out a cigarette and firing up a new one.

"Lighting, the weather, orientation and angle of the face," Besim chimed in. "As well as debris on the camera lenses."

"Right." I nodded curtly at her, then sat down. "I'm not going to ask how you know that."

Besim gave me a placid look but didn't respond.

"Not to mention facial anomalies, cheek angles, cosmetic surgery, out-of-date or doctored enclave IDs, people wearing masks or hats, you name it." I sipped at my coffee, then gestured toward Natalie's information. "The Global Population Database is filled with false information. As for EVI, she's good, but she's not that good, and right now she's not even close to mediocre. And don't get me started on civil liberties and invasion of privacy issues. That shit is a bag full of cats."

"Well, I don't reckon Vanessa really gives a damn about her privacy, being dead and all," Deacon remarked, flicking a tail of ash from the cigarette. "But I see your point. Still, y'all have it so much easier up here, Holliday. I tell you what, it's a helluva lot different down in Birmingham, that's for damn sure. Fuck your civil liberties, Citizen, 'cause the Church don't give two shits about them. They ain't gonna save your eternal soul."

"Never been to Birmingham," I said.

"Oh, it ain't so bad really, s'long as you don't break no Church laws," Deacon replied pleasantly.

"Sounds swell," I chuckled.

"It's just different, is all. Folks find their way to Birmingham, despite that. Called there, I reckon."

"Is that what happened to you?"

"Nah," Deacon drawled, tapping his foot against the bottom of the console. "Born and raised in Mercy, population one hundred and seventy-six. Or was it seventy-seven? Anyway, it's about ninety-seven miles southwest of the capital. You might like it, Holliday. It's got dirt roads, acres of farmland, and damn good fishing. I was a Protector there for eleven years. Spent the last seven after that abroad. Met Saranda when I did a couple jobs for Scotland Yard. She offered me work, and I've been on the payroll ever since."

My eyes widened in surprise.

"I thought you worked for Mahoney?"

"Nope," he laughed, amused at my reaction.

"I offered William the services of my personal head of security," Besim answered. "I knew he would find Deacon's particular skill set useful in the vetting process of potential Special Crimes candidates. Deacon is well-versed in the art of interrogation and information-gathering, as well as threat assessment and mitigation. I wished for William to be successful, and there are few better than Deacon in this regard."

Now that was a twist. The color rose in my cheeks as my irritation went up a notch.

"I find myself apologizing to you for a great many things today, Detective Holliday," Besim said, tilting her head to one side. "Everything that I have done has been to the benefit of William and the Special Crimes Unit. I assure you, my intentions are for the greater good."

"Sure." I stood up, glaring at the consultant. "Is there anything else you've neglected to mention?"

Besim appeared troubled, as if she were going to respond, but Deacon interrupted her.

"Back off, Holliday. We're here to help, that's all. Simple as that."

"Nothing is ever simple," I muttered angrily.

Deacon shrugged again and turned away to gaze out the window. Besim sat in-between, separating us, yet separate herself.

As the pod whisked along the 'way, I noted other pods along different tracks from ours. They bled through the shadows and fog, some of them remote blips heading toward destinations unknown. The misty city glowed brighter in response, pinpoints of scarlet and gold and blue and violet from windows and towers, holographic billboards, and other vehicles.

We arrived at our destination a half hour later. EVI's garbled announcement came out as a halting series of squawks, squeals and vowels. I grabbed an umbrella and moved to the hatch. I didn't offer one to either Deacon or Besim. I knew it was juvenile, but I didn't care.

"Where are we?" Deacon asked.

"Little Odessa," came my laconic reply. "Brighton Beach."

The old neighborhood wasn't pretty, even in good light. Thick metal support beams held the nearby mass transit pod tracks above the street. A multi-segmented pod surged past, its downblast sweeping the air around us with a loud whoosh. Ground traffic was sparse. A few beat-up old patchwork automobiles, powered by a blend of volatile chemicals, chugged their way along the pitted paved roads. Nexus energy fueled the sleeker vehicles in the better parts of the enclave. Down here, though, one of those cars rolling by meant it had been stolen from somewhere else.

When a sharp explosion blew out of the rear exhaust of a passing car, I jumped, reaching for my gun. Deacon assumed a defensive stance, with Besim behind him. We exchanged a sheepish look.

"Nice place," Deacon commented, raking the cars and neighborhood with a calculating glare. "You come here a lot?"

"Not as much as I should," I replied without further explanation, and headed down the block.

They fell into step beside me, heads turning, taking in the scene.

Gaudy lights flooded the street, advertising a wide variety of goods and services not welcome in the nicer parts of town. I walked too close to the entrance of one as a wave of pungent perfume covered me in a cloying cloud. A young woman wearing tight clothes and enough makeup to rival Besim waved at me with a gap-toothed smile. Vacant eyes stared through me. The needle marks along her bare arms told its own sordid tale.

We passed several ragged, homeless people leaning against the old brick of the one- and two-story storefronts scattered along the block. We weren't accosted, but I didn't look at any of them. They were beyond my help, scrounging a pitiful life amongst the seedy detritus of this banged-up place. The ugly underbelly of Brighton Beach was a flesh-eating disease, leaving little untouched by its corruption. As a result, police patrols were few and far between.

Not everything was lost, though.

Abner's Vintage Books was an anachronism from a bygone age living in a neighborhood that no longer cared. The store occupied a two-story brick strip between Frankie G's Tattoo Parlor and Mickey's Laundromat. A black canopy hung over the entrance, while a welcoming, warm glow spilled across its threshold.

Several fissures crisscrossed portions of the barred window, forming spiderwebs from where objects had struck the glass. The display held a neat array of genuine paper and ink books, artfully stacked, along with Halloween decorations. A sense of sweet nostalgia settled in my bones like good whiskey on a cold night.

"What's in here?" Deacon asked, gesturing at the books. "Besides the obvious."

"Family." I held the door open. The bright tinkle of a bell on the inside of the doorway greeted us as we went inside.

We stepped into the lair of a bibliophile. The interior was cozy and warm. Soft light from shaded lamps covered various tables and bookshelves filled to the brim with a treasure trove of paperback and hardbound books. Classical music filtered through the store in soft waves, the brooding rumble of Tchaikovsky's *Manfred Symphony* lumbering along *lento lugubre*.

A half-moon-shaped wooden counter anchored the center of the store, its surface holding more books and other odds-and-ends for sale. An old-fashioned cash register, the kind with push buttons and a drawer to hold hard currency, squatted on the counter between a drooping potted plant and a sign bearing the instructions to "Ring for assistance." Before the sign rested a grinning porcelain jack-o-lantern and a cheaply-made metal hand bell with a worn, flower-patterned plastic handle. The far wall held built-in shelving and an open doorway leading into the store's back room. A wrought-iron staircase spiraled up to a landing and another doorway. I caught the flash of a fuzzy tail as it fled from the landing in a puff of fur.

An old man perched precariously on a stool by the counter, his head bowed, arms folded, and his eyes closed. He wore a faded brown tweed jacket with patches sewn at each elbow, tan dress shirt, tan pants, and sensible shoes. His close-cropped, salt-and-pepper mustache and beard were matched by the same fringe surrounding a smooth head covered with liver spots. As we approached, I caught the faint buzz of his snoring. I strode to the counter, grabbed the hand bell, and shook it vigorously in his face. Startled, he jerked awake and almost toppled from the stool, but planted his feet on the floor in time.

"Rise and shine, Abner." I returned the bell to the counter. "You've got customers!"

"Thomas Henry Holliday," Abner grumbled in exasperation. "You of all people should know it is very impolite sneaking up on an old man while he ruminates upon the universe."

"Is that what they call sleeping on the job these days?" I asked with a fond smile, clapping the old man on the shoulder.

I made with the introductions.

"As I live and breathe!" Abner said with wide eyes. "A Vellan, and in my store! I'm quite certain my father never had a Vellan visit the store back when he was alive. I am honored by your presence." He bowed at the waist.

"The pleasure is mine, sir," Besim returned the bow with a polite nod.

The old man waved her away with a smile. "Please, call me Abner."

Abner Horowitz and my grandfather Harry had been friends since they were schoolboys. The bookstore had been with Abner's family for generations, surviving the Russian *bratva*, civil unrest and several drug wars. It was my second home.

With Mom dead and my asshole of a dad hopelessly drunk, my grandfather provided for most of my formative learning. When he worked nights, I'd get dropped off here. Between Abner and my grandfather, they taught me so many things about life, being a man, and the importance of family. As for Abner, he gave me the greatest gift of all: books.

I spent hours devouring every little literary bit I could swallow. I'd build small nests in a corner of the store, out of the way of the customers, and read until my eyes crossed. The bookstore was my sanctuary, a home away from home where I could flee into my imagination and forget life's travails for a while. After my grandfather died, I kept up with Abner, ensuring the neighborhood riffraff were aware the place was under my protection.

Abner was family, but he wasn't the reason why I was here.

"Is she around?" I asked the old man, a serious expression on my face.

"I presume you got my message?" Abner asked, his dark eyes wide with worry. "She didn't get home until late this morning. What's this all about, Tom?"

"The two of you, stay here," I addressed the others. "Besim, earlier you suggested we should do some research on our killer. Well, this place is as good as any library I've ever seen. Maybe you'll find something useful here. I won't be long."

And before they could respond, I ascended the spiral staircase.

CHAPTER 13

I found Leyla sprawled face-first on a bed littered with loose clothing and four cats. She wore a tight-fitting halter top, leggings, and a short skirt. Leyla's soft snoring was nearly indistinguishable from the purring symphony surrounding her. I caught the tang of cigarette smoke and other, less savory, things.

Beside the bed leaned a makeshift desk cobbled together from a variety of discarded old furniture. In contrast, a sleek portable holo-rig lay on its surface. I'd seen enough confiscated tech at the precinct to know that rig cost more than my annual salary. Scattered next to it were a few silver bracelets, and several deactivated enclave holo-ID cards. I crossed the room and sifted through them, noting names and faces.

Leyla had been busy last night.

Discarded beneath the desk were a black nylon bag and a pair of faded running shoes. There were no chairs in here, although one gray cat was fat enough to second as a nice cushion. A cold, damp wind blew through the open window.

The gray sauntered up to me and rubbed against my leg, purring like an overclocked engine.

"Hello, Carter," I greeted him fondly, scratching behind his neck.

Kneeling beside the bed, I regarded Leyla for a few moments. Her pale skin glistened from the flecks of misty rain blown through the open window, but she slept soundly as if wrapped in heavy blankets. A palpable chill radiated off her that made me shiver despite the layers of clothing I wore.

"No," she whispered suddenly, a small child's voice filled with fright. "Mom? Dad? Where are you?"

Leyla's body balled into a fetal position. The temperature in the room dropped, brought about by something more than the October weather.

"It's so dark. I can't see you."

She twisted on the bed. Her eyes moved rapidly beneath their lids. I was locked in indecision, unsure whether to wake her, or to let things play out.

"I'm cold. So cold. Why did you leave me?"

"I'm here. It's okay. I'm here."

"Why didn't I die?"

I made my choice. Reaching out carefully, I gently stroked her face, willing the terror she was experiencing to release her. My fingers went numb. At my touch, Leyla's eyes fluttered open.

"Hey," she murmured, her words slurred from sleep.

"You were dreaming again," I said.

"I was?" She blinked a few times. "I don't remember."

"Yeah." I hesitated, then said. "About your family again. You know, if you ever want to talk about what happened..."

"I know, Doc," she said. "I'll tell you, but when I'm ready, okay?

"Okay," I sighed.

"What time is it?"

"Time for you to get up, kiddo."

Leyla rolled over and propped herself up on one arm. Her snow-white hair held tiny frost crystals which drifted to the floor.

She appeared no older than a kid in her mid-teens, but I knew better. Tired, icy blue eyes regarded me curiously.

"Where's Abner?"

"Downstairs." I rubbed my hands together for warmth. "How are you feeling?"

"Tired," she yawned, rising from bed, the nightmare all but forgotten. "Anton's was doing another ten-credit beer night. I couldn't pass it up."

"Plenty of easy marks, eh?" I grinned.

Leyla returned the smile with a sly one of her own. "Guys wanted to buy me drinks. What's a girl gonna do?"

She stretched, clasping one hand to the other, and raised both arms over her head. Her back popped like soft gunshots. She walked barefoot to the desk.

"They're just a bunch of nobodies," she offered, gesturing at her collection. "They don't work for anyone important, and none of them are loaded."

"They'll be pissed once they realize their IDs were lifted by the pretty white-haired girl," I chuckled. "You're a hard one to forget, kiddo."

Leyla laughed and twirled like a mischievous sprite.

"Aw, c'mon. It's all in fun. I'm not actually going to do anything with them."

"Promise me you'll return them to Anton's." I was stern, but my eyes danced.

Leyla gave me an exasperated look. "Fine, Doc. I'll drop them off later."

"And no messing with their profiles either, young lady," I admonished, wagging a finger. "Remember what happened to the last guy?"

Her grin was wicked.

"Yeah, but that asshole deserved it," she sniffed indignantly. "He groped me, and then didn't tip Holly, which really pissed me off. Holly's a friend, Doc. You mess with my friends, then I'm going to fuck you up, my way. Besides, I'm sure the EC IRS is done auditing by now. I mean, it's been a year, right?" She scooped up the cards and put them in an inner pocket of her skirt.

"That has pockets?" I asked in surprise.

"Where else am I going to put things?" she replied, all wide-eyed innocence.

I left that one alone.

She gave me a critical look and said, "This isn't a social call, is it?"

"No, kiddo." I stood, folding my arms. "I need your help with something."

"Now there's a twist," she replied. "Usually I'm the one coming to you. Are you in trouble?"

"No, nothing like that," I smiled. "I'm working a case, and it's an unusual one."

"That's great, Doc!" she cheered. "About time those morons gave you something to do!"

"Not exactly, kiddo." I recounted the events of the past two days, leaving nothing out.

Leyla gazed out the window, chewing on her lower lip as she worked the angles in her head.

"You'll be my own consultant," I added. "Mahoney and Deacon won't like it, but they won't have a choice. I'll even pay you."

Turning back to me, her icy blue eyes glittered.

"Doc, you need my help, so I'm gonna help. How many times have you bailed me out of trouble?"

A warm feeling filled my heart as I regarded her with a soft smile.

Leyla might be a thief and world-class hacker, but I loved her all the same.

We weren't blood-related, but Leyla and I went way back, around the time I joined the 98th. I had worked a case involving money-laundering over in Flatbush. A small-time crime syndicate tried to set up shop using a bank as a front. Independent of my investigation, Leyla made the mistake of hacking into their system to abscond with their ill-gotten gains.

Unfortunately, she'd hacked the wrong family.

They hired a Cy-tracker to find her. When I arrived at the bank to ask some questions, I came upon a couple of thick-necked bad guys about to cause some serious harm to a very skinny white-haired girl in the alley next to the building. They cornered her, but I persuaded them to leave her alone with a heavy dose of Doc Holliday kick-assery.

The girl provided ECPD with a surprising amount of digital evidence to put away the syndicate for about thirty years. Leyla and I had been tight ever since.

I didn't discover just how special Leyla was until weeks later.

"So, what's the plan?" she asked, interrupting my thoughts.

"Grab your stuff. We're going to the decedent's townhouse."

Abner was regaling a disgruntled Deacon and an attentive Besim about something as we negotiated the spiral stairs. The Confederate looked up at our approach, dark eyes assessing Leyla with undisguised interest. One glance at her told him everything he needed to know.

"She ain't coming."

"That's too bad," I fired back. "I'm vouching for her, and that damn well better be good enough."

"Are you out of your mind?" he countered, eyes blazing. "This is a murder investigation, not some fucking field trip!"

"EVI's down," I responded as a strange calm settled over me. Having Leyla along felt right. She needed to be with us, although I had no idea why. "Which means we need an expert at manipulating data and researching things. Leyla is damn good at both. Worst case, she stays in the pod. That work for you?"

Deacon turned to Besim. They shared one of those invisible communication moments again. Abner and Leyla watched in silence.

"Fine," he grumbled. "But the kid's your responsibility. I ain't no goddamn babysitter."

Deacon stomped from the bookstore.

"'I ain't no goddamn babysitter,'" Leyla mimicked with a twang. "Jerk."

"Give him time," I chuckled.

She made a face and shifted the bag's strap on her shoulder.

"Thank you, Abner," Besim addressed the old man. "You are a wealth of knowledge."

Abner beamed, thick eyebrows bobbing up and down. Bowing at the waist again, he almost dashed his forehead into the counter.

"The pleasure is all mine, Madam."

Leyla embraced him.

"You be careful," Abner admonished as he held her tight. "You heard what Tom said. Stay in the pod, and out of trouble."

She laughed, pecking him on the cheek. Frost crinkled the skin where her lips touched him, but Abner didn't flinch.

I nodded to Abner and led the ladies outside.

Deacon stood beneath a burned-out street lamp smoking a cigarette. Rain spat down from above, but he paid it no mind. A few cars trundled past, their engines roaring like prehistoric beasts.

"And then there were four," I announced.

Deacon flicked the cigarette away, falling in with us as we walked back to the pod.

"Are you not chilled, Leyla?" Besim asked. "Do you require a coat?"

Leyla laughed gaily, turning her face to the sky as the rain washed her face.

"Oh, not at all," she replied. "I love the rain!"

She skipped ahead, jumping in puddles and soaking her clothes.

"You better be right about her," Deacon growled in a low voice. His flinty eyes bore into Leyla's back as she spoke with Besim.

I filled in Deacon on how I'd met Leyla.

"She stayed at my apartment for a few weeks in case anyone came looking for her," I finished. "She'd been living on the streets since she was twelve. Other than a stolen rig, Leyla had the clothes on her back and not much else. And she's a natural at hacking. Self-taught, if you can believe it."

I glanced around. Her last place was in a seedier section of Dyker Heights, worse than this one.

"Anyway, I knew she couldn't stay with me forever, so I called Abner," I said. "He lived alone, and loved to collect strays, so I asked him to take Leyla under his wing. She works at the bookstore during the day, and Abner provides her four walls, a roof, and a warm meal."

Deacon grunted.

"She's solid, Deacon. She'll be fine," I assured him. "What were you discussing with Abner?"

"Saranda asked about vampires," he scowled. "The old man recommended a few books, said he'd order them if we wanted. Told him Saranda can do the research on her own."

"We should go to Vanessa's brownstone," I said, changing the subject. "I'll put in a call to Natalie Bonner and set up a meeting with her tomorrow morning."

"Fair enough." Deacon stuck his hands in his jeans' pockets as he walked. "I reckon Bill is waiting on us to report in. He'll want to know about Little Miss Sunshine over there, too."

"Tell him whatever you want, Deacon," I said stubbornly. "We need her right now, we're short-handed, and we've got shit for leads. If Bill gets pissed because I brought in help, tell him he doesn't have to pay her. I'll handle that."

"Relax, Holliday," he barked a laugh. "If you think she's that useful, then she can prove it to me."

EVI transported us to Bay Ridge. I registered Leyla as an authorized passenger. Deacon parked himself in one of the back seats and made the call to Mahoney. Leyla and Besim sat next to each other, engaged in conversation. I stared out the window but kept an ear on them.

"So, you really are Saranda the singer!" Leyla said, sounding impressed. "What are you doing here with Doc?"

"Singing is but one of my interests." Besim gave the Leyla a modest smile. "Captain Mahoney is my friend. He required my help, and so I have given it."

"Yeah, but isn't it dangerous for you to be working the case, on the street I mean?" Leyla asked. "You don't look like the fighting type." She held up a hand. "No offense."

"None taken," Besim laughed. "No more dangerous than it is for you. Suffice it to say that I am curious about the investigative process and want to experience it for myself. I am in good hands with both Detective Holliday, and my very own protector, Deacon Kole."

Leyla glanced toward the back of the pod.

"I mean, Doc is one of the best. He's been on the force for years, and I know he's gotten himself out of a lot of bad situations. But your guy doesn't look like much."

"Do not be fooled by appearances, Leyla," Besim said with pride. "Deacon is a formidable opponent, both in body and mind. He is an exceptional individual."

"If you say so." Leyla wasn't convinced.

"Tell me more about yourself, Leyla. Do you have any family?"

"Besides Doc and Abner? Nah, not anymore. My parents died when I was very young. I have a sister but haven't seen her in a long time."

"I am sorry to hear this," Besim replied softly, a raw bleakness shading her voice. "Family is so very important, as it is in my culture. I can appreciate what it is like not to have your family surrounding you. The loneliness you experience every day must be unbearable. I did not mean to upset you."

"Oh no, I'm fine," Leyla laughed, and shifted her weight in the passenger seat. "It's been so long, sometimes I forget about it. My parents were engineers, involved with radiation land reclamation projects sponsored by a joint commission of enclaves including Empire City. They would take my sister and me on a lot of their trips to the other enclaves. I've been to Gateway City, New London, Roma Indomita, Les Habitens, you name it. They died in an explosion when we were visiting a site outside of Reykjavik. I remember it was really loud and bright, and I hugged my sister. Then the cold came, and everything went dark."

I'd heard the story many times before, but the sharpness of it never faded. I was surprised at Leyla's calm demeanor, as if she were talking about going to the store.

"We were rescued and shuttled back to a hospital in Reykjavik. My parents owned a place in Empire City, but they didn't have a will or anything. My uncle took their stuff, pissed it all away, then wound up dead. After that, we got placed with EC Social Services, and bounced around a bunch of foster homes for a few years. Eventually, I left and lived on the streets until the day Doc rescued me from the Carmichael syndicate. My sister stayed behind. The end."

Besim regarded Leyla with such sorrow, I thought she was going to cry. My eyes stung, and I rubbed at them.

"A tragedy for one so young," Besim said. "To have experienced this pain and heartache. I am so sorry, Leyla."

"Don't be," Leyla replied firmly. "It is what it is. Life sucks, and shit happens."

"Damn right," Deacon chimed in from the back of the pod. "You get knocked down, pick yourself up and get back on that horse. Ain't no point in crying about it."

"But it's all good now." Leyla nodded once at the Confederate. "I have Abner and Doc and the cats. I have the bookstore. What more is there?"

Besim sat in quiet contemplation, saying nothing. Deacon wandered up front, sliding into the chair next to me.

"What did Mahoney have to say?" I asked.

"Well, for starters, he ain't none-too-happy she's tagging along," Deacon lit a cigarette, and filled the front with gray smoke. "But I told him not to worry, you got it under control."

"Thanks," I replied in surprise.

"Also told me nothing worthwhile came from the neighborhood canvas," Deacon exhaled smoke from his nose. "Then he said your DA's been dealing with the media. Saying shit like the investigation is underway, not mentioning our names, and dazzling them with the usual run of bullshit."

"That's awfully nice of him," I said dryly. "That plausible deniability thing again."

"I reckon so," Deacon chuckled. "Mahoney said the mayor's expecting miracles, so we got to deliver. He'll keep everyone off our ass for as long as he can."

I tried not to let it bother me. Investigations took time and breaks in cases were the proverbial needles in haystacks. Pressure from the top brass wasn't anything new either and a gruesome murder case like this would put the spotlight on the mayor's office as much as ECPD. Mahoney said a lot was riding on this one, and I got the impression it wasn't only my career at stake.

While Deacon smoked, I pulled up all the data we had accumulated thus far, including the upload from the p-scanner. I entered notes from my interviews with the eyewitnesses, the bank security, Armin and Moonbeam, then added Deacon's findings at Hughes.

"At least that still works," I muttered under my breath.

"Incoming translation from Proctologist Staystrim, Detection," EVI's garbled voice announced over the speakers.

The pod filled with crunchy static, then cleared.

"Detective Holliday?" came Doctor Stentstrom's reedy voice. "Are you there?"

"Yes, Doctor, we hear you," I replied.

"I'm not quite sure where to begin," he hesitated.

There wasn't any music playing in the background.

"What is it, Doctor?" I asked, now concerned. "What's happened?"

"As I mentioned in our previous conversation, I had two further examinations to perform," he said. "I left to attend to them at a separate location and was away for several hours."

I didn't like where this was headed. My shoulders felt a crushing weight descend on them.

"When I returned, the lights were out," the medical examiner continued. "The room's power had been disabled for an indeterminate amount of time. Once EVI restored the power, I checked on the corpses in storage."

My throat went dry. I gripped the control console with both hands. The knuckles turned white.

"They were all accounted for," Stentstrom stated with finality. "All, except one."

I waited, holding my breath.

"I'm sorry, Detective Holliday," he said mournfully. "But Vanessa Mallery's body is gone."

CHAPTER 14

"What do you mean the body is gone?" I demanded, then glanced at Deacon uncertainly. "Dead bodies don't walk themselves out of morgues. Right?"

"There's gotta be a record of it," Deacon stated in a steady voice, ignoring me. "Don't y'all have cameras in there?"

"Indeed, Mr. Kole," the medical examiner confirmed. "When I reviewed the feed, there were no images. However, the diagnostic report I received detailed continuous outages over a span of three hours. These are in conjunction with the systemic breakdowns EVI has been experiencing since the explosion. It appears the body was taken between nine and ten-thirty this morning," Stentstrom paused. "Which also coincided with the building's fire alarm sounding a few minutes before nine. The entire building was placed on lockdown and evacuated."

A cold hand rested on my shoulder. Leyla stood behind me, concern mirrored in her eyes.

"*Someone* signed out the damn body," I said, scrambling to make sense of everything. "You can't just waltz in there, even if the building wasn't already on lockdown. Whose eSig is on the official registry?"

"Well, Detective, that is the most peculiar aspect of all," Stentstrom answered. "It was authorized by you."

"That's impossible," I scoffed, although my voice betrayed my anxiety. "I was following a lead. Our onboard log timestamps will show that, in addition to my own updates to the case file."

"I'll send you the registry," he offered. "But the signature page included your badge."

"While you're at it, forward the feed for the time between nine and ten-thirty," I said.

"As I already mentioned, the feed was blank," Stentstrom replied.

"Send it anyway," I grated between gritted teeth.

"Of course," he replied. "Detective Holliday, I take full responsibility for this, and will outline that in my report. When word of this gets out—"

"Stop right there," I ordered in a firm tone. "No one is hearing about this."

Deacon gave me an appraising look. Leyla's hand tightened on my shoulder.

"That is highly irregular," Stentstrom stammered in confusion. "An official report must be filed."

I rubbed at my temples, thinking furiously.

"Someone has gone through a great deal of trouble to steal the body," I said. "I'm willing to bet that same someone is involved with the explosion. With everything that's happened so far, there's too much coincidence here for my liking."

I moved from the chair and began pacing the floor.

"We're Special Crimes, right? Sanctioned by the mayor's office and authorized to apprehend criminals by any means necessary. Special dispensation needs to be given in trying to solve a case that has gone from a dead girl killed by a vampire, to a seemingly unrelated explosion at a power plant that just so happens to knock out most of EVI's functions and her redundant recovery systems right around the time when we need her most."

"I don't understand," Stentstrom said.

"He's saying we need to keep this on the down-low 'cause there's a lot more going on here," Deacon drawled, lighting a cigarette. "He's saying we've been fucked, and not in the Biblical sense, neither. We don't know shit right now, and someone's out there making sure things stay that way."

"And I thought I had conspiracy theory issues," Leyla quipped under her breath.

"What's going on here?" the medical examiner demanded. "And what is Special Crimes?"

I looked from Leyla, Deacon and Besim in turn, then made my decision and filled Stentstrom in on everything.

"I'm asking you to keep this under wraps," I urged, folding my arms. "We've got to figure out what's going on before every lead goes cold."

The silence on the line was broken by the occasional crackle of static.

"Doctor," I asked, eyebrows raised. "Are you there?"

"Mm?" he replied absently from a distance. "Oh, I'm sorry! Yes, I'm still here."

"What's going on? You all right?"

"Oh, quite fine," Stentstrom said, his voice fading in and out. It sounded as if he was strolling around the examination room. "However, while you were speaking," his voice strengthened as he returned to the communication outlet, "I have discovered something quite peculiar. There is the faintest hint of a strange odor in the air. It's quite distracting."

"Lemon freshener?" I asked.

"Yes!" the medical examiner exclaimed, as if he'd just discovered gravity. "That's it! I prefer more of a pine scent when cleaning the examination room. Lemon clears the palate just as easily but is a bit too bitter for my taste."

Deacon and I exchanged a knowing look. My mouth turned into a thin, grim line.

"Given our findings at Tony's apartment earlier today, I posit the scent is the same," Besim said from behind me. "Detective Holliday, someone is attempting to 'cover their tracks,' so to speak."

"And tie up loose ends while they're at it," Deacon chuckled mirthlessly, flicking ash from the end of his cigarette. "This case just got a helluva lot more fun. We got ourselves professional cleaners, Holliday."

"As if today couldn't get any worse," I muttered. "Doctor Stentstrom, send what you have as soon as you can."

"Of course," Stentstrom replied. "You will have it shortly. I also stored several of Miss Mallery's tissue samples. Whoever stole the body failed to account for my refrigerated storage unit. They may yet yield some more information about our victim."

"Thank you," I said, and cut off the call. Moments later, the registry appeared on the HUD along with the room feed. I frowned at the display. "This is bad."

"But it sure ain't boring," Deacon chuckled.

"No, I'm serious." I sat up to face the others and jabbed a thumb over my shoulder at the registry entry. "That's my old badge."

"Holy fuck," Deacon swore. "You left that on her desk."

"I did," I nodded grimly. "We need to pay Lieutenant Flanagan a visit."

"Detective?" Besim asked. "Given the speed with which these cleaners are operating, perhaps the lieutenant should wait."

I was about to disagree, but my mind raced with the implications.

"I hate to admit it, but you're right," I said. "If Flanagan is involved, she's not going anywhere anytime soon. Who knows what else they're using her for? Which means the cleaners will hit the victim's home, if they haven't been there already."

"Whoever they are, they must be on a strict timetable, unless there is more than one team, of course," the consultant added.

"And don't forget about Julie and Tony," Deacon said. "It'd be like shooting fish in a barrel."

I felt like I was trying to hold sand from an hourglass in my hand. I had to decide what to do, and fast.

"The security detail was assigned prior to Special Crimes taking the case, which means Downtown is responsible for providing those officers, not the 98th," I said. "Flanagan wouldn't have any jurisdiction."

"Given what's happened already, that ain't gonna matter," Deacon replied.

"Maybe," I said. "EVI, please contact the two uniforms on duty at Julie DeGrassi's apartment."

Moments later, a gruff man's voice spoke over the com system, "Afternoon, Detective Holliday. What can I do you for?"

"Just checking in," I responded. "Everything okay over there?"

"Yessir. Just me and Bolden. Nobody's been by."

"Copy that. Let me know if they get any visitors. Thanks." I closed the call.

"Do you trust them?" Deacon asked.

"We have to," I sighed. "I knew Bolden when he was just starting out Downtown. He wasn't caught up in the corruption probe. I don't know Humboldt, though."

"What do we do?" Leyla asked anxiously.

I realized during the call EVI had announced our arrival in Bay Ridge.

"We investigate Vanessa's home." I stood up, then moved to the evidence table. I handed everyone a pair of rubber gloves and put on a pair of my own. "Even if the cleaners have been through there, maybe we'll get lucky."

I retrieved the passkey from the evidence bag, then led the way out of the pod.

Midafternoon was cold and wet and filled with an intermittent drizzle, the kind that made you wish you were wrapped in three blankets, surrounded by heaters, and stocked with gallons of hot coffee.

Alas, it was not meant to be.

"There is nothing either good or bad, but thinking makes it so," I muttered to myself.

Quoting the Bard always made me feel a little better, and I sure as hell needed some better right then.

We were in a quiet residential neighborhood. A series of brick townhomes ran along both sides of the street, each one the classic brownstone, two-story variety with stone steps, metal railing and a small square of greenery. They were all enclosed by a swinging gate and four-foot metal fencing, the decorative utilitarian type with little fleur-de-lis caps at the tops. A couple of homes had been done up for Halloween, with pumpkins on doorsteps and even a scarecrow in one yard.

Several umbrella-wielding pedestrians moved aside as we approached Vanessa's place. A young woman wearing a dark rain-coat and holding a small carry-on bag and umbrella closed the door behind her. The exterior light revealed her face to be red and puffy. She shot me a suspicious look as I opened the gate.

"Can I help you?" her voice was rough.

I recognized her.

"Good afternoon, Miss Bonner," I introduced myself, with-drawing my badge and ID slowly so as not to frighten her. "I was going to call you. These are my...err...team. We're investigating the murder of your friend, Vanessa. May we come in?"

Her eyes widened, but to her credit, she turned back to the door, unlocked it and stepped inside. I held the gate open for the others, then made my way into Vanessa's brownstone.

As I neared the doorway, I inhaled.

The scent of lemon freshener was strong.

"Fuck me," I swore, swallowing the urge to slam my hand against the wall.

"Excuse me?" Natalie asked from inside the brownstone.

"I'm sorry, Miss Bonner," I recovered lamely. "I tripped on the welcome mat. It's nothing."

Deacon, Besim and Leyla were already poking around the interior as I closed the door. The short entryway led to a living room with a single siderailed staircase running up to the second floor on the right, and a small open fireplace opposite. The limited kitchen spilled out of the end of the living room across from the entryway. A water closet hid within the nook of the staircase. I spied a door with closed blinds within the kitchen.

A colorful rug sprawled across the hardwood floor, taking up most of the living room space, atop which rested an old couch, loveseat and coffee table. Floor lamps with sea-colored shades flanked the couch to either side. A fan, currently at rest with a long pull-cord, clung to the ceiling. Upon the walls hung framed paintings depicting seascapes, the same type and style as those found on Vanessa's website. There was no entertainment center or holo-vision.

I crossed the room to the kitchen, taking stock of the furniture and accessories. The kitchen boasted cabinet and counter space, a stove, refrigerator, dishwasher, and single-bowl sink. A small, round table holding an empty vase nestled in a corner surrounded by three armless chairs. One wall held a large picture window with closed blinds. I poked my finger through one of the slats, noting the tiny concrete patio hosting a long-necked ceramic fire pit on a metal tripod.

Everything was spotless.

Natalie stood nearby, arms folded across her chest. I gestured for her to join me at the kitchen table.

"I came here to feed Oliver and get a few of my things," Natalie sat down and gave me a tired smile.

"Anything else besides a bedroom upstairs?" Deacon called out.

"Two rooms," Natalie responded. "One is...was...Vanessa's bed and bathroom, and the other was her office. Everything's been tidied up, though. I never knew Van had a cleaning service."

Deacon's heavy boots clomped dully as he made his way to the upper floor. Besim and Leyla admired the paintings in the living room, affording us some privacy.

"Miss Bonner, I'm so sorry about your loss," I began.

Tears welled in her eyes. I handed her my handkerchief.

"Thank you," Natalie replied in a small voice, dabbing at her eyes. "Van was my best friend." She trailed off, staring at the living room, her face stricken.

I wanted to reach over, take her hand in mine, and tell her everything would be all right. Instead, I studied her reactions, body language, and cues that might tip me off as to whether there was more to Natalie Bonner than first met the eye.

But there wasn't any. True loss was hard to fake, and the young woman seated before me was as desolate as they came.

"I know this is very hard for you, but I need to ask you some questions," I said, and let her know she was being recorded. "When was the last time you saw Vanessa?"

"Last Friday night, here," Natalie answered immediately. "I brought takeout from Saigon Dragon, and we drank some wine. I'm in-between relationships and needed girl-time."

I let my eyes wander to the kitchen counter behind Natalie. Three bottles of wine were lined up next to the refrigerator.

"Had you spoken with her since then?" I smiled, hoping the expression would ease some of Natalie's discomfort.

"No, Detective. I spent the night on the couch, then left early the next morning. I tried calling her a few times, but she never answered."

The young woman began to sob.

I gave her a few moments to collect herself. Besim and Leyla walked slowly around the living room. The Vellan appeared to be distracted, head cocked to one side, as if listening. A familiar tingling formed at the base of my neck, but I turned my attention back to Natalie.

"Do you know anyone who might want to hurt Vanessa?" I

asked gently. "An old boyfriend, maybe, or co-worker? Someone she met online?"

Natalie wiped her nose with the handkerchief.

"No, Detective," Natalie sighed, offering me a wistful smile. "She lived alone so she could focus on her art. I had been pushing her to get out more, though. Kept telling her she needed to meet new people instead of being cooped up in here breathing all that paint."

"What about her family?"

My eyes shifted to Besim and Leyla, who had moved the couch and were staring up at a small ventilation cover. The tingling rose to my scalp, and the hair on my head stood on end.

Natalie shook her head and said, "Van's aunt was her only family, but she never visited. I think they both preferred it that way. Van's always been a loner, to be honest."

The floorboards above creaked as Deacon moved about. I heard a door open and close.

"Did the two of you go out much?" I asked.

"Sometimes," she replied, clasping her hands on the table. "We'd go to some dance clubs, catch a live show at one of the coffeehouses, that sort of thing."

"You ever hear of Armin's Coffee House?"

The young woman nodded. "We've been there many times."

"Were you at Armin's Sunday?" I asked.

"No," she said. "I haven't been back there in over a week."

"Did Vanessa have any other friends, besides you?" I asked. "Anyone she might go out to Armin's with, if you weren't available?"

"I was her only friend, Detective Holliday." Natalie regarded me with despondent brown eyes. "Van was shy, an introvert. She hated big crowds. I was all she had. We were like sisters. If there was anyone else in her life like that, I'd know."

I wanted to question her further, but the tingling bored into my skull, and it was all I could do not to scream bloody murder.

As I sat there, the feeling expanded into my mind. My vision blurred for a few seconds before clearing. My breathing shortened, and I became increasingly aware of the brightness in the room.

Besim called to Deacon. His heavy footfalls thundered down the stairs. She held out something in her palm for Deacon and Leyla, although I couldn't see what it was.

In that moment, the Insight burst unbidden through my vision. There was something at play here, but I needed space and time, and couldn't focus on it with Natalie present.

She noted my discomfort. "Are you all right?"

"I-I'm fine," I lied with a crooked smile, and stood up unsteadily. "Miss Bonner, I know the past few days have been very hard on you, and I won't trouble you anymore today. If you can think of anything at all relating to Vanessa and her murder, please don't hesitate to contact me."

I gave her my card and was relieved to see my hand wasn't shaking. Natalie and I returned to the living room where she picked up her bag and umbrella, then bid us all a good day. Besim and Leyla smiled, while Deacon glowered at the walls with impatience.

Once the door closed, I sat heavily in the loveseat, my head held in my hands.

Leyla rushed to my side, but I waved her away.

"That Insight about ready now, Holliday?" Deacon asked quietly.

I looked up with gleaming, silvery light searing my vision to stare at the tiny object held in Besim's hand.

"Yeah."

CHAPTER 15

I don't know where the Insight came from, but somehow, for some reason, I can work magic. To everyone else, my eyes appeared abnormally bright, with the pupils engorged and dilated. It's a look akin to goldjoy, but silver instead of gold.

"This is where the fun begins," I said, then frowned.

The device in Besim's hand wasn't the driving force here. Instead, I felt drawn upstairs, and staggered away as if drunk.

"Doc," Leyla called out to me. "Where are you going?"

I waved at her absently but didn't respond. Deacon had left the lights on upstairs, otherwise I would've crashed into everything. The Insight granted me true sight, not night vision.

Well, not yet.

A thin, mauve-colored carpet covered the floor, but was springy despite its worn look. I walked down the hallway, past Vanessa's office, and into her bedroom. A twin bed with a folded, handmade afghan blanket settled in between a faux-wood nightstand and narrow dresser opposite the door. A few odds-and-ends were scattered atop the nightstand and dresser, including a plain jewelry box and various keepsakes. There were no holo-frames or other mementos. To the right was the bathroom. Inside was a vanity with a mirror, toilet, and stand-up shower.

The bedroom doubled as her studio. Four seascape paintings hung along the walls in simple frames. The scent of lemon permeated the air, but underneath there were hints of fixative and other chemicals used in art supplies. An empty easel stood on top of a stained drop cloth in the corner by the lone window, with several canvases leaning against the wall, which was abutted by a narrow work table. It held a variety of plastic containers and bins, as well as different sizes and styles of brushes, a paint-spattered mixing tray, and dozens of small, labeled bottles. Attached to the top of the easel was a covered extension lamp. The window had a small lever at its base used to crank it open and shut. The glass was clear, but the rain and mist outside prevented me from seeing much, other than splashes of outdoor lights from neighbors' homes.

I heard the others downstairs discussing the tiny device, but I ignored them. I couldn't afford the distraction.

Bending down, I thumbed through the canvases. All of them were unfinished sketches of seascapes without a lick of paint on them. My preternatural sense detected the slight difference in size and weight between the last canvas and the others, something I would have easily missed otherwise.

I placed the canvas on the easel. It depicted a broad expanse of beach interspersed with scrub grasses, seagulls and a rolling tide. However, as my eyes swept the drawing, I made out subtle hints of another image hiding behind the first. I withdrew my pocketknife and made a narrow cut about the length of my index finger. Stowing the knife, I leaned in for a closer look, then stepped back. I pressed my fingers into the cut, tearing it wide to reveal another painting hidden underneath.

Unlike the seascapes, this one held the self-portrait of Vanessa seated in a chair opposite her reflection in a long dressing mirror. About half of the rendering bore light paint, with the remainder as penciled-in sketch work. Each woman wore different clothing and hairstyle. The level of detail involved was striking.

Vanessa's reflection was the unfinished rendering, a stark contrast to the completed, colored version opposite. And yet, the plain reflection held so much more depth and emotion. Although they were both seated, I felt the tension radiating from the unpainted version. The reflection's eyes were wide and her face full of expression, while the other Vanessa remained placid, an empty husk. It was as if the reflection wanted to leap through the mirror but was bound to her chair with invisible rope.

Even without the Insight, the artist's message was clear.

Fear.

But fear of what? Fear of whom?

As I drew closer to the painting, I noticed other, subtler details. Her unique style became apparent to me: the angle of her strokes, her effort and precision and the exact amount of paint she'd used.

Then the Insight took me further down the rabbit hole.

I stumbled backward in time. The window stood open. Soft daylight spilled into the room. I smelled fresh paint. A cool breeze wafted around, carrying with it the loamy aroma of autumn. Faint music played from down the hall, some catchy acoustic number sung with a woman's warbled voice.

Vanessa stood before her easel, red hair tied in a ponytail. A slight tremor shook her hand holding the pencil as she contemplated the blank canvas. Her white shirt and denim overalls were covered in dried color, and she was barefoot.

I lost track of how long she stood poised before the empty canvas with a determined look on her face, as if willing images to spring to life. A deep breath, and then she went to work, with quick, deft movements. The story of this unfinished painting unfolded, and I sensed her conflict, the turmoil in her life and the fear underlining everything.

I blinked.

My world shifted.

I stared at the unfinished painting, and I understood.

There was something else at play here, some hidden message unearthed by the Insight. I picked out discrepancies between the images of the two women, the curve of a lip here, the tilt of the head there, a stray lock of hair on the shoulder. This wasn't some self-portrait. These were deliberate details highlighting distinct differences between two women.

I wasn't looking at Vanessa's reflection. I was looking at someone else entirely.

Vanessa had a twin.

The Insight rushed from me like water from a broken dam. My legs turned to jelly, and I slumped to the floor. My eyes closed, but I couldn't shake the images of what I'd just seen.

As aftereffects went, this wasn't so bad.

I heard the others coming up the stairs but didn't bother getting to my feet. The floor wasn't going anywhere, and I was content to let the rest of the world get on with itself.

"Doc!" Leyla burst into the room with Deacon and Besim close behind. She knelt by my side. "You're burning up!"

My body was bathed in sweat. I felt the heat in my cheeks and ears, but Leyla's cold hand on my forehead evened me out.

Besim contemplated the unfinished painting on the easel, her arms folded, and a finger pressed to her lips. Deacon removed the paintings from the walls, stacking them on the bed.

"Found ya!" he crowed triumphantly.

I opened my eyes and winced.

"Fucking empty," Deacon complained. "Goddamn cleaners were thorough."

"Yeah, but not perfect," Leyla enthused. "Thanks to Besim!"

The consultant offered a small smile but didn't respond. She traced her fingers over the painting without touching its surface.

"Our girl was being watched," Deacon explained, standing beside a small hole in the wall about half the size of my open palm. "You can bet your ass there were more of them little fuckers here. Got three holes downstairs. And the device Saranda found is some serious high-grade shit."

He moved into the bathroom.

I rubbed at my temples. The world was no longer spinning. I rose unsteadily to my feet. Leyla shot me a concerned look. I returned it with a weak smile.

"I'm fine, kiddo."

She searched my face, then nodded.

"I'm going to check out Vanessa's workstation," she said, casting me one final look before leaving the room.

I moved to the hole in the wall. It was shallow and empty. I considered retrieving the scanner to look for fingerprints but decided against it. Judging by what we'd already seen at Tony's apartment, it was unlikely we'd find anything.

I walked back to the easel.

"May I see the device?" I asked Besim.

Besim reached into a coat pocket to hand me a clean white handkerchief. Within its folds was a small piece of inert technology with a tiny lens and casing. It bore no identifying marks or serial numbers.

"You heard this?" I asked.

"I heard the lens turn in its casing as it focused," she answered.

"Well it doesn't seem to be working now," I remarked while studying the little device. "Battery die?"

Besim glanced down. "It was disabled remotely. The moment the ventilation cover was removed, the device ceased functioning."

"Whoever's on the other side of that thing can't be happy we found their toy," I stated, depositing it in an evidence bag.

"Jesus Christ," Deacon swore, then stepped back into the bedroom. "There must've been a camera in her shower head. I found a hidden compartment there too. What'd you find?"

"It's a message," I replied, then paused for dramatic effect. "Vanessa has a twin."

I wasn't disappointed. Besim's eyebrows nearly jumped off her forehead.

"The Insight showed you that?" Deacon asked.

I pointed out the differences between the two drawings.

"Hot damn," Deacon whistled. "Can you run her image and ID her?"

"Already on it. Just give me a second," I said, then contacted EVI. "Hello, sweetie. How are you feeling?"

"Good evening, Detection Hollowsway," came her garbled reply. "My function...ality...remains impartial. Repairs are...spastic."

"You poor thing," I grimaced, glancing at the painting. "Listen, scan the image I'm looking at. I want you to run it through the GPD to find out who this is."

"Of course, Detection Hallowedway," she said in between several pops and crackles. "However, funk...shun...ality is limited. It will take several days."

"I know, sweetie," I said ruefully. "Do what you can."

"Doc, would you come in here?" Leyla called from the office. "You're going to want to see this."

I put the evidence bag inside my blazer pocket as both Deacon and I vacated the bedroom. Besim remained at her post, brow furrowed in concentration at the unfinished painting.

Vanessa's office consisted of a virtual workstation, more seascapes hanging on the walls, a daybed and not much else. An open window in the wall behind the workstation filled the office with cold air. Now that my internal thermometer had corrected itself, I went over and shut the window. Several holo-windows hovered before us, colored displays from Vanessa's workstation.

"It was just getting nice in here," Leyla grumbled, flicking her hand at several holo-windows, skimming them out of the air and replacing them with others.

One held the logo for Hughes Advertising, while others showed Vanessa's art homepage, favorite social media sites, and a variety of messages on colored stationery.

"What'd you find?" Deacon asked from the doorway.

Leyla waved her hand several more times, sending a kaleidoscope of images spiraling before me.

"That's just it," she said. "Everything appears normal."

"I don't understand." I gave Leyla a blank look.

She rolled her eyes in dramatic fashion. "Must I explain everything?"

"Please, oh guru of tech!" I pressed the flats of my hands together. "Please enlighten us poor, unwashed fools of the greatness that is you!"

"Jerk." Leyla punched me in the shoulder, hard, then turned to Deacon. "I went through all of her directories, registries, folders, caches, hidden caches, pretty much everything this workstation and her online history contained. Her security was about as complicated as Doc's love life."

"But I don't have a love life."

"Exactly," Leyla continued without batting an eye. "By the way, her passwords are all 'Oliver.' The point is, Vanessa's station looks ordinary, so ordinary that I'd say it was set up to fool the casual observer. Lucky for you, I'm now on the case. I think those cleaner guys came in here and wiped everything out. They probably used a cheap variation of a Vortex Hack to break her stuff apart, take the pieces they wanted, and rearranged the rest, without the lemony-fresh scent."

"Can you figure out what they took?" Deacon asked.

Leyla shook her head.

"Nope, all that data is lost. The hack strips the information from all of Vanessa's network data sources and rewrites the code. What's left is all surface stuff, and not worth looking at."

She lowered her hands, shutting down the workstation.

"Deacon, you said the device is high-grade," I said, eyes narrowing. "Are you talking military-grade?"

"Yeah," he nodded. "By my count, there was one in every room, probably one in that workstation and one at each exit."

"What do we do now?" Leyla's eyes were bright with excitement. "Should we call for backup?"

"No, kiddo, we don't need the cavalry just yet." I gave her an amused smile. "There's still a lot we don't know. For starters, why was Vanessa under surveillance? Who is this twin of hers? And what do cleaners have to do with our murderer?"

"Well, we can rule out anyone at Hughes," Deacon stated as Besim joined us. "She handled portfolios for boutique businesses like women's fashion and children's toys. A demographic analyst job may have gotten her access to sensitive material, but I reckon that ain't worth killing over."

"And the device isn't something you can just put together with tape and glue," Leyla said. "These guys could've picked them up illegally from any number of Black Web dealers. Also, sophisticated micro-tech like that requires a workshop with special tools. I doubt ad agencies have that kind of equipment. Even without a serial number, its architecture might give us a clue as to who made it. I'll take some pictures and send them to a guy I know."

Deacon gave her a flinty look.

"He's very discreet, Deacon," Leyla replied sweetly. "And he owes me a favor. I may have tipped the cops off to where they could find him, but felt really bad about it, so pinned it on this other really nasty guy who was after him instead."

We all looked at her.

"What?" she squirmed under our collective gaze. "The other guy had it coming. And besides, my new friend's kinda cute."

She blushed. I laughed and gave her a quick hug.

Deacon shook his head as I handed the bag to Leyla. She retrieved the bug and placed it on the workstation. After a few flashes from her phone, she returned it to the bag.

"There." She smiled at the three of us, displaying the images. "Give me a few minutes to put something together. I left my rig in the pod."

We made our way downstairs and into the living room while Leyla chattered on about her friend and the Vortex Hack. I missed most of what she said as I sorted out what I'd discovered through the Insight. I felt weak-kneed but made it down the stairs without breaking my neck, then wandered into the kitchen.

"Detective."

I hadn't noticed Besim follow me in here.

"What is it?" I replied, then opened the refrigerator.

Vanessa was into health food, but nothing else leapt out at me.

"Are you well?"

"I'm fine. The Insight wipes me out. I was just coming in here to get a glass of water."

After closing the refrigerator door, I checked out the cabinets below the counter. Inside one, I found a dozen cans of wet cat food stacked neatly to the side next to a small metal bowl. No litter bags, though.

"Miss Bonner said she came by to take care of Miss Mallery's cat," Besim observed. "However, the pet does not appear to be the indoor variety."

"Yeah, I haven't smelled a litter box, either. It's both ironic and sad. Our victim preferred to live alone, yet that was never the case. Someone was always here, watching. But who, and why?"

Besim nodded, moved to an upper cabinet and retrieved a drinking glass. She filled it from the tap in the sink, then handed it to me without comment.

I guzzled it in two quick swallows.

"Thanks," I said, placing the glass on the counter near the wine bottles.

My eyes strayed across the labels. Something nagged at my memory. All three read "Stettler Family Vineyards, 2098 Reserve,

Pinot Noir, New Hollywood." I felt a slight surge of the Insight and plucked up one, turning it in my hand.

"You notice anything familiar about this?" I asked.

Besim tilted her head to the side, studying the bottle.

Before she could answer, I blinked several times in rapid succession. The Insight sparked again. I set the bottle on the counter, moved to the back door, flicked the light switch by the window and stepped outside. Ignoring the cold and drizzle, I strode over to the ceramic fire pit. My breathing quickened, while my heartbeat thundered in my ears. My eyes burned again. I raised my face to the leaden sky. The rainwater sluiced over my irritated orbs, but it didn't help.

I knelt before the fire pit, peering inside to find a mound of burnt debris. Something was in there. I dug with my gloved hands, releasing small puffs of exploding ash. The Insight continued its pulsating insistence, urging me to dig further. Besim watched from the open doorway.

"I've seen that wine at Tony's," I explained in between gagging on the ash. My coughing worsened, and I stepped away to clear my throat. "In his wine rack. The exact same wine. Phooey!"

I spat out a gob of dark phlegm.

"C'mon, I know you're in here," I muttered.

Heedless of my mucked-up hands, I pulled out my holo-phone and activated the flashlight. Then I stuck my head inside the fire pit.

"And at Julie's place too," I said, my voice echoing hollowly. "I'm not a wine expert, but don't you think it's awfully convenient all three of them had the same taste in wine?"

At the very back, I found a small square lump pressed against the curved side.

"Gotcha!" I crowed in triumph, before slamming my skull against the lip of the fire pit. "Holy sonofamotherbloodygoddamnfuck! Ow!"

I rubbed the tender part of my noggin. In my other hand, I

held up a partially-melted metal cigarette lighter. It was empty. The word 'Kraze' was engraved on it in crimson and gold lettering. I tossed the lighter to Besim, who tried to catch it and missed. She gave me a sheepish look.

I stormed over and picked it up with a flourish.

"However, this?" I grinned, resembling some macabre chimney sweep from a Dickens' tale. "This is *very* interesting!"

CHAPTER 16

"What was that shouting outside?" Leyla asked.

"I cracked my head against the fire pit," I replied lamely, rubbing my head.

"Well, at least it's thick," Leyla said with a sly grin.

I reached toward her to rub my filthy hands on her clean clothes, but she skipped away with a giggle. Smiling, I used the sink and a wash cloth to clean myself off while the others studied the wine bottle and the damaged lighter. The Insight vanished, but I didn't feel any the worse for wear this time. I drank another glass of water to rinse the ashy grit from my mouth.

"Vanessa wasn't a smoker," I said.

"Maybe she used it to light the fire pit?" Leyla chimed in. "Then she threw it away because it was empty?"

"No, this is something else," I said while folding the washcloth, and dropped it on the counter. "The Insight pointed me to that lighter. Destruction of evidence, maybe?"

"Looks like our cleaners fucked up twice now," Deacon stated in satisfaction.

"Well, why didn't the cleaners just take it with them?" Leyla countered. "Why bother leaving it behind?"

I chewed on that a moment, then shook my head.

"I don't think the cleaners worked the patio," I replied.

Deacon moved outside and began poking around.

"Perhaps we were meant to find it," Besim offered in her quiet voice. "The cleaners' purpose was to remove all evidence of surveillance from Miss Mallery's home. Whatever devices that were present here would not be kept inside the fire pit. The heat would disrupt or destroy the device."

"Once we're back at the pod, I'll use the p-scanner on it," I said. "Although I doubt there'll be any prints."

"What manner of word is 'Kraze?'" Besim asked, gazing quizzically at the lighter. "I am unfamiliar with its etymology."

"You really like to use big words, don't you," I said.

"Shut up, Doc." Leyla glared at me before turning back to the consultant. "Kraze is a dance club. I've been to it a few times. It's off Mulberry, down in Chinatown. They do theme nights and drink specials to draw in bigger crowds. Oh, and no cover charge for ladies on weekdays."

"Natalie did say the two of them liked to go clubbing." I considered that for a moment, looking at Leyla. "And I saw the same bottle of wine at both Tony and Julie's apartments. Our eyewitnesses were dressed up for a night on the town, but they never said what they were doing *before* going to Tony's apartment. In fact, their night ended early, if they were really going out at all."

"Holliday's right," Deacon announced as he shut the exterior door behind him. "I checked all the places I'd hide a camera and didn't find shit. The cleaners didn't bug her patio. How far is Kraze from our crime scene?"

"A short Metro ride, maybe twenty-five minutes, tops," Leyla replied. "It's too far of a walk from here."

"And you know what else?" I said, regarding the three of them with wide eyes. "It's on the same route as Armin's. It's one of the stops along the line."

"Yeah, but Vanessa couldn't have been at Kraze that night," Leyla pointed out. "It doesn't open until after eleven."

"No, and Vanessa wasn't dressed up to go dancing, either," I responded grimly. "But our killer might have been." I looked to Deacon. "What if our vamp goes clubbing at Kraze? Perhaps they met there previously, or he sees her there one night and stalked her?"

"Maybe," Deacon replied slowly. "But that still don't explain what Vanessa was doing in Lower Manhattan Sunday night. And what's that got to do with the bugs? Or this wine?"

He grabbed the bottle and glared at the label as if he could intimidate an answer from it.

"Maybe we should crack one open and see what's inside?" Leyla moved to the drawers under the counter, rummaging for something.

A moment later, she tossed a stainless-steel bottle opener onto the table with a loud clatter.

"Allow me, please," Besim said. "I spent many years studying numerous vintages in the Bourdeaux Regime. I highly recommend visiting that enclave, as its residents take great pride in maintaining the highest quality of their vineyards."

Besim placed an empty wine glass on the table that she had found in one of the cabinets above the counter. Deacon handed her the bottle, and with deft, practiced motions, she stripped the cover around the bottle top. A moment later, the cork popped, and she poured a small amount of fragrant red liquid into the glass.

Besim swirled the wine, then bent her nose into the glass, inhaling deeply. She took a slow sip, swishing the wine around in her mouth as her eyes closed.

"You realize that's evidence," I pointed out.

"Keep your pants on, Holliday," Deacon chuckled. "There's two more bottles."

Besim opened her eyes.

"Bright, fruity, toasty aroma and flavors of honey-baked beets, caramelized cherries and nuts, vanilla cream, and peppery spices with an even, vibrant, dryish medium-full body and a warming, distinctive, medium-length cedar mulch and mossy earth finish with firm, chewy, earthy tannins and light oak. A sturdy, oaky pinot that needs a bit of time."

She spat the wine into the glass with a look of slight distaste. Leyla and I gaped at her. Deacon held a dour expression.

"It is a rather cheap wine," Besim said archly. "However, I do not detect anything unusual about it."

"The connection is the important thing," I stated, stifling a yawn. The use of the Insight had worn me down. I needed rest. "I think Tony and Julie lied to us earlier. They knew our victim."

Besim poured the bottle out in the sink.

"What are you doing?" I asked.

"The wine in this bottle is of no value," she replied in a calm voice. "And I do not believe these other two contain anything, either. In addition, there is no one to drink it. I am disposing of it. Then I shall clean both glasses. The dead deserve such courtesy."

"Suit yourself." I said, then followed Deacon and Leyla from the brownstone.

The weather hadn't improved in the few minutes since I was outside on the patio. I pulled my coat collar higher around my neck. My breath steamed before me in white puffs. A car split some puddles as it splashed along the road. Otherwise, the neighborhood was quiet.

Deacon was already headed back to the pod, talking on his holo-phone as he walked.

"You did good back there, Leyla," I said, smiling at her. I resisted the urge to pat her on the head. "Nice pickup on the hack."

"Thanks, Doc," she beamed at me, her blue eyes glistening with pride. "That means a lot."

I was about to say more when something crashed into my lower leg, bowling me over.

"Oh, oh, aren't you precious!" Leyla squealed.

I regained my feet. Leyla cradled something furry that wriggled in her arms. Besim stepped out the front door and stopped, eyeing my attacker with amusement.

"Why hello there, Mr. Fuzzy," Leyla cooed. An overclocked motor buzzed from the ball of fur. "Oh, you're all wet, you poor thing! Where did you come from?"

The cat wiggled free from her grasp and paced around the stoop. I saw the glint of something metal around its neck. A wisp of the Insight grabbed hold of me, and without thinking, I reached down to scoop up the cat. It squirmed, but I kept my hold as I unbuckled its collar, then let it go. The cat landed easily, raised its tail in disdain, and scampered away.

The Insight evaporated.

"Aw, Doc, why'd you do that?" Leyla complained. "He looked cold and hungry."

I stared at the cat collar in my hand and noted the name on the tag.

"That was Vanessa's cat, Oliver. He must've been lurking nearby." I pocketed the collar.

Exhaustion seeped into my bones. I needed a warm shower, dry clothes, and a big pot of coffee. Once inside the pod, Leyla sat in her chair with her holo-rig, working furiously. Deacon sprawled in one of the control chairs surrounded by a cloud of thick smoke.

"So, the eyewitnesses?" he prompted.

I collapsed in the chair next to his.

"Sure," I sighed.

"Damn, Holliday, you look like shit."

I waved a limp hand.

"I'm fine," I replied. My head was filled with foam. "Let's go."

"I would not advise that," Besim stated in a firm tone. "You need rest. A suite of rooms has already been prepared for our arrival."

I tried to protest, but my tongue didn't want to work. Instead, the world went sideways, and I slipped into darkness.

* * *

AS I WANDERED the twilight of my mind, lost somewhere between wakefulness and slumber, her face appeared.

Kate Foster had been everything to me. From her button nose, to her long brown hair, the dimple in her left cheek, the way she smiled with mischief twinkling in those hazel eyes when she was up to no good. She was fire wrapped in water, all fluid grace and burning passion. I had never met anyone like her.

She was my kind of girl.

And then she died.

I miss you, I thought.

Before Wallingbrooke, my life had been a joke. During my suspension, I didn't give a shit about anything. I lost count of the days, because it was easier that way. The places I'd go, the women I'd meet, the shit I'd put in my body, it all blended together into a self-destructive collage of excess and abuse. I'd somehow make it home alive, crash for a few hours, then start all over.

I can thank Abner for Wallingbrooke.

They both saved my life.

As I spiraled out of control, Abner refused to let me go softly into that good night. He'd leave messages, but I never returned his calls. When the old man finally came by my apartment, he found me lying in my own vomit. Emergency services carted me off to a hospital for a few nights of IVs, sedatives and stomach pumping. The doctors decided I'd live, but I was too broken to care.

Once Abner dumped my sorry ass off at Wallingbrooke, the real hell began.

Never in my life have I been more exposed. The overwhelming

shame fueled my resentment of Abner, ECPD and anyone associated with me or the scandal. My body was one raw nerve waiting to snap, and every sound made me jump. I didn't want anyone to touch, talk or look at me.

Wallingbrooke's doctors deconstructed me, piece by bloody piece. My body had to be detoxified, and my brain needed to be scrubbed with a wire brush just to take off the first layer of poor judgment. Between the group sessions, the evaluations, meds, self-loathing, anger, fear and pure stubbornness, I honestly didn't think I'd make it.

If Abner and Wallingbrooke saved my life, Kate Foster saved my soul.

Everything changed after I met her.

I ached from those memories, and a host of other old wounds.

My body twisted in the bed on which I lay, yet my eyes remained closed. Something was keeping me under.

Why, Kate? I howled into the shadowy void of sleep. *Why did you leave me?*

The void didn't answer. It yawned deep and dark and endless. It held secrets, too far to plumb, and answers, too opaque to see. The void mocked me with its silence, my broken heart and fractured soul seeking surcease and finding none.

Since Kate's death, I moved through life in a befuddled haze. Whenever I slept, all the despair I had suppressed in the waking world cloaked me in an armor of emptiness. My loneliness had buried my light, and my days became a series of mundane routines, each one without character or depth. Everything was mechanical, like eating stale toast without butter or jelly. Colors faded, I held little interest in anything, and when I wasn't at the precinct, I'd be home alone staring at chipped paint.

It wasn't much of a life, but I kept trudging along anyway, too damn stubborn to quit, I guess.

Yet now you have been given purpose, Thomas Henry Holliday, countered a voice.

It wasn't hers, nor the void, but I knew it anyway.

Her death forced you to live, it continued.

No, her death was the end of me, I raged. *There was no purpose to it. I should've died that night too. I should've gone with her.*

You did not, it said. *You could not.*

But why? Why am I still here?

To live, it answered with conviction. *You must rise now and seek justice for those who cannot.*

"What the hell do you think I've been doing?" I shouted, but there was no one there. "Dammit, answer me!"

Someone with very cold hands shook my arm.

"Doc," Leyla cried. "Wake up!"

"Go away," I groaned, swatting feebly at Leyla.

I lay face-first on a king-sized bed. Whoever had dumped my carcass there left me clothed.

Lucky them.

"C'mon, lazy bones!" She smacked my head with a pillow.

I rolled onto my back and cracked open an eye. A boring, off-white hotel ceiling greeted me. I turned my head and regarded Leyla, who sat on the edge of the bed with her white hair tied in a ponytail. She wore a blue and white floral-patterned halter top, a black leather miniskirt and glossy thigh-high boots. We must've stopped at Abner's on our way to wherever here was. The ensemble somehow made her appear younger, and more fragile.

"You all right?" she asked in concern, noting my expression. With a start, I realized I wasn't staring at her, but through her. "Who were you talking to?"

"Uh, nobody," I mumbled. "Was just a dream. Just give me a minute."

Behind her, I spotted an open doorway leading into a furnished sitting room. I caught the pleasant scent of brewed amaretto coffee with a hint of cinnamon. That was motivation enough for me. I washed up, then followed my nose from the bedroom.

We were in a posh executive suite with a central sitting area and small kitchenette. I counted two more bedrooms across from the one I'd occupied, plus a full bar, complete with holo-entertainment center, another bathroom and a balcony overlooking the city. A full-length tinted window filled one wall, with a glass double door at its center. Colorful lights from holo-billboards and other buildings glinted outside.

Elegant paintings decorated the walls consisting of surrealistic rip-offs, leaving the mind to decipher their hidden meanings. A large crystal chandelier hung from the ceiling overhead, glistening as if freshly-cleaned.

Besim rose from one of the sofas and handed me a cup, napkin and saucer. She was dressed in a loose violet blouse and a green and orange peasant skirt with a matching scarf around her neck. I also noticed she'd reapplied her makeup and removed the handkerchief from around her head. With her hair dry and free from the mist and rain, the Vellan almost looked human.

I thanked her and plopped down in an adjoining sofa, savoring the aroma. Several plates of fruit, some sandwiches, and all manner of junk food were spread on the table. It was clear who'd done the ordering. I slid a turkey sandwich on rye closer to me and scooped a few chips and a pickle on my plate.

"Nice place," I remarked between mouthfuls of sandwich. "Where are we?"

"The Lincoln Continental Hotel," Besim replied casually. "I own the penthouse suite. It is useful for private meetings and other social engagements."

"About time you got up, Goldilocks," Deacon said from the room's virtual workstation, glaring at me with impatience. His lank brown hair looked unwashed, although he'd changed into a clean navy t-shirt and blue jeans.

I downed half the coffee in one gulp before responding.

"What time is it?" I yawned.

"It's Wednesday, Doc," Leyla answered. "A little after seven."

"In the evening?" I sputtered.

"Yeah, and you snore something awful," Deacon growled, gesturing disdainfully at Besim and Leyla. "I wanted to wake you sooner, just to shut you the hell up, but the mother hens overruled me."

Nonplussed, I finished the coffee, found the beverage dispenser, and poured myself another cup. The dark liquid's magic flowed through my veins, energizing me. The conversation with my subconscious (or whatever the hell it was) faded, leaving behind a bitter aftertaste that I drowned with a pull from my cup.

"We heard back from Leyla's 'friend,'" Deacon continued, nodding at Leyla.

"He's not a friend, he's a guy," she responded primly, sitting down on the coffee table. "There's a difference."

Deacon waved her comment away with a mutter. She looked at me, ignoring him.

"He said the parts came from more than two dozen different electronics manufacturers, so there's no way to pinpoint who made the bug."

"There's a surprise," I sighed, slouching into the cushions. "We'd have to investigate all of them, but we can't spare the time or resources."

"True, but there's something else we can do instead," Leyla said. "Deacon and I spent the last few hours working on a tracking protocol. We think we can tap into their signal and trace it back to its source!"

I sat up, nearly spilling my coffee.

"That's brilliant!" I exclaimed. "What are we waiting for?"

"Keep your pants on, Holliday," Deacon warned. "It ain't as easy as it sounds. Given the level of tech, I reckon the signal gets bounced around a dozen or more satellites, not to mention any other ghosts or traps lying in wait for people like us trying to do this kind of thing."

"And it doesn't work fast," Leyla added. "Deacon showed me

how to alter the search scripts I use so the program is harder to detect. The program is very deliberate and methodical, inching its way along the virtual highway so as not to arouse suspicion. It pokes at any defenses until it finds a weak point, and then exploits it. That way, if our bad guys have sniffers, they shouldn't catch our bug."

"Is that anything like a fluffer?" I asked innocently.

"You're sick." She swatted my leg with a pillow. "No, it's just another word for a watchdog or sentry program. Most networks have their own protections to safeguard against unlawful entry. The rich and paranoid employ sniffers because they're like virtual bloodhounds and are good at tracking unauthorized hacking code. If their networks are ever attacked, they deploy counter-measures like sniffers and Cy-trackers to follow the intruder code back to the source."

"But they ain't infallible," Deacon added, giving me a calculating look. "As head of Saranda's security, we've been on the receiving end of them fuckers from time to time."

I glanced from Deacon to Besim.

"You've hacked other networks?"

"I engage in business with individuals whose global interests contain very sensitive data," the consultant explained. "I have built a great deal of equity with them, thanks in no small part to Deacon's efficacy. My office and laboratory are safe havens as a result, protected from satellite intrusion and other prying eyes."

"So, you've hacked other networks," I repeated.

"Damn straight," Deacon nodded with pride. "It's either them or us. I prefer us."

"Who am I to judge?" I chuckled, finishing my coffee.

"I've spent a shit-ton of time setting up a cloaking system to protect Saranda's interests," Deacon continued. "It didn't take much to alter Leyla's little tracking program by adding one of my own watchdogs to home in on the signal."

"In theory, it should work," Leyla added.

"Oh, it'll work darlin'," Deacon gave Leyla a wolfish grin. "Ain't nobody can hide from me once I set my sights on 'em."

"How long will it take?" I placed the coffee cup and saucer on the end table.

"Probably an hour to finish altering the code, then maybe two or three more for the search program to do its thing," Deacon answered. "Depends on how far they've bounced the signal. In the meantime, there's something else you need to see."

Intrigued, I walked over to the virtual workstation. Several holo-screens filled with text floated above it.

"What's all this?" I asked, leaning closer to get a better look.

"That's from the micro-drive you found." Deacon pointed at the screens.

"When did I find a micro-drive?" I did a double take.

"When you picked up that cat," he grinned. "It was hidden on the collar you filched."

I turned back to Leyla.

"It's my fault." She flushed, spreading her hands in a helpless gesture. "I watched you take off Oliver's collar and put it in your coat pocket. You passed out before I could ask about it. When I took a closer look, I noticed the charm with Oliver's name was big, like a bracelet. I poked at it, found the hidden catch, and out popped the micro-drive."

"What's on the drive?" I asked, turning my attention back to the screens.

"The dead girl's diary," Deacon replied. "Seems she'd discovered she was being watched too."

CHAPTER 17

"Some weird shit's going on, Holliday." Deacon pointed at one window set aside from the others.

I pulled it to the forefront, shunting the others behind it, and activated the feed. A moment later, Vanessa's face appeared with the eggshell white of her home office as the backdrop.

The luster of her long red hair struck me first. It shone with a vibrancy so unlike the dull and faded corpse I'd seen earlier, silent and still in death. Her eyes were gray-green and clear, the color of springtime. She spoke in a pleasant, husky *contralto*, and her face was expressive and lively. Seeing her like that reminded me of something, but I couldn't put my finger on it.

Vanessa's first few entries ran like a typical diary. She chattered about work, a couple of boring dates that didn't go anywhere, her opinions on art, her cat, wine, music, politics, and her neighbors. However, as the diary progressed, I noticed worry lines forming around her eyes, and her customary vivaciousness disappeared.

That's when it got interesting.

"It's July 10th, and last night I had a very strange dream. I'm lying on a table, and the lights were in my eyes, so it was hard to see. Then two people appeared, a man and woman, and they were wearing blue surgical clothes with white masks. The man had gold-rimmed glasses because they reflected the light. Anyway, they hovered over me, and it was really creepy. They just stood there, studying me, and there was no sound." She laughed nervously. "Better lay off the vino next time Natalie wants to come over and complain about guys!"

The recording shifted to the next with a buzz of audio and a flash of broken images.

"It's July 22nd, and I had that weird dream again," she said, a nervous bite tingeing her tone. "It was so vivid! This time, I heard a beeping sound, you know, like the kind in hospitals. Same people, same light. And then I woke up." She frowned. "I only drank one glass before I went to sleep. Better talk to Nat about this one."

Leyla came over to stand beside me, folding her arms as she watched the video stream move to the next installment.

"It's July 23rd. I spoke with Natalie. She's the best." Vanessa wore a wan smile. "She thinks the stress at work is getting to me, and the dream is just my subconscious trying to work things out. Maybe the man in the dream is Mr. Hughes?" Vanessa paused to consider it, then shook her head with a laugh. "No, he's too thin. I think Nat's right, though. I have a lot of accounts I'm working on, and they all have tight deadlines. I need some time off! Maybe go to that club Nat's been talking about. She also suggested I visit Doctor Ettelman and have her prescribe a sleep supplement. It couldn't hurt, right? Anyway, time to curl up with some pinot and a good holo!"

I paused the feed and looked to Deacon. "Did you interview Hughes?"

"Yeah, I met that fat fucker," Deacon growled. "He was too busy staring at his assistant's tits to care. Hell, he barely knew who Vanessa was, let alone she worked for the sonofabitch."

I nodded, then tapped the window again to resume the recording.

"Today is August 3rd. I finally went to see Doctor Ettelman today. She told me everything looks fine but wants to run a few more tests just to make sure." Vanessa absently brushed away her hair. She looked exhausted.

Oliver pushed his way across the screen, blocking my view.

"Hi, buddy," Vanessa laughed fondly, stroking the cat's tail. "He's the only man I need in my life. Right, O?"

I exchanged a glance with Leyla, who smiled and shrugged.

"She's right, you know," she said.

"About?" I arched an eyebrow.

"Just shut up and keep watching."

The recording skipped to the next entry.

"It's August 18th, almost a month since the last dream." Vanessa's eyes were round with anxiety. "Well, it's back, except this time it was different. A lot different. In it I felt small, like I'd been shrunk or something. I heard the steady beeping too. The man with the glasses was holding a syringe. He spoke, and I could tell because I saw the white mask moving, but I couldn't hear him. And I was cold. But worst of all was the fear, like I was swimming in it and couldn't get away."

Tears welled in her eyes.

"What's happening to me?" she whispered. "And the really weird thing? I felt connected to something, or someone. I don't know how I know this, but I do. Like there's someone else sharing the dream with me. But I can't turn my head to look around. I'm frozen in place, but I know they're there. And then I wake up."

Vanessa pressed her fist to her mouth and scrunched her eyes closed.

"What's worse, I think I'm being watched! When I was painting last night, I swear there was someone behind me, watching everything I did! And when I went to work today, it felt like everyone was looking at me, studying me, like I was an animal at the zoo."

Vanessa took several short, sobbing breaths. She fell back in her chair, shoulders slumped with exhaustion.

"I'm going to call Nat. Maybe we'll go to back to the club and dance the stress away. Hopefully, that slimy guy and his girlfriend won't be there. At least they have good taste in wine. So glad they recommended it! Aunt Jen said she'll ship some more in a couple of days. I'm not turning into an alcoholic, am I?"

She laughed nervously.

My brow furrowed, but I continued watching as the feed shifted to the next recording.

"It's September 12th, and I was followed today." Vanessa's complexion was several shades lighter than normal. Her hair was stringy, as if she hadn't washed it in days. "I went to the store for a few things. A man wearing a trench coat followed me for about four blocks. I kept looking over my shoulder, but he kept his distance and I couldn't see his face. When I got to my street, he was gone."

Vanessa stared at me with pleading eyes.

"Should I call the police? Can they even do anything? What am I going to do? *What am I going to do?*"

She sobbed uncontrollably, but the feed cut off as another edit led into the next entry. Leyla reached over, taking my hand in hers. Her touch chilled me, but I clasped it anyway, glad for her company. Vanessa no longer had that luxury.

"It's October 1st, and something amazing happened!" Vanessa could barely contain her excitement. "It was so surreal, like looking in a mirror! I still can't believe it! It was her, the one from my dreams! I *know* it was her. I could *feel* it. It's impossible to express in words, but we're connected. We're going to meet again tomorrow. But I'm afraid. What's happening to me? I know they're not dreams now. They're memories. But I don't remember any of it, so it must've happened a long time ago. I need answers. I need to paint. I need wine. I don't know what's going on, but I'm going to find out."

"Last one coming up," Deacon broke in solemnly.

A haggard Vanessa stared at the camera for several long seconds. The fear was there, but also resignation.

"It's October 21ˢᵗ. I've removed the bug they put in here, so they know I know."

Sunday. This was recorded Sunday. My eyes turned flinty as I caught the time stamp: 6:22 PM.

Three-and-a-half hours before her murder.

"I've left the others," Vanessa continued. "What's the point, right? They've listened and seen everything about me, my life, for *years*. So, this will be my final recording. I'm sure they'll come looking for this diary. Hopefully, you'll find it first."

Vanessa sobbed. My heart broke at the sight of her. I wanted to reach across and hug the distraught young woman, protect her from whomever it was that had done this to her. She settled down after a few moments.

"I found one of the cameras in my shower head! They were watching me while I...while I—" She cried again. "I feel so...so violated! How could they have done this? I can't trust anyone, not at Hughes, not at the store, no one. Well, except for Nat. But I can't tell her. That would put her in danger. I couldn't live with myself if anything happened to her."

Vanessa's harsh laugh skirted the edge of hysteria.

"They're coming for me. I don't know who they are, but they're coming for me. I know too much."

She paused, shaking her head.

"No, that's not right. I'm *remembering* too much."

Vanessa's phone rang in the background. Her eyes narrowed, and she hesitated before moving from view. It was faint, but I could just make out the conversation.

"You! What do you want?"

A few beats passed.

"Fine, fine, I'll meet you there. But you damn well better tell me what's going on."

I heard muffled footsteps approach as Vanessa appeared and resumed her seat.

"Well I didn't expect to hear from *her*. She actually made it sound like she wants to help me." Vanessa frowned and looked away. "It's probably not a good idea, but I'll meet her at Armin's tonight. Maybe I'll finally get some answers."

The young woman gripped the sides of her head with both hands and scrunched her eyes closed.

"Okay Vanessa, you can do this." She took a deep breath, lifting her head, and we locked eyes.

"I hid a portrait inside the unfinished sketch by my easel," she instructed, her cheeks flushed. "Once you see it, you'll understand. I don't know what else to say except find her. Save her."

Vanessa bowed her head.

"And whoever they are," she whispered. "Please, stop them."

The recording ended, and the screen went dark.

I stared at the blank window. Half of my body had grown numb while gripping Leyla's hand. I let go, and staggered against an end table, my legs unsteady and shivering.

"Oh no!" Leyla cried in dismay. "Doc, I'm so sorry!"

She rushed to my bedroom and returned with the comforter from my bed. I managed to fill a cup from the pot without spilling too much on myself or the furniture, then eased onto the couch. Leyla took the cup from me, and draped the comforter from my bed around my lower body and legs. She handed the coffee back. Besim sat across from me, studying Leyla with great interest.

"What?" I demanded. "I caught a chill from walking around in all this rain."

Deacon lit a cigarette. "That right?"

"It is," I responded with finality.

Leyla sat in the chair to my right with her arms wrapped around her knees, drawing them into her chest.

"She's a goddamn witch, Holliday, ain't she?" Deacon bristled. There was a dangerous cast to his eyes. "Something you damn well should've told me before we went and got her."

"I'm a minor talent," Leyla shot back. The air around us grew colder. I shivered despite the comforter. "Besides, what's it to you anyway?"

"It's *everything* to me, girl," the Confederate returned. "You're a fucking wildcard. I prefer knowing the variables before I work with anyone. Where I come from, you'd burn at the stake."

"Well, thank God we aren't in Birmingham," I retorted, standing up. "You're in *my* city, *Protector*, you got that? And Leyla's with me. If you've got a problem, we can settle it outside."

Deacon laughed in derision, but before he could respond, Besim spoke. "Although I am a mere consultant, it is my opinion Leyla has only begun to demonstrate her true value. She brings a fresh perspective to this investigation, something that is needed. And her technical skills are not inconsiderable, as the past few hours have already proven."

"Thanks." She smiled at Besim, and the temperature around us returned to normal.

"I ain't none too crazy about it," Deacon grumbled. He crushed his cigarette on the workstation.

"Get used to it," came my rejoinder.

"C'mon guys," Leyla said, gesturing angrily at the blank holo-window. "We've got more important things going on right now. Think of Vanessa! That poor girl, what they did to her, what she went through! It's like being raped."

She fixed me with a gimlet glare.

"Doc, we are going to find these bastards and put them away. Forever."

"It would appear Vanessa Mallery's entire life has been violated," Besim stated, calm and detached. Yet her cheeks were flushed, and I noticed one hand had closed into a fist. Some powerful emotion roiled beneath her placid exterior, and I sensed it was more than simply outrage for our murdered girl.

"Her observation of feeling 'small' suggests this occurred when she was young," Besim continued. Her closed fist relaxed. "Repressed memories from past trauma could explain the dreams, although such a general diagnosis is far from scientific. While cases of repressed memory are common, the memories themselves are not always reliable. An individual might be confused about events, their perception skewed by the emotions they experienced during that time."

"The memories could've been false, or even manipulated in some way," I supplied. "But the Insight wouldn't have led me to the cat collar if there wasn't something important for me to find. Vanessa was convinced her dreams were memories, and I believe her."

Deacon gave me an appraising look, then glanced at Besim. "Good enough for me."

That caught me off guard. "It is?"

"Somebody's gotta trust that gut of yours," he said. "Otherwise, why the fuck did Mahoney bring you on board?"

"So why now?" I asked, rubbing my temples. "And what triggered it?"

Besim paused to consider.

"The syringe in the dream-memory indicates the use of medication of some kind, perhaps an anesthetic or hormone," the consultant said. "The pinot noir could have been mixed with a catalyzing agent activating whatever had been done to her previously. However, I suspect more than one stimulus was involved, perhaps even a convergence of different stimuli to create the dream episode rather than a single instance."

"But you didn't taste anything in the wine back at her townhouse," Leyla pointed out.

"True." Besim nodded. "But it is highly probable the cleaners took the affected bottles, leaving behind clean wine. Detective, we should retrieve the pinot noir from both eyewitnesses' homes to examine the contents in a laboratory."

"We still have no idea what they were doing to her, though," Leyla lamented.

"Well, let's look at the victim for a moment," I said, thinking furiously. "There was nothing in her medical record indicating she was ever treated at a hospital. In fact, she's never had any health problems at all. Stentstrom confirmed she had strong musculature, healthy skin, no surgeries, scars, or blemishes —nothing."

I leaned forward with hands clasped and forearms on my knees. The comforter slid to the floor. Between the coffee and my rush of theories, my body warmed up.

"This Doctor Ettelman would know a thing or two about that," Deacon said.

"Vanessa lives alone, no significant others, and her only relative is in New Hollywood, over twenty-five hundred miles away," I said, nodding in agreement. "She was isolated, the perfect test subject who was under constant observation. Whoever they are, they followed Vanessa's progress remotely to make sure whatever it was they'd done to her continued to work."

Tension filled my body, and I knew I was getting closer. I could feel it.

"And Sunday night, ECPD gets an anonymous call about screams in an alleyway. ECPD arrives on the scene to conveniently find two eyewitnesses, zoned on 'joy, claiming to have seen a vampire. The officers soon discover the corpse of a young woman killed by severe lacerations to her neck, consistent with a bite wound. Upon examination by the coroner, it's confirmed the victim's body is devoid of blood."

"No shit," Leyla railed in frustration. "It's the one thing that's out of place. She was murdered in an alleyway by some freaking vampire? What does that have to do with everything else?"

The question hung in the air between us like a dead weight.

Leyla was right. The incongruity of it was almost laughable. Why a vampire? What's so special about that? They're supernatural creatures from stories and legend, and they feed upon...

"Blood," I stated. A different brand of cold ran down my spine, raising the hackles on the back of my neck. "It's her blood."

Besim's posture turned rigid.

"Yes, Detective Holliday," she breathed, her eyes bright with understanding. "Whatever procedure the individuals in her memory were performing involved injection into Vanessa's bloodstream. Presumably, its effect would impact her metabolism, down to a cellular level. If that is the case, then I would posit Vanessa Mallery was the unwitting participant of a biogenetic experiment. Over time, she has been engineered to the pinnacle of good health."

"Don't get me wrong," Deacon chuckled, flicking away ash. "I like science fiction stories about as much as a good proctologist with small hands, but ain't that a bit much, even for you, Saranda?"

"It's just one possibility, but it also makes sense," I said. "Mankind has been trying to eradicate sickness and disease for centuries. But there's never been such a thing as a universal cure-all."

"Until now," Leyla whispered.

"Well, let's not jump to conclusions yet," I said, raising a hand. "Still, how many more like Vanessa and her twin are in circulation? Is her twin even in the same condition as Vanessa? Whoever did this was still in the experimental phase, otherwise we'd all have heard about the miracle drug by now."

I looked over at Besim.

"I need to know who has the capabilities to perform this kind of experiment."

She considered the request.

"There are several operations within Empire City with the facilities, personnel and resources who could manage it. More than two dozen in the Northern Hemisphere alone. However, within my circles, I have not heard of such a thing."

She paused as something occurred to her.

"Detective Holliday, I would also posit her recovered memories and newfound awareness sparked action on the part of those responsible, to eliminate the possibility of revealing this knowledge to not only the authorities, but anyone interested in such an enterprise."

"She was no longer an experiment," I stated flatly. "She became a threat."

"Yeah, but who would do such a despicable thing?" Leyla asked. "And why?"

"Corporations, darlin'," Deacon growled angrily. "And they don't give two shits about your sensibilities. To them, it's all about credits, power and influence. Just imagine how much synthesizing genetically altered blood like this is probably worth. No more sickness. No more disease. It'd be a goddamn medical miracle!"

"It's enough worth killing for, kiddo," I added. "All her blood was taken, down to a cellular level. But I've got a hard time believing whoever is behind all this has a vampire on the payroll. There has to be another explanation."

"If the tales of the *vampyr* are to be believed, then it is possible," Besim remarked.

"You're a damn scientist, for chrissakes!" I snapped back. "Aren't you supposed to be governed by logic and all that?"

"Even your most famous literary detective said, 'once you eliminate the impossible, whatever remains, no matter how improbable, must be the truth,'" she said.

"Sherlock Holmes wouldn't have believed in vampires, either," I countered.

"Well, we do live in interesting times, Holliday," Deacon quipped. "And Stentstrom confirmed the wound around her neck was caused by something sharp, like fangs."

I shook my head but didn't argue.

"I think it's time we head out," I said, thoughts of a hot shower and a change into fresh clothes now the furthest thing from my mind.

"Doc, you need to rest," Leyla admonished. "You look terrible."

"I'll be fine," I said with what I hoped was a reassuring smile. "Besides, this temple runs on coffee."

"And a whole lotta bullshit," Deacon chuckled.

"That too," I laughed.

"But we still don't know who the mysterious 'they' are," Leyla countered.

"And we ain't going to sitting here." Deacon cracked his knuckles. "But I think we got a good idea who does."

"Julie and Tony," I finished for him. "They're now accessories to murder."

CHAPTER 18

"*E*VI, who are the two active officers handling the security detail assigned to Julie DeGrassi's apartment?" I asked aloud as the pod sped along the *'way*.

"Accessing," EVI replied. "Officer Stanley and Sergeant Romero were dispatched to the DeGrassi apartment at twenty-one hundred hours."

Despite several hours' worth of repair, EVI remained at a low level of functionality. She'd been unable to identify Vanessa's twin, either. The ECPD tech staff was having difficulty restoring her, which brought into question the overall benefit of employing a single AI to oversee the day-to-day operations. Based on several inter-department messages I'd read, the proverbial eggs in one basket moment had arrived. The higher-ups weren't thrilled that a single explosion had crippled our law enforcement, social, and emergency services in one fell swoop. Even the DA weighed in on the subject. Would she get shut down once and for all? ECPD had relied on EVI for a long time, but a situation like today reinforced either the need for better protection of our systems, or the AI's elimination in favor of something decentralized.

The prospect of losing EVI made me sad. Sure, she's all circuits and code, but to me, she'd been the one stable constant in my police career, never critical of my life's choices. I'd miss having her stuffy presence in my head.

"Thanks, sweetie," I said. "Now connect me to Julie DeGrassi."

I sipped on my coffee as the line rang several times before Julie's automated message picked up. After five minutes, I had EVI call again with the same result.

"She could be asleep," Leyla offered.

"Maybe," I said. "EVI, patch me through to Romero."

I knew Nicolas Romero from my days working downtown but didn't know Stanley at all. Nico never gave me grief during the corruption investigation, which put him on my short list of good people.

After two rings, Romero answered. "Yo, Holliday! Been a while, man. What's a washed-up, good-for-nothing detective like you doing on this case?"

"I'm like a bad penny, Romero. I always turn up," I replied with a smile. "How'd you get stuck on protection detail? Lose another bet?"

"You know me and the holo-ponies," Romero said slyly. "Anyways, I got this kid Stanley here with me. He's shit at rummy, so I'm makin' the most of my night."

"He must be really bad if you're winning," I teased. "Listen, I'm on my way over with my team. Be there in about twenty. Just wanted to give you the head's up. Good to hear your voice, amigo."

"I'll keep the cards warm for you," Romero said. "I always loved takin' your credits, Tommy."

We hung up.

With Deacon hovering over her shoulder like some steely-eyed raven, Leyla worked her digital magic on her holo-rig. The small surveillance device lay on the evidence tabletop. Besim sat near the back of the pod, lost in her thoughts.

"How's it coming?" I asked.

"Just about done," Leyla replied. "For this to work, I'll have to reactivate the device to refresh its signal."

Her fingers were a blur of movement as she created a series of glowing numbers and letters in patterns on the holo-screen that were beyond my puny mortal's comprehension.

"What about the video feed?" I frowned, pointing at the device's small camera facing.

"I already removed the lens," Deacon chuckled. "Whoever's watching ain't seeing shit."

"And the audio?" I asked.

"The inner circuitry's damn sophisticated," he replied. "I couldn't disable the audio without damaging everything else. You do want this to work, right?"

I glanced at the pod wall by the evidence table, opened a small storage cubby and placed the bug inside.

"The cubby's insulated," I said. "That'll muffle the sound. The signal should still pass through."

"There," Leyla announced, tapping two holo-keys in quick succession. "Hopefully, we'll get a hit in the next few hours."

We rode the rest of the way in silence. Leyla dozed in her chair, head lolling from side to side as the pod made a turn or was jostled by a gust of wind. Deacon stared out the window, a shadowy silhouette cloaked in wispy smoke. Besim appeared to be meditating. I was wired, my mind overflowing with burning questions for the two eyewitnesses. There were still too many holes, although our theory that Vanessa was an unwitting guinea pig in some biogenetic experiment to produce a magic master cure explained a few things.

I failed to imagine a world where sickness and disease no longer existed. It was just too good to be true. And even if someone had discovered it, the socio-economic fallout would be disastrous. I doubted the finished product would be something you only needed to take one time, either. That's not how industries like big pharma made mountains of credits. Whether they manufactured real medicine or a placebo, the perception the product could fix whatever ailed you was just as important as the actual cure itself.

Of course, this wasn't something new. Most people in Empire City, hell, anywhere for that matter, were more interested in a quick fix so they could get back to whatever it was they were doing before they got sick. I envisioned thousands of people selling everything they owned to buy this mysterious cure-all, followed by protests and riots, and culminating in a bloody revolution to overthrow the establishment.

Okay, so maybe I was exaggerating a little bit there. Still, the idea one mega-corporation controlling a product that everyone might want frightened me a lot. Who wouldn't want to live a life free from illness? Some people were desperate enough they'd do just about anything to get their hands on it.

But what if we were wrong?

My thoughts shifted to Vanessa and her mysterious twin. How long had this been going on? Vanessa was twenty-five years old. Her parents had died when she was young. The elusive Aunt Jennifer raised her, then moved to New Hollywood. Yet, there were no photos of her in Vanessa's brownstone. Did the woman even exist? Or was she some fiction fabricated by those responsible to establish the illusion of a family member for Vanessa to create a sense of normalcy? The insidious manipulation of Vanessa's life was heartbreaking. Had everything about her past been a lie?

Vanessa believed it to be real until the memories resurfaced and things unraveled. Now she was dead, the price for learning the truth. This hadn't been some random killing. It was premeditated, a calculated action on the part of someone who valued their secrecy above the life of one innocent girl. Even the manner of her death was disturbing. Hell, they stole Vanessa's body right out of the damn morgue in broad daylight! The inhumanity and arrogance of it all sickened me.

As I watched the liquid light of the city streak past, my stomach twisted into knots.

Julie and Tony had a lot to answer for, of that I was certain. Even if they were unwitting accomplices, I knew they possessed critical knowledge that could blow this case wide open.

"Detective Holliday, we have arrived," EVI announced. "Outdoor temperature is thirty-six degrees, with rain, moderate wind gusts out of the east, and fog."

I woke Leyla with a light touch to her shoulder.

"Huh?" Leyla gave me a bleary-eyed look. "Oh, okay. Let's go."

I kept my hand on her shoulder.

"No, kiddo," I instructed in a gentle voice. "I want you to stay in the pod and keep an eye on that program of yours. The minute it finds something, contact me, okay?"

"Yeah, okay," she nodded, throwing her arms out to stretch. "I figure you wouldn't want me to turn them into popsicles anyway."

I chuckled and exited the pod accompanied by Besim and Deacon.

A solid breeze kicked up, blowing cold rain in my face. I raised the collar of my blazer. Other than the occasional passing car or the distant thrum of a pod, the neighborhood slumbered.

A night doorman stood beneath the canopy leading into the building. He was younger than Phelps, looking a little rough around the edges, which I suppose wasn't a bad thing. Although what kind of trouble you'd expect to find in a cozy neighborhood like this was anyone's guess. Still, it didn't hurt to be cautious.

"Can I help you?" the night doorman asked in a surly voice, eyeing us warily.

"Police business, pal," I answered, producing my silver badge. It gleamed with ghostly light, illuminating his nametag which read "Donovan." "So, if you would please let us through, I'd appreciate it."

Donovan gave it a thought, grunted, and unlocked the door to let us inside. There was no sign of Romero or Stanley, other than an empty card table and two chairs. A half-eaten sandwich and chips cluttered one end. I frowned and looked back at Donovan. He had resumed his post.

Something was off.

"What is it?" Deacon asked.

"Nothing," I replied absently, then moved across the narrow foyer toward the open elevator.

"Must be interesting, being a doorman and all," Deacon commented as we piled inside. I tapped the holo-screen for Julie's floor, and the elevator hummed. "Probably seen all kinds of shit coming in and out of this place."

A moment later, the door opened. I stepped out.

The hallway was empty.

I raised my hand in warning and drew the SMART gun with the other. Besim and Deacon held their position. The gun was lightweight and warm to the touch, and I felt the connection activate through the implant in my head.

"Safety off," I murmured. "Load standard rounds."

"Confirmed," came the hollow reply in my ear.

"What's the play?" Deacon asked softly.

"Hang on," I replied. "EVI, give me the location and status for Stanley and Romero."

"Accessing," she said.

Half a heartbeat later, she confirmed the two men were in the building.

"Detective Holliday, their vital signs no longer register."

"Shit," I muttered.

Adrenaline surged through me as my heart rate accelerated, but I managed my breathing and remained cool and calm. I studied the thin carpeting on the floor. Faint scuff outlines in the material revealed something had been dragged away from the elevator. No sounds from a holo-vision, music, or voices from any of the apartments. Other than the buzzing from the antique torch lamps along the walls, and the occasional thrum of the elevator machinery, it was quiet.

I crept down the hallway following the drag marks, glancing back to see Deacon a few feet behind blanketing Besim. She seemed distracted, and I realized Besim must be concentrating on her other senses. The marks led to the apartment two doors down from Julie's. There was no welcome mat nor any other sign someone lived there.

"Lemon, Nitroglycerin," Besim stated succinctly, tilting her head with a meaningful glance at the door. "And something else." She gave us a stricken look.

I tested the door handle. It was unlocked. Deacon and Besim stood to the side as I turned the handle and pushed, gun at the ready.

Stanley and Romero lay in a pool of dark crimson several feet inside the apartment. The fresh scent of lemon mingled with the sickeningly sweet metallic tang of blood.

"They were both shot from behind at close range," I noted with professional detachment, scanning the bodies with my eyes, then the darkened apartment.

Other than the corpses, it was empty. I had a feeling the other apartments weren't occupied, either.

"Their guns are holstered," I continued. "And judging from the wound splatter, they were led in here and shot."

"Tony?" Deacon supplied.

"Maybe," I replied, feeling uneasy.

Just then, the elevator dinged out in the hallway. Somebody had arrived.

"Get behind me," I hissed, ushering Deacon and Besim into the apartment. I edged the door open enough to peer out, gun held close.

I heard their approach before seeing them. Donovan crept in a half-crouch past the crack in the door armed with a .9mm capped by a suppressor. Three beats behind him stalked a bald, black man, tall and muscular, also carrying a .9mm. He wore a grey uniform with a patch on the back that read "Quality." Each step they made was deliberate and wary. As the Quality man passed our door, I braced myself. He paused, head cocked to the side. I held my breath. He resumed moving.

I shivered. A droplet of cold sweat seeped slowly down my spine. Taking short, shallow breaths, I gripped the gun tighter.

"EVI, dispatch backup to my position ASAP," I instructed through the neural communication we shared, describing the two men in quick detail.

"Order confirmed, Detective," EVI replied. "ETA is nine minutes."

I wasn't sure if we'd still be around in five minutes, let alone nine, but played the odds anyway. I had no doubt these two were our cleaners, which meant they held answers I wanted. The trick was finding a way to incapacitate them without getting us all killed in the process. We were trapped inside the apartment, but we also possessed the element of surprise. And if I was right, the only innocent people remaining on this floor were behind me.

Glancing at Deacon, I held up two fingers, then three. He nodded once.

I whispered the count, then pushed out into the hallway.

"ECPD, assholes," I shouted and opened fire, not waiting for a reply. I figured they'd already waived their rights the moment they showed up armed.

The bullet hit Donovan behind the knee, but I missed the other guy.

Even worse, the recoil from the SMART gun's discharge took me by surprise and knocked me against the wall. Somehow, I managed to keep my grip on it. Dazed, I watched Donovan collapse to the floor clutching at his leg, screaming in pain. He dropped his gun, but the other cleaner didn't hesitate, drawing a bead on me with his as I blinked stupidly at my handiwork.

"Gun!" Deacon warned.

He leapt past me, grappling at the cleaner's wrist. As they struggled, the gun went off several times, spraying bullets down the hallway. I ducked as bits of plaster rained on my head. Deacon drove the cleaner to the carpet, leveling punches to the man's face. But the cleaner was tough and strong, absorbing the blows. He blocked Deacon's next strike with a meaty forearm. Using his shoulder, he slammed the former Protector against the opposite wall, winding him. Deacon staggered, lifting his arms, but he was too slow. Quality struck him in the face, then punched him in the gut. Deacon collapsed to the floor.

Finally, I came to my senses, ears echoing badly. I felt like I was moving through mud. Despite his wound, Donovan lurched to his gun and scooped it up. His partner brought his to bear, training it on me. I had to do something now, or we were all dead.

"Don't," I threatened, raising the SMART gun.

They didn't listen.

And I didn't miss.

It happened so fast. One moment they were in motion.

And in the next, they were dead.

I stared blindly at the bodies of the two men I'd killed. A cold weight settled in my stomach.

"Nice shooting, Holliday," Deacon wheezed as he rose unsteadily to his feet. "Those fellas weren't interested in getting caught, that's for damn sure."

He shook his right hand out a few times, the knuckles scraped and bloody.

"No, they weren't," I replied hoarsely, aware Besim had moved into the hallway with us.

I passed a trembling hand over my face, ignoring the look of concern she gave me. The adrenaline rush faded. Sand weighed down my arms and legs.

For some people, killing was easy, but not for me. I understood it came with the job, and was necessary when the situation called for it, like it did just now.

But I don't like it.

And I'll never get used to it.

Ever.

"Had to be done," Deacon said as he gingerly bent over each body, rifling through their pockets. "A damn shame, too, 'cause we ain't learning shit from these fake IDs they got."

He tossed me two enclave identification holo-cards, stood, and exchanged a glance with Besim. I studied the images.

"Donovan Fleming and Cecil Darby," I read, then pocketed the cards. "Well, when the uniforms get here, I'll have an officer pull their prints. See if they show up in any of our databases."

"Where are the other tenants?" Besim asked, looking around.

None of the doors opened during the fight, confirming my suspicion the floor was vacant.

"Ain't nobody living here, Saranda." Deacon spat a gob of blood onto the floor in disgust. His eyes blazed with fury. "This whole fucking place is a trap. We've been had, Holliday."

I nodded mutely.

"Officers have arrived, and are on their way to your position," EVI announced. "Will you require medical assistance?"

"No, we're fine," I instructed in a cold voice. "Call the coroner's office. We need some bags."

I moved to Julie's door. It was ajar, and an incongruent thought leapt into my muddled head of an old riddle involving a door that wasn't a door. I pushed it open anyway, not bothering to announce my presence.

The interior was dark. Holstering the gun, I strode into the apartment, Besim on my heels, and Deacon not far behind. The smell of gunshot, blood, piss, and shit greeted us as we entered the living room, but no lemon freshener.

"Fuck me," Deacon swore.

Tony Marrazzo slumped in a chair.

I crossed the room and lifted his head.

A small hole had been blown into his skull.

CHAPTER 19

*M*y earpiece buzzed as I pressed against one wall to let two men from the medical examiner's office pass.

"Doc are you okay?" Leyla's tinny voice sounded nervous.

"We're fine," I replied, heaving a heavy sigh. I kept my voice low and filled her in on what happened.

"Jesus," she breathed. "Things just got serious."

"They already were," I stated grimly. "Sit tight. We'll be out soon. Anything from the tracker?"

"No, not yet," Leyla said. "It's going to be slow, though. The signal's bounced a bunch of times already! I'll let you know if anything changes."

We hung up.

I was at the center of a maelstrom. ECPD and PIS milled around poking at furniture, scanning for prints, and searching every cabinet and closet. It was surreal watching them, as if I weren't the one handling the investigation. I guess in a way, I wasn't. It'd been years since I was last involved in a gunfight, and it took several minutes for my body and brain to settle down. The splitting headache from the gun's discharge dimmed to a dull throb.

I stood outside Julie's bedroom. The faint remnant of her pleasant-smelling perfume clung to the air. But where was she now? Had she left the apartment of her own free will? The apartment didn't contain the scent of cleaning fluid which meant the cleaners never stepped foot inside here. And the bullet hole in Tony's head suggested a small handgun, something that could've been kept in a purse. Had Julie killed him? This case was getting murkier by the hour.

An honest-looking, plain-clothes detective from the Police Involved Shooting Unit named John Fredericks stepped up to me. I didn't know him. He had a dark face and darker eyes. Fredericks asked me to go over what happened in the hallway. His eyes glittered with the tell-tale signs of EVI recording my statement.

Mahoney had said SCU would be off the official books, but after my OK Corral lovefest with the cleaners, our unit's clandestine status was out of the bag now. With the way this investigation had progressed so far, that was the least of my worries.

"No sign of a struggle, nothing broken," Fredericks observed as his eyes swept over Tony and the room. "GSW from a revolver, maybe a .38? And, to confirm, this relates to the Vanessa Mallery murder you're investigating? I checked with EVI, and you're not on record, Detective."

"Run it by Captain Bill Mahoney, then," I said. "He'll vouch for me."

Fredericks nodded, and after a silent moment of consulting with EVI, he regarded me with renewed interest. "You've been cleared. And I was told to let you do your job. You've got friends in high places, Detective. So, who were these two?"

"Tony here and his missing girlfriend were the eyewitnesses." I gave him the bare bones, enough to justify my role in things, but my mind was elsewhere.

I studied Tony, slack-jawed and staring at nothing. Was that a look of shock on his face, or fear?

"So, kidnapping is off the table?" Fredericks asked.

"Hold that thought," I replied.

My eyes strayed over to the wine rack underneath the breakfast bar. A bottle was missing from the lowest rack, and I had a damn good idea which one.

"EVI, please upload Julie DeGrassi's image to Detective Fredericks here," I said aloud. "Put out a BOLO and let everyone know she's now a person of interest for both the Vanessa Mallery case and the murder of Tony Marrazzo."

Fredericks' eyes glazed over as he received the data. Seconds later, he regained focus and nodded at me.

"Thanks," Fredericks said. He gestured at all the activity around us. "Must be a nice change from working a desk, eh, Detective?"

"Excuse me?" I asked, taken aback.

"I know who you are," Fredericks replied. "Or, who you were. Heard you're with the 98th, though. You get a transfer?"

"Um, yeah, something like that," I replied evasively.

Fredericks chuckled, taking note of my discomfort.

"I was a first-year at the Academy when all that shit went down about you," he explained. "Back then, me and a bunch of the guys thought you were a modern-day cowboy, making collars and bustin' heads. It's kinda funny to say now, especially with you standing right here, but we looked up to you. Even followed your cases, figuring we could learn a thing or two. Maybe somehow make us better cops, y'know?"

"Yeah, well, I never wanted to be a role model," I mumbled. "I was just trying to do my job."

I stood there, bracing for the punchline. It never came.

"You used to be a helluva cop," Fredericks said with a scowl. "It was a damn shame what happened to you back then. We still think you got a bum rap. I'm glad to see you're back on your feet and working cases again. I'll let 'em all know I ran into you."

A strange feeling swept over me, something I hadn't experienced in a long time.

"Yeah, well, shit happens, right?" I replied with a half-smile, rubbing the back of my neck. "Look Fredericks, I appreciate what you said, I really do. But I've got a fugitive to find, and the trail is getting colder by the minute."

"I understand, but I've still got some more questions for you," Fredericks said, all business again. "It'll only take a few more minutes."

"Your people can handle this," I said in an even tone. "In the meantime, we're leaving."

Excusing myself, I pushed past him and stormed from the apartment beneath a dark cloud. Besim was on her holo-phone. Deacon thanked the paramedic attending him. The Confederate caught my look, then steered Besim by her elbow down the hallway toward the elevator. I watched two techs lift Romero's corpse into a vinyl bag. Romero had been my friend. The cleaners might've killed him, but my credits were on Julie behind what went down here.

A cold anger surged through me.

I'm on to you now, bitch.

Outside, uniforms secured the area amid the blinking lights from emergency and law enforcement. A small knot of curious neighbors formed on the opposite side of the street. The media would be here soon. I wanted us to be long gone before that happened. I showed the badge a few times before breaking free from the cordon ECPD had set up. As we made our way back to the pod, my eyes surveyed the parked vehicles on either side of the road.

"There." I pointed at a van across the street.

I jogged to it, kicking up cold water from the multitude of puddles littering the ground.

The decal on its side read Quality Commercial and Residential Cleaners, including a list of services as well as a phone number. I put my hand on the hood and found it warm to the touch.

"The cleaners hadn't been here long," I stated, giving Deacon a pointed look.

"I reckon something bad went down between them and Julie," he said, then spat on the ground, rolled his tongue around in his mouth and grimaced. "But I don't think killing Tony or the cops was part of the plan."

"What do you mean?" I asked.

"It's too damn sloppy," Deacon pointed out, his breath streaming out in front of him. "They're both eyewitnesses, but instead of getting ganked by the vampire the same way Vanessa did, Julie's nowhere, and Tony takes a bullet to the head. And why kill Stanley and Romero? They trying to make it look like a kidnapping? That's bullshit. I'm thinking Julie snuffed Tony, snuck out the back, and was already gone before the cleaners got there. Those mercs arrive to clean Julie's apartment, panic, kill the cops, and then we show up to really fuck things up for them."

"You might be right," I said, nodding. "So why take the risk?"

Deacon lit up a cigarette despite the falling rain. He took a long drag, then blew twin plumes of smoke from his nose like some disheveled dragon.

"What if there's more than one player involved?" Deacon offered, narrowing his eyes at me. "What if Vanessa was at the center of some corporate game, and Tony, Julie and the cleaners are just pieces on a damn board?"

"Competition," I mused, and considered the implication. "Maybe we've been looking at this all wrong. What if the 'vampire' is a special wet-works operative employed by their closest competitor? You know, a different brand of cleaner. And what if that competitor figured out what was being done to Vanessa, and wanted it for themselves?"

I began to pace, ignoring the rain and the cold as the idea sprouted big, hairy legs in my mind.

"It's all a setup. They send their wet-works guy to eliminate Vanessa, hoping to cripple the other interest by destroying their experiment. Millions of credits down the drain now that Vanessa is dead. The police investigation that follows exposes the ones behind Vanessa's gilded prison, and all eyes are now on them."

I folded my arms across my chest as I paced, my mind racing through the details. "The ones behind Vanessa realize their opposite number knows what's going on, so they send Julie and Tony to follow her. Unfortunately, they arrive at the alleyway too late to help Vanessa. But they get a good look at who did it and are saved by the police arriving on the scene. Otherwise, there are three corpses in that alleyway instead of one."

"Yeah, and a fuck-load more questions on the table too," Deacon replied dryly.

Why else would Julie and Tony make themselves vulnerable to questions by the police? They couldn't run from the murder scene as that would've aroused suspicion. Instead, they received treatment from the paramedics, answered everyone's questions, and acted the part of terrified eyewitnesses. They knew they'd be afforded police protection while the investigation continued, which deflected any immediate suspicion. If the killer or his bosses tried anything, they'd have to go through the police. Still, of the two, Tony had been genuinely frightened during our interview earlier in the day.

Why kill Romero and Stanley? Had someone panicked? Or was it something more?

"Tony didn't strike me as the tough-guy type," I said after a moment. "Maybe he lost his nerve, didn't like how things were going down, so he wanted out. Julie decides to get rid of him before he can blow the whistle."

"Could be," Deacon coughed, wincing as he did so. He spat on the ground again. "Tony tries to leave, so Julie kills him. The cleaners show up to report to Julie, but she's already in the wind. Stanley and Romero are the collateral damage."

My eyes narrowed.

"And the cleaners wait around for whoever shows up and take them out too? No, guys like them aren't sacrificing themselves, no matter how much they've been paid. Maybe Julie suckered the cleaners into coming there? A double-cross?"

"One or both of them's trying to clean up a big fucking mess," Deacon grunted, flicking his finished cigarette into the wet street, then lighting up a new one. "So, where's Julie now?"

"Kraze," I answered. "That's where they all met. One of the pinot bottles was missing back at her place too. Kraze might be the contact point."

"Worth a shot," he said. "And you still think it's about the blood?"

"I'm sure of it." I stopped pacing to regard the former Protector.

"Vampires feed off human blood, Holliday. What's the fucking point of murdering Vanessa that way? Your theory's all well and good, but it's a damn thin one."

"Dammit, Deacon! There are no such things as vampires!" I bristled with anger and frustration. "For chrissakes, you seriously believe it too?"

Deacon puffed on his cigarette before answering.

"I've said it before. I've seen a lot of weird shit. The Vellans came through a goddamn dimensional portal! For all we know, a vampire could've jumped here too! Hell, before you used the Insight on Reynolds and saw that *fetch* latched to him, you had no idea something like that existed. Now, do I think our murderer is one of them blood-sucking fuckers? Maybe, maybe not. But we both heard Stentstrom's report and got a good look at the body. How else do you explain the missing blood? Did it magically disappear? No, something really fucked up happened in that alleyway."

He was right. We were missing too many facts, piecing together what little we knew in a vain attempt at understanding the truth. It was like trying to build a sandcastle on the beach during a hurricane.

"And we don't even know if this miracle drug you and Saranda went on about even exists," Deacon said.

"Maybe they haven't finished it yet," I answered, but without confidence. "Or maybe it's something completely different, and we're barking up the wrong tree. But I'm telling you, the blood is the key."

"Look, I believe in your Insight, or I wouldn't be standing out in the fucking rain yammering on about this goddamn case," the Confederate said. "But we don't have the body anymore to corroborate any of this!"

As he uttered the words, something clicked in my mind.

"Holy shit!" I exclaimed. "This wasn't just a homicide. It was a goddam theft!"

Deacon gave me a blank stare.

"Don't you see?" I resumed pacing, excitement in my voice. "Whoever murdered Vanessa didn't eat her blood. *They stole it!*"

"With what?" Deacon asked. "A tube and an air pump?"

"Maybe," I said, rubbing at my dripping nose. "Look at the surveillance we found at Vanessa's brownstone. You said it yourself that was some serious tech. Maybe these guys built a machine capable of draining all of the blood from a body."

"So, *everything* Tony and Julie told us was bullshit," Deacon said, eyes widening as the realization dawned on him. "Son of a bitch! They saw what the murderer did, and how he did it!"

"Has to be." I nodded with certainty, then remembered something else. "Stentstrom kept some of Vanessa's tissue samples. We need to have Besim examine them. Maybe she can discover what was being done to Vanessa."

I paused and glanced at Besim, whose face was aglow with the white and blue light from her holo-phone. She returned my gaze, her eyes glinting like a cat.

"She'll need her lab for that," Deacon said slowly. "Stentstrom won't take kindly to having more of his stuff removed from his custody."

"I'll just ask nicely," I replied with a grim smile. "Besides, we need to get after Julie before she skips town."

The rain pattered around us. I stared at the van, feeling equal parts cold and tired. A steaming cup of black brew with a mountain of sugar would've been real nice right about then.

"Let's see what's in this van." I turned toward the driver's side door.

Deacon stepped up to the window, took off one boot, and smashed the heel of it through the glass in three rapid blows. He grinned, put the boot back on, and moved to the side with a flourish. I chuckled, looking around to see if anyone noticed. All the attention remained on the apartment building half a block away.

"Ain't nothing here," Deacon said after we searched the interior. "No records, no notes, nothing. Real pros."

"EVI checked the main office number, but it was disconnected," I said, folding my arms across my chest. "Guys like this are paid in hard currency. I bet the serial numbers on their guns were filed off, so no way to track that, either. And the IDs you gave me could've been made in any number of places."

I slammed my hand against the side of the van in frustration with a loud thud.

"Jesus Christ, Deacon! Who were these guys?"

"Excuse me, Detective Holliday," Besim called from outside the van.

I poked my head out the back and said, "Yeah, what is it?"

"I have made a few inquiries with some business associates who are involved with local commercial real estate," Besim said.

Prolonged exposure to the rain hadn't been kind to her hair or makeup. She looked like a drowned mime. Foundation ran down her face in tragic lines of dark tears.

"Oh?" I managed to keep a straight face.

"The prior owner of the apartment building died in early April of this year, and the building subsequently put up for auction," Besim explained, running a hand through her hair. She paused, regarding the dark dye covering her fingers with a frown, then looked up at me and continued. "It was acquired by Hyman and Associates LLC, an apartment management company. The new owner evicted all of the tenants, the last of whom vacated the premises less than three months ago."

I wasn't surprised. If my theories were correct, these were bad people with deep pockets and little spending sense.

"Furthermore, Hyman is a shell corporation. Its owner, Franklin Hyman, is a fictitious name drawn from the enclave identification number of an Empire City businessman who died ten years ago. There are no other employees, or an office, other than a phone number that is no longer in service."

"You got all that from one call?" I asked dubiously.

"My contact can be quite informative, when presented with the proper incentives," she sniffed haughtily.

"I don't want to know," I said, jumping out of the van. Deacon followed a moment later, shutting the doors behind him.

In the distance, the exterior lighting increased outside of the apartment building. I pointed in the direction of the light. The media had arrived.

"Leave the van," I instructed. "Let's get back to Leyla. We've got work to do."

CHAPTER 20

*L*eyla sat cross-legged, frowning at her holo-rig, arms folded across her chest. She glanced up as we came aboard. The temperature inside the pod was noticeably chillier than outside. The internal digital thermometer displayed a balmy twenty-seven degrees. I raised the temperature. Small ice fragments flittered off my wet blazer like sparkling crystal raindrops. I turned to the beverage station, punched a button, and watched a steady stream of brown liquid gold pour sunshine into my mug. EVI confirmed the two dead cleaners were mercenaries whose last known whereabouts were somewhere in the Euro-Bloc.

"At least the cleaners are gone," Leyla commented, a slight quaver to her voice. "Score one for the good guys, right?"

"Sure," I muttered, taking the other command chair with a heavy sigh.

The potent aftermath of adrenaline sloughed away bit by bit. My hands trembled as I replayed the deadly fight in my mind. It'd been a long time since I killed anyone, but I knew there'd be others before this case was over.

Besim resumed her place near the back of the pod. I stole a

glance toward the Vellan. She was composed, at ease, as if nothing out of the ordinary had happened. If Besim hadn't smelled the blood and gun residue, we would've been caught flat-footed in the hallway when the cleaners arrived.

She saved our lives.

"They knew we were coming," I stated, staring hard at the white knuckles of my clenched fist. I swallowed the coffee in two gulps. "We were lucky."

"Jesus," Leyla breathed, eyes wide.

Adding caffeine to my frayed nerves was probably not one of my brightest ideas. I had a penchant for collecting bad habits and decided not to turn a new leaf just then. It'd been a long day, and despite my catnap earlier, I was far from rested. A dull ache took up residence in my shoulders and neck. Thankfully, the caffeine was quick to reignite my internal engine.

"So where does that leave us?" Leyla asked.

I explained my latest theory on Julie and Tony, and Vanessa's blood.

"It's a work in progress," I conceded, pouring myself a second round. This one was noticeably colder than the first, but I chugged it anyway. Besides, I never questioned the java. I merely obeyed.

"What if Kraze is just some random meeting place?" Leyla gave me a dubious look.

"That is a distinct possibility, Leyla," Besim chimed in softly. Her cosmetic travel kit rested unopened on her lap. "However, the digital evidence provided by Vanessa's journal eluded the cleaners' search of her premises. While the surveillance cameras would have continued to monitor Vanessa and her journal entries, it is unlikely the journal was ever discovered. You confirmed the workstation at the townhouse had been scoured. Vanessa had already removed the journal, leaving behind no trace of its whereabouts. It is also improbable the cleaners determined Vanessa secreted the micro-drive on the cat collar. Therefore, they would possess no knowledge of our awareness of its contents. Finally, Detective Holliday's discovery of the lighter reinforces the night-club as a place of interest, presuming it is indeed used for nefarious purposes."

I pointed two fingers at the consultant and belched, "What she said."

Leyla snorted in distaste, wrinkling her nose at me.

"The Insight drew me to the lighter," I continued, my tone sobering. "Planted or otherwise, it's important."

"What if Julie isn't there?" Leyla asked.

"She'll be there," Deacon snarled with angry conviction.

He removed a faded black baton from inside the jacket he wore and placed it on the control console with a loud thud.

"Killing Tony created a shitstorm, and she knows it," he continued, staring at the blunt weapon. "Time for her to cut bait and get the fuck out of Dodge."

I nodded in agreement. "Her image is out to all of the precincts in the enclave, so we'll have more eyes than ours keeping a lookout. She's not leaving Empire City."

I finished my coffee and poured a third cup.

Third times the charm, right?

"Keep an eye on that program." I laid my hand on Leyla's shoulder, giving it a reassuring squeeze. "Rest up, if you can."

We exchanged a glance, and I hoped the apprehension I felt remained hidden.

I instructed EVI to take us to Kraze, then moved to a command chair and set the mug down on the console near the baton. We sat in silence, me staring out the window at a massive, remorseless city made of steel and stone, and Deacon boring holes into the baton laying on the console with dark, brooding eyes.

"How're you holding up?" I asked, taking note of the ugly purple swelling around Deacon's jaw.

He regarded me with equal measures of amusement and annoyance.

"I'll be fine, Momma," he chuckled. "It's gonna take more than that to slow me down."

I gave him a wry smile.

"Nice toy," I remarked, turning my attention to the baton. "Was wondering what you were packing."

Deacon grinned fiercely. He hefted the baton by its worn grip.

"Oh, this little darlin'?" he said in a sly voice. "She ain't much to look at, but she got it where it counts."

"It looks solid enough," I observed, taking special note of the strange shallow markings etched around its business end. "Why didn't you use it against the cleaners?"

For a moment, the markings gave off a soft silvery-blue glow. I blinked, and it was gone. A trick of the light?

"It ain't meant for them." Deacon's voice turned melancholy.

"It reminds me of the old night sticks beat cops used before stun batons became all the rage," I prompted. "Is it made of real wood?"

The former Protector glanced at me with a sly smile.

"There was this big ole oak in a corn field near where I grew up." Deacon chuckled, lost to the memory. "My brother and me used to play there. Called it our 'sanctuary,' treated the place like it was holy ground. My old man even hung a swing on it."

Deacon stared at the old and battered piece of worked oak, a dark gleam to his eye. I caught a brief glimpse of the man behind the tough-guy façade, bearing an indomitable will, deep-seeded convictions, and profound scars. His fingers hovered above the weapon, his eyes lost to a faraway field, a tree, and people long gone.

"And then, wouldn't you know that goddamn tree got struck twice by lightning in the same night. Twice! What're the odds? Anyways, after the storm, I took an axe to it. Harvested the wood myself."

His voice faded. The worry lines on his brow deepened.

"This here is a consecrated weapon, Holliday," he continued

with a hint of reverence. "We don't fuck around where I come from. I've only ever had to hit someone once with it to make my point. Blessed by the holiest of holies himself, the Grand Inquisitor, back when I was still wet behind the ears. Each Protector on his final communion is tasked with crafting a weapon that best fits his disposition, to signify the completion of their training. The materials that make up the weapon bear significance of some kind to the maker, like a point in time, or a place. And we got all sorts of tools to mete out church justice, Holliday. Some messier than others."

His voice trailed off as a he regarded the truncheon.

"So, I got me this," he stated coldly. "The Grand Inquisitor blessed it and me in front of a few hundred of my former brothers and peers. There was a ceremony, lots of prayers, and all kinds of hootin' and hollerin'. That fat bastard used to say the truncheon was just like me, a blunt instrument. Fucking asshole."

Deacon handed the truncheon to me, grip first. I held it with momentary trepidation, anticipating a bolt of lightning to streak down from the heavens and smite me dead.

"It's not heavy," I remarked in surprise.

"Yep. Ain't no metal in it, neither," Deacon said. "It don't register with detectors, which comes in handy sometimes."

He lapsed into silence. I didn't want to push him. Instead, I studied the man's lined face. Some of those lines blended with old scars so you couldn't tell where one ended, and others began. After this brief glimpse into Deacon Kole, I wondered how many more lay underneath.

"Is that what the scrollwork represents?" I pointed at the markings. "Part of the consecration process?"

"They're more than ceremonial, if that's what you're wondering," Deacon chuckled harshly. "When my righteous wrath comes down on my enemies, and if my cause is just, those runes'll light up like a fucking Christmas tree and bring about some serious retribution."

"Wait, like Biblical proportions kind of wrath?"

I'm not overly religious, but even I've read enough of the Old Testament to hold a healthy respect for what the Almighty could do if sufficiently pissed off.

Deacon didn't smile.

"Ain't nearly so dramatic," he replied with that same sober expression on his face. "Trust me, Holliday, you ever get hit by a Protector's weapon, you'll know it."

I finished what was left in the mug and looked out the window, watching the city flow by in a blur of light and movement. We finally arrived about a block from the nightclub. The place was in full swing, even for a weeknight. Deacon stood up, tucked the truncheon inside his jacket, and gave me a look.

It was go time.

Leyla giggled, studying me with amusement.

"What's so funny?" I frowned.

"Well, you're sure going to stand out, dressed like *that.*" She suppressed another laugh.

"Like what?" I sniffed indignantly and donned my coat. "Unlike some of us, I dress for the weather."

"Yeah, and it also screams 'I'm a cop!'" She tapped her lips with a finger, thinking. "We don't have time to stop somewhere and trick you out." Leyla's face brightened. "But I've got a better idea. Why don't I go in separately? I've seen Julie's image, so I know who I'm looking for. I can blend in with the crowd a lot better than you two. I'll snoop around, look for Julie, and call in anything I find."

"You promised Abner you'd remain in the pod if anything got dicey," I reminded her sternly. "And someone needs to stay here and keep an eye on the tracker program. I can't keep you safe if you're running around the nightclub, right?"

"Aw, c'mon Doc," Leyla said, crestfallen, yet determined. "The program runs itself, and there's been no update. I've got it linked to my phone anyway, so if something pops up, we'll know about it right away. Besides, you're going to need me in there."

My mind raced with all the things that could go horribly wrong. Not to mention how awful it would be explaining to Abner what happened, and me somehow living with that and not losing my mind.

"No kiddo," I replied firmly. "You're not going in there alone."

Out of the corner of my eye, Besim stood.

"I shall accompany Leyla," she announced.

As I turned toward Besim to remind her yet again she wasn't a cop, I stopped and stared.

Besim had removed all her makeup and the soaked bandana from around her head. Gone were the garish streaks of dark colors and mismatched layers of foundation, powder, blush, lipstick, and mascara. Her hair remained a patchwork dichotomy of painted black, bleach, and auburn-gold, as the rain had been unable to wash out all the dye. I was struck by how luminous her short, natural hair appeared, even in the shadowed confines of the pod. It was like a living thing.

The prominent architecture of her sharp features, with high cheekbones and almond-shaped eyes slightly wider than a human's, was clean and clear. The dark tattoos running along her scalp and down the sides of her face bore stark contrast with her pale features. Looking on her fully, I was taken aback yet again by her physicality, the long arms and legs proportionate to her size, and the similarities she shared with a human woman. There was a powerful sensuality to her as well, hidden beneath the layers of makeup. It was raw, almost primal, yet held in check by the firm grip of a cold, logical mind.

"You, ah, clean up good," I stammered.

"Thank you, Detective." Besim offered me a brief, almost hungry smile that was gone in the same instant. "As I was saying, I will accompany Leyla into the nightclub. In this way, we can, as you say, 'cover more ground.' Two eyes are better than one, yes?"

Deacon's frown deepened to a glower.

"I don't like it," he snapped in irritation. "If Julie's in there, she's probably armed and expecting trouble. You ain't ending up like Tony."

"Perish the thought, Deacon. I have no intention of that occurring," Besim explained with long-suffering patience. "Leyla and I will enter the nightclub first. We will establish our presence through the normal fraternizing young women exhibit in such places and belay any suspicions. Once we have integrated ourselves with the rest of the patrons, we will be considered two females amongst many attempting to satisfy our bohemian desires. The two of you will enter an appropriate amount of time afterward. I suspect a member of the on-site security will accost you, at which point I am confident in your abilities to successfully circumnavigate the situation. Meanwhile, Leyla and I will reconnoiter the premises to ascertain the whereabouts of Julie DeGrassi."

Deacon and I gaped at her.

"You can't be serious," he spluttered.

Besim held up a hand to forestall any further arguments.

"It has the virtue of simplicity." Her lips curled into a slight smile. "Of course, should the situation become untenable, Leyla and I will extricate ourselves from the nightclub by exiting via the front door."

I shook my head as I considered her idea. "There are too many unknowns."

"On that we agree, Detective Holliday," Besim replied primly. "However, time is short. The longer we debate, the more opportunity Julie DeGrassi has to elude us."

"Besides, we're a team, right?" Leyla added, moving to Besim's side and linking arms. "You came by Abner's because you said you needed me, so here I am. Let's do this!"

I looked to Deacon for help, but he stood with a vacant expression on his face.

"I don't like it," he said, his voice troubled. The former Protector winced as he rubbed his right side. "Give Leyla an earpiece. Saranda has hers. Just don't forget to use it."

His answer caught me by surprise.

"Fine," I sighed, throwing my hands up in the air. "But the moment anything gets hairy, you two ghost out of there. Am I clear?"

"Sure, Doc," Leyla laughed. "What could possibly go wrong?"

CHAPTER 21

"This is a terrible idea," I muttered for the third time.

"You agreed to it, so it's your own damn fault,"
Deacon replied dryly, his dark eyes fixed on a distant point
beyond the rain-streaked window. "Least they ain't dead yet."

I narrowed my eyes at him, suppressing the urge to pull out
my gun and shoot him.

Leyla and Besim had been gone no more than ten minutes, but
it felt like an eternity. The consultant provided marginal details of
their approach, describing the nightclub's exterior in clipped,
emotionless tones. We heard the rhythmic rumble of bass-heavy
music through their earpieces. The sound grew louder after each
heartbeat. I adjusted the speaker control to reduce the noise
before my eardrums exploded.

"Sorry, what was that?" I asked, missing whatever it was Besim
said.

"...commenced...Holliday," she repeated, her soft voice
drowned out by the roar of dance music.

"Come again," I repeated, exchanging a confused look with
Deacon.

Leyla shouted something unintelligible, followed by a few

muffled thumps. A sudden squeal of feedback shrieked over the pod's comm system. The nightclub music fell away, replaced by a dull, undulating throb.

"This any better?" Leyla's voice came through clear. "I made a slight adjustment."

"What'd you do, smash it against a wall?" I grumbled in irritation.

"Lighten up, Doc, I know my way around cheap electronics," she replied cheerfully. "Besides, the wall was padded. Boys and their toys. Am I right, Besim?"

I rolled my eyes and shook my head but didn't argue. We heard someone ask if they wanted anything to drink. Leyla ordered a vodka tonic, while Besim requested the wine menu.

"We've got a table upstairs along the railing," Leyla provided a moment later. "There's a staircase on either side just past the entrance to the club. We're on the left, six tables down the row. No sign of Julie. We've got a good view, but there are a lot of dark places she could be hiding in, and we'd never know it."

"EVI, please check Resources and pull the architectural designs for Kraze," I ordered.

"Accessing."

The heads up display fizzled to life, producing the original blueprints, as well as colored images of the nightclub and three-dimensional graphics of the interior. I studied them all, rubbing my stubbly chin with fingers and thumb.

Kraze was a big place.

Past the entrance, the club opened into a two-story mezzanine, framed by square pillars. The main floor contained a three-tiered inverted terrace with railings around the perimeter. The images revealed cozy leather booths arranged at regular intervals along the terraces around a massive dance floor which lay at the club's center, like the bottom of some gladiatorial arena. Three sets of short, broad steps ran from the topmost tier down to the dance floor, one several feet inside the main entrance, and two further along to either side. Several round tables, scattered throughout the bottom, left most of the area open for dancing. Doors in the back wall of the second tier of the terrace led into an area for the bathrooms, commercial kitchen, a storage room and an office. The bar stretched along the right-hand side at the top of the terrace. A raised stage stood at the far end to provide ample space for a DJ or live acts. Even in today's world of magic-powered technology, artificial intelligence and digitized music, you still needed a live someone to keep things fresh, raise a roof, and bring the funk.

Or whatever current crap young people partied to these days.

"Kids listen to such shitty music," I lamented. "Doesn't anyone care for the classics anymore?"

"You're a fuckin' fossil, Holliday." Deacon exhaled a long plume of smoke and chuckled. "What's that?"

He pointed at a short series of stairs accessed via a door in the back wall of the stage.

"Basement and boiler room," I surmised. "Old building like this probably still keeps its mechanicals down there. If the nightclub owner is anything like Armin, they're more interested in maintaining the lightshow and speakers than the refrigeration and heat. Leyla, I want EVI to connect to your phone so that we can see what the scene looks like tonight."

"And give ECPD access to my stuff? Not on your life, Doc," she replied scornfully. "Besides, it's just people out having a good time. No one I recognize, though. Half of them are wasted, and the rest are well on their way. The place itself is pretty decent, and there's a retro feel to all of it, the décor, the sound. It's a throwback to one of those decades in the late twentieth century. The eighties, I think."

The people of Empire City loved resurrecting fashion trends, and often outfits that hadn't been worn in a while would make a surprising, and sometimes unfortunate, comeback. Clothes were never a thing for me, although the music from back then was a different story.

I thought back to Armin's, and the conversation I had with Besim when we looked at the band advertisements posted to the windows.

Maybe Deacon was right. Maybe I was a fossil. I should probably get out more.

And maybe I should just put my head in an oven and turn it on broil.

"I've watched enough history holos to recognize where mullets, hoop earrings and hairspray came from," Leyla continued, breaking me from my half-baked reverie. She thanked a server for bringing her drink. "There was one girl wearing a pair of those rainbow-striped leg warmers. You know, the kind that glow in the dark?"

"We don't give a shit about what everyone's wearing, girl," Deacon growled into the communicator.

"Mm, this tastes good!" Leyla exclaimed, ignoring Deacon. "Besim, let's order another round!"

"And don't you get shit-faced on your first assignment," Deacon warned.

"Focus, kiddo, focus," I urged, stifling a grin. "Do you see anything else?"

I had pulled up Julie's profile on our ride over here. As expected, there wasn't much to it, other than her image, a brief employment history and little else.

"Nope, nothing," she replied with a slur to her voice. "But you and Deacon, you're gonna fit right in."

She giggled, and I swear Besim chuckled.

"What's that supposed to mean?" Deacon snapped.

"Oh, nothing," Leyla giggled again, and hiccupped. We heard the clink of glasses. "You'll just have to see for yourselves. C'mon Besim, let's go dancing!"

"This ain't no fucking field trip, girl," Deacon admonished angrily, but Leyla's reply was cut off by a loud surge in the music.

He blessed me with a baleful glare and said, "She's your fucking responsibility, Holliday."

"Thanks for the reminder," I grimaced, and went to refill my mug.

As I resumed my place, I had a thought.

"EVI, who owns the club?" I asked, leaning back in the chair.

There was a moment of rough static as the nightclub schematics and photos were shunted to the side of the display.

"Kraze is owned by David Crain, of Westchester," EVI's voice crackled and popped as an image of Crain appeared.

A brief biography of the man dribbled along a panel as EVI relayed a bland summary of an unassuming background for a local businessman.

But I stopped listening.

The Insight burned around the edges of my vision as it reacted to what I saw on the HUD. Crain was a pale man in his early thirties with sharp features, light blonde hair and blue eyes. His image wasn't smiling, yet I felt the hunger lurking behind the calm exterior, a chained and calculating beast, remorseless and cold.

I didn't need the Insight to tell me David Crain was a predator.

Throughout my career, I'd busted men just like him for all manner of horrible crimes involving women and children. These men held no fear of the law nor gave a shit about anything. They felt no contrition for the vile acts they performed, no remorse for the innocent people they harmed. They cared only for the power they held over the weak, feeding an insatiable need to inflict pain and suffering. And on the rare occasions when a few of those scumbags made parole, they went right back to where they left off, hurting someone, anyone, perpetuating a never-ending cycle of hatred and violence.

Oh, I'd seen that look before. I bore several white-puckered cigarette scars on my forearms, friendly souvenirs courtesy of my very own personal parental demon. It was also the reason why I never picked up smoking.

For a moment, I became lost in a myriad of tender memories involving my father's alcoholism, and the things he'd done to me when I was young. A sheen of sweat formed on my brow. I trembled, my body reacting to the memories, deeply accentuated by the Insight's power.

"What the hell's wrong with you, Holliday?" Deacon demanded, noting my reaction. "You look like you've seen a goddamn ghost."

I stared wide-eyed as Crain's face mocked me, a living reminder of my past, weighing heavy and dark. And I found myself blazing back, angry and defiant, and full of bitterness. A very dark emotion surged through me. It was all I could do not to draw my gun and put a bullet through the image of a man I'd never met.

"The girls are in danger," I grated between clenched teeth. I turned to the Confederate with a flinty stare. "We've got to get them out of there. Now."

One look from me was all Deacon needed to tap out his cigarette and lurch into motion. I checked the SMART gun, and without another word, we left the pod. A steady rain pelted us, but I didn't pay it any attention.

"Meet us at the entrance," I ordered. "We're coming to you."

"Why, what's the rush?" Leyla responded without a hint of concern. Fast-paced music pounded in the background. "This place is great!"

She was drunk.

Stupid, stupid girl.

And stupid, stupid me for letting it happen.

It took us less than five minutes to cross the soggy distance to the nightclub. The entrance was empty except for one bouncer standing beneath the stoop of the door. At our approach, he stepped into our path.

"Hold up," the thick-bodied man ordered, eyeing us with a hard stare.

"Move," I said, and shoved my badge in his face. I wasn't in the mood for this.

He hesitated for a half-second, then looked between me and a grim-jawed Deacon, but that was long enough to get past him and into Kraze.

An explosion of sound greeted our arrival. The girls weren't there to meet us, a fact that fanned my growing unease. A young man, dressed in matching black shirt and pants, shouted at us about paying the cover charge. I waved the badge at him and glared. He backed away with his hands held up, not wanting any trouble.

About ten steps later, I came to a dead stop.

Leyla was right. Many people were dressed up in styles from the late twentieth century.

But what she'd failed to mention was how the rest of the crowd looked.

Halloween had come to Kraze.

A scantily-clad vampire in a blood red corset and very little else wandered past us. She blew me a kiss.

"Oh, you've got to be fucking kidding me," I groaned.

Deacon guffawed, eyeing the gathering with amusement.

We stuck out like sore thumbs that had been covered in gasoline and lit with a flamethrower. In between the eighties retro outfits, priests, princesses, and witches mixed it up with pirates, celebrity doppelgangers, and other costumes whose meanings were lost on me. I counted ten different versions of zombie ranging from gaunt to cadaverous. And all of them drank and partied, danced and talked, and were having themselves one helluva night.

"Oh, ain't this a sight!" Deacon chortled.

A thick veil of wispy, gold-flecked smoke filled the interior, reminding me of incense. Bright, multi-colored lights flickered and flashed throughout, creating a disorienting strobe effect. Halloween decorations littered the floor and ceiling, some with light and sound. The temperature was several degrees warmer as well, a sudden change from outside. As we moved deeper into the nightclub, the air tasted strangely familiar, but I couldn't place it.

"There," Deacon shouted to be heard, breaking into my thoughts. He pointed to a side staircase to our left leading up to the mezzanine. "The girls said their table was upstairs."

"Weren't they down on the dance floor?" I asked.

I felt lightheaded, rubbing my eyes with the back of my hand. What was happening to me? Was Deacon feeling this too?

"Then tell them to meet us back there," he replied. "I hate crowds, and I'm thirsty, so you're buying me a drink. Let's go."

Grabbing my elbow, he directed me along while my head teetered around on a broken swivel. As we pushed our way through, I licked my lips and found my eyes wandering, soaking in the sights and sounds of the nightclub. A slow smile crept across my lips. Tension leaked out of my taut muscles in slow, luxurious waves. The sense of imminent danger I'd felt for Besim and Leyla evaporated, replaced by a languid indifference.

We navigated through skeletons cavorting with ghosts and werewolves. Rowdy superheroes in painted-on spandex laughed and drank and twirled. The music was awash with synthetic sounds and slick beats. A curvy devil with a plastic pitchfork and a lot of cleavage leaned against the railing post of the stairs. She leered at us with a 'come hither' look. I blinked, feeling a powerful urge to tear off her clothes and take her on the floor.

"Time for that later, Casanova," Deacon said, dragging me unwillingly up the stairs. "We got shit to do."

Moments later, we were seated. To either side sprawled costumed people in various stages of intoxication. A few asked us to join them, but Deacon waved them away.

An unattractive waitress with pale skin, frizzy hair, black eyeliner, and heavy red lipstick sidled up to our table.

"What can I get you two?"

With a start, I realized the waitress was a waiter. He wore a leather corset and garters that revealed more than it concealed. His fishnets were torn in places, and he bore the long-suffering look of someone who needed the job despite all the aggravation that went with it. Deacon ordered something I couldn't hear, and before I could respond, the waiter left.

"Don't worry, Holliday. I got you something," Deacon said as I started to protest, draping his arms over the armrests.

I gave an indolent shrug and glanced past the railing down to the dance floor below. Between the flashing lights and the fog shrouding everything, I imagined I was atop the crow's nest of an ancient mariner ship from a Jules Verne adventure.

"Leyla, we're upstairs. Where are you?" I asked, although I didn't really care.

I tapped my foot in time to the rhythm, humming to myself. I didn't recognize the song, but that didn't seem to matter, either.

"Was about to ask you the same thing, Doc," she replied, appearing a heartbeat later with Besim in tow.

Leyla plopped into her chair with a merry laugh, pale cheeks flushed with excitement. Besim took the seat next to mine, a look of discomfort on her face. She produced a small flask from her coat. Tilting her head back, she drank deeply, then stowed the flask away. I noticed her skin glistened, heightening the dark tattoos around her face and neck. I leered at Besim, admiring the curve and angles of her face, and the way the light reflected in her strange, gray eyes.

"Glad to see you're both enjoying this," I remarked as Besim held my gaze with an appraising one of her own. Right then, thoughts of the murder investigation, Julie DeGrassi, and David Crain were the last things on my mind.

"I find dancing to be deeply satisfying, Detective Holliday, and not solely for its health benefits," Besim answered. Her discomfort was gone. "The body's movements stir up instincts and senses buried below the mundane demeanor, reminding the mind and soul there are more things in life than work, responsibility, and duty."

"I just think it's fun!" Leyla chimed in, laughing. "It feels good to kick it!"

Besim nodded, smiling fondly at Leyla.

"It is a catharsis, to be sure." Her voice held the same resonance as her singing back at Armin's. "Such movement draws upon the primitive nature in all of us, both intimate and powerful."

The sound of her voice stirred feelings and desires in me, base emotions that had lain dormant for a long time. I idly wondered what lay beneath all that bulky clothing she wore, and whether the stories I'd heard about Vellans and their appetites were true.

"Is everything all right?" Besim asked, her eyes narrowing in concern.

"I feel fine," I replied with a lopsided grin. "Everything's fine. Now where the hell's my drink?"

CHAPTER 22

A bottle and glass were set before Besim, who examined the label with a critical eye. The server offered to pour, but Besim declined with a languid wave of her hand, performing the honors herself. She let it breathe, then swirled the contents of her glass. The consultant sipped, sloshing the liquid around in her mouth before swallowing. She nodded in clinical satisfaction, then refilled the glass.

Deacon watched in mild amusement as Leyla grabbed her colorfully-mixed cocktail and downed it in two gleeful gulps. She twirled the empty glass between her fingers, and whooped as it slipped from her hand, tumbling to the floor without breaking. She laughed again at her clumsiness and lost her balance while bending over to retrieve it. Deacon reached out to catch her, but she fell backward and onto his lap. Her eyes widened in surprise, then narrowed with lewd mischief as she writhed seductively in time to the music. The mortified look on Deacon's face was priceless.

"Sorry Deacon," Leyla laughed as a wicked smile played across her lips. She returned to her seat and winked at me.

He knocked back his rye whiskey, then glared at the empty glass.

"Oh, for fuck's sake!" the Confederate bristled. "Where the hell's that server?"

My shoulders sagged as I settled deeper into my seat, breathing a heavy sigh, content and at ease. I was captivated by all of it, the music, the people, the atmosphere, and could've sat there for hours. I glanced from Leyla to Deacon and Besim with a crooked smile.

"*I count myself in nothing else so happy, as in a soul remembering my good friends,*" I murmured.

It was nice having friends again.

I laced my hands behind my head and took a deep breath. The air up here tasted sweet despite the acrid admixture of sweat, booze and cigarettes. Leyla summoned our server and rattled off a series of drinks, many of which even I'd never heard of before.

I was sipping some shitty, watered-down bourbon when David Crain strolled up to our table, along with three of his stooges.

Our waiter rushed over to him, nodding furiously as Crain gave him instructions, then hurried away. A pointed glance from the nightclub owner was all it took for the adjacent table to empty as if poured from a bucket, affording us additional space.

I took another swig, studying Crain. He was a lot paler in person. Average height and build, and unlike his profile, he sported a trimmed beard and mustache. Tonight, he wore a dark evening jacket, slacks, and a slate grey turtleneck.

That threw me.

A turtleneck? I nearly choked on my drink.

Who the fuck wears a turtleneck to a nightclub?

Apparently, this guy.

As I swallowed my drink, I imagined a younger David Crain walking around my old neighborhood wearing that stupid-looking turtleneck. My old *bratva* "friend" Ivan Kruchev and the rest of his gang would've kicked the shit out of him just on general principle. For some reason, the thought warmed my belly.

"Good evening, Detective Holliday." He smiled pleasantly, an expression that never reached his cold, blue eyes. "My name is David Crain, the owner of this establishment. May I join you?"

My head was stuffed full of cotton candy, but I managed to nod and return the smile. Something tickled at the back of my mind, but I ignored it, concentrating instead on the music and drinks. A welcome tide of inebriation washed away any of my lingering concerns.

"Marko, bring that over here." Crain motioned at a chair by the empty table next to us.

As Crain sat down, his flunkies fanned out in a half circle behind him, pinning us against the banister. All three eyed us with arrogant disdain. They reminded me of historical images I'd seen of rock bands from the eighties, with the big hair, feather earrings, ripped t-shirts, and acid-washed jeans. Marko, the shorter, curly blonde-haired one who had brought over the chair, wore a high-collared jacket covered in colorful patterns and bits of flair, and a leather glove on one hand. A permanent sneer was plastered to his face.

Crain nodded at Leyla, and the two exchanged pleasantries. She chattered brightly about the music and the decor, stumbling over her words in her excitement. A deep scowl crawled across Deacon's stony face, his new drink untouched. Besim withdrew deeper into her chair, more interested in the wine than the new arrivals. She casually swirled her wine with a practiced bored expression, drank it, then filled her glass again.

"We need more drinks." Leyla glanced from Crain to his men with a broad grin. She waved frantically for another server a few tables down the row.

"I've already taken care of it," Crain said. "The next round is on the house."

His voice was soft, yet forceful, and smooth as silk.

The server returned with a helper to deliver whatever it was Crain had ordered. Leyla's eyes gleamed lustily as she took in the distilled festival laid out before us. From glow-in-the-dark bright blue cosmopolitans and pastel-colored daiquiris, to robust red wine and a more sedate gin and tonic, the table brimmed with bottles and glasses filled with all manner of alcoholic concoctions. Leyla whooped with delight, clapping her hands like a little girl. Deacon glared at Crain as if the man had just pissed in his whiskey.

"What do you think of my club?" Crain asked me, gesturing expansively with an outstretched hand. "I've spent a lot of credits to make Kraze one of the premier hot spots in Empire City."

His quiet voice mingled with the music, alcohol and sweet smell of the place, lulling me further into a deep lethargy. Crain chose one of the small glasses containing a golden liquid and handed it to me with his compliments. It tasted like honey fresh from one of those Bioclone beehives, yet flavored with a hint of cinnamon, cayenne and something else. The flavor was remarkable, and while my body sagged, my mind wandered even further away, lost in all the sensations I was experiencing.

"It's nice," I replied, my speech slurring. "I mean, really nice. I like the lights, and the music is great!"

I sounded like a complete idiot to my own ears but didn't care. The world swam around me. I rubbed at my eyes, but that didn't help. The music billowed, becoming less distinct. My throat constricted. What the hell was wrong with me?

"Sorry," I said, frowning in consternation. "Never had a problem holding my liquor before. Haven't touched the stuff since I left Wallingbrooke though. When was that, anyway? Wasn't that long ago. Seems like yesterday. Or was it the day before? Oh, who gives a fuck, right?"

"I'm glad you are enjoying yourself, Detective," Crain replied, adjusting the cuff of his dark jacket. "It's not very often I have one of Empire City's finest come through my door."

"That right?" I mumbled.

"Health inspectors and the fire marshal, to be sure," he continued amiably. "Rarely one of the boys in blue, unless they're off-duty, of course."

I laughed, slapping my knee as if Crain had made the funniest joke I'd ever heard.

"But you aren't off-duty tonight, are you?" he asked quietly, a hint of menace creeping into his voice. "What brings you to my club?"

"Cut the bullshit, Crain." Deacon took in Crain and his hair band crew with a measured look. "What the hell do you want?"

"Oh, lighten up, Deacon," Leyla wheedled plaintively. "He got us free drinks!"

"Fuck that shit," the former Protector grated. "Pull your head out of your ass, girl. There ain't nothing free in this fucked-up world. Just a lot of assholes looking to sell you something you don't need."

Leyla's smile melted, her pale skin flushed with anger. She crossed her arms and turned away from us, focusing on the dance floor below. The temperature dropped several degrees. I swallowed the rest of my drink hoping the liquid gold would warm me up.

Deacon growled something unpleasant, but a sudden swell in the music made me miss whatever he'd said. Crain smiled as his eyes slid toward the Confederate like a lizard, cold and bereft of emotion. Deacon shifted in his seat, then reached into his coat for his lighter and cigarettes and lit up. He blew a thick plume of smoke in Crain's direction, glaring daggers with a spidery smile. With one elbow on an armrest, his other hand trailed by the side of the chair.

Crain waved the smoke away dismissively.

"Detective, my doorman informed me you're here on 'police business,'" the nightclub owner continued, handing me another glass of gold. "What sort of business?"

Syrupy thoughts sloughed inside my head like a Catholic priest on an all-night bender. I felt the sudden urge to tell Crain about Vanessa Mallery, the investigation, our chase for Julie DeGrassi, everything.

"Oh, you know, the kind where we chase the bad guys," I managed to say, motioning with a lazy hand. "Arrest 'em, read 'em their rights, and all that happy horseshit."

I snickered, pointing my finger like a gun, and mimed shooting Crain. As my head lolled about, somewhere in the back of my mind a small part of me panicked. My arms and legs felt like dead weight. It was all I could do to maintain my grip on my own glass. The last thing I wanted was to spill my drink on Crain's ridiculous turtleneck.

The nightclub owner was not amused.

"And your investigation has led you here," he pressed.

"You could say that," I graced him with an indolent smile.

Crain's eyes narrowed to slits. Anger radiated from him in waves. He leaned in, our heads mere inches apart. I felt his breath on my face and wrinkled my nose. It smelled like rotten flesh. My stomach turned. I almost threw up but managed to hold it together.

"*Why* are you here?" Crain hissed at me, loud enough so only I could hear him. "Tell me."

I tried. I really did, but something held me back despite the strong desire to speak.

Do not give in to the poison around you, a faint whisper echoed in my mind.

"Tell me," Crain repeated.

He held an armrest of my chair in a white-knuckled grip. I thought I heard the crack of splintering wood but chalked it up to my wayward imagination. A song blared in the background. I snorted at its absurd lyrics. The tune was catchy, so I hummed along, tapping my foot in time to the music, my moment of nausea forgotten.

"Who brings a dead man to a party anyway?" I laughed. "That's against the law. I should arrest your DJ, Crain!"

"What do you know?" Crain said, his frustration growing with every word. "Why did your investigation bring you here?"

"Mr. Crain, you have an excellent eye for wine," Besim broke in suddenly.

Her clear voice rang both vibrant and strong. The sound of it cut through the strange fog clouding my mind. I shook my head in response, trying to clear the stuffing. Leyla turned away from the railing to regard Besim, her head cocked to one side as if listening to a conversation only she could hear. It reminded me of the shared communication between Deacon and Besim.

The air around us grew colder. I took a shuddering breath, releasing it in a cloud of white.

Crain reluctantly faced Besim with hooded eyes.

"Thank you," he replied with a brittle smile.

Besim held the glass before her, raised it in salute, and drank the rest. She returned his gaze with an unblinking stare of her own.

"A rather interesting tincture," she mused almost to herself, and placed the empty glass on the table with exaggerated care. "A peculiar maceration of crushed grapes infused with something else. A foreign element, meant to heighten more than the flavor of the wine, to be sure."

The sound of her voice remained level, yet something about it attacked the malaise wrapped around my brain. I rubbed at my eyes several times. They felt sticky, as if I had a bad case of hay fever. Glancing at my hands, a thin layer of film glistened there, glittering like gold.

Crain leaned toward her, his face registering surprise.

"I thought it a costume at first, but I see I was mistaken," he said with raised eyebrows. "You're a Vellan."

Besim inclined her head in acknowledgement.

Deacon shifted his weight in his seat. He crushed the cigarette on the armrest, then flicked the butt away with disdain. His other hand rested inside his coat.

"It has certainly imparted the desired color and proper amount of tannins and aroma," Besim continued, unperturbed. "In fact, it is a fair facsimile to the real thing."

Crain's hand clenched into a fist. A vein throbbed in his temple. Two of his goons looked at each other, yet Marko observed the Vellan in a detached manner, his sneer lost somewhere during the conversation.

"How curious then to discover the very same wine at both Julie DeGrassi and Vanessa Mallery's apartments," she said, gray eyes smoldering with fire. "However, the bottle at Vanessa's townhouse was conspicuously devoid of this additional element. Alas, I was unable to examine the one at Julie's to corroborate my findings. It had disappeared, along with its owner."

Staring hard at Besim, my slumbering mind struggled against the sickly-sweet shroud covering it. The Insight scratched at the edges of my vision, desperate to burst through my submerged senses. I clung to Besim's every word, urged on by the burgeoning Insight. The distinct sounds of her voice were rungs in an audio ladder. Using it, I clawed my way out.

"And yet, the vintage I just drank is rife with the new element," Besim raised an eyebrow. "The beverage you provided Detective Holliday is another example, as is the peculiar aroma your club's ventilation system continues to produce. A purer form, if I am not mistaken."

Besim paused.

Crain froze in place.

She held his gaze.

"Of goldjoy."

The word crashed down like a tidal wave in my mind, snapping me out of the drug-infused haze. Everything came back to me in a mad rush, the murder investigation, the chase for Julie DeGrassi, and the horrible realization that we'd been drugged.

Crain stood, but Besim was unmoved. Deacon stormed from his chair, placing himself in front of her. He brandished his truncheon, his mouth set in a grim line.

My own eyes blazed from the Insight's fury as I reached for the SMART gun. Leyla snarled something, her hands rimed with frost. The air surrounding her crackled like ice shattering on a frozen pond.

"You asked Detective Holliday why he was here," Besim declared in a strident voice, back straight and chin held high. "Instead, I shall ask you. Why did you murder Vanessa Mallery?"

And before I could say anything, all hell broke loose.

CHAPTER 23

*A*s I pulled the gun, Crain sucker-punched me in the jaw. Stars exploded in my vision. The weapon fell from my nerveless hand while the rest of me met the floor, momentarily stunned. Crain followed that with a sharp kick to my side, below the ribs. And then another, for good measure. I jerked into a fetal position, breathless and wheezing.

"That blonde bitch!" Crain bellowed, eyes blazing with mad realization. "We've been set up!"

For a skinny guy in a turtleneck, he packed one helluva punch. A quick inventory of my injuries revealed nothing broken.

"Surprise," I quipped, relieved I could speak.

At least, that's what I think I said. It probably sounded like a mumbled groan followed by short gasps for breath, and a sob for good measure. I hurt like hell. My head rang like a church bell, but at least I was still in one piece.

"No wonder she wanted to meet tonight," Crain said, ignoring me for the moment.

He was lost to a volcanic anger. Behind him, two of Crain's goons menaced Deacon and Besim.

"How could I have been so blind?" Crain ran a hand across his pale face, quivering with rage. "All their talk of partnership. It was all bullshit!"

I refrained from another of my patented pithy rejoinders, deciding that literally armed was more important right now than figuratively. The gun lay a few feet away. Besides, if the bad guy wanted to monologue, who was I to argue? Those extra seconds of pontification would mean the difference between my life and my death.

"'Orpheus wants to discuss our options,'" Crain ground on, mimicking Julie's nasally voice while laughing in derision. "What 'options?' We said we'd take care of it, and we did. We paid those goddamn mercenaries a bloody fortune! If they'd done their jobs right, there would have been nothing left for the police to find."

I stored that nugget away, inching my way over to the SMART gun. I had no idea who or what Orpheus was, but they were climbing up my public enemy number one list faster than you could say "Straight outta Hades."

"We still don't know who killed the girl, but—" Crain paused, then smacked his fist into his open palm. "But now we know who took the body from the morgue. That goddamn, fucking bitch!"

Appreciate you clearing that up, Crain.

Presuming he wasn't lying—and I didn't think he was at this point—Crain and company weren't our killers. Now if I could just get up and arrest them. Unfortunately, my body struggled to move, sluggish from the pain and the last vestiges of goldjoy in my system.

Then another thought hit me.

If Crain knew about the body's theft from the morgue already, whatever intelligence network he possessed was downright scary. Only authorized access to EVI could provide such information about an active case file. The short list included ECPD officer-level, and certain high-ranking enclave officials. And with her functionality at an all-time low due to the explosion...

The enormity of that thought ballooned in my mind, sending a cold sliver down my spine.

"None of that matters now," he stated. "We still have the other one. She's not going anywhere."

Just a few more inches. My trembling fingers reached for the gun.

"DeGrassi and Orpheus can go fuck themselves," Crain laughed again, more maniacal than before. "We don't need their support anymore. We don't need anyone!"

Keep flapping your gums a little bit longer, jerk-wad.

"As for that double-crossing bitch bringing the police to *my* place?" Crain paused, glancing in my direction, hungry blue eyes focused and full of bloody murder.

That was my cue. I took hold of the weapon, drew it close, and aimed it at Crain's ridiculous turtleneck.

"Doc, stay down!" Leyla shouted from a million miles away.

Pure instinct forced me to duck, although I moved more like a pregnant yak than a trained police detective. As I did so, the temperature plunged, nearly stealing all the warmth from my body. I almost blacked out from the sudden shock to my system.

A wave of writhing, black shadow engulfed Crain, knocking him off his feet. It buffeted him against the banister. I lurched away from Crain, staring without really looking at Leyla, caught between the strong desire to see her through the Insight and the need to avert my eyes. Despite my better judgment, I caught glimpses of midnight-blue and black ripples of dark energy rolling from her extended right arm through her upraised, open palm and splayed fingers. Leyla's lips moved, uttering words I couldn't understand, but whose power I felt with my own senses charged by the Insight. Her young face was tight with concentration as she maintained the stream of undulating darkness and cold.

I sucked in a breath. Leyla's eyes were pure white, the sclera devouring both iris and pupil.

Something enormous with wings stretched above and around her, enfolding her within its dark embrace. It was vast, its mere presence a crushing weight against my psyche. My eyes were forced toward the shadowy expanse. As I focused on whatever this thing was, more of its outline became apparent to me. Because of the Insight, I knew I was the only one who could see it. My thumbs pricked, while the hair on the back of my neck stood. My skin buzzed with both excitement and dread. I licked my dry lips in uneasy anticipation. Heart racing out of control, my blood pounded like kettle drums in my ears with each passing beat.

I was about to look on it fully, when that voice echoed in my mind again, breaking the spell.

Away! Look away! Now is not the time!

I crushed my eyes shut, blindly obeying the voice. My beleaguered brain needed time to process what was happening, but things moved around me too quickly. Again, instinct made me act. I centered myself, forcing the images I witnessed into a compartment deep inside my mind, to review another time.

"*You are idle, shallow things,*" I whispered, offering the Bard's quote up like a prayer. "*I am not of your element.*"

Somehow, that worked.

I opened my eyes and willed my heart rate to steady itself. Strangely emboldened, I gave the SMART gun a mirthless smile.

Deacon had engaged the two long-haired goons, his truncheon an extension of his arm. He battered one to the floor, but the other closed in quickly, hoping to take advantage of Deacon's inattention, and swung at the back of his head. Quick as thought, Deacon spun on the balls of his feet like a dancer, sidestepping and evading the attack while smashing the second man in the back, shoving him roughly away.

As soon as he was clear, Deacon yanked Besim from her chair and placed her behind him. However, the two men recovered quickly, much to Deacon's surprise. They exchanged a glance, then rushed him together. They tried to tackle him, but Deacon lashed out low at one, cracking the truncheon against his leg, then pivoting to bring its tip into the stomach of the other.

"Leyla, behind you!" Besim warned, but she was too late.

Marko grabbed Leyla by both shoulders and threw her two tables down the row, as if she were a rag doll. She crashed into another table, sending glass, people, and drinks flying. Leyla didn't move, but the other partygoers screamed and rushed toward the stairs, fleeing the scene. As soon as Leyla struck the table, the silhouette of darkness surrounding her along with the bitter cold vanished. The oppressive weight dissipated as if it had never been.

"You son of a bitch!" I snarled, aiming at Marko.

Before I could pull the trigger, the gun was kicked from my hand by Crain, no longer immobilized by Leyla's power. It landed near the railing behind me. I made a mental note to apply some adhesive or Protoglue or something on my hand to prevent that from happening in the future, presuming I lived through this. Losing my gun during a fight was getting damn inconvenient.

I stole a glance toward Leyla. Seeing her crumpled beneath the table filled me with rage, but before I could act, Crain channeled his own fury to give me a good ole-fashioned ass-kicking. He'd recovered quickly from whatever hex Leyla had hurled at him. Shards of ice crystals crackled over his clothing. His pale skin was tinged blue. Despite the caked frost on his arms, he drove a fist into my stomach with such staggering impact, I doubled over. Crain followed that with a knee to my face, then an uppercut to the jaw. Blood gushed from my mouth as I crashed against one of the chairs and onto the floor.

I gasped for air, the wind knocked out of me again. The Insight seethed around my eyes, intent on revealing to me something about Crain and his motley crew of rejects. My face throbbed as blood flowed freely from multiple cuts. I wiped some away with a shaky sleeve, unable to focus on the Insight.

Damn, I hurt like hell.

"You're…under…arrest," I managed from the floor, trying to get back up.

"Contrary to what you may think, we don't possess the girl's blood." He was composed, the raw fury replaced by an icy malice. "But we'll discover who does soon enough, after we're finished with you."

I didn't doubt him. Crain's apparent infiltration of EVI and ECPD's information highway would see to that. Between the surveillance tech, the stolen corpse, the hired cleaners, presumed genetic tampering of Vanessa's blood, and now, unauthorized access to EVI, that reeked of Big Money.

However, something didn't fit. David Crain acted the part. Hell, he even looked the part, right down to the holo-B-movie repertoire. It was like something straight out of an old crime serial. But the clues we'd uncovered spoke of a diabolical subtlety and methodical cunning that Crain lacked. No, Crain had to be a middle man, and the nightclub was a staging area for something else. But what? Yet, Crain's over-the-top reaction following Besim's question was the kind you saw when the cat's out of the bag, and he had nothing to lose. Threatening me was one thing but having the stones to assault a police officer in public was something else.

Crain either didn't fear the police, or he didn't care.

"The Master needs to know," Crain muttered almost to himself. "We have to tell him. *He needs to know!*"

I crawled toward the gun, but my movements were too slow. Crain grabbed me by the lapels and lifted me off the floor. He jerked me toward him until I was up close and personal. As my head snapped forward, the petty kid in me hoped some of my blood spattered all over his stupid turtleneck.

The sight of my blood excited Crain. His eyes bored into mine as he licked his pale lips, nostrils flaring.

"You should never have come here," he hissed with cold hatred.

Crain's fetid graveyard breath filled my nostrils.

"And you should brush more often," I replied with a sickly grin, hoping to stall him with my witty repartee.

"Is that right?" he smiled. I noticed he had perfectly even white teeth. Or at least I thought so at first, but now it looked like two of them had grown longer.

What the fuck? C'mon, Tommy boy, get your shit together!

"Soon this will all be over." His blue eyes glittered with hungry anticipation. "I will make certain your body will never be found. And then we'll take care of that conniving bitch and her employer."

My innards went cold. Despite Crain's pulpy dialogue, I believed him.

"You have...the right," I continued through clenched teeth, blood streaming over my lips, "to remain...silent."

"How charming," Crain sneered, holding me easily, his strength belied by his slim size.

He laughed disdainfully as he battered me against the banister a few times. I toppled to the floor.

"Anything...you say," I mumbled, head bowed, eyes unfocused, "may be used...against you...in a court...of law."

The SMART gun lay next to me, and I reached for it with a shaking hand.

I became dimly aware of Deacon slugging it out with Crain's men. Besim rushed to Leyla's side, where Marko was hovering over her like an angel of death. My heart wrenched in fear, but a sudden blast of cold and darkness smashed into the curly-haired freak, knocking him away from her. Leyla shrieked something incomprehensible. My skin crawled again from the otherworldly sound.

Marko staggered forward, holding one arm in front of his face to shield himself. Leyla raised her voice, the sound setting my teeth on edge. She redoubled her efforts, but Marko slid to the side and away from the girls. Once outside the radius of Leyla's power, Marko bolted for the stairs.

Adrenaline surged through me, generated by my fear for my adoptive little sister. I struggled to my feet. Crain stalked toward me, slow and seductive, as if everything around him was reduced to a crawl and he had all the time in the world to murder me. His features blurred and shifted as he moved, stretching over his flesh. The bones of his stark face grew sharper and more pronounced. Something moved beneath the surface of his skin.

I concentrated, and the Insight roared in my ears while my eyes filled with silver fire. A calm detachment filled me, as if my entire body had been dipped in a vat of anesthetic. The air shimmered around Crain, and I saw the veil masking him. The Insight tore it away to reveal a vile, ravenous creature fashioned from things foul and unclean. A sickly aura of gold and verdigris hung on the creature like a mantle of despair, smelling of corruption and desiccated flesh. It still owned Crain's blue eyes, though, although no humanity remained. What I saw instead was an overwhelming need to feed on the living.

It leered at me. Two long fangs sprouted from its mouth.

My brain reeled at the sight.

"You are one ugly sonofabitch," I whispered in awe and fear. "What the hell *are* you?"

"The next phase in human evolution," the Crain-thing purred, its sibilant voice intermingled with that of its host. "Thanks to Vanessa Mallery, and the poor fools before her. Their sacrifice has changed the world."

With one hand on the railing to steady me, I brought the SMART gun to bear. But I was woefully slow, my arm moving through mud. The creature stepped with preternatural speed, slapping my arm away like an afterthought. It held me with an unnatural strength, and try as I might, I couldn't escape.

"And now little man, I shall drink from you, and end your pathetic life, so it may sustain my own."

It lowered its head slowly, almost lovingly, to sink its fangs into my exposed neck.

"Then I hope you like coffee, Crain," I blustered in a trembling voice, pushing against its hold on me with every fiber of my being. "'Cause it ain't decaf running through these veins."

I knew I wouldn't be able to stop it from tearing out my throat, but I struggled anyway, refusing to give in to the inevitable.

"*Oratio ad Sanctum Michael Sancte Michael Archangele!*"

And then Deacon was there, the former Protector's truncheon aflame with a pure white fire. Brandishing the weapon before him, Deacon's face was aglow with holy zeal.

"*Defende nos in proelio, contra nequitiam et insidias diaboli esto praesidium!*"

He lay into Crain, and the creature's grip on me vanished. I slipped to the side as Deacon slammed Crain against the railing with his shoulder. The former Protector was limned in holy glory, his face triumphant and true. I shaded my eyes from the brilliance surrounding him, but watched the fight, captivated all the same. Where Deacon struck Crain, the truncheon's purifying fire charred both the man and the creature wearing his skin. They both shrieked in dark agony. The creature was no match against the truncheon, its body now wreathed in white flame. It clawed at the air, its flesh and bone eaten away by the fire, and fell to its knees. With a mighty heave, Deacon lifted Crain and threw him over the banister.

Crain's body made a sickening impact as it struck the floor below. The crowd erupted in shrieks and screams. The music screeched to a halt. The main lights flashed on, momentarily blinding me. A sea of Halloween costumes rushed toward the exit as if expelled by a giant vacuum cleaner that had gone from suck to blow.

"I'd say they waived their fuckin' rights, wouldn't you, Holliday?"

Deacon strode up, clapping me on the shoulder as a triumphant grin spread across his face. Behind him lay Crain's two other goons, both consumed by white flame.

It hurt to laugh, but I did it anyway.

The Insight departed the moment Deacon threw the creature overboard, but it didn't leave behind the wasted lethargy I normally felt.

So too was the glorious light encompassing Deacon.

I felt invigorated despite the pounding I'd taken. The golden muck inside my head was gone. This was something new, a facet to the Insight I hadn't experienced before. I felt protected, insulated, and surrounded by an invisible suit of armor I somehow knew, without knowing how or why, the Crain-thing could never have penetrated.

"The girls—" I began.

"We are unharmed," Besim announced from several tables down the row.

The consultant held Leyla around the shoulder in a protective embrace.

She exchanged a knowing look with Deacon, who nodded, and headed toward the stairs. I hesitated, staring at the wreckage that were once creatures like Crain, then followed Deacon down. Moments later, in the glare of the main lights, we stood over what was left of David Crain.

"Don't fuck with a Protector of the Tribulation, asshole," Deacon pronounced, his voice full of satisfaction and disdain.

"Former Protector," I corrected, breathing heavily.

Ignoring me, he spat on Crain's corpse.

"Still don't believe in vampires, Holliday?" he asked, then walked away to leave me with my troubled thoughts.

CHAPTER 24

"Yes, I know what time it is." I stood near Crain's smoking remains and shook my head at the sight, immediately regretting it as my face throbbed. "You know I wouldn't have called if it wasn't important."

"Detective Holliday, I cannot simply leave my girls," Stentstrom admonished me in his singsong voice. "Shayna and Lucy are on a very strict schedule, and any disruption to their training regimen, however minute, could prove disastrous. The Poodle Club of Empire City Grooming Competition is scheduled for mid-November, and I'm certain you can appreciate the salutary effects a good night's rest has on the body."

"I completely understand," I replied, squeezing the bridge of my aching nose with two fingers. "But I need you to get here right away. There's been a break in the case, and I've got bodies. Or what's left of bodies."

"That sounds like something the coroner-on-call Doctor Cohen can perform for you," he continued in the same tone.

"Doctor, I—"

"There is simply no need for this interruption at such a dreadful hour."

"But Doctor, I really—"

"After all, why bother establishing work hours if anyone can call at any time—"

"Gilbert, these are *very* special bodies."

Silence.

"Oh," he whispered conspiratorially. Suddenly, the image popped in my head of a googly-eyed Stentstrom creeping around his living room stalking assassins and unicorns.

"My apologies, Detective," he continued in breathless excitement, shuffling about. A door closed with a loud thud amidst a fanfare of indignant barking. "I'll be there as soon as I can."

"I'm forwarding images right now to your private box," I added, working the virtual commands on my phone. "This needs to stay off the books. There's a lot going on right now, and I need time to sort it all out. I want you to have a head start before anyone from ECPD starts asking questions."

"I'll be there within the hour," the medical examiner said. "Now girls, don't you worry, Daddy will be right back."

"Ping me when you get here." I ended the call, exhaling a heavy sigh.

"Front doors secured," Deacon said in passing, breaking into my thoughts. "That bouncer was gone, but there were a couple of gawkers outside. Told them to skedaddle, club's closed due to a kitchen fire. Should give us a little time before anyone tries anything. You call Mahoney?"

"He's ten minutes out," I replied, rubbing the back of my neck to massage taut muscles full of tension. "Was monitoring channels, heard the noise and figured it was us once he checked EVI for my location."

EVI had informed me that several 911 calls were made minutes after Crain's fiery crash to the dance floor, which meant ECPD, fire and emergency would be here soon. I needed Mahoney here to pull his weight, take charge and keep everyone off my ass for a while. I didn't want the specific details getting out through EVI on the main ECPD feed. The sinking suspicion there were "ears" listening in on anything she transmitted was something I couldn't ignore. I needed the time and freedom to delve into this further.

If the mayor and DA wanted results, I couldn't just hand them a half-eaten shit sandwich.

Hey Mr. Mayor. Listen, turns out there really are vampires. We lit a few on fire at this nightclub. I think they're part of a conspiracy involving weird genetic experimentation that is linked to the murder in some way, but we still don't know who's doing it, what was done, or why. Anyway, we're about to look for their lair, so if you don't hear from me, send in the Marines because we're probably dead.

Yeah, that'd go over like a stale fart at a job interview. Hell, it sounded ridiculous even to me, despite what we just went through.

"This is one fucked-up case," Deacon chuckled while lighting a cigarette.

"With a lot of moving parts," I said. "Let's consider what we think we know. Crain hired the mercenaries. Whatever fallout caused by Vanessa's murder included the bad breakup between Crain and his mystery boss, and Julie and Orpheus. I think Julie hoped Crain and his gang would eat us. With us dead, the investigation gets put on a temporary hold, and Kraze is on ECPD's shit list. Either way, bad times for Crain and company, and good times for Julie and Orpheus.

"Normally, that would've put Julie and Orpheus at the top of the suspect list. But why would Julie be in the alleyway at the time of Vanessa's murder? For plausible deniability? Of what? What did she and Orpheus gain from all of this?"

"Beats the shit out of me," Deacon replied.

"Crain's villainous soliloquy confirmed two very important things," I said. "He didn't know who murdered Vanessa, which I believe, and he tabbed Orpheus with stealing her corpse, which he believed. Either the body held some other clue that we'd missed, or the bad guys didn't know either, and were afraid it might."

"And don't forget there's a third party involved now," the Confederate pointed out.

"Yeah." I nodded soberly. "Somebody else murdered Vanessa to steal her blood. But who? And why?"

The sick feeling that I was some pawn being manipulated around a chessboard by an invisible hand was really pissing me off. I'd be damned if I let that continue for much longer.

My window of opportunity was short. I needed to make some moves of my own.

Deacon wandered over to talk to Besim and Leyla. The young hacker clutched one of Besim's crumpled, colorful handkerchiefs in her hand. She nodded at whatever Deacon was saying, then looked gamely over at me with a tremulous smile. I returned it with an encouraging one of my own and a wink, although inside my mind was awhirl with what the Insight had revealed to me about her.

Then there was Deacon, and his convincing impersonation of an avenging angel. The purity of the light that had surrounded him still blinded me. What was he, and why was he here? And I didn't even want to think about the Vellan.

I stared at the charred corpse of David Crain.

Angels and vampires.

Jesus Christ.

"You okay, Doc?" Leyla asked in a soft voice. I hadn't noticed her approach.

"I should be asking you that," I replied.

"He…it…really beat you up," she said, and ran a chilled hand down my face.

"Yeah, but I've had worse." I tried to sound brave. "You remember that time Ivan and his *bratva* jerks beat the shit out of me at Eddie's? That hurt a lot worse than this."

"Yeah, I remember," Leyla laughed. "I helped Eddie clean up the mess. You bled all over her nice, dirty floor."

I hugged Leyla close. She lay her cold head against my chest. My tender ribs cried out in pain, but nobody heard.

"I won't let anything happen to you, kiddo," I whispered into her hair. "That's a promise."

Her hug tightened, but I didn't mind. "I know."

"And I should never have brought you along."

"S'cool," she sniffled. "You needed me here tonight, Doc."

I wasn't convinced, but squeezed her hard and then let go, giving her a sad smile.

"Holliday, finish up, 'cause we've got work to do," Deacon called. Both he and Besim stood by one of the doors leading to the back of the nightclub.

I hesitated mid-step.

"You think leaving him...err...'it' here is a good idea?" I nodded in the direction of Crain's corpse. "What if it, you know, gets up or something?"

My experience with the undead was unsurprisingly limited.

"Then shoot it harder." Deacon flicked his expired butt away with a grin. "Relax, Holliday. He ain't goin' nowhere."

I decided to trust the professional.

"Stentstrom's on his way," I announced as we rejoined Deacon and Besim. "He's discreet, and I need him to take out the trash before the rest of ECPD crawls over the place and contaminates everything."

Despite the beating I took, I felt remarkably good. My body ached, especially my nose and jaw, but my mind was clear.

"Smart," he said, surprising me.

Before I could say anything, Deacon pushed through the door. I handed a pair of gloves to the girls and tossed another to Deacon, who pointedly ignored them as they bounced off his chest and hit the floor. Leyla retrieved the gloves and gave them back to me with a shrug.

"Fine, don't touch anything," I instructed him.

Deacon snorted but said nothing.

We followed the short corridor leading past two doors marked as bathrooms. It ended at a small commercial kitchen with a cooking surface, several fryers, two prep tables, a large double sink with hoses suspended from the ceiling, a dishwasher, and a walk-in refrigerator. The area reeked of burnt food and old cigarettes, with layers of grease caked on all the surfaces. Packed shelves and cabinets lined one of the walls, while half-filled serving trays and a mountain of unwashed dishes and cutlery lay in piles around the sink.

Besim wrinkled her nose at the sight. She'd been quiet since bringing Leyla down to the dance floor. I glanced at her, but she appeared aloof and composed as usual.

"Where'd everybody go?" Leyla asked, looking around.

"They must've bolted after the screaming started," I supplied, doing a quick circuit of the kitchen.

The cook had failed to shut off the burners before fleeing the scene. Turning a couple of knobs did the trick, otherwise we would've had a real fire instead of the story Deacon had fabricated outside.

"That way." I pointed to the left where another short corridor led to what I presumed was Crain's office. We followed it past a storage room to a closed door at its end. Besim paused in front of the storage room door, while Leyla and I continued to the office.

"What the fuck are you doing, Holliday?" Deacon hollered from the kitchen.

He leaned against one of the tables with arms folded across his chest.

"It's what we police-types like to call 'looking for clues,'" I retorted, irritated by the question. "Shake down the premises, go through his sock drawer, locate the virtual workstation, and mine it for information. You should try it sometime."

"I get that," he replied amiably. "But I doubt a vampire's gonna hide its secrets inside an office, do you?"

Scowling, I tried the door handle and found it unlocked, with the room beyond lit.

Crain's office was small and organized. A bank of closed-circuit holo-monitors was arranged in a neat row along one wall near the ceiling. I didn't see a potted plant, holo-frame, personal items, or even a coffee mug with "Blood-Sucking Asshole" on it. The office contained all the surface trappings, but none of the lived-in feel one would expect from an occupied space. The monitor feeds displayed the front entrance, a back exit attached to the kitchen, the bar, the mezzanine, dance floor, both bathrooms, the check-in counter, kitchen, and different angles of the stage. The desk contained nothing worthwhile, just scraps of useless junk. The chair bore an impression in the seat cushion, so someone came in here to monitor things at least.

Leyla plopped down before the workstation, powered it on, and manipulated the holo-windows. I took a seat opposite her and stretched out my legs.

"Work your magic, kiddo," I said as a wry smile spread across my face.

See what I did there?

The workstation's screens flashed in front of me but winked out before I could get a read on them. Leyla worked faster than I could keep up. The speed with which the screens appeared and departed made my head swim. After several minutes of this, she shut it down.

"Nothing here, Doc," Leyla announced, sounding more annoyed than defeated. "It wasn't hard either. His security was crap. I hacked the entire system, front to back, and even went looking for hidden drives, backdoors and caches. Didn't find a thing. It was just messages from vendors, budgets, food and beverage orders and expenditures, payroll, tax forms, upcoming events, and a lot of junk mail. Everything you'd expect from a legit operation. I guess Crain was the world's most boring vampire."

That was unfortunate, but unsurprising. Crain had to maintain appearances.

"What are you hiding here, Crain?" I muttered in frustration, staring at the walls of the small office.

"Excuse me, Detective Holliday," Besim called from the hallway. "I believe there is something here you should see."

"I'll keep digging through his box," Leyla announced as I disentangled myself from the chair. "Maybe I missed something."

I nodded once and left. Besim hadn't moved from her position before the storage room door. Deacon came down the hallway to see what was up.

"There is a particular scent emanating from behind this door," Besim said. "However, there are too many variables in the way. I attempted to identify it from here but was unsuccessful. And I did not wish to open the door in case certain...undesirables...lurked behind it."

Deacon and I exchanged a look.

"We've made plenty of noise already," I observed, drawing the SMART gun, "but it doesn't hurt to be careful. Marko's still at large."

I tried the door knob. It was locked.

For the second time in as many nights, I picked it with my handy-dandy set of tools. The door swung open, revealing a darkened room. Several metal shelving racks held containers of kitchen supplies, extra flatware and cutlery, pots, pans, three mops, a couple of brooms, and a partridge in a pear tree.

Okay, I made that last part up.

Still, nothing unusual about the room's contents. I flipped on the light. A single fluorescent bulb came to life, buzzing happily, and illuminated the room. Besim moved past me. With deliberate steps, she made her way to the opposite wall where a mop sat inside a metal bucket with wheels. The shelving ended a foot from the wall. Hands at her sides, she studied the mop with an unreadable expression on her face. I was about to say something when Deacon shot me a look and shook his head.

"Here," Besim announced. "There are chemical agents at play. They are below, but not far. And I hear the sound of machinery."

"That could be the boiler," I said.

Besim looked over her shoulder at me, raising a critical eyebrow.

"No, Detective," she replied. "This is something else."

As I made my way back down the hall toward the kitchen, I called out to Leyla to join us.

A few moments later, we were downstairs inside a dank and murky boiler room. The machinery dominated the space with rusted piping that penetrated the concrete foundation, running along the ceiling and down the walls. Although the pipes appeared to be the original copper, the chiller, boiler, air handlers, heat exchanger, water heater, tanks, and pumps were all new.

"A shit-ton of equipment for just one nightclub," Deacon commented. "Why would a dump like this need all that?"

I stepped to the far end of the room where I spied a small metal panel installed in the wall, hidden behind a thick copper pipe.

"Let's find out." I grinned, pushing the white button.

A door-sized panel of false concrete detached itself from the wall and slid silently to the side.

"Going down?" I uttered in a sepulchral voice.

CHAPTER 25

*T*he elevator door opened.

Nothing with big nasty teeth leapt at us, and I took that to be a good sign.

With both hands on the SMART gun and a round in the chamber, I crept from the elevator and into the lit corridor. My breath ghosted before me in thin puffs. The air was thick with mildew. A dank chill settled into my bones, and I shivered.

"Clear." I nodded once to the others.

The elevator was set in the middle of a long, slate-gray corridor of worked concrete. A continuation of the thick, rusted pipes from the floor above snaked along the length of the wall starting at shoulder height. Condensation dripped from them into small pools here and there. Small bulbs in metal cages were interspersed evenly along the ceiling, providing plenty of light. Other than the faint buzzing from the bulbs, silence reigned here like a tomb.

"By the pricking of my thumbs, something wicked this way comes," I murmured low. Goose bumps flocked on my skin.

"Doc, you've got some serious issues," Leyla snorted quietly from behind me.

Grinning ghoulishly, I stuck my tongue out at her and moved to the right. As Besim and Deacon edged away from the elevator, the consultant tilted her head to the side, listening for something, her eyes closed. After a moment, she faced left, opened her eyes, and gave the empty corridor a speculative look. It stretched a good twenty feet, then veered right.

The Insight had been quiescent so far, but that didn't make me feel better.

"What is it, Besim?" Leyla asked in hushed tones.

"I am not certain," Besim replied tentatively, her brow furrowed. My unease boiled as she turned back to me, concern written on her face. "Detective, I—"

She paused in mid-sentence to stare at something past my ear.

I followed her gaze. A pinpoint of red light flickered at the far end of the corridor. Its source was a small security camera, wedged into the upper right corner of the wall, just above the pipes. I whipped my head around to discover its twin in the opposite wall.

Both faced our direction.

My hackles rose.

"Shit."

Just then, a door swept open around the corner from the first camera, followed by men's voices and the snap and click of weapons being readied.

"Holliday!" Deacon hissed. He placed himself protectively before the girls, truncheon in hand.

"C'mon, c'mon!" Leyla mashed the elevator button in the wall panel, blue eyes round as saucers, but the door refused to open.

Besim looked expectantly at me, a calm expression on her face.

"Tactical," I ordered.

An instant later, the three-dimensional HUD of the SMART gun appeared in my vision. Back when we'd encountered the cleaners, I had forgotten about the combat-guided assistance the SMART gun provided.

Not this time.

My eyes tingled as I focused on the targeting display. I noted the proximity sensors tracking the distance between me and the incoming welcoming committee, blockages of sightlines, as well as options for round type, sniper scope, infrared, and night-time modes. It was like being thrown into one of those virtual first-person arena games the kids all raved about, except with live rounds and real-life bad guys. I felt a momentary queasiness while my eyes adjusted, but adrenaline overrode it as instinct and training took hold. With gun and badge in hand, I stalked across the short distance between us and certain death, then rounded the corner.

"SCU!" I announced in a commanding voice, brandishing the badge. "Drop your weapons, get on your knees, and put your hands behind your heads."

Two rough-looking men wearing black camouflage, combat boots, and carrying semi-automatics stopped in their tracks.

"Do I need to draw you a picture?" I growled, the anger rising in my voice. "You're under arrest. Drop your goddamn weapons and get on your goddamn knees!"

In that moment, confusion fled from their eyes, replaced by desperation.

They didn't hesitate, and neither did I.

Using the precise aiming guidance of the targeting sensor, a red line visible only to my retina which ended at the center of the first man's forehead, I shot him before he could pull up the weapon in his hands. The gun exploded with a loud crack and a jerk of my arm, but I was ready for the recoil this time. He crumpled, blood and bits of brain decorating the wall like an Escher drawing. In the same motion I fired again, and the bullet tore through the second man's chest.

I faced the camera on the wall and blew it to smithereens.

"Holy shit, Doc!" Leyla exclaimed as she and the others caught up to me.

Her pale features turned a shade greener at the sight of the two dead men and the twin pools of blood saturating the corridor.

"So much for them," Deacon stated.

"Yeah," I replied, and holstered the gun, my mouth set in a grim line. "Watch my back."

A quick search of the first man's pockets produced a holo-ID that displayed the name John Adam Smith and a local address. Crackling communication broke the echoing silence. I looked for its source and noted the earpieces each dead man wore.

I grabbed the other guy's piece since it was less messy.

"Mahoney needs to get me one of them when this is over," Deacon said.

"You'd give up the truncheon?" I asked, some tension leaving me as I reattached the badge to my belt.

Deacon shifted, twirled the consecrated weapon, then offered me a sunny smile.

"Not on your goddamn life, Holliday." His tone sobered as he gestured toward the bodies and the camera with one hand. "They'll come in force now."

"Let them," I said. "But if I'm right, that won't matter. This place is about to become a ghost town."

"Where's the fun in that?" Deacon chuckled dryly.

My gaze softened.

"Crain's been using mercs, and it looks like they're all wired to the same network." I held up the communications device. "There's got to be a control room here, and at least one or two exit routes to the streets above."

The earpiece spat and popped with life again as several people hollered at once.

"Clear the line! Clear the fucking line!" a man's voice shouted. "Facility is compromised! Repeat, facility is compromised! Initiating shut-down protocol, and alerting gold command."

"Rumpelstiltskin," I muttered darkly. "Has to be."

The man repeated the order, then the communicator went dead.

"What has goldjoy got to do with any of this?" Leyla asked.

"Not sure, kiddo," I answered, glancing back at the earpiece I'd discarded. Things started to make a little more sense, just not enough for me to connect the dots. "But I think I know at least one thing Crain's stashed down here."

Our run-in with the cleaners and the theory that the ECPD communications network had been compromised by meddling third parties was one thing. But armed mercenaries in a secret underground complex run by vampires and who-knew-what-else was entirely different.

Wait, did I just think that?

"Vampires and drug lords." I took a deep breath, then gave Deacon a rueful smile.

"Oh, you ain't seen nothing yet, Holliday," he chuckled. "Come down to Birmingham someday. I'll show y'all a good time."

I shook my head in bemusement.

"What now, Doc?" Leyla asked. "You think Rumpelstiltskin is even here?"

"I doubt it," I replied. "I don't think Rumpel hangs out with the hired help."

No more guards came at us during our brief respite, which meant Crain's mercenaries were following the evac order. And there remained the odd feeling Besim picked up from whatever lay down the opposite corridor.

"Those men were stationed in there for a reason." I nodded toward the door, sounding more confident than I felt. "We need to keep the pressure on them while their pants are down."

I checked the ammunition counter on the HUD, although I hadn't used much so far. All systems were operable and at full efficiency.

Good, because we were going to need it.

I set the gun to semi-automatic with a satisfying click.

"Shoot our way through?" Deacon grinned. "Now you're talking, Holliday!"

I grimaced, looking from Leyla to Besim, and finally back to him. "Stay behind this door until I say it's okay to follow."

Before I moved, Besim reached out and wrapped her hand in mine.

"Be careful, Thomas Henry Holliday," she said, surprising me.

We locked gazes for a moment, then moved to stand beside Deacon. I nodded to them, crouched low and pulled the door open carefully, gun leading in my other hand. I crept forward, poised and calm. Warmth tingled through my hand where Besim's fingers had rested.

It felt both strange and soothing.

The room beyond was dim and quiet, broken only by the soft and steady thrum of working machinery from below. I switched to night vision. The world around me became tinged in a heavy, grainy yellow-green. On the far wall was a closed metal door, twin to the one I had passed through. A raised metal catwalk high above the floor ran the length of the room's outer perimeter. Double security cameras were placed at each corner near the ceiling, pointed at a door, or to the room below. They oscillated slowly, red lights fluttering above each device.

I was about to signal the all-clear when movement across the way caught my eye.

A cascade of bullets peppered the wall and door inches above my head. Crying out, I dove to the side. Several more bullets splattered the railing and catwalk, sending up sparks, just missing me. In an instant, the SMART gun's targeting system locked onto the gun-toting maniac who was using the opposite metal door for cover.

Lying on my side, I bellowed, "Armor piercing!" and squeezed the trigger.

A violent burst of heavy-duty shells blasted both door and man. The satisfying squeal of metal was music to my ears as the bullets obliterated the obstruction, and the mercenary hiding behind it. I counted a slow three, holding the gun toward the door with a steady hand. Smoke wafted from its nozzle in a lazy spiral. No answering gunfire greeted me. I took note of the messy smear painting the wreckage that once housed the door, then looked around.

The subdued lighting cast long shadows, creating pockets of darkness in the corners. I slunk low along the catwalk toward the lone stairway leading to the room below. Indistinct shapes moved, but no one shot at me. The ambient sounds of the room became more pronounced—the clink of glass, liquid bubbling and frothing, the thud of something heavy being dropped, and a steady, whirring grind of gears and machinery.

I reached the top of the stairs, gun at the ready. Night vision revealed humanoid-shaped outlines shuffling between dozens of long tables. I switched back to normal vision to get a better look at the room.

The metal tables were covered with all manner of equipment, from beakers, flasks, and tubes to small distilleries, burners, condensers, and receivers filled with liquid. A working conveyor belt crossed the room lengthwise. As I watched, covered plastic tubs trundled along and through a square depository hole in the far wall. Two large steel coolers stood to either side of a closed door near the back of the room. None of the shapes let out a cry or said anything.

Jackpot.

"All clear," I whispered into the earpiece.

I found it strange no one came rushing up the stairs or reacted in any way. Whoever was down there seemed content to wait on me.

Despite my previous misgivings, it was time to call this one in.

"EVI, send an emergency message to Lieutenant Sam Gaffney in the Downtown Narcotics Division," I instructed in a clear voice. I figured if anyone were listening at this point, we might as well give these guys something more to worry about. "Tell him the Special Crimes Unit has discovered some hard evidence regarding the goldjoy case, and to get here right away."

"Detective Holliday, Lieutenant Gaffney is not scheduled for duty at this hour," EVI's garbled voice explained. "He is currently at his private residence, and his life signs show he is asleep. Should I contact the active officer on duty instead?"

"EVI, you wake Gaffney's sorry ass up, provide my current location, and have him bring his entire narcotics team," I ordered harshly. "Officers have engaged heavily-armed personnel and need backup right away. Transmit the recent fire fight to help motivate him."

"My apologies, Detective Holliday," EVI replied.

"It's fine, sweetie," I said, softening my tone. No need to take anything out on her. She was just doing her job. "Please relay the message first to Mahoney, then wait five minutes and send it to Gaffney."

There was no point in keeping Special Crimes on the downlow now. Between our encounter with the cleaners, and now this, we were officially on the board. Bill would handle whatever fallout followed. That's why he got paid the big credits. Hell, I'd let Gaffney and the narcotics team take all the glory. Mahoney could spread the love around, call the whole thing a joint effort between the newly-formed SCU and those guys, and a huge win for ECPD. Knowing Gaffney, he'd eat all that shit up anyway. That self-absorbed prick never shrank from the spotlight. Besides, we had bigger fish to fry, presuming we made it out of here alive.

Deacon and the others joined me at the top of the stairs. The former Protector stopped cold and pointed to the floor below.

"Lord Jesus," he swore, aghast. "Look at them!"

The indistinct shapes I'd seen through the night vision resolved themselves into full-grown women and pre-adolescent girls. All were naked and emaciated, stick-like scarecrow figures with scraggly hair and sunken eyes. I watched in horror as the women worked mechanically—like stringless, macabre marionettes. They filled small syringe tubes with golden liquid from thin, dangling hoses, and stacked them neatly into small plastic containers. Once full, the other girls covered the containers and placed them on the conveyor belt.

My jaw set in a firm line as my temple throbbed.

"I'm going down there."

Leyla's hand on my arm stopped me. A sliver of intense cold followed her touch. I shivered.

"If any guards were still around, they would've shot at us already," I said, removing her chilled hand gently, while indicating the cameras throughout the room. "Just keep an eye on the doors in case someone decides to crash the party."

As I slowly descended the narrow metal stairs, none of the workers reacted to my arrival. It was eerie watching them labor in silence. There were no smiles or grimaces, no grunts of effort or small talk, and none of them ever looked at each other. Their slack and drawn faces held little more than dull resignation, as if even an end to their misery would be as meaningless as everything else.

One pale-haired little girl paused in her movements, and watched my approach with dead, indifferent eyes. She couldn't have been more than eight or nine. A closed container was clutched in her skinny arms. I gave her what I hoped was a friendly smile. She dismissed me without blinking and placed the box on the conveyor belt.

"Hey there, sweetie," I spoke softly, holstering the gun as I approached her. "My name's Tom, and I'm a police officer. I'm going to get you out of here, okay?"

I kept my movements slow and deliberate, and crouched before her with a creak of old knees. She regarded my silver badge with the same dead expression, then resumed stacking the small golden tubes into a new empty container.

I noticed a thin hose filled with a dull crimson and gold liquid running from her inner thigh into a squat metal machine set in the floor beneath the table. The machine's face held a monitor indicating what I took to be her vital signs, as well as other numbers whose purpose I could only guess. Even to my untrained eye, the numbers appeared low.

I craned my neck to see all the workers were attached to similar devices, with dozens of hair-thin filament hoses connecting each monitor to the next. Long glass tubes sprouted from the tops of the devices, and up through the bottom of the table into other pieces of hardware. From there, additional hoses full of the mixed liquid were connected to more machinery. The whole thing reminded me of the George Washington Bridge linking Washington Heights to Fort Lee, except instead of using steel cable and concrete, this was puzzled together by some mad scientist using tubes, hoses and wires.

The child moved past me to deposit another container onto the conveyor. As she did, I noticed dozens of cuts and abrasions marring her face.

I peered at her more closely, and gasped.

"What the hell?"

"Holliday, what's going on?" Deacon's voice floated down from the catwalk above.

I brought the badge closer to the girl. In its silver radiance, the number 9 was etched in what I hoped was ink on her forehead, just below the hairline.

"What's happened to you?" I whispered hoarsely.

She didn't respond.

I drew the badge down and along her body. Puncture wounds decorated her malnourished and bruised neck, wrists and inner thighs, as if she'd been bitten repeatedly by a large animal.

Or a vampire.

"Get down here!" I shouted, choking on the hot tears boiling down my face. "All of you, get down here now!"

CHAPTER 26

The light from my badge limned the little girl's thin face in silver, the number 9 stark against her pale skin. I stood up, took a steadying breath, and edged backward a few steps. Once outside the range of the light, hungry shadows fell on her like a tide, restoring the gloom. She resumed her work, while the embers of my anger settled into a slow, dull ache.

Leyla rushed down the stairs to my side, crystal tears forming on her cheeks. I drew her close. She sobbed into my shoulder, and the onrush of her despair was a physical blow. My legs buckled, but I held up and lay my cheek against the top of her head briefly, my own spirits diminishing in return.

The Insight was absent. I was glad there wasn't a need a for it. Rumpel's drug lab and his zombie workers were bad enough. Seeing this unfiltered through the Insight's magical lens would've sent me over the edge. The Insight had always been finicky, and I was never certain when it would show up, or why. Some days I thought I had it under control, and others, like right now, was just a crapshoot. I knew madness lurked at the end of my road. It was the price I'd eventually pay for everything the Insight had indelibly printed on my soul.

"But not today," I muttered with grim resolve, shelving those thoughts for another time. *"Though this be madness, yet there is method in 't."*

There was no rest for the weary, or the wicked. Besides, rest was for quitters.

And I had a job to do.

Besim moved past us, calmly taking in the room, the equipment and the workers. She knelt before the girl who had stopped working at the Vellan's approach. Still and mute, the child's eyes were downcast and lost.

Leyla stepped away from me. The negative feelings she had projected onto me vanished like an afterthought. Only the bitter chill, my smoldering anger and a burning desire to hunt down Rumpelstiltskin, Orpheus, and anyone else involved in the case remained. Glancing over my shoulder, I noticed Deacon had taken a position on the last two steps. He appeared ready to leap into action, taut as a wire.

"Have you ever seen anything like this?" I asked him, hooking the badge to my belt. The silvery halo surrounding me winked out.

For the first time since I'd met the man, Deacon Kole was at a loss for words. I had expected some profanity-laden tirade about my ignorance of the wider world, and how monsters were very real. Instead, a strange look crossed his face. Deacon shifted his weight, as if unsure how to stand. His eyes locked with mine. We shared a moment, two men helpless in the face of unspeakable abuse and pain.

"Number Nine," Besim addressed the girl in a soft voice, breaking our trance.

My skin prickled. At the mention of the name, the child looked up.

"I am Besim. I will not hurt you."

She gently examined Nine, lifting one stick arm after the other before leaning toward the little girl's chest, head tilted. After a few breaths, Besim traced the fingers of her left hand over and around the crown of Nine's head several times, then tenderly down her cheek. Despite the shadows, Besim's face and neck tattoos stood out prominently, the whirling patterns filled with a strange, ambient light. A faint humming sound grew at the edge of my hearing. It grew in timbre and depth, and I realized it wasn't coming from the machinery.

Besim had begun to sing.

It was an ethereal melody akin to the one back at Armin's. The song's gentle fingers reached deep inside of me, tugging at memories of people and places long past. Besim's music carried me to all the nooks and crannies of my mind where those memories slept, knocked off the dust, and coaxed them to life.

I saw my mother, hale and whole, when her cheeks were still rose-colored, and her blue eyes were filled with joy. I watched Harry grumble good-naturedly while playing another round of cribbage with Abner at Uncle Mortie's. Long nights at the ECU library poring over stanza upon stanza of iambic pentameter, and the joy of discovering Shakespeare and the other literary giants for the first time. The mouth-watering aroma of an original Vito's meatball pie pulled hot from the oven at his restaurant down on Brighton Beach Avenue. My mouth filled with the phantom flavors of oregano and garlic as if I'd just taken a bite. Images of Kate surfaced, of those secret moments when we'd steal away from Wallingbrooke for a few quiet hours together.

I took a shuddering breath, savoring every sensation as I relived it. Other fond memories followed, half-remembered slivers and pieces of neighborhood swing sets and carefree laughter, of blue skies and bright smiles, of family holidays and lazy daydreams. There was springtime and flowers in bloom, the fresh scent of Kate's hair, soft summer breezes, and the gentle reminder that the world wasn't such a terrible place after all.

My anger sloughed away and lost its edge, clearing my mind. My hand tingled again from the memory of Besim's touch. A comforting warmth tumbled throughout my body. Even Leyla was buoyed by the melody. She wiped her eyes, staring at the Vellan with admiration and wonder.

Yet, despite the healing music, Nine remained unchanged, immune to the haunting, uplifting sounds of Besim's song.

Her melody echoed once, then faded. Diminished by the effort, Besim's shoulders sagged. A soft sigh escaped her lips like a farewell.

"You all right?" I asked.

"I will manage," she replied hoarsely, raising a trembling hand.

"What...what was that?" Leyla asked, but the Vellan didn't respond.

We waited while Besim knelt on the floor, her head bowed low. Nine resumed her work, stepping around the consultant as if she were a piece of furniture. Finally, Besim lifted her head, made a slight gesture with her hand, and Nine approached her again, docile and obedient. Besim studied the catheter attached to the child's inner thigh without touching it. Her eyes flicked over to the nearest monitor and its readout, and then up at me.

They were dark pools in the dim light of the room, conveying an infinite sadness.

"Detective Holliday, Number Nine and the other drones require immediate medical attention." She sounded exhausted. "Although, it will make little difference. Their lights are gone."

"What are you talking about?" I demanded, gesturing in outrage at the laboratory. My anger returned, and I wanted to smash something, but Crain was already a congealed puddle of goo. "What the hell did Crain do to them?"

Besim stared at the floor before answering. "These drones are empty, bereft of their humanity, their very souls. They are—"

"Blood dolls," Deacon stated flatly, his worn face bleak and filled with worry.

"It is possible," Besim conceded, looking up at him and

nodding. "Although I suspect there is a far more sinister application at play."

"What the hell is a blood doll?" I asked, feeling lost.

"Some people ain't victims, Holliday," Deacon explained grimly. "Some people give themselves willingly to the Dark. They allow themselves to be fed upon, believing someday they'll transform into one, and live forever."

I stared at him.

"You're serious," I whispered, the color draining from my face. "Jesus Christ."

Deacon didn't blink.

"He ain't got shit to do with it."

Besim ignored us. She stood, brushing invisible wrinkles from her clothing with precise movements.

"The *vampyr* fed upon them," she said simply, her customary composure reasserting itself like a surgeon's mask. "As did his coven. The condition of these drones, however, goes far beyond that."

"Explain," I frowned, and folded my arms.

Besim moved toward the nearest table.

"The apparatus connecting the workers and the tables, along with their associated pumps and output lines, appears to be a modified version of dialysis." She indicated the monitor and its web-like attachments with a wave. "The basic principle behind dialysis is the removal of waste from the blood across a semi-permeable membrane when the kidneys are unable to do so on their own. It seems this apparatus performs a very similar function."

"Are you saying all these people suffer from kidney failure?" Leyla asked, incredulous.

"No Leyla." Besim shook her head. "While these machines assist in maintaining life to some degree, Number Nine and the other drones are essential cogs within the overall production mechanism."

By way of explanation, she pointed across the room at a row of four tall tanks with blue-colored top caps and yellow stickers containing the words "concentrate storage."

"Those are dialysate solution tanks, which would normally contain water, a critical component to the cleansing process. However, I suspect the water has either been modified or replaced with other agents to act as the dialysate, or the fluid normally used to remove impurities."

She took a half-step forward to study the squat upright box beneath the table.

"This monitor here provides output for the workers' vital signs, as well as volume pressure and other indicators with respect to the efficacy of the mixing compounds and the cleaning process."

Nine hadn't moved or registered any emotion. She just stared at the floor, submissive and unseeing. I balled my hands into fists, then unclenched them. The red furrows burned from where my fingernails had dug into the skin.

"So why are they standing?" I asked, clearing my throat roughly, trying to wrap my head around it all. "I've been to EC General and seen patients hooked up to dialysis machines. They were all sitting or lying down. Wouldn't all the movement make these catheters pop out?"

"Someone surgically created the arteriovenous fistula, a type of vascular access for hemodialysis," Besim answered as if lecturing to a class of medical students, and not while standing in some darkened room surrounded by designer drug equipment and a herd of docile zombies. "Whoever is responsible for affixing the catheters must have reinforced the femoral connection in a way to prevent the devices from accidentally detaching from the drones."

Besim paused, brow furrowed.

"Yet, I see no sign of infection, which is quite remarkable," she said. "Perhaps whatever the *vampyr* injects into the drones it feeds upon provides an increased ability to fight infection?"

Besim was intrigued, her detachment and exhaustion replaced by genuine curiosity.

"What are the catheters for, then?" Leyla asked as she stared forlornly at the lab.

"The intake-line catheter feeds the admixture of blood and other compounds into and through the various machinery," Besim explained. "The process must require continuous cleansing, or a recycling of the fluids. At first, I hypothesized these drones were as Deacon believed, willing cattle to be fed upon by their captors. But now I believe a living, biological component is the essential ingredient to all of it. Number Nine and the other drones not only facilitate but are, in fact, critical to the proper synthesis of the completed product. The *vampyr* infects the drone to establish a chemical base, and the machinery, coupled with whatever compound is contained within the dialysate tanks, is combined to refine the process."

She indicated the array of thin tubing connecting the devices.

"These chains of tubes are a pooling arrangement, so that a large volume of blood is cleansed simultaneously to maximize output of the synthesized product. I can only conclude the process removes undesirable content from the blood in favor of an admixture of unknown elements resulting in the narcotic goldjoy."

"They're using these people's blood to *manufacture* goldjoy?" Leyla gasped, horrified.

"They're fucking mules," Deacon growled in disgust.

"My understanding of that term refers more to smuggling contraband, but there are similarities," Besim conceded.

"But you said their light was gone," Leyla pointed out. "Your song didn't do anything to Nine. What has that got to do with any of this?"

"In my experience, only creatures without souls, lacking any sense of emotion or feeling, are immune to my...voice," Besim replied softly. "All of them failed to respond emotionally to the sound, a clear indicator to me that their lights, their very souls, have been taken from them."

She looked at me, and there was genuine fear reflected there. But then she blinked, and it was gone.

"Only a functional biological subject is required to complete the process. A drone's soul, therefore, must be assimilated as part of it. Perhaps this is the reason why goldjoy is so addictive to you humans."

"Quit calling them drones, Besim," Leyla bristled, intense cold radiating from her. "They're still people."

"I meant no offense, Leyla." The Vellan was taken aback, holding up a placating hand. "I merely wished to elucidate on the condition of the drones to provide a complete—"

"I said, quit calling them drones!" Leyla blazed.

For a moment, she appeared ready to unleash frosty hell on Besim. Ice crystals formed in the air around her, and the temperature plummeted.

"Why don't we table the existentialism debate for another day?" I managed in a calm, steady voice, and stepped between them. I gave Leyla a pleading look, despite the sinking fear settling in my gut. My heart pounded in my chest and sweat froze on my brow. "C'mon kiddo, pull yourself together for me. Nine needs our help."

Leyla blinked several times, as if waking from a daydream. She took a deep breath, then relaxed. Whatever darkness had settled inside of her was gone, along with the cold and frost. Deacon gave me a solemn nod, and I saw him lower his truncheon.

"So, what now?" I sighed heavily, giving the laboratory a grim look.

"I will require raw samples from one of these drones...apologies, workers," Besim replied, nonplussed. "With it at my disposal, I believe I can determine the precise metabolic and molecular structure of whatever is contained therein and confirm my theory."

"You want to draw blood from one of them?" I was dubious, staring at the mess of catheters, lines, and tubes.

"My own apartments at L'Hotel Internacional possess the appropriate equipment necessary to study the samples," Besim confirmed. "Once Doctor Stentstrom arrives, he can assist me."

"Naturally, you have a lab in your apartments," I deadpanned, rolling my eyes at Leyla. "Doesn't everybody? I bet you run around the city at night in spandex fighting crime too."

The young hacker offered me a wan smile. Some of my unease faded as I smiled back.

"Excuse me?" Besim asked perplexed, eyebrow raised.

"Nothing," I replied. My holo-phone vibrated as EVI's crackling voice in my ear announced both Mahoney and Stentstrom's arrival. "The captain's almost here, and Stentstrom's at the front door. Deacon, you mind leading him down here?"

The former Protector nodded, then gave the room one last, deep scowl.

"We'll be fine," I assured him.

"I ain't worried about you," he grumbled in irritation, and climbed the stairs two at a time.

"Well, what if one of them attacks me and I get turned into a blood doll?" I asked. "You'll just knock me out with the truncheon, right?"

"Yep," he replied easily as he headed toward the exit. "And after that, I'll stake your heart, cut off your fucking head, and *then* light your infected ass on fire."

For some reason, that didn't make me feel any better.

CHAPTER 27

"*No matter where, of comfort no man speak,*" I whispered to myself. "*Let's talk of graves, of worms, and epitaphs. Make dust our paper and with rainy eyes write sorrow on the bosom of the earth.*"

It was spooky standing around Rumpel's drug lab while Nine and the others worked in silence. I tried not to imagine the horrible things Crain had done to these people, yet I couldn't ignore Besim's words.

Their lights are gone.

These poor people had suffered. Their trauma was raw, and very real. I'd seen plenty of cases where the survivors of rape and abuse spent years trying to recover some measure of themselves, if they ever recovered at all. EC Social Services did the best they could with their limited resources, but some wounds never healed. As I studied Nine, I was struck again by how slack and lifeless she appeared.

Their lights are gone.

The longer I watched, my sense of her emptiness grew. It reminded me of staring at the sun in winter, how its pale radiance made everything it touched faded and dull, as if all the color in the world had bled away. Would Nine and the others ever find solace? Could they? Or was Besim right, and more than just their will to live had been taken?

James Reynolds had been one. The Insight had revealed a soulless man, devoured by the *fetch*. What was done to Nine felt the same. If Nine and the others couldn't be saved, then it was a fate worse than death.

Until my own near-death experience at Wallingbrooke, I'd left spirituality alone. Father Jack Davis from the Holy Redeemer Church where my grandfather had worked was better-equipped for an exploration of the immortal soul than some poor schmuck like me. As far as I was concerned, God and I weren't on speaking terms, and hadn't been in a long time. After Kate's death, I hadn't given the Almighty or organized religion much weight. And Kate's afterlife, let alone mine, hadn't been something I spent time pondering on my days off either.

Then the Insight entered my life, and everything changed.

I couldn't deny Besim's song, nor the profound effect it had on me. Despite my past hurt, anger, and bitterness, Besim's song was a soothing balm on all those old wounds. My sense of self had been rejuvenated, if only for a brief moment. Even my previous ass-kicking at the hands of Crain had become a dull ache, as if I'd spent several days recovering.

What her voice had accomplished was nothing short of magical.

In the dim light of the lab, I watched Besim follow the conveyor belt to the end of its line. She poked her head carefully through the space where the containers trundled along.

Who *are* you?

"I have located a door to the storage area for the packaged goldjoy," Besim said, her muffled voice carrying across the room. "Two workers are inside. With your permission, I shall investigate further."

"Knock yourself out," I called back, then addressed Leyla in a quiet voice. "Keep an eye on the professor here while I look around."

"Sure, Doc," she replied, chewing on her lower lip while her eyes flicked between Nine, the workers, the laboratory, and the catwalk.

"It'll be okay, kiddo," I said, squeezing her shoulder before moving toward the two large coolers flanking the door. "Besides, Deacon and Stentstrom will be here soon."

I opened the coolers, one after the other. A blast of chilled air greeted me, and I rubbed my hands for warmth. Inside were dozens of bags full of clear and dark crimson liquids. Each bore marks corresponding to a blood type and the unique number etched on the heads of the workers.

"Looks like a blood supply," I called over my shoulder. "Not sure about the clear ones, though."

"Unsurprising, Detective Holliday," Besim responded. She had returned to the main floor. "The workers need continuous trans-fusions while their blood transforms into the final product. The clear liquid must contain essential nutrients, such as glucose and amino acids, for sustenance, to maximize work output without causing delays due to stoppages for meals. This complex undoubt-edly houses a medical facility to modify and correct sudden fail-ures to the equipment, as well as any other relevant medical procedures. A trained staff of two or three would be sufficient to manage the medical operations, given the number of workers present in the laboratory. It is highly unlikely the guards we have encountered thus far were capable of such action. Nor were, I suspect, the *vampyr* and its minions."

"Yeah, well, whoever they are, I bet they're long gone by now," Leyla pointed out.

"Probably," I replied, shutting both coolers. "You find anything in that storage room?"

"A service elevator to the surface," Besim said. "I presume it leads to a staging area for the transportation of the product."

"Makes sense," I grunted, turning toward the metal door set between the coolers.

After a quick peek through its small window, I pulled open the door with care. Inside, a dozen live-feed holo-screens were inset along the far wall. They cycled through different angles of the dance floor, bar, stage, kitchen, boiler room, the drug lab, part of the entryway and elevator, another hallway, and an alleyway, either next to Kraze or nearby. The faint whiff of burnt rubber and circuitry caught my attention. Two of the projectors were smashed, with glass, metal, and wiring littering the top of the lone virtual workstation. A rolling chair with a bent wheel strut lay on its side nearby, surrounded by more debris.

"The murder weapon, I presume," I murmured, folding my arms across my chest.

A second chair was parked beside a small trashcan, refrigerator, and a table holding a coffee maker whose pot was half-filled. Above the table was a small cabinet with a single door. A quick look inside revealed two empty mugs, artificial sweetener packs, and powdered creamer. Both trashcan and refrigerator were empty.

"Don't mind if I do," I said, filling one mug.

It was disgusting, but after a couple of fortifying cups, I almost felt like a new man. As the last drop poured down my throat, I offered a silent prayer of thanks to the coffee gods. Java was the only religion I could get behind.

I called out to Leyla, who appeared a few seconds later. She placed her holo-phone on the desk, then manipulated the workstation controls. A smaller display hovered above the phone, a miniature clone of the larger one. Like a conductor before her symphony, Leyla maneuvered between the devices. Music filtered from the phone, a song I didn't recognize. She started to hum. Realizing there was an audience, Leyla looked up at me and smiled.

"I'm good, Doc," she replied, round face pinched in concentration. "I'll let you know when I find something."

I strode back to the laboratory in time to watch Stentstrom and Deacon hasten along the catwalk and down the stairs. Stentstrom was smothered inside a heavy winter coat, white designer gloves, and a white *ushanka* with the earflaps down. He carried a steel briefcase. A sticker was affixed at an angle on one side displaying a symbol of two poodle heads back-to-back, one black and the other white, with the tagline "Proud member of the PC of EC".

"Doctor—" I began, but the medical examiner stared at the laboratory, eyes round as the moon.

"Sweet Westminster's Kennel Club!" the little man exclaimed.

"Gilbert!" I said, snapping my fingers in front of his face. "Over here."

"Oh, yes, my apologies," the medical examiner said, fast blinking eyes focusing on me. He took a deep breath. "It's just so...so..."

"Awful," I supplied.

"Magnificent," he breathed.

"Um, right," I said, steering him back to the foot of the stairs.

"And a Vellan," he squealed with delight. "How extraordinary! Is she your assistant?"

He twisted his head around to catch another glimpse of Besim and the laboratory.

Once I got his attention, I introduced him to Besim and Leyla, then summarized what had transpired since our arrival at the nightclub. His eyebrows merged with the *ushanka*.

"Make sure these people are cared for," I finished. "And don't mention anything about the vampires to anyone else. Not in your report. No one."

The medical examiner stiffened.

"Well, I have to provide an explanation of some sort," he sniffed in professional indignation. "I have a reputation to uphold, after all, not to mention hours of paperwork to complete. I take pride in being quite thorough, after all. What on earth am I supposed to say?"

"Make something up," I countered. "Look, just gloss over the details. Say it's a case of kidnapping, abuse, and drug dealers employing slave labor. That's pretty much the truth anyway."

"Detective Holliday, this is highly irregular." He wasn't convinced. "Lieutenant Gaffney and his narcotics team will have their own forensic investigators, who will be equally thorough. I appreciate what we did regarding the theft of the body from the morgue, but withholding evidence is—"

"There's a lot at stake here," I implored in a quiet voice. "Delay things for a little while, until I can figure out what's really going on. Lives depend on it. I'm asking you to trust me, Gilbert. Please."

Stentstrom searched my eyes for a moment. "Of course, Detective. I'll take care of it."

He winced when I clapped him on the shoulder.

"That's the spirit!" I grinned. "Oh, once you've finished assisting Doctor Saranda, head back upstairs to scoop up whatever's left of Crain and his two goons. That white fire from Deacon's truncheon melted them to the bone, and I'd rather you hold onto their remains."

"I thought I recognized the foul stench of burnt hair when I was led through the club above." The medical examiner's eyes lit up with interest. "I had presumed it was from all the hairspray young people wear these days. How terribly repugnant, not to mention flammable! Fortunately for you, Detective, I came prepared, and brought a full complement of forensic paraphernalia, as well as a spatula, a rather useful tool. Blood and fluid splatters find homes in some of the more unusual and dirty places. Why, I recall one particular case involving a triple homicide at a sperm donation facility—"

"Yeah, Doc," I shuddered. "We get the picture."

"A rather nasty bit of business, that one," Stentstrom tittered, turning toward Deacon. "And since we're on the subject. Mr. Kole, perhaps you could explain the properties of the white fire you used to melt the decedents?"

The former Protector glowered but said nothing.

"Another time, then," Stentstrom said quickly, offering me a nervous smile as he joined Besim. "Doctor Saranda, how may I be of service?"

Stentstrom set the briefcase on the floor, removed his hat and gloves, and placed them on top. Nine stood unmoving nearby, a tiny rag doll next to the towering Vellan and the shorter medical examiner.

"Hey, Doc," Leyla called. She was in the doorway between the two refrigerators. A troubled expression crossed her face. "You're gonna want to see this."

I glanced at Deacon, then followed her into the control room.

"Crain's security did a good job clearing out their virtual, cloud, and hard records," Leyla explained as we entered. "They initiated a self-destruct sequence to their systems, wiping out whatever data they kept. They got rid of a lot of it, too, but not all."

Deacon walked over to the holo-screens to stand before the one depicting the entrance to the club. Flashing lights and dozens of figures milled outside, but no one had gone through the door yet. Mahoney was at the center of it all, directing traffic.

"You get any of the archived footage these cameras picked up?" Deacon asked.

Leyla flicked through a side holo-panel of the workstation.

"Not a lot," Leyla replied, squinting at the screen. "The latest date stamp is from two nights ago. I did a facial recognition sweep looking for Vanessa, but she never came up."

"Well that's about as useless as tits on a bull," Deacon grunted in irritation. "You found nothing better than that, girl?"

"As a matter of fact, I did," Leyla sniffed haughtily.

She shunted the side panel away, drawing to the fore a single window. A series of characters, numbers and symbols ran along the screen like falling rain.

"What the fuck is all that?" Deacon demanded.

"*That* is the result of our tracker program." Leyla pointed a triumphant finger at the streaming data. "*That* is where the signal from the surveillance cameras we found in Vanessa's townhouse went to."

"Where does it go?" I asked.

"Here," she replied, stepping to the side of the screen. "And what you're looking at isn't one signal, it's three. Or, more accurately, the telemetry from three different signals. The first is the initial code. That one isn't very elegant or discreet. You see that most commonly used in one-way transmitting devices. It still took a lot of time to hunt down because of all the false paths whoever wrote it had set up. I've uploaded the remaining data that didn't get wiped and transmitted all of it to some extra micro-drives I keep handy. From what I can tell, it goes back *years.*"

My eyebrows rose. I exchanged a grim look with Deacon.

"You said there are three different codes," Deacon said with grudging respect. "What about the other two?"

Leyla nodded. "Wrapped around the first one was a second, transmitted to an office building in Queens. I'm still working on triangulating its exact location, but I've got a pretty good idea. Anyway, this code is much more involved, written by someone very skilled. I don't think Crain and his security team had a clue it was even there."

"That's gotta be Orpheus," I declared. "Keeping tabs on their business partner, no doubt. What about the third one?"

"That's the weird part, Doc," she answered, her face clouding over. "I have no idea where it goes. My program traced it to a point somewhere in Manhattan. But then it stopped, like the signal disappeared into a black hole or something. It reappeared sometime later in the Bronx, and then disappeared right after. I think the signal is mobile."

"Any good security company can hide a signal," Deacon growled. "That ain't nothing new, girl."

"I know that," Leyla replied testily. "But this one is...different. Doc, you know how good I am at this kind of stuff. I've kept both ECPD and ECBI off my tail for years. But when I study the code involved with that third signal, it's decades ahead of me. It's so complex, and full of all kinds of subtle sub-routines, that it's more than just some signal sending back information to whoever wrote it. And I think it's two-way, made up of multiple signals, not just the one. The signal ends not because it's coded to disappear if discovered, but because it was never there in the first place. It's like a ghost."

"How can you track something like that?" I asked, rubbing the bridge of my nose. "How did you know it was there in the first place?"

"More military-grade tech, Holliday," Deacon grumbled. "If that's the case, then that's some serious shit. Although I ain't never heard of a signal able to do what girlie here just said."

"Well then what is it?" I asked.

"Magic."

Besim stood in the doorway.

"Excuse me?"

"Whoever is responsible for that third signal has employed magic to keep it hidden," she answered calmly. "Only magic can defy physics. The signal is there, but magic has been employed to obfuscate its presence, fool modern technology, and prevent anyone from finding its transmission source."

"I get what kind of world we live in," I said, folding my arms across my chest while giving Besim a skeptical look, "but I've never heard of anything like that."

"There are many mysteries still undiscovered, even after all this time, Detective Holliday," Besim said cryptically. "Perhaps whoever is responsible for the third signal remains hidden through a blend of magic and technology? Regardless, Leyla has discovered its presence, and it cannot be ignored."

"She's right," Leyla said. She hugged herself, becoming increasingly uncomfortable.

Something clicked in my mind. I didn't need my Insight to figure this one out.

"That's how you stay hidden, isn't it?" I said, keeping the accusation from my tone. "It's why so few people have been able to find you. Your cold ability is one thing. And you're a skilled hacker, great with holo-tech, too, but there's always been more to it."

"Yes," she replied in a small voice.

"Like knows like," Besim said. "You can see what lies within the code where others cannot."

"Fine, then how do we figure out where it goes?" I asked.

"I'm working on it," Leyla said in earnest. "I just need time, that's all."

I placed my hands on her shoulders.

"You got it, kiddo," I smiled, and she returned it, but then her face clouded over.

"There's more," she said, turning from me to flick the screen away with her hand. The display changed to a dark image.

"What are we looking at now?" I asked.

"This is from several hours ago." Her lip began to tremble. Crystal tears formed in her eyes. "Just listen."

She activated the recording.

Something shifted in the blackness of the screen. Moments later, a door opened, and an aisle of light spilled into a large room. Two mercs stepped into view, each carrying a naked body. They came to a short wall and dropped the corpses over the side. Muffled cries arose from below them. The two men ignored the sounds, and shut the door closed behind them.

That's when I heard it.

"Help us," a faint, tremulous voice cried. "Please. Help us."

The transmission ended.

Silence descended on the room like cold, unrelenting death.

"That is what I sensed from the other hallway, Detective Holliday," Besim said. Horror filled her eyes as she regarded me. "That is where the *vampyr* keeps its larder."

CHAPTER 28

"We're too late."

My badge illuminated dozens of naked forms, limbs and bodies twisted in grotesque parodies of life. All of them women, or girls of an age with Nine. Dozens of nameless victims had been cast into this black pit, never to see the light of day again. Now reduced to an unmoving pile of grisly shapes, they'd been carelessly strewn on a bed of skulls and bones like some forgotten assemblage of childhood rag dolls. The stench was unbearable, yet I willed myself to remain at the lip of the pit.

I stared at the collection of corpses, wondering who they'd been. How they came here. What had been done to them.

And why.

Leyla's choking sobs echoed from the passageway behind me. Besim comforted her, but even her voice rang hollow, like empty air. Deacon stood beside me, a grim specter at the edge of the badge's light. His eyes blazed. A flicker of white fire flared along the truncheon, as if responding to the roiling emotions of its wielder.

When I heard the little girl's plaintive plea for help from the salvaged feed, I burst from the control room in a mad dash. I felt

Nine's dead, knowing eyes follow me as I bolted across the catwalk and through the door. My legs chewed up the distance in long strides, heedless of whatever lurked ahead. At the end of the hallway, I broke right and crashed through another metal door. Beyond was a small operating room containing empty tables and beds, glass and metal cabinets, all manner of medical equipment, and another door on the far side. A smashed virtual workstation sat dark next to a water cooler and cup dispenser. Ignoring the room, I pushed through the other door and down a shadowy corridor, my badge lighting the way.

Crain's larder was at the end of the line through a thick metal door, but the rotten stench of human detritus still reached me well before I got there. The others arrived shortly after. Besim ushered Leyla from the charnel house before she could catch more than a glimpse of the horror below. But she'd seen enough.

We all had.

The little girl's desperate voice from the recording echoed in my mind.

Help us.

Closing my eyes, I focused on the case, blocking out Leyla's devastated sobbing and my own rising anger. I reviewed all the information our investigation uncovered so far. The facts and evidence, our theories, anything that would pull me temporarily from that pit. Yet Nine and the bodies below intruded on my thoughts, taunting my inability to stitch together this intricate web of murder and lies. And then Vanessa's still face floated before me, the ghastly wound on the side of her neck a chilling reminder that unfinished business remained.

EVI announced the arrival of Gaffney and his team, as well as the media swarm.

"Time to leave, Holliday," Deacon said quietly. "Ain't nothing left for us here."

I tore my eyes from the bodies in the pit and nodded my agreement.

"We already got the sonofabitch," he continued, placing a firm hand on my shoulder.

"No, Marko's still out there," I grated in a hard voice. "So are Rumpel-fucking-stiltskin, Julie, Orpheus, and whoever else is involved. I'm putting an end to this, Deacon. One way or another, I'm putting an end to this."

Deacon's mouth formed a thin line.

"Then let's get these motherfuckers before they hurt anyone else."

We returned to the darkened hallway. Besim held Leyla in a protective hug, the white-haired girl's head buried in the Vellan's chest. Leyla's sobbing had subsided, but her shoulders still trembled. Even Stentstrom's customary enthusiasm was gone, replaced by an uncharacteristically grim countenance I found comforting.

"Doctor, head back up and collect those remains," I said, addressing them all. "Mahoney's expecting you, so look for him, follow his lead, and just do what he says. Try not to answer too many of Gaffney's questions. And contact me on my private number if you find anything new. At this point, I want to keep any further communication between us away from the regular channels. EVI's been an open party line, compliments of Rumpelstiltskin and his inside man. Let's not tip them off to what we're doing any more than we've already done. The rest of us are getting the hell out of here."

They murmured their assent. We returned to the elevator in silence. I pressed the button, staring back at the empty corridor. I felt the weight of the entire world settle on my shoulders, like Poe's raven. The door slid open. Stentstrom stepped inside, both hands gripping the handle of his briefcase. Before it closed, the medical examiner stuck his hand out, forcing the door open again.

"Detective," he called.

"Yes, Doctor?"

He fixed me with a steady look.

"Stop them."

The elevator door closed.

We returned to the catwalk above the laboratory to discover Nine and the others had resumed their mindless work. I paused, observing the activity below with a frown, and wondered what her life would now be like once she and the others were freed from the goldjoy laboratory. Was there a family out there still searching? A desolate mother and father to be suddenly reunited with their missing daughter? EC Social Services would put Nine into foster care if no one claimed her. And then what? Would there be a return to the light for this little girl? Or was she doomed as well?

She and I were kindred spirits in that, I supposed. But I was lucky. I had stared into that abyss and come back, for better and worse, with the help of Abner and Leyla.

I'd lost nearly everyone important to me. I couldn't fathom truly losing everyone.

Or, if Besim was right, losing my very soul.

"You got everything you could from here?" I asked Leyla.

"Yeah," she replied tentatively. Her sad eyes met mine.

"But you made sure there's nothing for Gaffney to find either?" I pressed gently.

"Um, yeah," she sniffled, pulling herself together. "I figured you'd want me to do that. I added a worm that wiped out everything it found relating to the surveillance footage and vampires. It's already infected all of Crain's virtual drives, the cloud and all the backups. By the time Narcotics gets down here, their holo-tech forensics team will assume Crain's people did it."

What Leyla did was illegal, and I'd lose my badge over it if anyone ever found out. Given how this investigation had gone, it was a gamble I had to take.

"Good."

I gave Nine one last, pained look.

"*O, why should nature build so foul a den,*" I murmured, "*unless the gods delight in tragedies?*"

She turned her head up toward me, and our eyes met a final time.

I led the way along the catwalk to the blasted door on the opposite side. I didn't bother sifting through the bloody wreckage. There wasn't much left of the mercenary I'd shot. The corridor beyond was less worked compared to the rest of the complex. As we walked, I smelled refuse and rain. The corridor inclined steadily, then leveled as we reached another metal door. My phone buzzed, but I ignored it. I pulled the door open. A blast of bitterness greeted me.

A narrow back alley filled with trash led to the street, about half a block from Kraze. Cold rain fell from the leaden sky of morning. We were drenched in seconds. I glanced over my shoulder. Another small camera perched above and to the right of the door frame. A little red light blinked, barely perceptible in the gloom.

I see you, Rumpelstiltskin. And I'm coming.

"EVI, bring the pod around," I said, breath streaming out before me. "Keep it away from the nightclub. We need immediate evac."

"Affirmative," the AI's voice sounded grainy. "You also have several messages from Lieutenant Samuel Gaffney, and one from Captain Mahoney. Shall I play them for you?"

"Sure," I grimaced, bracing for an unflattering verbal barrage.

Sometimes, I hate it when I'm right.

"Holliday, what the fuck do you think you're doing?" Gaffney's snarky, outraged voice blasted in my ear. "Goldjoy is *my* fucking case, asshole! The 98th has no jurisdiction here, and you can bet your ass both Flanagan and IAD will hear about this the first chance I get. Call me ASAP."

His other messages were shades of the same. I cleared them before moving on to the one from Mahoney.

"Tom, I'll take care of things here. Call me when you're some-where we can talk."

Surrounded by gloom, fog, and rain, we were wisps on the wind, stealing away from the complex unseen. The pod emerged from the early morning mist like a dream, and out of sight of the circus that had set up shop around Kraze. Once inside its cozy, climate-controlled confines, I collapsed onto one of the command chairs, and looked to Besim.

"L'Hotel Internacional," she replied, taking one of the passenger seats.

I had EVI rev the engines, and we high-tailed it over there.

L'Hotel Internacional looked like some giant had dug up an eighteenth-century German castle and dropped it next to Central Park. Its sprawl engulfed four city blocks, protected by a massive wall of bedrock and granite towers lit by faux watch fires. The place boasted rising spires, conical glass domes, and gold-plated statuary of radiant angels and regal men on horseback guarding its entrance. A fancy walkway, illuminated by flickering torches in sconces, connected the hotel to the Central Park Shopping Mall across the street.

It remained one of the most sought-after destinations in Empire City for the rich and shameless. The place was an anachronism. It dwelled in a part of the city where all the other more modern buildings surrounding it had been torn down and rebuilt using spell-forged steel, glass, and concrete. With the trees of Central Park as its backdrop, the place stood apart from the other tall, gleaming structures like a white swan in a sea of pigs.

Marble and stone were its armor; elegance and opulence, its currency. I was more than a little disappointed when Deacon confirmed the hotel didn't have a moat and drawbridge.

EVI maneuvered the pod into the half-moon shaped entrance. I was conscious of the bright lights and curious stares from several hotel employees and guests, still up and about despite the early hour. The incongruity of our drab ECPD vehicle parked next to the sleek personal chariots of Empire City's upper crust wasn't lost upon me. I looked for the red carpet to be rolled out, and a fanfare of horns trumpeting our arrival. Instead, a single puffed up, rosy-cheeked middle-aged man in red, white, and gold livery, tall black hat, and white gloves greeted us as the pod's hatchway extended. He stared down his nose at my disheveled appearance, eyes narrowing in disdain.

My fingers fumbled for my badge. Damn, I was bone tired.

"Good morning, and welcome to L'Hotel Internacional," he said in bored tones as I slunk down the steps, Leyla on my heels. "I wasn't aware of any issues at our hotel requiring the attention of the police. How may I be of service?"

I was about to respond, when Besim appeared at the pod hatchway.

A beatific smile blossomed like the dawn across the bellman's lips. His sudden transformation from disinterested arrogance to fawning deference was so sudden, he nearly fell over himself.

"Doctor Saranda!" he gushed with oily delight, stepping past me and bowing. "What an unexpected pleasure! Welcome home! It would be my honor to assist you with anything you require."

Besim glided down the stairs and toward the gleaming glass of the hotel without a word. Her haughty eyes dismissed the man and gilded entryway. She moved toward the gleaming lights of the hotel foyer as if she owned the place.

Maybe she did?

"Giles," Deacon greeted the bellman without warmth. He blew smoke into the other man's face. "Tell your people Doctor Saranda is not to be disturbed. These two are her personal guests. Am I clear?"

"Of course, Mr. Kole! I shall see to it personally! Discretion is my middle name!" Giles bobbed his head several times, stifling a cough. "Is there anything else? Could I interest you in a fresh breakfast whipped up by our world-renowned chefs? Or perhaps a fine Bourdeaux, warmed to perfection, to whisk away the damp and chill?"

"Yeah," Deacon growled, flicking ash at Giles. "Shut the fuck up, and make sure nobody goes near the pod."

We left the bellman and moved after Besim.

"Friend of yours?" I asked with a crooked smile.

Deacon gave me a pained look.

"Fuck no. This goddamn place is a disease."

Despite the rain and cold, the entryway was kept at a pleasant temperature beneath its broad expanse of metal and stone. I gawked openly as we passed through the entrance to the hotel. My pride was relieved to see Leyla doing the same. We were tiny fish swimming around a massive bowl, surrounded by a lavishness and grandeur we rarely encountered.

"Not the kind of place I'd expect you and Besim to call home," Leyla said.

"Girl, there's lots you don't know about me and her," Deacon shot back, his brow furrowed in annoyance as he took in the hotel, a sour expression on his face.

He picked up the pace.

Leyla and I exchanged a look and shrugged.

The grand foyer opened into a broad, airy hall filled with dazzling chandeliers of crystal. Long stretches of thick carpeting displaced white marble veined with gold. Dust was apparently not allowed past the front door. The air was warm and tinged with cinnamon, while soft strains of delicate music from stringed and wind instruments circulated around us. An enormous fountain that could easily have filled the main floor of the 98th precinct was inset at the center of the vast room. Its centerpiece was a theatrical display of men on horseback charging into some nameless fray with flowing cloaks and drawn swords. Water poured from spigots cunningly crafted along the base of the marble, conveying the illusion that the statuary rode atop the liquid surface as if held there by some invisible hand.

A gallery of floors rose above us, each with its own little balcony and waiting area. Two banks of elevators held court in the back, the sheer walls creating the illusion that the machines were fashioned from light and air, and not glass. Holo-tapestries hung on the walls to our left, cycling between hunting scenes and panoramic vistas. Periodically, new images melted into view, replete with different colors, fabrics, inlays and settings. Additional torches along the walls burned without smoke, more holograms to add to the ambience of wealth and excess.

"Style without substance," I said sadly, offering Leyla a rueful smile. *"All the world's a stage, and all the men and women merely players."*

Besim stormed across the hall. A few well-manicured guests offered pleasantries, but she ignored them as completely as she had Giles the Pompous Bellman. The hotel employees we encountered were drawn to wealth like sharks smelling blood in the water but wilted under Deacon's withering glare.

Past the elevators, we turned a rounded corner down a long hallway with two empty dining rooms and an ostentatious gift shop filled with Halloween bric-a-brac. The sounds of the busy foyer and its music faded in the distance. Another turn found us in a side alcove. A man and woman dressed in matching gray pant suits and wearing earpieces stood at its end, hands clasped behind their backs.

"Gaff, Bryant," Deacon greeted them with a slight nod.

An elevator door in the wall slid open between them.

"Nothing to report, sir," the woman replied. She had a severe face and calculating brown eyes that strafed Leyla and me before returning to Deacon. "Orders?"

"Keep the area secure," Deacon instructed. "No one goes upstairs."

"Understood, sir."

He nodded once as Besim stepped first into the elevator. We followed, the doors closing behind us. There were no buttons in the steel interior. A sudden push from below indicated we were underway. I felt my ears pop from the movement.

A moment later, we arrived.

A tall, handsome woman with close-cropped brown hair streaked with gray greeted us. She wore black slacks, a violet top and an unamused expression.

Besim tossed her longshoreman's coat at the woman, who caught it without flinching. She moved past the woman wordlessly. Deacon made straight to the wet bar. Concern mixed with irritation flashed across the woman's face. It dissolved as she turned back to address us.

"Welcome, Detective Holliday, Leyla," she said in an accented voice I couldn't place. The woman smiled, but there was little warmth to it. "I have rooms prepared for you, and refreshments should you require. Please, follow me."

I had a million and one questions, but the sludge in my brain ground any rational thought. We entered a spacious living room filled with comfortable furniture and a roaring fireplace. All manner of artwork, from genuine paintings to busts and sculptures, were tastefully arranged so as not to impose one piece on the other. A mix of authentic Oriental and Arabian fabrics clung to the polished tile of the floor in patterns that added to the collection of color and comfort. What the hotel lobby lacked in substance, Besim's apartments more than made up for it.

Heavy drapes of dark gold covered the far wall. Three open doorways exited the room, two to the left, and one to the right. A large holo-vision hovered before one wall, currently dark, with several lounging chairs arranged around it. My head swam in circles from the scent of lilac and chamomile that mingled with the warmth of the room. The woman led us to the right and down a short hallway toward a pair of well-appointed bedrooms.

"You'll find that everything you need has been provided for you," the woman instructed in clipped tones. "Please place your coat and clothing on the chair, and I will see to it that they are laundered."

Leyla staggered into her room and fell face-first on the bed.

"Thank you," I replied, raising my eyebrows in silent question.

"Mamika," she answered, and left me alone. "Get some rest, Detective. You've had a long day."

I shrugged off my coat while taking in the king-sized poster bed, a virtual workstation, holo-vision, lounging chair and closet. An open doorway led into a marble washroom, stand up shower, vanity, and brass tub. A fuzzy white bathrobe hung on a peg inside the door, with the letters *LHI* written in calligraphy along one sleeve. I found a matching pair of white slippers underneath the vanity. Several different flavors of shampoo and body wash were arranged neatly, along with a toothbrush, toothpaste, mouthwash, a fresh blade, and a can of shaving cream.

I don't remember falling asleep, only that at some point, I did.

And with it, came the dream.

CHAPTER 29

*T*he park was quiet and cold.

Old playground equipment sat lonely and unused. Rusted metal creaked as swing chains shivered in the late afternoon breeze. Ashen-gray clouds covered the winter sky. The few trees scattered around the area were naked, their limbs bare of leaves.

"I can't do it," I whined. "Ma, I can't do it!"

The distance separating me from the far side of the jungle gym yawned like adolescence. I hung from the metal rungs with aching arms. My cheeks burned from the frosty wind billowing about.

"Yes, you can, Tommy," my mother called from the park bench.

She wore her old faded blue-and-pink down coat. The blue and white scarf she'd knitted two Hanukkahs ago was wrapped around her neck. Its tassels fluttered in the breeze.

She gave me an encouraging smile, all warmth and love and tenderness.

"You can do anything, Tommy. You just need faith."

"But it's so hard," I complained. My fingers ached. "I'm not strong enough."

"Yes, you are," she replied in a gentle voice, walking toward me. Her blue eyes shone, deep and wise. "It's all there, deep inside."

"If you say so," I grumbled in the way only an eight-year-old could.

Shifting my grip, I took a deep breath and stretched out a hand, bare fingertips brushing the other bar. The movement made my grip slip more. I reached back frantically with my other hand to catch myself before I fell.

"See?" I cried. *"I just tried, and I couldn't do it. It's too far. Can you help me?"*

My mother stood next to me. The scent of her body wash reminded me of so many nights cradled in her arms as she sang me to sleep.

She stroked my cheek with cold, dead fingers.

"Oh Tommy, how I wish I could. But I can't. You have to do this on your own."

"But it's just so hard, Ma," I sobbed, disconsolate and defeated. *"I'm not strong enough!"*

"You're stronger than you know. Don't give up, honey. Don't ever give up, no matter how bad things seem to be."

I stared into her eyes, soaking in everything I found there, the love, the caring, the knowledge, warming my heart and strengthening my arms. I reached out toward the bar again and gripped it with a firm hand, then grabbed the next one.

"That's it, my love," my mother whispered. *"Now, go. Find her, before it's too late."*

I awoke with a start.

Light filtered into the room between the slit of the heavy drapes cloaking the window. My body was stiff, and I ached all over, but I felt alert and refreshed. I reached for my holo-phone on the nightstand, flicking it on to check the time.

It was nearly four o'clock in the afternoon.

I grabbed a pillow and smothered my face with a groan, then checked my messages. Three more from Gaffney. My stomach rumbled in protest, its gurgling reproach reminding me of how I'd been neglecting it.

After a quick shit, shower, and shave, I found my clothes

neatly folded on a chair. I put them on, marveling at how clean I felt. Maybe it was time I took better care of myself.

As I made my way to the main room, the glorious smell of freshly ground beans tickled my fancy.

"Good afternoon," Mamika greeted as she handed me a piece of delicate white china filled with the black nectar of the gods. "I trust you slept well?"

Leyla was parked on a couch staring at her rig, several empty plates covered with crumbs decorating the table in front of her. Her innocent dominatrix outfit from last night had been replaced by a somber, plain black cotton top with matching mini-skirt and dark canvas slip-ons. Leyla looked up and smiled before returning to her screen. The heavy drapes were drawn away from the long series of windows on the far wall. Grey and gloom covered the outside world, hiding everything beyond except for the continuous rain streaking the glass.

I sat opposite Leyla and sipped my coffee.

"I did," I replied.

"Very good," she continued pleasantly. Whatever irritation was plaguing her yesterday was gone. "Should you require something more substantial than these refreshments, please let me know, and I'll have our chef prepare it for you."

"Thank you," I said, saluting her with my cup.

Mamika nodded once, then moved from the room and out of sight.

"Dammit!" Leyla swore.

"What's the matter?" I asked.

Leyla placed her rig on the table with a loud thud.

"That third signal." She looked at me. "Every time I get close, it disappears!"

Deacon strolled into the room and took the chair beside Leyla. His hair was combed, but sleep hadn't been kind to him judging by the family of luggage stacked beneath his eyes.

"It's not going very far," she continued. "It hasn't left Manhattan for hours."

"Can't you triangulate it based on past hits?" Deacon yawned, leaning forward to look at her screen.

"I've already tried that," she snapped irritably, gesturing at the screen. "There's just no pattern to it, and like I've said before, it jumps around a lot. I've cross-referenced specific street names and compiled a list."

"Don't mean shit to me." Deacon studied the list, then shook his head.

Finishing my coffee, I moved over to them. My eyes raced across the screen, taking in the names associated with the coordinates shown. I nearly turned away when something caught my eye.

"No shit," I breathed. "Leyla, can you provide the names for all the local businesses at the street corners you've got here, as well as dates and times for when the signal was tracked to them?"

"Sure," she replied, manipulating the holo-windows. "I've already done that. Which ones?"

"Just the last twenty," I said.

I got up and paced the room, anticipation and excitement filling me.

"EVI, I need you to pull up Vanessa Mallery's bank statements," I said out loud. "I want you to focus on the week before her murder."

A series of banking entries appeared, projected directly to my retina. I used the movement of my eye to scroll through the entries until I found the ones I was looking for.

"Do you have that information yet, Leyla?" I asked intently.

A map of the city, including a series of specific latitude and longitude coordinates filled the rig's holo-screen. Leyla complemented it with the new list.

"Deacon," I said. "Please give EVI and Leyla access to your HV."

The Confederate pulled his phone from his jeans pocket. He

swiped a few swift commands across its screen, then nodded back at Leyla and me.

"Thanks," I said. "EVI, use my current location to connect to the HV in the living area. Show the list of Vanessa's most recent purchases. Include the address, date and time stamps."

The holo-vision flickered. A second chart appeared next to the one Leyla put together. I walked over to the large screen and gestured.

"What do you see?"

Deacon stepped forward, narrowing his eyes.

Leyla caught her breath.

"Three of those track the same!" she declared.

"A doctor's office, Armin's Coffee House, and some art supply store," Deacon said, and then his eyes widened. "Well I'll be damned."

Leyla stared at the screen.

"The doctor's office!" she exclaimed with a laugh. "That tracks with the second signal from Queens."

She opened a separate window and drew up the building as well as the name of the practice.

"Doctor Tamara Ettelman, General Practitioner," Deacon read, placing his hands on his hips. "That's Mallery's doctor. And we already know about Armin's. What's so special about the third place?"

"Make Me Blush Art Supply," I stated with a fierce grin. "That's where we'll find Vanessa's twin."

The three of us left L'Hotel Internacional in a hurry. Besim remained behind to study the samples she and Stentstrom had taken from the workers. She hadn't provided Deacon any further details other than that she would contact us once she had time to analyze everything.

The pod skimmed along the 'way, avoiding most of the early evening ground traffic already slowed by the continuous rainfall.

Splotches of color emerged from the fog as we came upon billboards and buildings. I wondered if the rain would ever end.

Deacon sat next to me at the control panel, another cigarette smoldering between his fingers. Leyla was plugged into her rig, the tracking program consuming her attention. She sat in the back, humming some nameless tune while she worked. The hacker wore a pair of old headphones that were nearly the size of her head. She claimed they were necessary for her concentration. Apparently, Deacon and I made too much noise.

She missed me sticking my tongue out at her.

"Tom, you created one helluva shitstorm back at Kraze," Mahoney's image spoke above my phone's display. I had called him on his private line. "Gaffney wants to press charges. He's demanding your badge."

I popped several grapes I'd taken from Besim's apartments into my mouth, relishing their sweet tang as my teeth crushed the soft skin of the fruit.

"He can fuck off," I stated between bites. "He's still jealous I graduated ahead of him at the academy. Besides, how was I supposed to know we were going to take down the goldjoy mother lode? Isn't he getting all the credit for the bust anyway?"

"He is, but he's not happy about it," Mahoney chuckled mirthlessly. "I've done what I can to keep him off your ass for now. The DA's office is also doing their part. This case has become a helluva lot bigger than any of us anticipated. I've already spoken with Stentstrom but tell me what you know."

I recapped everything, sparing no detail.

"All right," Mahoney said. "In the meantime, I'll get eyes on Flanagan. I've asked someone reliable to check into EVI's diagnostic. If her security protocols have been compromised, we'll get her back on track as soon as possible. Stentstrom used a ground courier to deliver Besim all the biological evidence, notes, and data he's gathered on Vanessa Mallery since his initial examination."

"My people will make sure the penthouse is secure," Deacon stated, blowing a steady stream of white smoke.

"Good," Mahoney said. "Incidentally, I had a nice talk with Stentstrom. He'd make a fine addition to SCU, if we can ever afford him. But that's a problem for another time."

"Just getting paid would be nice," I grumbled, but without heat. "A man's gotta eat."

"Keep up the good work, Detective," Mahoney chuckled mildly, ignoring my comment. "And let me know what you find."

"Copy that," I said, and cut off the call.

I stared at the phone for a moment, then shook my head.

"He's got faith in you, Holliday," Deacon said. I glanced at him with narrowed eyes, as my mother's dream-voice echoed in my ears. "Saranda too."

"Well, then that makes two people," I grumbled.

"Lighten up," Deacon chuckled. "We've done some damn fine detective work in a short amount of time. We're closing in on them sons of bitches. I can feel it."

Leyla had connected her rig to the onboard nav-system. She superimposed her signal-tracking program over the map, then highlighted all three signal trace histories. A smaller window appeared next to each showing a current view of the street and building, along with its associated latitude and longitude. I had EVI tap into the closest street cams, but with all the mist and rain, there wasn't a lot to see, just vague blotches and shadows with little detail. The third signal hadn't appeared yet, but it was only a matter of time. If anyone was using EVI to keep tabs on us, that was just a chance I had to take. I was banking on Mahoney's man to fix that problem sooner rather than later. There was no way on our end to disable the tracking feature for the implant in my head short of removing it painfully with a spoon.

EVI informed me that ballistics confirmed the .9mm used to kill Stanley and Romero belonged to the mercenaries. However, the bullet that killed Tony was from a .38. I wondered if Julie had changed the plan midstream. Crain was convinced it was she who had directed us to Kraze. It sounded like Julie and Orpheus were cutting bait. But why lead us there? Maybe I hadn't figured out a clear motive for the murder yet, but I had my suspicions. The link between goldjoy and the human experimentation performed on Vanessa Mallery could not be denied. I expected Besim's examination of the samples to corroborate that. There remained so many other questions, though. Why had Vanessa been killed down in the Financial District in the first place? Why not at home, and in private? The more I chewed on it, the more I felt she had been running toward something, rather than away from it.

The grapes were gone, and I picked up my coffee.

"Rumpelstiltskin, Orpheus, and Julie have been one step ahead of us the whole time," I said between sips.

"Well, Julie certainly fucked Crain and his crew," Deacon snickered without mirth. "You think the loss of that lab will shut Rumpelstiltskin down?"

"No," I replied. "Look at everything we found there. That reeks of long-term planning, and a shit-ton of credits. Unless there are more vampires hiding beneath the city streets kidnapping kids and turning them into mindless drug slaves, busting that lab is a major setback for him. But I doubt he's done for good."

"He'll have a helluva hard time hitting back," Deacon said with a wolfish grin. "Taking out Crain has to hurt just as much as losing the 'joy. Rumpelstiltskin is vulnerable, maybe even desperate, and desperate people do stupid shit."

"I'll always count that as a win anytime drugs are taken off the streets. But is Rumpel even our murderer?" I asked pensively. "Or is he something else?"

"The fuck if I know," Deacon replied, blowing little smoke rings.

"I think Julie and Tony knew something was going down the night of the murder, but arrived too late to save Vanessa," I said. "Then there's the 'joy-contaminated wine Besim drank at the nightclub. It's the exact same vintage as the bottles found at all three apartments, except the wine at Vanessa's turned out to be plain Jane. Whatever is in that wine must be really important."

"Well, we don't have any," Deacon pointed out. "Those cleaners got it all before we arrived."

"True. Which brings me back to Tony." I rubbed my jaw and sighed. "We've assumed he became a liability at some point, and I've been asking myself why, but I still don't have a good enough answer."

"Killing him was sloppy," Deacon reaffirmed with a sour note. "Julie knew we'd find him. But if she hadn't done it, we'd never know about Orpheus, or their ties to Crain and Rumpelstiltskin."

"Yeah," I conceded. "His murder pointed us right at Kraze. Julie knew what we would find there. With Crain gone, and the goldjoy lab under wraps, at least one mess got cleaned up."

My voice trailed off as I considered the circumstances. One dead witness killed under the watchful eye of the ECPD. Two dead cops, and another witness, now a major person of interest, running from the law.

Then something clicked into place.

"Julie wasn't just trying to clean up a loose end," I said. "If I'm right, she planted the lighter in that fire pit. Somehow, she beat the cleaners there, or had someone do it for her. She might even know about Vanessa's diary. Eventually, we'd turn to Kraze. Regardless, the lighter was a subtle manipulation to get us to where she wanted us to go sooner rather than later. But that wasn't enough for her. She had to ensure we'd follow her, so she killed Tony to direct our focus on Kraze and *away* from him. She knew we couldn't resist once we puzzled it together. Our murder eyewitness gets killed execution-style just as we realized we have more questions for him. And once we find his corpse, we're hell-bent on hunting Julie down."

"Marrazzo was a fucking addict, Holliday," Deacon countered. "His testimony would've been invalidated in court because of his toxicology report. Your little theory is nice, but it don't explain why she killed him."

Deacon was right. No, the only person who could've corroborated it was Julie, and she wasn't about to help us.

So why kill him?

Unless...

"Yeah," I said slowly as another piece fell into place. "Yeah, he was. EVI, bring up the emergency responder's report on Tony Marrazzo and Julie DeGrassi for me."

A separate window appeared on the HUD, displaying both reports. They outlined in succinct fashion the conditions at the scene, statements from both Tony and Julie, as well as the care provided to both eyewitnesses. My eyes scoured the reports like a drowning man clawing for his last breath.

"Goddamnit, I am such a fucking idiot!" I slapped my hand against the control panel in frustration, knocking my empty mug to the floor.

"Look at Tony's report!" I pointed at several lines of text. "'32-yo/m no sign of injury, answered questions clearly' and 'Pt calm, no signs of intoxication.' Tony wasn't high on 'joy. And you can bet your ass Julie wasn't either. Hell, that probably isn't even her real name."

"No shit," Deacon grumbled. He retrieved the mug and tossed it to me. "Just like Rumpelstiltskin ain't a real name, or Orpheus. Just a bunch of fucking clowns hiding behind masks."

I moved to the beverage station to refill the mug.

"Crain was right," I muttered to myself. "Julie doesn't care if we know about her, or Orpheus, or their ties to Rumpelstiltskin! We've all been played like a fucking violin."

"Come again?" Deacon asked.

"It's all been a set up," I stated as I came back front, holding the mug with one hand as I gestured at the holo-map. "You said it before, Deacon. This whole thing is an elaborate game. I think Julie and Tony went to the club that night, partied with Crain, then Tony jacks up on goldjoy, and Julie somehow gets tipped off something bad was about to happen to Vanessa. Julie pretends a headache, they leave Crain hanging, but instead of going back to Tony's apartment she leads him down the alleyway, knowing Vanessa is in trouble. Hell, I bet Julie called it in to ECPD that night, just as a safety precaution in case things went south. Then they arrive at the scene and are bailed out by the first responders. Only Julie didn't realize the massive adrenaline rush Tony got from seeing the killer offset the effects of the 'joy in his system. Instead of being impaired by the drug, Tony *sees* everything, raw and unfiltered. Julie discovers this when he's checked out, bides her time, and then strikes."

"It don't explain nothing we don't already know," Deacon said, flicking ash on the control panel.

"Because he didn't just see Vanessa in that alleyway," I responded triumphantly. "He recognized the murderer, and that was bad for Julie's business. I bet Tony didn't know shit about Julie's dealings with Crain and Rumpel, the secret experimentation with Vanessa, all the surveillance, the nightclub, the wine, the goldjoy operation. But I also think he was more than just Julie's boyfriend. He was an easy alibi when she needed one, and her eventual fall guy. He and Julie were together for a few months. Now, why cultivate a relationship with Tony Marrazzo? For a quick fuck during her off-hours when she wasn't doing Orpheus' dirty work? No, everything we've seen from Julie so far indicates a very cold and calculating person. She must've needed him for something else, something that connects Tony, Rumpelstiltskin, and Vanessa together."

I set the mug down on the control panel and folded my arms across my chest.

"EVI, please replay our entry into Tony Marrazzo's apartment...minus the breaking and entering, of course," I added quickly, "even though at the time I did have probable cause. Make sure you delete that part."

Deacon shook his head, eyeing me with amusement.

The ER's report was replaced by the recording. We watched it in silence. The high-resolution rendering was from my point-of-view.

"There," I pointed at the screen. "Pause play."

It was in front of me the whole time, right in plain sight.

My grandfather used to say the devil always played in the details.

"What?" Deacon asked, brow furrowed. "What are we looking at?"

"EVI, enlarge and enhance this section I am circling," I instructed, drawing my finger across the image.

"There's the wine rack," the former Protector stated, narrowing his eyes. "And a coffee table with a bunch of shit on it. So?"

"Don't you see?" I said as a slow smile spread across my face. "That 'shit' is marketing material for Wrigley-Boes Pharmaceuticals. Tony worked for Wrigley-Boes. That's the connection! This pharmaceutical company is somehow wrapped up in all of this."

"Julie used her relationship with Tony to get into Wrigley-Boes," Deacon said, as comprehension lit up his eyes.

"That has to be it!" I replied. "Tony's the furthest from their research and development team. A front-man, one of dozens on the payroll, pushing the product, but with no clue as to how any of their pills are produced, or what's in them. To allay suspicion if anyone at Wrigley-Boes got worried, Julie picked some young stud with no brains and a penchant for getting off, who couldn't possibly know anything important. So now she has access to his workstation, his badge, anything to gain entry to their system and facility. Tony must've somehow figured this out after the murder, and she had to take care of him before he blew the whistle on her and the whole goddamn thing!"

"Ho-lee shit!" Deacon laughed. "Assuming you're right, of

course. But that still don't answer who murdered Vanessa, or what Wrigley-Boes got to do with this."

"You're right, it doesn't," I replied, my heart racing. "But it's a damn good start."

The coordinates designating Make Me Blush Art Supplies blinked.

"Gotcha!" Leyla shouted from behind us. "It's the third signal, Doc! Transmitting from the art supply store!"

"Great job, kiddo!" I cheered.

I finished two more mugs of coffee, then checked the SMART gun in its rig.

My skin prickled with excitement. I sensed we were closing in on Vanessa's killer, and finally unraveling the mystery behind it all.

CHAPTER 30

$\mathcal{M}$ ake Me Blush Art Supplies was a quaint corner storefront on the first floor of a twelve-story building surrounded by retail boutiques and cafes. The store boasted a glowing holo-sign of rainbow calligraphy as well as two red awnings for two separate entrances, one on Broadway and the other along Dey. Behind the glass frontage sat pretty displays of half-painted canvases on easels, paints and brushes, and all manner of clays, frames, ceramics, mosaics, furniture and other crafting tools for the artistically-minded. The place appeared to be the fabled Shangri-La of all things artsy in Empire City, at least to my philistine eyes.

With a PhD in English Literature, I'm a devout follower of the written word. When it comes to art, I'm as ignorant as the next guy. I couldn't tell you the difference between abstract, contemporary, hyperrealism, Chagall, Picasso, the guy with syphilis, or the other guy. Visual expression had always been Kate's area of expertise. She enjoyed dragging me around the Metropolitan Museum of Art on shitty days like today in the vain hope of teaching me culture.

"I would not wish any companion in the world but you," I whis-

pered wistfully, my white wispy breath streaming from me before it was carried away by the October wind.

The thought tasted like ash in my mouth. I sighed as thin raindrops pelted my bare head, each one a jarring reminder of the business at hand.

"You say something, Doc?" Leyla's voice buzzed in my ear.

She was playing quarterback from the pod and had already hacked into the store's security feed.

"No, kiddo," I replied. "Just admiring the view."

A Metro pod whooshed past several stories above me. Setting my shoulders, I crossed the street, weaving around vehicles stopped at the holo-traffic signal while avoiding the larger puddles. Despite the weather, a steady stream of pedestrians flowed along the sidewalk, mostly young, up-and-coming business types, and trendy fashionistas wearing the latest outfits, all searching for the next distraction.

A pleasant blast of warm air mingled with the musty odors of wet hair and clothing met me as I stepped inside the store. Deacon waited nearby, glowering at a pair of twenty-somethings who chattered animatedly about last night's raid on Crain's nightclub.

"They say the guy was melted," a blonde with pigtails and tight leggings gushed excitedly. "Like someone lit him on fire!"

"That's so fucked up!" the other exclaimed, a skinny brunette with more face hardware than Kaplan's jewelry store over on Fifth. "Wish I'd been there to see that shit!"

I wandered over to Deacon, who gave me a perfunctory nod. He eyed the place with ill-concealed suspicion and distaste.

"Deacon, try not to look so menacing," Leyla admonished in a motherly tone.

"Shut the fuck up," he growled back, a bit too loud.

The two young women glared at the Confederate.

"Fuck off, old man," the brunette said, bristling with annoyance. "Go find some nursing home to die in."

The blonde made a rude gesture at us as she and her friend exited the store.

"You sure do have a way with people," I observed wryly.

Deacon grinned. With an unspoken word, we made our separate ways deeper into the store.

Along one aisle, I poked at small containers and tubes of paint stored in the tall metal and plastic racks lining the sides. Each showed branding labels highlighting pigmentation, type and style. Soft, folksy music played in the background, pumped through little speakers strewn throughout the store.

"Remind me again how we're going to find the signal?" I muttered under my breath.

"The signal is coming from somewhere in the back of the store, within two hundred feet of your current position," Leyla replied. "The store has a second floor above for classes and workshops. There should be some stairs leading to the second floor, located behind the main checkout area."

"You still can't pinpoint its exact location?" I asked, surprised.

"No," she sounded troubled. "Whatever is cloaking the signal is constantly re-modulating its frequency. It's all I can do to adjust my program on the fly to keep up. I can tell you the signal is there, but that's about it."

"Which means someone's carrying it," I grumbled.

"You can't body search everyone in the goddamn store, Holliday," Deacon snapped in irritation.

"I'll think of something," I muttered darkly. "Just keep looking."

The aisle spilled out into a large open space where the store's salesforce held court. Off to the left was the exit leading out to Broadway. Several customers stood in a queue before a circular checkout counter. Holo-signs hovered above the counter detailing daily sales as well as a list of current and upcoming art workshops. One of the classes, "Fun with Watercolors" hosted by Patricia Sullinger, had started ten minutes ago.

Several feet beyond the counter was a staircase leading up to

the second floor. Past the stairs lay an open space containing long tables upon which sat canvas, frames, and other samples. A closed door with a hand-written sign on it that read "Employees Only" was on the far wall.

I profiled the customers and employees. Some held the age-old bored expression so common to people accustomed to waiting in line for their turn. Others stared at their holo-phones or were engaged in friendly banter. Even the employees appeared polite and mild-mannered.

Just another day of buying art supplies, I suppose.

I reached for the Insight to summon its power, but it slumbered, and I wondered if it needed to recharge, like a battery. So far, the mercurial ability had worked like a champ, but I was in unfamiliar territory now, unaware of my own limits, worried it wouldn't be there when I'd need it the most. The past few days had been a rollercoaster of events full of emotional and physical wear and tear, leaving behind scars I'd need time to process. For now, I couldn't let up. If I stumbled, those responsible for the exploitation and murder of Vanessa Mallery would get away unpunished.

Insight or no Insight, I wasn't about to let that happen.

Deacon sidled over to me.

"My gut's telling me it ain't one of them."

"All right then. Back door, or upstairs?" I asked, indicating the door with my chin.

"I'll take the door," he replied.

"Always took you to be a backdoor man," I joked.

Deacon grunted, giving me a blank expression before moving away.

Nobody got my humor. Their loss.

I swept the area again before climbing the stairs, absorbing the sounds of different voices drifting down from the second floor. At the top, I found another open space separated by clusters of easels, worktables, and several virtual workstations. At the far end, opposite the stairs, squatted a massive oven made from heavy stone and brick. Even from this distance, I felt the heat it generated. Three people wearing gray smocks and heavy gloves pulled out pieces of pottery with flat, fire-scarred wooden spatulas.

I turned away from the kiln to explore the rest of the room.

A class was underway in one corner. More than a dozen easels atop paint-splattered drop cloths were set up in a semicircle facing several tall windows. Rain patterned the glass. Some of the fog had lifted, revealing indistinct images of the buildings across the street. The coffeehouse music was louder up here, reminding me of Armin's. The people behind the easels ranged in age, from late teens to a couple of grandmothers. All of them sat on stools or stood by their canvas, focused on their work. I wandered up to an elderly woman holding a palette in one hand and a thin brush in the other. A deep frown troubled her lined face.

"Afternoon," I greeted in a friendly tone, linking my hands behind my back as I inspected her work.

"Hello," she said absently, then realized I'd spoken to her. She had a nice smile. "Oh, hello! I'm sorry. I didn't realize you were standing there."

"Having trouble?" I asked, offering a critical glance at the partially-painted canvas.

"Nothing behind the door," Deacon reported in my ear. "Employee break room, a bathroom, and an exit out to a side street. I'm headed your way, Holliday."

"Well, this is my fifth class," the woman sighed, her face downcast. "And I still cannot figure out how to blend the shadows and light evenly, without making it all look like one giant mess! The strategy of the composition can be so overwhelming, don't you think?"

"Umm, yeah," I replied, trying to sound knowledgeable and failing. "Maybe if you used more white paint and less black paint, that would help things?"

Her eyebrows shot up, and then she laughed.

"That might do the trick!"

"Is everything all right, Miss Talbot?" a woman with a pleasant voice asked from behind me.

"Oh yes, Patricia," Miss Talbot replied, her smile shy and embarrassed. "I was just telling this gentleman how difficult it's been to come up with the right blend of colors. Your classes are always so insightful, but I just can't seem to put it all together!"

"That's all right," the woman replied, moving up to study the canvas. "These things take time."

My jaw dropped.

Standing next to me was Vanessa Mallery.

"Art may be in the eye of the beholder," she continued. "But true art is born from our hearts and imaginations. I'm certain you'll find what you need. Just keep at it."

I stared. A pod could've rolled through my gaping mouth.

"Hello, I'm Patricia Sullinger," the red-haired woman said with a bright smile. She had gray eyes. "Did Rory send you up? We've only just started, so you can take one of the empty easels over there and set up your things."

She was the spitting image of the murdered girl. A handkerchief, not unlike one Besim wore, wrapped Patricia's radiant red hair above her neck. She wore a colorful blouse and matching skirt, a few hand-crafted bracelets on each wrist, and a long silver chain with small baubles and beads that clicked whenever she moved.

"Um, yeah, Rory," I fumbled, staring at her like some awestruck kid meeting his idol for the first time. Where the hell was Deacon?

Patricia's smile faltered.

"Are you all right?" she asked, concern etched on her face.

Gooseflesh tickled my arms.

"Fine," I said with a weak smile, and stumbled away from them. "I'm fine. Sorry, just getting over a cold. Would you please excuse me? I...I need a moment."

"Doc, what's going on?" Leyla asked in alarm. "What's happening?"

Deacon materialized next to me a moment later.

"Holliday's fine," he said, glancing toward the class before returning his attention to me. "He's just seen a ghost, is all."

Deacon led me to an empty chair over by the kiln. I sank into it heavily, kicking out my legs as I stared at the ceiling tiles.

"A ghost?" Leyla was excited. "What's that supposed to mean?"

"It means we've found Vanessa's twin," I replied, shock and awe coloring my voice.

"Holy shit!" she exclaimed. "You mean the one from the portrait? She's real?"

"Yeah, she's real," Deacon replied sardonically. "Like seeing the dead walk again, only different."

He looked down at me, folding his arms.

"You gonna survive, Holliday? Or do I need to carry your sorry ass?"

"You mind?" I whined with wide-eyed innocence, recovering quickly. "My feet are really tired."

Deacon snorted.

"What do we do?" Leyla asked.

Patricia returned to the front of the class, but I caught her casting curious looks our way.

"Where are we on that signal?" I asked.

"You're right on top of it," Leyla replied. "It hasn't moved in a while."

"Maybe she's wearing it?" I shifted my eyes to Deacon. "A piece of jewelry? One of those bracelets?"

"It could be planted in a light fixture, or in that kiln over there," he grumbled in frustration. "Who the fuck knows?"

A sudden thought hit me.

"Leyla look up the home address for Patricia Sullinger and see if the signal originated from there. It might give us an idea if she has it on her person."

"Hmmm," Leyla said. "It's a Manhattan address. The third signal definitely propagated there. It's on the list of places I made. But from what I can tell, it doesn't seem like the signal ever went into or out of her apartment."

"Well, that's something," I said. "Vanessa had her entire brownstone bugged. If this signal hasn't been inside Patricia's apartment, then maybe she wasn't under as much surveillance as Vanessa."

"Or maybe Crain's cleaners already took out all that tech," Deacon countered.

"Deacon's right," Leyla said. "The original signal from those cameras shut off and hasn't reactivated. Once I discovered the third signal, I've been focusing on it, and ignored the other two. But when I go back over the history of the original one, Patricia's apartment was definitely one of the more active transmissions."

"Which brings us back to here," I sighed, running a hand over my eyes. "Do I walk up to Patricia, tell her she's under secret surveillance by some shadowy organization with a nefarious scheme, and ask her to come with us?"

"Why the fuck not?" Deacon said. "The woman's in danger, Holliday. She just don't know it. Vanessa said she'd found her twin. Maybe she didn't get a chance to tell her what she knows?"

The man had a point.

I slapped my hands on my knees and stood up.

"Stay here," I ordered. "And keep an eye out."

I made my way back to the workshop, passing the students at their easels. Miss Talbot was using more white paint than black. I smiled. Maybe Kate's art appreciation had rubbed off on me after all?

Patricia noted my approach with raised eyebrows and an uncertain smile.

"Feeling any better?" she asked solicitously, tucking a loose strand of her hair beneath the handkerchief with a trembling hand.

"Uh, yeah, about that," I replied, presenting to her my badge and ID and introducing myself. "Could I have a moment of your time, please?"

Patricia opened her mouth to respond when someone with enormous strength shoved me hard from behind, hurling me into the wall with a loud crash. Blank canvases, bottles of paint and palettes flew everywhere.

"What are you doing? Let me go!"

I rolled to my side and into a crouch, gun in hand.

Marko stood behind Patricia, holding her hostage. Gone were the eighties rock star clothes from the night before, replaced by jeans and a flannel t-shirt covered in splotches of paint. One hand gripped her neck easily, while the other was wrapped around her waist. Patricia was white as a sheet, her eyes rounded with terror as tears ran down her cheeks.

Crain's flunky betrayed little as he stared at me with empty, dead eyes.

"You've got nowhere to run," I said in a deadly voice, training the gun on him.

Marko edged a few paces backward, Patricia in tow. I advanced slowly, ignoring the panicked art students as they scrambled from us. Deacon moved opposite me, truncheon ready, blocking Marko's other avenue of escape.

"We can do this in one of two ways, Marko," I said evenly. "Let her go, I'll take you back to the precinct, and then you can tell me all about Rumpelstiltskin, Orpheus, and the murder of Vanessa Mallery. Or I can shoot you right now, you'll bleed all over the place, and we'll just do the rest anyway. Choice is yours."

In response, Marko bent his knees, lifted Patricia off the floor, and jumped backward using his back as a battering ram. The tall window shattered in a shower of glittering shards and broken support struts as Marko and Patricia dropped from sight.

A blast of cold wind and rain buffeted me. I rushed to the sill. One story below, Marko raced along the alley, carrying Patricia over his shoulder like a sack of potatoes.

"Holliday!" Deacon shouted. "Move!"

The Confederate flew out the window after him, landing in a tumbler's roll onto the wet pavement. He recovered instantly and pelted after Marko and Patricia.

"You're not getting away this time, motherfucker," I swore, and leapt out after Vanessa Mallery's killer.

CHAPTER 31

*M*y teeth mashed together painfully as I hit the pavement and rolled the way I'd been trained. It hurt like hell, but I lived, so I had that going for me, which was nice. The fall didn't have to look good so long as you didn't break anything important. With my heart pounding, I limp-ran after Deacon and Marko.

"Doc!" Leyla's high-pitched shriek screamed through my earpiece. "What's going on?"

"Marko's got the girl," Deacon explained before I could catch my breath. "Grabbed her and jumped through the goddamn window."

I tried to add something, but all I could manage were grunts and wheezes.

"Holliday, you taking the slow boat to New Shēnchéng?" he demanded in an exasperated voice. "Where the fuck are you?"

"Right...behind...you," I puffed, slowly gaining speed as my knees settled into something just short of agony.

Flickering lights from vehicles, billboards, storefronts and street lamps painted everything in chiaroscuro. Early evening's gloom had settled in, casting everything else at the edge of the city's coruscation in a shrouded gray slate. The effect made the world appear like I was stuck inside the curved walls of some giant fish bowl.

I reached the end of the alley and banged right following the commotion caused by the foot chase. The rain wasn't helping, but the mist lifted at ground level to give me a better idea of what was happening ahead. Marko's progress was hampered both by the bulk of the woman he carried and the intervening pedestrian traffic, although he still held the lead. Deacon was closing in, shouting for everyone in his path to clear the way. I lurched along, passing loose clumps of startled people waving excitedly in the direction I was moving. At one point, the slight-bodied Marko lowered his shoulder and bowled over several surprised pedestrians as if they were paper dolls without slowing down.

"The signal is on the move," Leyla chattered excitedly. "And it's transmitting and receiving. Tracing it now."

"Determine the signal's point of origin first, girl," Deacon interrupted with a growl.

"I can't," she replied, frustrated. "There's a lot of interference, and it's messing with my program. I'm having a hard time locking onto anything specific. I need to get closer to you guys."

"Son of a bitch," Deacon swore. "Someone's jamming the line. Stay at your post, girlie."

I shook my head as I ran, trying to catch up. Deacon smoked like a chimney yet didn't sound winded chasing after Marko these past few minutes.

And he was also half a block ahead of me. Show-off.

Scowling, I picked up my pace. Somehow, we needed to slow the skinny little bastard down in a way that didn't involve mixing pedestrians with a hail of bullets. Suddenly, I had an idea, and prayed EVI's functionality would be up to the task.

"EVI," I huffed between breaths. "Lock onto...my position... and give me...a current layout...of the streets near me...in a ten block...radius. Include...traffic patterns, irregularities...and account...for the weather."

A split-second later, a color-coded map of the area was uploaded into my visual center, along with a colored dot assigned with my name.

It was hot pink.

I grinned. *That's my girl.*

"Leyla," I puffed again. "Jack...into...EVI's map...and add your...tracking program...to it. EVI, upload...the new program."

I shifted part of my attention to the map as two new colored dots appeared, blue for Deacon and red for Marko. Taking a quick note of Marko's current heading, I made a call.

"Mahoney here."

"Cap'n...it's Holliday," I blurted out in a rushed mess. "No time...for 'splanations. Need you...to get me...override control... for all ground...and pod...traffic signals...for my current...location...in a...ten-block...radius. In pursuit...of suspect...on foot."

He said without hesitation, "You'll have it."

A woman with a gaggle of three screaming kids poured out of a store to my left, and I nearly collided with them. Twisting to the side, I pirouetted around them before careening painfully off a light pole and into the street. I managed to dodge the oncoming self-driving car as its brakes squealed in protest.

Angry shouts floated after me, but I ignored them. I patted the hood of the car with one hand and raced along the sidewalk, checking the map to see how much ground I'd lost. Marko had turned a corner, moving rapidly east along Liberty, with Deacon close behind.

"Detective Holliday," EVI's calm voice announced. "You now have access to emergency traffic control."

Stopping at the intersection of Liberty and Nassau, I bent over with my hands on my knees to catch my breath.

"Deacon, get ready, because the shit's about to hit the fan," I stated between huffs, then stood up straight, appraising the long corridor of mist-enshrouded buildings. "EVI, on the count of three, I want you to change to red all traffic signals at the next two intersections along Liberty Street east-to-west and north-to-south based on my current trajectory. Activate emergency warning sirens and holo-signs, then inform local police and emergency services of the sudden traffic malfunction. Return all traffic signals to their normal settings ten seconds after you've done it. Ready? One, two, *three!*"

The result was immediate. A fanfare of horns exploded around me amidst the squeal of rubber tires, hydraulic brakes, and the shouts of hundreds of very angry people. The frenetic buzz of electromagnetic pulse engines spat with rage as Metro and private pods decelerated suddenly to avoid a collision. A mass of vibrant metal and technology came to a screeching halt, while a wave of humanity surged inexorably toward it like a lodestone to a magnet. Emergency sirens blared, red and orange holo-signs and voice response issued traffic warnings, and EVI informed me more uniforms were on their way. Both Deacon and Marko's dots halted a block ahead. Confusion and noise melted the immediate cityscape into chaos, and I stumbled into action.

"Nice job, Holliday," Deacon proclaimed with grim satisfaction. "He's got himself a crowd now. He ain't going nowhere."

"Deacon, don't engage," I ordered. "I'm almost there. We'll take him together."

I pressed forward, making steady progress as throngs of people milled about in confusion. My chest burned with fire. I crushed my fatigue, refusing to let up now.

"What the fuck!" Deacon exclaimed. A wave of surprise undulated from the onlookers ahead of me. "The bastard leaped across the goddamn street!"

Marko's red dot shifted to the opposite street, moving steadily away. Without responding, I changed direction in a break in the crowd and crossed in time to catch Marko with Patricia still over his shoulder racing down a darkened alleyway. Deacon and I converged at its entrance, and together we pelted after them.

We reached the bend and turned to find Marko facing us several feet away, Patricia lying in a heap at his feet. Seeing her there, so helpless and alone, filled me with rage. Vanessa Mallery must've looked the same several days earlier, in that other shitty alley not far from here.

No one was there to help Vanessa then.

I wasn't going to let that happen to Patricia now.

"End of the line, Marko!" I barked, drawing both badge and gun. "You're under arrest for kidnapping, assaulting an officer, resisting arrest, conspiracy, and the murder of Vanessa Mallery."

The badge flared a brilliant silvery light, bathing Marko and Patricia in its radiance and illuminating the alley's end. The young woman's face was haggard. I couldn't tell if she was still breathing.

I replaced the map with the gun's tactical display. Marko's outline blinked at its dead center. He made no move, and I studied him in the clear light of the badge, taking note of how little expression ever crossed his pale face. Crain's flunky tracked our movements; his cold, emotionless eyes slid slowly from side to side, betraying nothing. He wasn't winded from the chase, or uncomfortable despite the rain and cold.

Uncertainty gnawed at me. Something wasn't right. Marko was already at the art store before we arrived. It made me wonder how long he'd been keeping tabs on Patricia. Why would he need to do that if Patricia's home contained the same surveillance tech as her twin?

Unless Marko wasn't working for Orpheus or Rumpelstiltskin.

I recalled our fight at Kraze, the way Marko handled himself, and how quickly he'd fled when the situation shifted our way. At one point, Marko felt the full brunt of Leyla's frosty wrath, which deflected him aside, yet caused him no discernible harm. Even Crain had been slowed by her icy power.

Deacon witnessed Marko leap across a city street in a single bound, carrying the unconscious girl like she was a stuffed animal. Maybe Marko was cybernetically-enhanced? The account from the cops at the murder scene reported that the suspect jumped straight up, lost in the fog. From my recollection of the alley, the fire escape was more than twenty feet high. Uniforms tried to pursue, but by the time officers reached the rooftop, the suspect was long gone, and without a trace.

Could vampires really do that?

Apart from old wives' tales about night stalkers turning into bats or mist and flying away, this was all new territory for me. But this case was chock full of weird shit, and at that point, I wasn't about to put anything past Marko.

As I surveyed the scene, it was two against one, yet it still felt like the odds were in his favor.

What the hell was he?

"Holliday," Deacon hissed. "Look at the girl!"

Two discolored holes, each the size of my fingernails, marred Patricia's neck.

Marko had already fed upon her.

Dark stains covered his mouth and lips. I watched as Patricia's blood dissolved, devoured by his flesh.

Enough was enough.

With my gun trained on him, I took a few cautious steps forward. Had he tried another jump, I would've poured several rounds in him before he could get away.

Yet Marko didn't so much as flinch.

Worry knotted the muscles of my shoulders.

"Put your hands where I can see them," I ordered in a harsh voice. "And move away from the girl. Now!"

As if in response, a shimmering wave pulsed from Marko, bathing us in its wake before winking out.

"Umm, guys," Leyla's tinny voice burbled in my ear from a long distance. "...interference...centered... not sure...happening... on...way—"

Her voice cut out. The SMART gun's tactical followed a breath later. I reached out to EVI, but there was no response. I tried for the Insight again, but it remained out of reach.

Anxiety and dread settled like bad donuts in my gut.

Somewhere in the distance, the mournful sound of a church bell tolled seven times.

Seven o'clock.

The time triggered something in my mind. According to the sign at the checkout counter, Patricia's class started a little before six o'clock.

Before sunset.

That had to be all kinds of wrong. My heart clenched.

"Uh, Deacon?" I asked, my voice uneasy. "You're the vampire expert. How is it Marko's at large during the day?"

"I've had enough of this shit," Deacon grated, ignoring me.

He held the truncheon easily, body loose and ready for a fight.

"No, seriously," I pressed, more anxious. "Even with all this rain and fog, I thought vampires hated sunlight? Don't they turn to ash or something?"

"Yeah, so what?" he spat. "It's night-time now, and there he is, so let me purge this motherfucker with righteous fire, and call it a day."

"That's just it, Deacon," I replied. "Your truncheon isn't glowing."

The instant he glanced at the weapon in his hand, Marko moved.

Crain had been fast, but Marko made him look slow. Before I could shoot, he crossed the distance separating us and drove his fist into Deacon's stomach. The impact hurled the former Protector against the far wall. Deacon slid to the ground, eyes wide and tearing as he gasped for breath.

I dropped the badge and squeezed the trigger. The gun exploded, blanketing the opposite wall with bullets, but Marko had already dodged, rushing at me with both arms extended. The slippery pavement made him lose his footing enough that I ducked before his hands smashed into the wall, sending concrete shards flying. I rolled sideways and fired again, narrowly missing him.

Even as he moved, Marko's expression remained unchanged. I thought he would've worn the same look folding his laundry. While naked. In the middle of Times Square.

Jesus Christ, what the fuck is he?

"Leyla!" I shouted, but there was no response.

"EVI," I tried via my implant. "EVI, call for backup!"

Again, nothing.

The silvery nimbus of the badge drowned the alleyway, cleansing it of shadows. The sounds of the bustling city were drowned and muted, like echoes from a seashell. EVI had said officers were on their way, but they were probably held up by the traffic kerfuffle I'd orchestrated. By the time they arrived, we'd be dead, and Marko long gone.

Score two for the bad guys.

I fired another burst. Marko evaded it easily. He came at me in a fluid dance. A backhanded slap across my face sent stars swirling in my vision. A second strike clipped my shoulder at the joint. My arm instantly went numb. The gun slipped from my nerveless fingers as Marko shoved me roughly against the wall with one hand.

He pushed against my chest, dead eyes boring into mine.

Slowly, inexorably, I felt my sternum giving way beneath the irresistible pressure against it. I gripped his wrist with my one good hand, pulling with all my fading strength.

There was nothing I could do.

"*In nomine Christi cogimus!*" a strident voice called out, piercing the haze of my agony. "Be rebuked and depart!"

Deacon smashed Marko behind his right ear with a loud snap. The crushing weight against my chest receded and I collapsed to the ground, struggling to catch my breath. Marko faced Deacon.

The Confederate eyed him warily. No white fire coursed along the length of the truncheon.

Needles of pain shot up my arm as feeling returned to it. A bleary-eyed search of the wet pavement revealed the SMART gun scant inches from where I lay. I reached out with my good hand, pulling it toward me. Scrabbling along the wall, I created some distance between myself and the two combatants. I staggered upright on trembling legs and raised the gun to a firing position. I hesitated, lamenting the loss of the tactical display, and anxious I'd shoot Deacon by mistake.

"C'mon, man, get your shit together," I muttered. "You don't need a computer to shoot this guy. You're fucking Doc Holliday!"

Deacon lashed out at Marko, delivering what should have been a debilitating onslaught against the slimmer man. Instead, Marko ignored it, maneuvering with a languid grace as he toyed with his opponent. Infuriated, Deacon redoubled his attack, but the other man was too agile and quick. A lunging feint to Marko's left was met by a matching sweep to the right, enough that Deacon lost his balance and stumbled forward. Marko easily sidestepped, then seized Deacon by the arm and shoulder.

With little effort, he snapped Deacon's arm at the elbow, then drove his face against the wall. The former Protector dropped the truncheon. He slumped to the ground, blood gushing from his nose and mouth. It was the opening I desperately needed.

I shot Marko in the side and leg just below the waist, shredding his shirt and jeans.

But there was no blood.

"What the fuck!" I shouted, firing again.

Marko took several rounds to the chest, their concussive force knocking him back a few steps. He shrugged it off, and in a blur of motion rushed toward me. He grabbed my throat and lifted me off the ground as if I weighed nothing. I couldn't breathe. My entire world wept red with pain.

I slapped futilely at Marko with my hands, but it was like punching the moon. Darkness bled into my eyes.

Then everything went cold.

"Let. Him. GO!" Leyla commanded. Her young voice reverberated with power.

Tendrils of writhing shadow arose from the ground to curl around Marko's arms. The pressure against my throat released, and I gasped for air. The tentacles flung Marko across the alley, but he landed on his feet.

Leyla stood beside me, her body wreathed in a blue and black nimbus of swirling energy. Her eyes where white, and while I couldn't see the monstrous winged shadow surrounding her, I knew it was there. My body ached in places I didn't know could hurt. I could barely move.

"You'll never hurt anyone again!" Leyla shrieked.

She strode toward Marko, arms stretched wide and her fingers splayed open. Jagged, dark crystals of ice appeared in her fingers, and she hurled them at him.

Marko danced between them, twisting his body in ways that defied logic. The ice daggers smashed into the wall behind him. Leyla swept her hands and fingers in intricate patterns, mumbling words that made my ears bleed. More tentacles rimed with ice gathered around Marko, tearing at him, but he leapt to the side and against the building wall, then pushed himself over them to plant his foot into Leyla's chest. She fell to the ground hard, the tentacles melting into harmless wisps. Marko landed beside her and Deacon, then picked up Leyla by the arm and hurled her against the alley wall. I heard something break.

"NO!" I raged, and trained the SMART gun on him, but I was too slow.

He rushed at me, but Deacon swept his leg out at the last second, and Marko crashed to the ground. Gripping the truncheon in his good hand, Deacon hammered the back of Marko's skull. There was a tremendous crack. White sparks surged from the point of impact. Suddenly, EVI's voice was in my ear, and the gun's tactical display came back online.

And with a roar and a rush, the Insight was there.

Everything slowed to a crawl. I made out individual raindrops as they scrawled down from the darkness above, each one unique with its own shape and texture. The light from my badge lying on the wet pavement became a collection of thousands of tiny dots strung together by gossamer threads of ghostly brilliance.

Deacon rolled away from Marko, struggling to stand, his bloody face a map of scars and pain from years of physical and personal abuse. The shadowy white silhouette of a winged man surrounded him, broad yet cloudy. Unlike the black, soulless thing that enshrouded Leyla, this one radiated justice and retribution, loss and failure, and I held no fear of it.

Before I could study Deacon further, Marko regained his feet. I observed the colorful Nexus energies swirling around him, released by the blow to his head. A powerful magic had been blended with inhuman technology to bind and power Marko, unlike anything I'd ever seen.

Marko wasn't a vampire.

He was a machine.

I admired the structure of the synthetic man before me. Fashioned by an exoskeleton of spell-forged steel, Marko was a marvel of magic, advanced robotics and bioengineering. Every part of him was crafted by a singular cunning mind to forge the appearance of both human and vampire. The engineering of his exoskeleton made him proportionally stronger and faster than his flesh-and-bone counterparts. Yet his flesh was organic, as were his hair, eyes and tongue. The intricate network of pores around his mouth, fangs, and jaw could draw away all the blood from his victim down to a cellular level, leaving no trace behind. The blood was safely stored in his lower torso. Even now, Patricia's own swirled within, but not enough that Marko had drained it all.

Which meant Patricia could still be alive!

But something was wrong. Through the Insight's clear vision, I discovered Patricia's blood had already lost its efficacy. Whatever had made it special was gone.

Thin, dying streams of Nexus energy trailed off from Marko and into the night. The damage to his head had disrupted the electromagnetic dampening field responsible for blowing up the bank cameras, shutting down my access to EVI, our link with Leyla and the SMART gun.

Time sped up.

I faced him, my hands steady on the gun. With a start, I realized someone else now lurked behind Marko's eyes. One eye blue and the other red, a cold and calculating intelligence appraised me, then vanished, as if it were never there.

The owner of the third signal.

And the murderer of Vanessa Mallery.

"Heavy ordnance," I snarled.

As Marko came at me, I let him have it, both barrels blazing, shouting with unbridled fury. The powerful explosive rounds shattered his slim form, detonating on impact. Searing heat and shrapnel showered me. I ducked, covering my head with both arms.

The sound echoed and died. Silence crept into the alleyway like a partially-remembered dream.

"That got him," Deacon chuckled painfully.

I grimaced, turning away from the wall to find tiny fragments of Marko smoldering on the ground. A small piece of glittering metal simmered in a puddle next to me. With the last vestiges of the Insight, I caught the outline of a symbol I didn't recognize etched on its surface. I scooped up the fragment and placed it in my blazer pocket.

My phone buzzed. Ignoring it, I rushed to Leyla, returning the gun to its shoulder rig. Blood trickled down her scalp, but she was alive. Relief washed through me as frosty tears dusted my cheeks. Despite protests from every part of my body, I picked her up with great care. Her breathing was shallow. She shivered in my arms.

I hugged her close.

"EVI, get the pod over here," I ordered, heading back the way we'd come. "Also, don't accept any incoming transmissions from anyone. Even Mahoney."

"Affirmative, Detective Holliday."

Deacon managed to carry Patricia with one arm. His other hung at his side, useless and dangling. The former Protector's nose was broken, and both lips had been split wide open, but his blue eyes shone with a fierce fervor.

"We need to get Patricia to safety," I answered. "She's lost a lot of blood."

"I'll let Saranda know to expect company."

"Yeah," I replied in a grim tone. "And they might have itchy trigger fingers."

CHAPTER 32

The pod hurtled along an emergency 'way, one of many dedicated to critical services transports when speed was required. Unlike the municipal 'ways, traffic was very light along these paths. Taking this route back to L'Hotel Internacional would halve the trip time. I poured myself the dregs of what remained in the beverage station, making a mental note to pick up more grounds from Uncle Mortie.

An unconscious Patricia lay on a gurney in the back, wrapped in several thick blankets. Her breathing had stabilized, but her face was still too pale for my liking. The pod contained all manner of emergency medical equipment, including oxygen masks and a defibrillator, as well as a small pharmacy with enough medication to make a tidy profit on the streets. But if Patricia became worse, my PhD in literature wasn't going to be worth a damn.

Leyla sat beside the gurney, a bandage around her head and grave concern etched on her bruised face.

"You sure we shouldn't be taking her to a hospital?" she fretted, chewing on her lower lip.

"Positive, kiddo," I replied. I took a long sip from the black sludge caked in my cup. It tasted awful, but I needed the jolt.

"Enough people have been killed already because of the stuff flowing through her veins. No sense in bringing that kind of trouble to the nice people at EC General. Besides, Deacon says Besim's little private palace has an infirmary."

"Why am I not surprised?" Leyla said with a wan smile. She grimaced as she shifted her weight in the chair. She claimed nothing was broken, but I had a hard time believing her.

"You and me both," I answered with a wry one of my own. "You and me both."

"I wonder how many of these places Besim has?" Leyla mused.

"Who knows?" I shrugged, studying Patricia in the subdued light. She bore neither freckle nor mole, the poster child for perfect skin care.

Throughout the ride, my phone buzzed, but I ignored it. I wasn't ready to discuss anything with Mahoney right now and needed time to digest what I'd seen with the Insight. Meanwhile, Deacon had been attached to his since we left the alley. He refused any help, accepting only the air-sling I'd found in the medical supply kit. I didn't feel like bashing my head against his wall of stubborn pride, either.

When we arrived, neither Giles nor any of the other regular hotel personnel was there to greet us. Instead, five of Deacon's security team, led by the severe-looking woman with brown eyes, waited outside, each carrying a holstered sidearm.

"Gaff, report," Deacon grunted as we piled out of the pod.

Leyla guided the gurney. One of Deacon's security team tried to take over. She fixed him with a warning glare so frosty it would've frozen the sun. I conceded my spot and moved beside Deacon.

"All's quiet, sir," the woman stated in clipped tones. She gave a cursory glance at his arm, then added, "The infirmary's been prepped for your arrival."

Deacon's eyes were bright with pain. His complexion was the color of curdled milk. Nodding once, he led the way into the lobby at a brisk pace. Inside was a ghost town. No guests lounged about, no music played, and none of the employees were present. We moved briskly to the penthouse elevator. Two more security personnel stood guard to either side of the door.

Mamika waited inside the elevator. Some color touched her cheeks when she laid eyes on our cargo.

"This way, please," she instructed. "We will do this in two trips."

Mamika gestured for Leyla and her helper to wheel the gurney into the elevator. She gave Deacon a critical look.

"I'll wait for the next one," he said stoically.

She arched an eyebrow.

"It is my understanding you ran several blocks in the cold and rain, took yet another beating, and had both your arm and nose broken," Mamika replied in a hard tone that brooked no argument. "You are in no condition to wait for anything. Get into this elevator. Now."

They glared at one another for several seconds, neither about to budge.

"Patricia isn't getting any better, so table your biggest dick contest for another day," I said. "Now isn't the time."

Deacon said something very unflattering even for him, then stomped into the elevator. As the door closed, Mamika glanced in my direction with a brief nod and a slight curve of her lips.

Moments later, I found myself occupying one of the thick leather couches of Besim's living room, drinking a tasty *café au lait* and wondering when my muscles would relax. Leyla connected her rig to the workstation and sifted through the data she'd collected during our chase of Marko.

"Shouldn't you be in the infirmary too?" I asked.

"Not now, Doc," Leyla waved me away. "I've got shit to do."

Besim stood by the windows. A fresh bandana covered her head. The drapes were drawn. Squiggly patterns of rain decorated the glass. The penthouse was subdued except for the soft *tap-tap-tap* of the precipitation as it died against the windows.

"How is she?" I asked, setting the porcelain cup down on the table.

"Patricia Sullinger is stable," Besim spoke in her quiet voice. "The *golem* caused her great harm, but I do not believe the damage is permanent."

My eyebrows shot up, intrigued.

"Interesting choice of words," I observed. "I'm not current on Jewish folklore, but even I recognize *golem*. My grandfather used to tell me boogeyman stories by the campfire when I was a kid. Where'd you hear that?"

Besim hadn't moved. Tall and austere despite the rustic clothing, she stared ahead as if deciphering all the secrets hidden within the fog.

"Before I went out into your world, I studied the major religions of your people to gain a better understanding of your various belief systems," she replied. "I felt the knowledge would prove useful in my future interactions with humans."

"Naturally," I said, then changed the subject. "What about Deacon?"

"He is in surgery," she explained, turning toward me. "The break caused internal bleeding and ruptured all of the tendons around his elbow. Detective Holliday, I am afraid Deacon Kole will be unavailable until he has recovered sufficiently to be of use to your investigation."

"Deacon doesn't strike me as the kind to sit idle while someone else does the heavy lifting," I replied. "Do you have a timetable for his recovery?"

"His wants are irrelevant," she answered, and I knew she wasn't solely referring to him. "I require Deacon Kole to operate at optimum efficiency at all times. In his current state, this is impossible. Do you have any other questions for me, Detective Holliday? If not, I must return to my laboratory. Several tests on the tissue samples provided by Doctor Stentstrom require further examination."

My eyes narrowed, but I bit back on the retort simmering in my mind.

"Don't let me keep you," I acceded. "I've got to update Mahoney anyway."

"Very good," Besim replied, breezing past me. "Please pass along my regards to William. Now if you will excuse me, I have work to do."

She exited the room without another word.

"Man, she can be such a bitch sometimes," Leyla said.

She hadn't turned away from the dozens of holo-windows hovering before her. Several of them held a variety of charts displaying signal strength, wavelength, and a few other categories that were all Greek to me.

"Ain't that the truth," I muttered, standing up. "Hey, I'm going downstairs to make the call. You need anything?"

"No, I'm fine," she responded with an absent-minded wave, intent on the information. "Just trying to figure out where Marko's signal went. The break created a tiny window of opportunity, because the signal wasn't ghosting like it had been. Unfortunately, this is going to take a while."

"Let me know if anything pops up," I said, and made my way to the elevator.

Five minutes later, I stalked through the now bustling lobby, across the valet entrance with a one-fingered salute to Giles, and inside the police pod. I had EVI fire up the converters, and we were underway.

"Please take me to the office of Doctor Tamara Ettelman," I answered, sinking into the command chair.

"Her practice is closed at the current hour, Detective," EVI advised. "I can provide you with her patient after-hours emergency number, if you would like?"

"That won't be necessary, sweetie," I replied. "Just display her profile."

It was no surprise there wasn't much on Tamara Ettelman. Her image appeared, an attractive woman with shoulder-length, dark-brown hair and a friendly, freckled face. Everything I read about her was exactly what I'd expect from a fictitious medical professional. She had no criminal record. Her demure educational background contained the obligatory nods to good, but not great, schooling. And she held a laundry list of memberships to professional and social organizations one would expect from a middle-aged doctor living in Empire City. It was a classic smoke screen, like the useful series of half-truths a philandering husband tells his unsuspecting wife.

Ettelman's backstory was so full of shit, her eyes really were brown.

My mind drifted back to Vanessa's diary. Staring at the HUD, I pictured the young woman paying a visit to Ettelman, describing the nightmares plaguing her since July. Yet, despite the prescribed sleep supplement, Vanessa's nightmares had grown increasingly more visceral and distinct. Why would that be? Did the sleep supplements make things worse? And what was Ettelman's part in all of this? Could she be the one responsible for the experimentation on both Vanessa and Patricia?

Then there was the wine. What was in it that was so important? Besim believed it contained something else, a trigger or enzyme of some kind integral to whatever had been done to Vanessa. Had Vanessa's body been a vessel for the final synthesis of the finished product? After all, she was in peak physical condition before her death. Nine and the others had been hooked up to all that equipment as part of the manufacturing process. A single body capable of doing what that entire laboratory did seemed implausible, but then I'd seen a lot of improbable lately. The more I chewed on that though, the more it didn't feel right.

I went back to the diary again. Vanessa had received a phone call. She'd instructed whoever it was to meet her at Armin's. As I regarded the doctor's image, the realization struck me.

Tamara Ettelman was Miss Ponytail. She was the woman Moonbeam described accompanying Vanessa the night of the murder. At some point, Vanessa discovered her doctor's involvement in whatever was going on and demanded the meeting.

I waved the holo-window away.

It was time to call Mahoney.

"Where the hell have you been?" he demanded.

"Sorry sir, but I've had a really long day."

I related most of the details regarding Marko, as well as the condition of both Deacon and Patricia. The bit of metal sat inside my blazer pocket. I didn't mention it, or my final encounter with whoever, or whatever, lay behind Marko's eyes.

"So where does that put us?" the captain asked. "Marko was the murderer, but from what you've said, he was just a tool for someone else. Do you have any suspects?"

"I think we're close," I replied. "But I need to flush out one more lead before I come to any conclusions. I know I've asked a lot already, but can you get me a digital search warrant for Doctor Tamara Ettelman's office? At this stage, I think I have plenty of probable cause."

"Get used to being with with Special Crimes now, Tom," he said. "That badge I gave you is all you'll ever need."

"I understand, sir, but it would be nice to have something official besides that, just in case," I said. "I'd hate to put it to the test, then fuck up the DA's case because I got called out for not doing things by the numbers."

"I'll see what I can do," he said. "What do you think you'll find there?"

"I'm not sure," I replied. "As far as I can tell, Rumpelstiltskin and Orpheus are wrapped up together in this. If the second signal is coming from there, it could just be a remote data collection site for Orpheus. I sneak in, have a look around, maybe get a better idea of what's going on. Any word on Flanagan?"

"None," Mahoney soured. "No one has heard from her, and she hasn't called in to the 98th either. I sent officers to her apartment hours ago, but so far, nothing. I'll call you if she turns up. The good news is EVI's repair is done, but nothing was found in any of her code. If she was compromised, whoever did it got away. And by now you've probably heard about the push for shutting EVI down permanently. Not sure which way that's going to go."

"Yeah, me neither," I said. "I think it's a mistake if that happens. She's far too useful."

"Be that as it may, it's out of our hands now," Mahoney said. "Tom, this investigation has turned into more than just the hunt for a killer. What you've uncovered so far is nothing short of incredible. Human genetic manipulation? Drug trafficking and slavery? Honest-to-God vampires? What's next, a zombie apocalypse?"

"I hope not," I answered. "Although Deacon might get a kick out of that."

We both shared a chuckle.

"I've always known bringing you in was the right call," Mahoney said with pride. "If you can solve this one, we'll surely get the funding we need to make SCU a permanent fixture in Empire City. But watch your back, son. Whoever created Marko can't be happy you broke their toy."

"I'm counting on it. Angry people always make mistakes," I grinned, echoing something Deacon had said earlier. "I'll let you know what I find."

Mahoney nodded once and closed the call.

Staring out the window, I lapsed into a brooding silence, then nodded off.

EVI's announcement of our arrival jolted me awake. Wiping drool from the corner of my mouth, I stretched and yawned, then checked the status of the SMART gun. I had used plenty of its firepower in Rumpel's laboratory and against Marko. The inventory display showed armor-piercing shells were empty, and regular rounds were below half. The gun's readouts also indicated it needed a recharge and cleaning as well as a reload.

"Well, here's to hoping I don't get myself into too much trouble," I muttered, doubly annoyed for not plugging the damn thing into the pod during the ride.

The pod came to rest. A cold drizzle hell-bent on drowning me and the rest of the world one wet drop at a time greeted my arrival. Ettelman's office was down on Sullivan Street along with a little restaurant, across from the Kowalski Medical Center.

I dug both hands in my pockets and dashed across the street. An awning provided me welcome refuge, and I surveyed the neighborhood. A couple wandered past, huddled close beneath their umbrella while speaking in hushed tones. The delightful smell of gravy and garlic bread floated around me. My stomach roared in protest. I glanced longingly at the restaurant. Maybe if I finished up quickly, I'd hit Cacciatore's for some take-out.

The thought of homemade chicken parmigiana and pasta fagioli soup warmed me as I pushed through the door and into the office building lobby. A holo-directory along one wall displayed the names of the various practices and other businesses housed in the building. After a quick search, I discovered Ettelman owned a suite on the third floor. An elevator opened at my approach. Several people filed out wearing heavy coats and speaking animatedly about their evening plans. I smiled politely, then stepped inside once the car was clear.

The third floor was well-lit and quiet. I glanced at my phone. Still no warrant. I hadn't expected Mahoney to come through quickly, even if he or the DA had managed to convince a judge to sign one this late in the day.

I heard the hum and grind of elevator machinery as the car returned to the lobby. Turning to the right, I walked to the end of the white-walled hallway where a blank closed door greeted me.

It was the keyless entry kind, requiring a retina or fingerprint match to open, a surprising level of security given the neighborhood. A small holo-sign next to it proclaimed the office of Doctor Ettelman, and her scheduled hours.

Given the type of door I faced, and without Leyla's technological wizardry, the only way through was blasting it off its hinges. I didn't think the building owner would take too kindly to that.

As I considered my options, the door crept open on silent hinges.

Someone was expecting me.

With gun in hand, I stepped carefully into a small waiting area, complete with coffee table, holo-vision, and two comfortable chairs with thick padding. Three framed paintings hung on the walls, each depicting a seascape scene, similar with those that were found at Vanessa's apartment. A second open doorway across the waiting area led to a carpeted hallway.

Opposite the entrance was an empty receptionist office behind two panes of tall glass. Small signs and disclaimers were affixed to the nearby walls and panes, outlining accepted health insurance plans, standard health service disclaimers, and numbers to various clinics around the area. An end table held several pamphlets describing different health problems, and the types of treatment available.

A lone pamphlet on the receptionist's counter caught my attention.

It was for Wrigley-Boes Pharmaceuticals. "Live life the way you've always wanted" its cover read in bold type.

Frozen in place, I stared at it, the perfect, handsome couple on one side, and the old man in the white lab coat on the other.

"Be welcome, Guardian," a pleasant lilting voice called from down the hallway. I nearly jumped out of my skin. "We would be honored if you would join us."

CHAPTER 33

I pressed against the side of the doorway and peered around the corner. The Insight suddenly roiled behind my eyes, but I couldn't summon its power. I sensed an unfamiliar force at play here, dark and sinister. Strands of an unseen web wrapped around me, suffocating my preternatural senses.

That wasn't good.

My grip tightened on the gun.

"Come now, Guardian, let us parley," her laugh tinkled with genuine amusement. "Had I wished you dead, it would be so."

I stole a glance at the clear glass facing the receptionist's desk. Unless someone was hiding below the counter, I didn't think anyone was lying in wait. Still, there were several other offices on this floor, which meant plenty of places to hide an ambush. Any one of them could contain un-friendlies. I verified my connection with EVI was active. Backup wasn't out of the question, but by the time anyone arrived I'd already be a greasy smear.

I imagined Deacon's voice in my head.

Quit being a fuckin' pussy, Holliday.

In that moment, I really missed the crusty sonofabitch.

"Your fallen Protector cannot aid you," she cajoled, picking through my thoughts like some old spinster at a yard sale. "There is no harm in acting civilized. You have much to gain, and so little to lose."

Cinching up my courage, I crossed the short hallway and strode into the other room.

Ettelman's office was small and cozy, reminding me of my grandfather's book-filled study at the old house in Brighton Beach. It had wood paneling, and more framed seascapes draped the walls. Two padded chairs were arranged before a desk made from real oak polished to a fine sheen. There was no virtual workstation or anything else on its surface. A closed door with a holo-placard reading 'Examination Room' was off to my left.

The delightful scent of freshly-cut roses clung to the air like prom night.

I stifled a sneeze.

Doctor Tamara Ettelman sat behind the desk wearing a white lab coat and round glasses. Dark brown hair was pulled back in a ponytail, stray fronds artfully loose below one eyebrow. Her elbows rested atop the desk, hands clasped together as a look of mischievous anticipation danced on her face. A gold ring bearing a startling emerald was on one finger, sparkling with a captivating inner fire.

Julie DeGrassi stood at ease next to her, a satisfied smirk plastered across her designer face.

"You!" I snarled.

"Nice to see you too, Holliday," Julie said, folding her arms across her chest, daring me to make a move.

"On behalf of the Empire City Special Crimes Unit, you are hereby under arrest for the murder of Tony Marrazzo, and accessory to the murders of Officer Stanley, Sergeant Romero and Vanessa Mallery," I grated between clenched teeth. "Put your hands where I can see them, and don't make any sudden moves."

"Fuck off," she sneered, eyeing me with cold disdain. "You can't arrest me. All you've got is circumstantial evidence, no proof, and no witnesses."

"I've got probable cause." My ears burned as my eyes narrowed. "You were nowhere to be found when I arrived at your apartment. Thought you'd been abducted, but there was no ransom note, and no sign of a struggle, so scratch that off the list. Then poor Tony takes a .38 between the eyes at close range. And now I find you hours later alive and well, and in the office of Vanessa Mallery's doctor, resisting arrest. I can't wait to hear you explain it all to the DA after I bring you both in."

"I don't give a flying fuck what you think," she replied haughtily. "I'm not going anywhere with you, asshole."

"Those officers assigned to protect you? They were my friends, you goddamn bitch," I roared. "You have the right to remain silent."

I yanked the SCU badge from my belt. Its light halted several inches from the two women, held back by an invisible barrier.

What the hell was that?

"Now, now children," Ettelman chided with a matronly smile. The air around her shimmered as the silver played along its edges. "The Guardian only has a short amount of time here, and there is so much we need to discuss!"

"What the hell are you talking about?" I demanded. The Insight hammered to be unleashed, but whatever held it at bay tightened its grip. I winced in sudden pain. It felt like someone had shoved sharp needles directly into my brain. "And who the hell is the Guardian?'"

"Why that would be you, my dear," Ettelman replied, noting my discomfort with amusement. "Such is the role you play in this Game, and might I say your unexpected return to the Board has exceeded my wildest expectations! Now put away that filthy weapon before you hurt yourself."

My vision swam. The pain was excruciating, stabbing everywhere at once.

"Fuck off," I snapped in anger, but my arms lowered as if they possessed a mind of their own.

The emerald glittered. Staring into its depths, the world around me became wreathed in a green, gauzy haze.

"My dear Guardian, there is no need to be rude," Ettelman purred in a voice dripping with honey. She gestured with a languid wave of her bejeweled hand at one of the chairs. "Your quest for the truth has brought you to my parlor. Now, sit."

My resolve slipped. I ran my fist clutching the badge across my eyes, and lurched backwards, bumping into one of the chairs. The slight contact sent a stream of agony shooting along my leg. I staggered, catching myself on the arm of the chair before I fell.

"What...what are you doing to me?" I stammered, staring down at the champagne-colored carpet.

Cold and heat alternated for control of my body. I shivered, wracked by a sudden fever. With unsteady hands, I holstered the gun.

"I have done nothing, my dear," Ettelman replied mildly, although her eyes told a different tale. "However, you seemed bent on a most distressing course of action. One that would have ended poorly for you, I'm afraid."

I sat down. The moment I touched the chair's padding, the pain vanished. I sucked in a deep breath. Sweet relief washed over me.

"Much better," she said primly, adjusting her spectacles. "Now, I believe introductions are in order. You are already acquainted with my Handmaiden."

Julie inclined her head, watching me intently.

"You're Orpheus," I spoke haltingly, heart racing.

My thoughts scattered like sand in a breeze. The emerald filled my vision, engulfing everything else. The Insight pounded at the fringe, a chained force desperate to be unleashed.

"Very good!" Orpheus clapped her hands in delight. "I found the tragedy of the original story appealing and adopted it for this little charade. To bargain with Death, only to be thwarted in the end! Melodramatic, and utterly human."

"Who are you really?" I managed. My tongue was thick inside my mouth. "Ettelman can't be your real name."

"Well, of course it isn't," came her cherubic laugh. "No, my dear, my name is not important. After all, what is in a name, hmm?"

My head swam, but my body was made of lead. I was anchored to the chair, arms and legs unable to adjust. The scent of roses was overpowering. I reached for the Insight again only to run into a barrier, a fortress of pure will dwarfing anything I'd ever encountered. My thoughts railed feebly against it.

"Oh no, Guardian." Her smile turned sad and cruel as she observed my struggle. "You are not ready for that. Another time, perhaps."

"Then just kill me," I spat in anger, furious at my body's futility. "You've got me where you want me."

"And spoil all of my fun?" Orpheus pouted, with a dismissive wave of her hand. "Absolutely not. No, my dear Guardian, your return to the Board has changed the entire complexion of the Game. It has brought an unexpected and delicious wrinkle, one that I find most intriguing."

"What do you want?" I agonized, unable to do more than squirm in the chair. "Why are you doing this?"

"Because I enjoy it," she answered mildly. "And because I am curious. It was my desire to lay these tired, old eyes on you, and take your measure, as in days' past."

"What the hell does any of that mean?" I tried to get comfortable, but my body wouldn't cooperate. A lump of clay had more mobility than I did.

"It means nothing to you, yet," Orpheus replied, folding her hands neatly together. Her smile was filled with malice. "By now you've deduced Rumpelstiltskin is responsible for poor Vanessa and Patricia, as well as those wretched abominations he kept at that despicable nightclub. Despite the knowledge I bestowed upon him, Rumpelstiltskin is bound by certain constraints, and thus limited in scope. The fool was tasked to create life, and like the tragedy of my name, he failed to keep faith. Sadly, his works are all flawed, and he thought to hide this from me. Playing at God is not for amateurs, Guardian. Such audacity cannot go unpunished. Rumpelstiltskin lacked vision, and his mishandling of this entire enterprise is unacceptable. It is now my wish for him and all his works to be removed from the Board. You are but one of my instruments."

My taut muscles strained against the invisible bonds coiled around my body. I clutched the SCU badge in my fist, unable to let it go. I closed my eyes, but the image of the emerald was there, something I couldn't erase. Trapped within its endless expanse of green, I was vulnerable and exposed, a marionette held by twisted strings.

"Poor Vanessa. Innocent until the very end," Orpheus continued with a hint of sadness. "When she discovered the truth, she demanded we meet at that deplorable coffeehouse. And for what? To accuse me of ruining her life? I saved it! If not for me, Rumpelstiltskin would never have developed the enzyme to sustain his faulty creations! Alas, there was nothing more I could do. What was done, was done. When I discovered the truth, Vanessa's usefulness, her purpose, no longer mattered. A blessing, perhaps, that her life was taken while she remained vibrant. Poor Vanessa and Patricia, like Eurydice before them. They are mere shadows whose lives are specks of light in a vast ocean of nothing."

"I...don't...understand," I said. My will was fading. Orpheus' voice sounded far away. "What...was...her...purpose?"

"Why, to sacrifice herself for me, of course," Orpheus answered with a small smile.

"You're…insane," I mumbled.

"How provincial." Orpheus frowned, her lilting singsong voice lulling my mind further down a dark emerald hole. "I had expected more from you, Guardian. A man of vision, perhaps. A worthy challenger to the Game. Alas, I see I am to be disappointed again. No matter. Like Vanessa, so too shall you turn to dust. *Thou know'st 'tis common all that lives must die, passing through nature to eternity.*"

Helplessness and despair seeped in, freed by the collapse of my will at the hands of whatever power Orpheus held over me. Those feelings flourished, a wasting disease that attacked my faith, and devoured my conviction. My past arose to haunt me, the constant abuse to my body and mind through drugs and alcohol, the loss of friends and family, my career, everything relived again moment after excruciating moment. A whirlwind of sensations rushed through, unimpeded by any sense of structure or purpose. I was a drowning man in a desert, unable to escape the prison of my own failures.

There was no one here to help me, no ally I could call on.

I was alone.

Images of Kate appeared, lying lifeless in a tub full of water and blood, and I broke.

"He's weak," Julie said from afar, scorn lacing her words. "What threat could he possibly be? Let's be done with him."

"Perhaps you are right, my Handmaiden," Orpheus pouted. "And he had such promise!"

"He's outlived his usefulness anyway," Julie scoffed. "Grant me the pleasure of ending his life, mistress. I deserve as much. Then I'll find Rumpelstiltskin, and finish this."

"Make it so, my Handmaiden," Orpheus sighed dramatically. "Rumpelstiltskin must know the price for his failures. However, the theft of the blood by the servant of my brother is an insult that will not be tolerated. My plans must change."

"Must they?" Julie asked. "How did he even know?"

Orpheus chuckled without mirth.

"How quickly you forget, we are family. My brother and I, and the others yet to come, breathe cunning and deceit like you draw air. It matters little how he discovered our arrangement with Rumpelstiltskin, only that he did. And so, let my brother keep the blood of Vanessa Mallery, for what little good it will do him. Still, it would have been far more exquisite had the Guardian thwarted both Rumpelstiltskin and my brother simultaneously. My designs shall continue regardless of his interference."

Choked with emotion, my eyes ran hot with tears, and I opened them.

The familiar sight of old white scars crisscrossing my wrists greeted me, stark mementos of one of the worst moments of my life. Seeing them, raw and real, was a bucket of cold water splashed in my face. I shook my head, clearing some of the emerald fuzz caking my mind. The hold Orpheus had on me sloughed off, enough for me to get my bearings.

Instinct told me the more I struggled, the tighter became her grip. Instead, I concentrated on the stone sparkling on her finger. As my vision plunged further into it, I discovered the tiniest imperfection at its swirling heart. It was a fissure so gossamer thin, not even the finest jeweler in the world could have noticed it. Something about that imperfection filled me with hope. My hand squeezed the badge tighter. Its edges bit into my palm. A trickle of blood rolled off my flesh. The sudden sting jolted my senses. I relaxed my grip without dropping the badge. A rush of cool thought filled the vacuum of my mind, and clarity returned.

The Insight remained under wraps, but my tongue loosened as I settled more comfortably in the chair. Full range of movement was restored, and with it, a dull anger whose heat I directed at the women before me.

"I'm not done yet, not by half," I grated, narrowing my eyes. Although I could've reached for the gun, I left it in its holster, instead folding my arms across my chest. "But since we're on the subject, why don't you fill me in on what's really going on?"

Julie bristled, but Orpheus raised a silencing hand.

"Very good, Guardian." She nodded in approval, appraising me again. "Very, very good. I see now why you were chosen."

I ignored the comment.

The green of the gemstone slowed to a crawl, no longer drawing my attention.

"Who is Rumpelstiltskin?" I asked. "The name isn't in keeping with the whole Greek theme you're peddling. He another one of your hand-men?"

I grinned at Julie who answered it with a petulant scowl.

Orpheus' lazy smile returned.

"It suited him. An imp of a man spinning human waste into goldjoy," she replied, leaning forward, licking her lips in anticipation. "Shall you guess his name, then? Three tries, like the story? Should you guess true, then I shall answer one question! And if you fail, then a debt shall you owe me."

"I'm not interested in playing your game, Orpheus. And besides, I already know who he is," I bluffed with conviction. After seeing the Wrigley-Boes brochure in the waiting room, I had a pretty good idea where to look. "I just came here to close out a lead."

"Bullshit," Julie said. "You've been running around with no idea what's really going on. Fucking amateur."

"Then why don't you enlighten me, sweetheart?" I kept my eyes on Orpheus as I delivered my rejoinder. "You're dying to do it. You can't help yourself. And it's why you haven't let your hand-bitch here take me out."

"Oh, Guardian, I have missed you so!" Orpheus cackled with glee, clapping her hands again. "It has been far too long since we last faced one another!"

"What the fuck are you talking about?" I exclaimed, exasperated. "All this 'Guardian' and 'brother' and 'Game' bullshit? What the hell does any of it mean? And what does that have to do with Vanessa Mallery?"

"Why, nothing, and everything," she smiled enigmatically. "Your world has changed, doorways have opened, and old things return that have not seen this sun in an age." Her eyes took on a dreamy, romantic cast. "Humanity is upon the brink of a new era, Guardian, one it has forgotten through the vast span of time and technology. Pieces such as Vanessa, Patricia, and David Crain are but harbingers. However, with your return, the Board is now set."

Her fingers traced patterns over the smooth surface of the desk, traversing the whorls and knots of its wood with a lover's touch.

"And the stakes?" Orpheus breathed with excitement. "They go far beyond base, material things such as reputation or land or wealth."

"Such as?" I asked, although I already knew the answer.

"Why, power, of course," she said with a Cheshire grin. "What else is there? But no matter. Our audience is at an end. It is time for you to finish what was set before you. As for my brother, he is already on the losing end of this round. I shall savor every tasty morsel of it."

"That's it?" I retorted, the color rising in my cheeks. "You spout a bunch of nonsense, and then you think I'm going to let you and your hand-bitch waltz on out of here?"

"You desire justice for the murdered girl!" she replied with a deep, cruel laugh. "And all those poor scraps of crude flesh Rumpelstiltskin kept in his basement! How rich! I had forgotten how much I've missed your probity, Guardian! The self-righteous can be so tiresome, but you wear yours like a badge of honor. No, Guardian, I should think your next course of action is obvious. Since justice is what you seek, then you shall find it in the lair of Rumpelstiltskin."

The gun was in my hand faster than thought.

"You aren't going anywhere," I growled, pointing it and the

badge at the two women. Once again, the silver light halted inches from them.

Orpheus regarded me with cool detachment.

"Until we meet again, Guardian."

"Next time Holliday, you won't be so lucky," Julie taunted, laying her hand on Orpheus' shoulder.

Then they vanished as if they had never been.

CHAPTER 34

The scars on my wrists throbbed with a hollow ache. I stared dully at the cuffs of my shirt sleeves, wondering if the pain would ever recede.

"As tyme hem hurt, a tyme doth hem cure," I muttered.

The years passed, but time had healed nothing. Sorry Chaucer.

"You barely touched your bagel!" Myrna admonished, rousing me from my troubled thoughts. "Whatsa matter, bubbe?"

She refreshed my mug, wearing a frown so deep you could bury treasure in it.

"Just got a lot on my mind, that's all," I sighed, offering Myrna the wrinkle of a smile. "Don't worry about me."

Myrna wasn't convinced.

"I been worrying about you since deh first day Heschel brought you here," she said. "You were so pale and skinny! Look at you now. Nothing's changed. Have you slept? All dis running around. Is not healthy. You need to eat."

Myrna stepped close, and with a familiar gesture, brushed the hair from my eyes.

"I know just deh ting." Her eyes brightened. "Mortie baked a fresh batch of rugelach. Dey are to die for! I go in deh back and fetch you a plate."

"How can I refuse?" I replied in weary amusement, suddenly nine years old, and just as awkward.

"Don't." She'd already turned away, heading for the kitchen. "And don't go running off!"

"Where would I go?" I mumbled, but Myrna was gone.

My eyes strayed back to the table, falling between the twisted piece of Marko-metal and the Wrigley-Boes pamphlet. My mug separated the two, filled with the perfect blend of bean and sugar, enticing me with its promise of wholesome goodness.

I wasn't thirsty.

"What are you?" I asked the metal fragment. "Who made you? And why?"

The alloy stared back at me unimpressed, mystifying me with its silence. The fragment held no voice, yet the secrets it contained spoke volumes. And then there was the pamphlet. I studied the pictures on its glossy surface underneath the blue, white and gold Wrigley-Boes logo.

The young couple in the prime of their lives, smiling and happy.

The older man in the white lab coat off to one side, hard at work surrounded by his lab equipment. I imagined him conjuring alchemical magic to produce the innocuous little white pills Wrigley-Boes foisted on a populace craving prolonged health.

Their catchphrase in big, bold letters promised improved stamina, weight loss, increased sexual prowess, and keeping you that way.

Just take our products, see the results, and stay healthy forever. What a crock of shit.

I'd ridden in the pod around aimlessly for hours before realizing I was hungry. I had waited beneath the stoop to the backdoor of the deli until Uncle Mortie and Myrna arrived. Thankfully, they always opened shop at five on the nose every

Friday to get a jump on the Jewish sabbath crowd. The rain hadn't let up, and the early morning had plunged to near freezing. After one look at me, Mortie unlocked the door and held it open. Myrna fired up the coffee pots without a word.

I sat in a booth by the long window, while Mortie went about his daily routine doing prep work in the kitchen. Dozens of customers would be coming by to pick up their deli orders in a few hours. Their daughter Shayna wouldn't be in for another hour, so it was just Mortie, Myrna and me holding down the fort. Outside was dark and dismal, but inside the deli was warm and quiet, and right then, I really needed both.

My mind drifted back to Orpheus. After their disappearing act, I did a quick search of the office. It revealed nothing I didn't already know. Two holo-projectors were concealed in the upper corners of the ceiling, aimed at the desk and chair.

Had everything been staged?

Your quest for the truth has brought you to my parlor.

The echoes of Orpheus' voice intruded upon my quest for calm.

Sadly, his works are all flawed. A blessing, perhaps, that her life was taken while she remained vibrant.

Not for the first time, the image of Vanessa lying cold on the metal table of Stentstrom's examination room came across my mind. It haunted me, her red hair framing a body without scar or blemish, other than the vicious tear by her throat that ended her life. Patricia might have wound up like her, if we hadn't intervened.

And for what? If Orpheus was to be believed, whatever experimentation that had been performed on Patricia would eventually end her life too.

Your world has changed, doorways have opened, and old things return that have not seen this sun in an age.

My eyes roamed out the window. A low morning fog draped the streets in its clammy embrace. Here and there, people shuffled along wrapped in their own solitude, thin shadows flitting in and out of the mist.

As if they'd been reborn.

I shivered without understanding why.

With your return, the Board is now set.

Orpheus had made the word sound like it was something concrete and tangible, and not some prosaic metaphor. She made no bones about wanting power, or at least something as profound. But what? And why?

Whatever this game was, she'd been playing against her brother for a very long time. Who knew how many others were a part of it? And how did Vanessa and Patricia figure into it all? Or were they just collateral damage, some by-product of the twisted machinations of your not-so-average, garden-variety megalomaniacs?

I had thought we'd stumbled onto some sort of secret corporate war, competing financial giants who had routinely crushed the little guys on a whim to achieve a more profitable balance sheet. The further this investigation went, the more convinced I was that it ran deeper than that, with stakes far more malevolent.

And what was up with that weird emerald on her finger? The way Orpheus had manipulated my mind frightened me, and I still wasn't sure how she'd done it. She and Julie had been holograms for chrissakes! Could a gemstone really possess uncanny power, a talisman you'd read about in some fantasy story? Or was it all parlor tricks, using light and smell and sound to confuse and disorient me? Regardless of the method, her influence over my mind had been real enough. And I hadn't imagined the monstrous will hiding behind that pretty smile either.

Who the fuck were these people?

As usual, too many questions and not enough answers. However, I was certain of one thing.

I'd been set up from the start.

Orpheus was both surprised and pleased at my return to her

board. That meant someone else wanted me in play, someone who already knew about Orpheus, probably her brother, and a helluva lot more besides, but hadn't bothered to let me in on any of it.

Someone who had wagered big that I'd shake things up.

I shifted uncomfortably in my seat at the thoughts crowding inside my head. The hum of Mortie's meat slicer buzzed its soft, steady song, mingling with the drip-drip-drip of the battalion of coffee makers at Myrna's command. I needed to wash the scent of roses away. The homely smell of the deli was the perfect antidote.

Myrna returned carrying a plate brimming with chocolate-filled pastries sprinkled with diced walnuts. They looked divine, and my mouth watered. I popped one into my mouth, savoring the blend of cinnamon and nut and cocoa. The second and third one went down without much of a fight.

The little bell above the front door jingled, but I didn't move.

Besim slid into the seat opposite me. She wore the heavy long-shoreman coat. Her head was bare, the tattoos prominent and dark. Somehow, Besim managed to look both old and young all at once. Her race was so different from humans, and yet, with far too many similarities I simply couldn't ignore.

"Get you anything, dear?" Myrna asked.

"No, thank you," Besim replied.

"Can you give us a minute?" I asked.

Myrna searched my face briefly, then walked back to the kitchen.

I didn't offer Besim any rugelach. Lifting the mug with both hands, I held it before my lips. I savored the warmth as wisps of flavored heat radiated upward. Besim glanced at the metal frag-ment and pamphlet, a slight frown creasing her brow.

"You disabled your phone," Besim stated in a quiet voice, a bit of reproach tainting her tone. "No one knew your whereabouts, not even Leyla. I nearly instructed Mamika to find you. Instead, I waited, trusting in your safe return."

"What are you, my mother?" I snapped in irritation. "I wasn't in the mood to talk. Besides, Mahoney could've had EVI track my location."

I sipped at the scalding coffee, wincing in appreciation.

"Damn, this is good. You sure you don't want any?"

"I considered contacting William, but the hour was late, and I was aware he had other administrative items of import requiring his attention," she said. "Instead, I speculated you would return to a place of comfort, somewhere you could gather your thoughts unimpeded by any outside influences. From there, it was not difficult to deduce where you would go. Given the hour, and your predilection toward that particular beverage you enjoy, I chose here."

"How very logical of you," I muttered darkly. "You'd make a great profiler for the ECBI."

I grabbed the sugar and poured some into the mug. Besim observed with her customary detachment as I stirred the contents with a spoon. The white crystals were devoured by the black abyss of java, leaving behind no trace.

Seemed like there was a metaphor there, but I wasn't in the mood.

"Deacon Kole agreed."

"The surgery went well?" I asked casually, hiding the sudden concern I felt for the former Protector.

"He is resting," she replied, tilting her head. "The damage has been repaired. He will have full range of movement after he convalesces for several weeks."

"Good," I said, returning to my coffee.

"Leyla also wished to accompany me, but hide it though she might, her injuries suffered at the hands of the *golem* required observation and rest. In addition, I felt her continued research into the communication signals outweighed any worry she might have for your well-being. How went your investigation into the physician of Vanessa Mallery?"

"Ah yes, that," I placed the mug down, wiped my lips with a

napkin, and leaned across the table so that inches separated us. "Maybe I am in the mood to talk after all."

Unperturbed, Besim studied me behind her Vellan veil, enigmatic and aloof. Her placid demeanor was really getting on my nerves.

"I met Orpheus, and wouldn't you know Julie DeGrassi was with her," I stated, the blood rushing to my face. "Seems Orpheus and Doctor Ettelman are one and the same. At a guess, probably as a way of keeping tabs on Rumpelstiltskin's experiments. Anyway, we had a nice chat about Vanessa, Patricia, Rumpel, something about a game, a board, and her brother. Seemed damn important, but I couldn't tell you what any of it meant."

I paused to let that sink in, but Besim didn't respond, so I plowed ahead.

"I heard all about how pathetic I am, and that I know nothing about what's really going on, which is certainly true. Come to think of it, my favorite part was getting mind raped by whatever magical whammy she threw on me. Still haven't figured out exactly how she did that, but I'm a strong-willed guy, and managed to break her hold all the same."

"Oh, and she kept calling me 'Guardian,'" I continued, my voice lowering, every word laced with outrage. "She went on about so many different things, as if we were old gym buddies or something."

Besim regarded me.

"Aren't you going to say anything?" I snapped, then fell back in the booth with a heavy sigh. "It wasn't coincidence I was chosen for SCU. And all that bullshit Bill fed me about doing good and helping others? Oh sure, it sounded nice, but it was all for show, wasn't it? Were you ever going to tell me what's really going on?"

Besim blinked once, then reached out and took the Marko fragment between her forefinger and thumb, rubbing it thoughtfully.

"After the case had been resolved," she replied. "It was neces-

sary for you to approach the investigation free from any precon-
ceived prejudices. My concern apropos your past record of
substance abuse, rehabilitation, and attempted suicide outweighed
the critical success you enjoyed as a downtown homicide detective. Further testing was required to ensure you were no longer
tainted by your prior transgressions."

"Wow, I'm not sure whether to thank you or punch you in the
face," I retorted. "You're telling me this investigation has been
some goddamn experiment?"

"A test of your faith and resolve, if you will," came her mild
reply. "As well as confirmation that none of your skills had atro-
phied since your time in rehabilitation. And thus far, you have
performed admirably."

"Jesus Christ, woman!" I exploded, throwing up my hands in
disgust. "What the hell does that even mean?"

She placed the metal piece on the table.

"It means there remains an investigation to conclude."

I sucked in a deep breath, held it, then let it out slow.

"I'm not interested in being your tool that you can order about
like Mamika and the rest of your goddamn puppets. And I'm not
doing jack shit until you give me some insight into what's really
going on."

I picked up the mug again, held it, but didn't drink.

"Insight," she said as a smile curved the corners of her lips. "A
singular ability you possess, Detective. In my experience, no other
on this world sensitive to the mystical energies of the Nexus
wields it. Have you ever considered why the Insight chose you?
Why you are a part of it?"

The hair on the back of my neck stood up. My heartbeat
throbbed loud in my ears, and behind my eyes I felt the Insight
stir.

"After the family of William Mahoney was slaughtered by the
shade of the serial killer Mark Madsen, he left Empire City and
explored the world," Besim continued before I could answer.

"Little did he know a greater purpose had set him on this path. William had been a worthy protector of your enclave, an upright man known for his honesty, a man of the law and the people. The death of his family, however, made him realize more was needed to defend his enclave from threats pedestrian methods could no longer handle.

"Many years before, I left Vellas, wandering the human enclaves of the European Block, learning from your people, their similarities and differences. When William and I found one another, what he considered serendipity, I knew was something greater. Our paths intertwined, destiny called, and we answered."

I tried not to roll my eyes but didn't succeed.

"Maybe you should've let destiny go to voice mail."

"I understand your skepticism," Besim said primly. "But please hear me out."

"I'm still drinking my coffee," I said, and nodded toward the window. "And technically I'm not on the clock yet. Fire away."

"There are many things on which my people and I disagree," Besim stated with conviction. "My interest in humans and your culture being chief among them. Such a remarkable species, you humans. Full of creativity and pettiness, hatred and love, passion and principle, mired in both altruism and cruelty."

She paused, and for the first time I witnessed her internal struggle, a tightening of the eyes, a slight quiver of the lips.

"Our own sordid past," she explained slowly, gazing down and away at something only she could see. "Our rise and fall from our home of Evenir, and the adversary from which we fled, is a guarded secret not to be shared with anyone outside of the Pure Blood."

She looked up at me, and her gray eyes filled with resolve.

"But I sensed a change here after decades of silence, hints and reminders of things from our past, and I could not sit idly by and watch your world suffer the same fate as ours. I knew something had to be done, and thus began my search."

"Your search," I asked. "For what?"

"Why, for you, Thomas Henry Holliday," she said with a sad smile. "It is why Orpheus called you Guardian, for she recognized you for who and what you are. Only the Guardian may wield the power of the Insight, and truly see the fell, dark forces at play in this world. It is why you were chosen for Special Crimes, and why you are the only one who can bring justice for the fallen, for Vanessa Mallery, and those like her."

CHAPTER 35

"*G*ive me a break," I scoffed. "You expect me to believe this horseshit?"

"The Insight is a gift," Besim responded calmly. "How it is bestowed, and who is deemed worthy, remains a mystery, even to me. Know that you were chosen, and as Guardian, to you falls the task of safeguarding Empire City from fiends such as Orpheus and Rumpelstiltskin."

I shook my head and said, "Sorry, Besim, but I'm not buying into fate, your Vellan mysticism, or whatever the hell this is."

"You are the Guardian of Empire City," she stated. "The Insight is within you. There is no other. That is a matter of indisputable fact. Deny it if you wish, but even you must wonder why you possess it."

"I refuse to accept that, let alone the notion there's only one 'Guardian of Empire City,'" I shook my head at the absurdity of it all. "I'm not some golden child, Besim. I live and work in the real world. I go after criminals, arrest them, then do it again, and hope I don't get killed in the process. I do it because it's my job, I've got the training and it's the right fucking thing to do."

"What I speak is the truth," she replied firmly. "Whether you accept it is your own decision. I cannot compel you to be the Guardian."

"I see, so free will and all that, eh?" I said full of scorn. "Well, at least I have that going for me. For a second, I thought I was being railroaded into my new career. I actually get to choose how I get fucked. I mean, it's not like you've manipulated this whole thing from the start. Oh wait, you did."

"Detective Holliday." Besim managed a reproachful look, infuriating me further. "I had hoped your decision to join the police force would be sufficient cause to accept my word. Despite a life as tumultuous as yours, your law enforcement career has been a testament to your conviction to the sanctity of protecting those who cannot protect themselves."

"Oh yeah, pushing paperwork around and being everyone else's errand boy has been a real dream these last few years," I said. "Seriously, why are we still talking about this?"

"Because now you are needed," Besim urged. "Vanessa Mallery, an innocent girl murdered through means both technological and arcane. Her body, and that of Patricia Sullinger, used for unnatural experimentation as part of a nefarious scheme, the purpose of which has yet to be revealed. Diabolical forces engaged in some larger game with human lives used as pawns for their amusement. *This*, Detective Holliday! This is what you were meant to do! To protect, and to serve. Surely the untimely death of Kathryn Foster would possess sufficient inspiration for you to assume the mantle of Guardian, if nothing else?"

My world burned black and red. The Insight's distant thunder had been rumbling in my ears since Besim started talking. Now it roared, drowning out whatever Besim said next.

"Don't you dare bring her into this!" I shouted, angry tears streaking my cheeks.

I rubbed the scars, painfully aware of the puckered flesh beneath my trembling fingers. The Insight seethed, but I exerted my will and refused to let it overtake me. I had no desire to see

Besim as she truly was right now, or anything else, for that matter. All I wanted to do was crawl down some deep, dark place, curl up, and never be bothered by murdered girls, vampires or tattooed Vellans again.

"She's none of your goddamn business," I jabbed a finger at her. "You got that?"

"As you wish," Besim replied. She placed the fragment atop the Wrigley-Boes pamphlet.

Although the rain hadn't lifted, the early morning gloom settled into a somber shade of dull gray heralding yet another soggy day. Myrna and Mortie were engaged in small talk, but I could feel their eyes on me. Their voices carried through the open service window separating the counter space from the kitchen.

"Rumpelstiltskin remains at large," Besim said quietly. "He must be stopped before others suffer the same fate as Vanessa Mallery."

"On that we agree," I stated, my anger settling into a dull rage as I drank the last of my coffee. "I'll finish this, and then I don't want to see you, or any of your people ever again."

I pulled out my phone and called Leyla.

"What's up, Doc?" I heard the concern the moment she spoke. "You okay?"

"Yeah, kiddo," I replied with false cheer. Besim regarded me, her expression unreadable. "I'm fine. Listen, I need you to pull up every Wrigley-Boes Pharmaceuticals facility in Empire City, owned, rented, triple-net, vacant, you name it. Specifically, any of their properties containing laboratories or distribution centers."

"Got it," Leyla replied.

Several seconds passed while I waited.

"There's five," she piped up with excitement. "The main corporate office is in the Financial District. Now what?"

"Downtown, eh?" I said, eyes narrowing in thought. The Insight dimmed as I focused my attention on the conversation. "Anywhere near the alley where Vanessa was murdered?"

Leyla sucked in a sharp breath. "Holy shit, Doc! It's two blocks away!"

"What about former R&D sites?" I spun the fragment on the pamphlet, watching it twirl before it slowed and stopped. "Distribution centers, old offices? Where are those?"

"Let me see..." She hummed a tuneless melody while she worked. "Oh, here's something. There was a fire last night in Hoboken. I'll send you this morning's feed."

The holo played above the display of my phone. A pretty, brown-eyed reporter wearing a raincoat and carrying an umbrella stood before the smoldering ruins of a windowless one-story building.

"A three-alarm fire destroyed this building last night down in Castle Point," the reporter explained in a perky voice, as new footage appeared showing the property engulfed by flames. "Firefighters responded to the call shortly after midnight, battling the blaze for several hours. The cause of the fire remains unknown, although arson is suspected. A spokesperson for the building owner, Wrigley-Boes Pharmaceuticals, issued a statement that the building had been vacant, and was up for sale. Wrigley-Boes Pharmaceuticals is a manufacturer and seller of healthcare and nutritional supplements, with headquarters—"

I killed the feed with a sullen swipe of my hand.

"Isn't that convenient?" I muttered. "Credits to donuts that's where Rumpel hid his secret lab. Now what?"

My eyes strayed to the pamphlet on the table, lost in thought.

"I'll search the other buildings," Leyla replied.

Rumpelstiltskin had been a ghost, evading everyone for years. Once he realized we were closing in on him, he'd covered his tracks and melted into obscurity to start all over again. There had to be some way to catch the slippery son of a bitch. Something I'd missed that could bridge the gap, bring me closer and take him down once and for all.

But what?

"Check this out," Leyla said. "All the buildings are for sale, even the corporate headquarters. There's been an ongoing battle between the Wrigley-Boes parent company and another corporation attempting a hostile takeover of its pharmaceutical operations. I bet the lawyers' fees are astronomical!"

I shot a glance at Besim, who watched me with hooded eyes.

"Wrigley-Boes is owned by somebody else?" I asked suspiciously.

"You've got to be shitting me!" Leyla laughed. "Their parent is Orpheus Financial Group, a private, multinational holding firm engaged in pharmaceutical and disease research, development, marketing, and distribution. Three guesses who their CEO is."

The image of Tamara Ettelman appeared above the phone, mocking me with her dancing eyes.

"Her name is M. Fatima," Leyla said. "Not sure what the 'M' stands for, and her bio is really thin. I mean, like there's just her name, an image and not much else other than she grew up all over the world."

"What's the name of the company trying to take over Wrigley-Boes?" I glowered at the Vellan.

"Azyrim Technologies," Besim replied in a thoughtful voice before Leyla could respond. "Azyrim is a privately-held European-based company. They maintain a strong presence here. It is curious to see them thus engaged."

"Why?"

She folded her hands on the table. "Azyrim holds controlling interest in various industries including energy, waste disposal, food production, and holo-technology. Billions of their credits are engaged in subsidizing and sustaining governments and their infrastructure. As a result, Azyrim-branded products proliferate throughout Empire City. Until now, pharmaceutical manufacturing has not been within their spectrum of investments."

"Well, I guess Azyrim decided to branch out," I said, my anger at the Vellan fading as I returned my focus to the investigation.

"But it sure as hell could explain the advanced technology that built Marko."

"It might," Besim murmured, almost to herself.

"Leyla, I want you to hack into the Wrigley-Boes personnel files," I began.

"Wait, you're *asking* me to commit a felony?" she interrupted, barely containing her excitement.

"There's always a first for everything, kiddo," I suppressed a smile. "Bring up anyone in research and development over the age of fifty who's still on the active payroll or receiving retirement benefits within the last twenty-five years."

"Why twenty-five?" Leyla asked.

"Because that's how old Vanessa and Patricia are," I stated with cold certainty.

"Then why fifty?" the hacker asked.

I was about to answer when the transmission cut off. The bell above the front door jingled. A man in an overcoat and hat stepped into the diner carrying an umbrella under one arm. Something in the way he moved caught my attention.

"Get down!" I shouted in alarm and ducked beneath the table.

Bullets erupted above my head, shredding the back of the booth. I rolled to my left, and opened fire, but the assailant had already moved away from the door. A quick glance revealed Besim crushed low against the window and booth, fear spreading across her face. I pushed over the heavy table next to me for cover. More bullets ricocheted off its surface. Thank goodness Uncle Mortie had stuck with heavy-duty steel tables instead of the old wooden kind. Otherwise, I'd be Swiss cheese.

Cold sweat beaded my brow. I hoped there were enough regular rounds remaining, or this was going to be a very short day.

A second barrage bounced off the table's surface. My makeshift barricade wasn't going to last for long.

Suddenly, Uncle Mortie appeared at the kitchen door brandishing a wicked-looking butcher knife.

"Get outta my place!" the old deli owner shouted.

"Mortie, no!" I yelled in desperation, but I was too late. The gunman fired twice, and Mortie fell away, blood staining the door behind him.

Myrna shrieked.

"What kind of a fucking moron brings a knife to a gun fight?" a familiar voice derided from the other side of the room. Two tables crashed to the floor.

"Flanagan!" I howled in fury.

As I leaned around the table edge, several more bullets smashed into its top. I jerked back and covered my head with my hands as jagged table shards burst around me.

Desperate, I tried accessing EVI to call for backup, but my connection was cut off.

"Holliday!" Flanagan shouted. "You goddamn, self-righteous son of a bitch! You should've stayed at the 98th! But no, not you! You had to get involved! Well, guess what, asshole? It's going to cost you, and I've come to collect."

"That's the kind of bullshit all desperate people say, Flanagan!" I retorted, stalling as I assessed the situation.

Besim looked to me, but I gestured for her to stay put.

"With Rumpelstiltskin's goldjoy operation out of commission, your gravy train's run out of track," I continued, eyes darting around. "The way I see it, your options aren't pretty. Give yourself up, turn state's evidence, and maybe the DA will go easy on you."

"And give up my life of luxury?" she barked back. "Fuck you, Holliday! Oh, and good luck calling this one in. I've disabled EVI and every other device in the building. Including the sensors in that little gun of yours."

I sucked in a sharp breath. If she had something similar to what Marko had used in the alleyway to take out our tech, it would explain how her movements stayed hidden from ECPD. A flick of the switch, and the signal from the microchip in Flanagan's head would vanish in a puff of smoke. And with her rank, she had access to sensitive systems and material, the perfect inside man. She could feed Rumpel everything, and no one would be the wiser.

Which is precisely what she'd been doing.

I had never liked Flanagan. Every day, the fat bitch complained to anyone who'd listen how I was taking up some better cop's spot at the precinct. To her, I was a washed-up has-been, little better than the criminals we booked.

Her hypocrisy sickened me.

"What? No witty comeback, Mr. PhD?" Flanagan taunted as she reloaded her gun. "Thought maybe you learned something from that halfway house for jerk-offs and addicts. Your 'joy-whore girlfriend probably killed herself just to get away from you. Hide it all you want, but deep down, you're dirty like me."

"At least I use soap," I shot back. "By the way, nice job using my badge to steal Vanessa Mallery's body from the morgue. Didn't want to pay for sex anymore?"

"Fuck off, Holliday," she retorted. "All I did was give the badge to your eyewitness. She did the rest."

"Oh yeah? Well, she doesn't work for Rumpelstiltskin," I laughed derisively. "I'm sure your boss won't be happy when he finds out about that. Better pack your bags, Flanagan. I hear New Riker's is nice this time of year."

"Bullshit!" she shouted. "I'm protected, Holliday. I got too much on everyone. They need me, or I'll blow their whole operation."

"Whatever you say," I said. "From where I sit, there's not much of an operation left, so I wouldn't strike up the band just yet. You're going down with the rest."

This stand-off was pointless. Somebody outside must've heard shots fired and called 911, right?

Yeah, and if wishes were fishes, we'd all live in submarines.

In the meantime, I had to do something. I needed a distraction.

Flanagan had a helluva lot more bullets than I did. I recounted the number of shots I'd fired since I first used the SMART gun. I took an inventory of everything on the floor next to me. A salt and pepper shaker. Ketchup. Deli mustard.

I grinned.

Good ole Uncle Mortie and his penchant for keeping things classic at the diner. He employed an old-fashioned deli meat slicer in the back. His cooking surfaces were the same his forefathers had used, with an ancient cleaning system that was in disrepair more often than it worked.

And he filled his homemade kosher mustard in small glass jars.

I stared at the mustard, calculating angles, distances and trajectories as I once had back at the academy for ballistic classes. Flanagan couldn't be more than thirty feet away. If I timed it right, I could get one shot off before she realized what was happening.

It wasn't my brightest plan, and would probably get me killed, but desperate times, right?

I hefted the mustard jar.

Breathing deeply, I unleashed the Insight roiling around inside of me, waves of power fueling all my senses. My body tingled with raw energy. It suffused my muscles with vitality, sharpening my sight, my hearing, my touch, the way I breathed, and quickening my reflexes to something beyond human.

Reality crystalized. I noticed the finest detail in everything, from the individual rolls of paint on the walls, down to the hair-line crack fissuring the jar in my hand.

With my back to Besim, I switched to a half-crouch and tossed the jar toward Flanagan's position. I watched it fly in slow motion, catching the fluorescent ceiling light on its glossy surface, knowing it would reach its intended mark. It crashed to the ground in a shower of glittering fragments, smearing the floor a dark yellow.

I stood up, moving with a preternatural celerity, and reached the makeshift barricade Flanagan had made, faster than thought. I overtook her before she could react. She fixed me with an expression of loathing and fear.

That's when I saw the *fetch*.

It perforated her with foul coils of smoky darkness, concentrated around her heart, neck and head. Fathomless eyes glared back at me, while its lipless rictus twisted in a ghastly expression of joy, hunger, and need. It issued no sound, yet a soulless echo surrounded it, as if the creature was embraced by the cries of everyone it had feasted upon before Flanagan.

"Help me," Flanagan gasped.

I jerked backward, aghast at the sightless horror drawn on the poor woman's face. Knocking her out wouldn't stop the creature. Its hold was too rooted within the fabric of Flanagan's very being. The Insight revealed how the *fetch* had grafted itself to the lieutenant, someone who carried deep-seeded anger at being one of only a few females in a male-dominated department. Disgruntled and disenchanted, Flanagan felt that she had earned her place and deserved more. The creature had played upon her low self-esteem, fanning the flames of her bitterness. It had heightened every single dark thought Flanagan had, leading her down this path of self-destruction. She'd betrayed her fellow officers, losing pieces of herself over time under the influence of the vile creature. However, buried beneath the lieutenant's gruff and brusque exterior lurked the real Joan Flanagan, trapped by the parasite devouring her. Stark terror now shone in her eyes, but the *fetch* held mastery, and she was powerless to stop it. And so long as that thing remained attached to her, any hope of escape was lost.

Pity at her plight welled in my heart. Knocking her out wouldn't stop the creature. Its hold was too rooted within the fabric of Flanagan's very being. And even if I could somehow separate the *fetch* from Flanagan's body, there would be nothing left of the woman's soul except madness and pain.

I recalled Deacon describing the *fetch* back when we'd first met at the precinct, how only consecrated weapons could harm it.

Glancing at the SMART gun, I realized the creature was proof against it.

But the woman wasn't.

"I'm sorry," I whispered.

I shot Flanagan in the head.

The *fetch* shrieked in silence, severed from its dead host. It rushed away, sliding through the long window by the booths and out into the morning gray.

The Insight fled the instant Flanagan's life left her eyes. An enormous weight crashed against my shoulders. I slumped to the floor opposite the woman who had once been my boss.

"Detective?" Besim called out tentatively.

"Give me a minute," I replied, enervated by the release of the Insight.

I noticed a small device next to the lieutenant's nerveless hand. Levering myself unsteadily to my feet, I studied it with a dull expression, then stomped on it several times. It was probably a dumb move, but right then I didn't care. The gun's tactical flared to life as my connection with EVI returned.

Besim moved to the kitchen. Myrna sobbed while Besim spoke in quiet, calm tones to someone on her phone.

"Your uncle Mortie is wounded, but I believe he will survive so long as he receives appropriate medical attention," Besim explained as she came to my side. "He avoided the worst of it by wearing a baking pan beneath his shirt. My people are on their way and will ensure his safety while they transport him to Empire City General."

I staggered toward the door, unsteady hands holstering the gun.

"Then it's time to go," I stated with shaking breath.

"Where are we going?" Besim asked, eyebrow arched quizzically.

I gave her a level look.

"To find Rumpelstiltskin."

CHAPTER 36

"**Y**ou want me to do what again?" Father John Davis asked.

It was early, but I knew the pastor at the Holy Redeemer Church would be awake, preparing for the eight o'clock mass. Rain or shine, his morning ritual always included a brisk walk around the grounds of the massive cathedral located a few blocks from the waterfront down in Brighton Beach. We'd caught up to him as he was unlocking the front door. Once he overcame the shock of meeting a Vellan for the first time, he ushered us inside with a cordial smile.

I'd always known him as Father Jack. On the rare Sundays my dad was sober, the old bastard dragged me to the Holy Redeemer for morning mass. Maybe he thought I'd learn something. Or maybe it was just his goddamn stubborn pride getting in the way, like it did with everything else involving us. To me, it was another half-assed attempt at assuaging the shame he felt. I'm told abusing your wife and son can sometimes do that.

I attended the parochial school at the church, thanks to my grandfather's job as its janitor. My dad showed little interest in me after my mother's murder, so Harry took it upon himself to handle my education, among other things. Harry made a deal with Father Jack, and to the Holy Redeemer I went.

My grandfather's devotion to his Jewish faith ran deep, and he worried the school's heavy religious slant would rub off on me. So, he filled me up with as much Jewish pragmatism as I could stomach. Some days I listened, and others, I tuned him out, along with Father Jack and everyone else. The result was muddy, like a fruity cocktail with too much juice and not enough booze.

To say I'd experienced all the guilt two major religions could offer, and none of the fun parts, would be an understatement.

Thankfully, Father Jack had always been good to me.

He was a tall man, rail thin, with a pronounced widow's peak at both temples and salty gray hair. But his brown eyes were shrewd and full of a good-natured humor that had served him well over the years.

Today, they reflected concern for my sanity.

"I need you to bless the bullets," I repeated for the third time.

"So that you can battle the forces of evil?" Jack was dubious, giving me a sidelong glance. "*Genuine* evil. As part of your investigation into the murder of that poor young girl I saw on the feeds the other day?"

We were in the small breakroom down the hall from the nave. A coffee maker percolated happily on the counter next to a double sink and a large holo-frame cycling between hundreds of images of various church-goers and their families. It was a warm, inviting place, with soft lighting and two windows along one wall overlooking an old, familiar playground.

Besim remained in the vestibule. Father Jack was content to leave her there.

"That's right," I nodded with vigor.

A warm coffee mug beckoned to me, but I refrained. Its twin sat across from the pastor, also untouched.

"And you've already encountered one of these—what did you

call them?" he asked, folding his arms across his chest as he leaned back in the chair.

"A *fetch*," I supplied with a hopeful smile.

"Yes, *fetch*," he chewed on the word with a frown. "And let me make sure I have this right, a Protector from the Church of the Tribulation, a religion, I might add, that considers every other faith heretical, informed you they can only be killed by consecrated weapons?"

"Yes, his name is Deacon Kole," I replied, then added quickly. "He's a good man, really rough around the edges, but he means well."

"I'm sure he is." Jack licked his lips, blinking in rapid succession. "And why is this important, out of curiosity?"

"There's a man out there, Rumpelstiltskin, the goldjoy drug lord. He performed illegal genetic experimentation on the murdered girl, as well as her twin and who knows how many other victims. I'm *this* close to catching him. Today. As soon as I can get you to bless my bullets, or the gun, or both, whichever you think would work best. But I need them in case there are any more vampires or other, well, things like the *fetch* protecting him."

"Vampires?" Jack's eyebrows shot up in alarm. "I thought that was something the media invented to generate interest. You're saying an actual vampire murdered that girl?"

"Well, yes and no." I shifted in my seat discomfited. "The vampire that killed her wasn't a vampire. Well, he was, and he wasn't. I mean, he stole her blood, but he was an android, and not some honest-to-goodness Nosferatu or anything like that."

"I see," he said, staring past my shoulder as he absorbed everything I said.

"I know how this all sounds, Father Jack," I spread my hands wide with a deprecating smile. "But I'm not crazy. The shit...err... stuff I've seen over the past few days, well, I don't know what to think anymore."

He rose from his seat and moved to stand at my side, placing a hand on my shoulder. A troubled frown creased his worn face.

"Tommy, when was the last time you talked to someone?"

"I'm not using again," I snapped, and brushed his hand roughly away.

I reached for the coffee, hesitated, then stood up.

"And I've got nothing to confess to you, or anyone else. I need your help to bring a supernatural murderer to justice. Jesus Christ, after everything we've been through, and you still don't trust me?"

We stood there, facing one another, a vast gulf of emotions separating us by mere inches.

"Tommy Holliday, I have known you since you were in diapers," he said, regarding me with a fond melancholy. "Your father and I grew up together, were close friends for a very long time, even after he, well, yes, that."

He hesitated, and I saw his eyes cloud over with regret.

"And your mother was a lovely woman, God rest her soul. You've always possessed a vivid imagination, and it healed my heart to see how well you've recovered. But this is a bit much, even for you. What you ask, I cannot do. To bless a weapon, any weapon, purposed to kill is not something I can condone, regardless of the reasons. I'm sorry, but there must be another way."

"I wish there were," I muttered, glaring at him. "Thanks for nothing."

He took a step back, clasping his hands behind him as he'd done so often when addressing his congregation.

"Tommy, sometimes when we lose our way, a cold splash of water to the face can help clear up any confusion or doubts," he chided in his pastor's voice. "I want to help you, I truly do, but not in this way. Through Christ, anything is possible so long as you possess the faith in your heart and your mind to try. I urge you, find another way."

"Maybe for you," I said, storming from the breakroom before he could respond. "But not for me."

I found Besim by one of the massive, polished stone support pillars outside the nave. The silence was an obtrusive companion, poking its nose into everything without apology or excuse. Thick shadows surrounded her, as the dozens of holo-candles set in their brackets several feet above her head had yet to be lit for the morning. Tall, intricately stained-glass windows reached to the heavens along the upper walls, capturing the essence of the divine for those worshipping beneath them. A carved font with a head-stone containing the likeness of Jesus rested on a simple pedestal next to her. Besim traced her long fingers around the lip of the font, gazing in quiet contemplation at the architecture.

"He would not bless your weapon," she said without turning.

"No," I groused, chafed by how the conversation with Father Jack had ended. I shoved my hands in my pockets. "I shouldn't be surprised. Hell, I would've said no too."

"Then why did you come here?"

"I don't really know," I admitted, removing my hands from my pockets to grip the sides of the font. "I guess I feel exposed without Deacon here to back me up."

I peered into the clear water. My face was reflected on its surface by the dim light of the morning. Worn, tired eyes blinked back at me. Threadbare lines streaked the corners, and I worried not for the first time that I resembled my father more than my mother.

"If Rumpelstiltskin is a *fetch*, or something worse, how am I going to deal with that? How am I going to protect any of you?"

"Your inadequacy is an illusion," Besim spoke quietly. Her voice resonated, the words palpable and telling. "It is a tool of the enemy you chase, to drag you down and subvert your strength. Instead, draw courage from your conviction. Your sense of self will protect and guide you. The events of the past few days have been more than a mere investigation into the murder of Vanessa

Mallery. They have been your rite of passage. Whether you accept that you are Empire City's Guardian or not, you have proven your resolve and resourcefulness over Rumpelstiltskin. It is through your intervention his minions were slain and the goldjoy laboratory uncovered. You are now on the cusp of apprehending him. Do not let the fear of the unknown cripple you. Instead, find your strength inside yourself. That is why you came here. You chose a place with faith steeped in the very bedrock of its foundation, its identity unquestioned, and its compassion endless. Whether you believe in that effigy over there, or in something else entirely, what you need now is to draw upon all of your past experiences, all of your training, and do what is right."

I bowed my head.

"There are no tricks in plain and simple faith," I whispered, immersed within Besim's voice, buoyed by whatever power it held. *"But hollow men, like horses hot at hand, make gallant show and promise of their mettle. But when they should endure the bloody spur, they fall their crests and, like deceitful jades, sink in the trail."*

The candles flickered to life above us, bathing the sanctuary and vestibule in golden illumination. I wiped my hands on my pant legs, then put them back in my pockets.

"Boldness be my friend," I stated with finality. "Let's go."

Already, a thin flow of people was filing in, drenched from the constant rain outside. Besim nodded, and together we left the church. A brisk walk down the block brought us back to the pod. We were underway a moment later.

After collapsing into one of the command chairs, I checked in with Leyla.

"So now we're headed to Wrigley-Boes' corporate office," I finished. "How's Uncle Mortie?"

"Your people arrived just in time, Besim," she replied. "He was rushed into surgery but should pull through. Myrna's still a wreck though."

I exhaled sharply.

"That's good news," I replied with relief. "Thanks, kiddo. What else is going on?"

"Not much," Leyla said. "Patricia hasn't left her room. I've tried talking with her, but I think she's still in shock, so I've left her alone. And Deacon's been a real pain in the ass. He won't rest like he's supposed to, he refuses to take his medicine, and he's been ordering everyone around!"

"Sounds like he's feeling better," I chuckled.

"'It's just a broken elbow,'" Leyla said, impersonating Deacon's voice. "'Quit treatin' me like I'm some fuckin' baby!'" She laughed. "If Mamika hadn't isolated the elevator controls, he would've already left to find you."

"Mamika has been given explicit instructions that Deacon is to convalesce," Besim's said sternly. "No one is allowed into or out of the suite without my express permission."

"That's like telling the sun not to shine," I responded with a smile. "Glad you're there to keep an eye on things, kiddo."

"Yeah, but I'd rather be with you," Leyla said, her voice filled with worry. "You need me, Doc."

"I know," I replied. "But you need to rest too. If Rumpel sees us all descend on Wrigley-Boes, he'll go to ground before you can say 'once upon a time.' Rumpel's made a living feeding off insider information, using it to stay three steps ahead of the authorities. He's been under everyone's noses, hiding in plain sight. Now, his operation is in disarray, his allies are scattered, and his network has crumbled. He knows we're coming, but he won't know when or how, so we have the element of surprise on our side for once."

"Well, what will you do if he's one of those things, like Crain?" Leyla pointed out.

I exchanged a glance with Besim.

"I'll improvise," I said grimly, then changed the subject. "Were you able to hack into Wrigley-Boes?"

"I sure did," she snickered. "Their encryption is, like, so ten years ago. Anyway, I sent their personnel directory to your box.

Just those people that fit the description you were after. You think Rumpelstiltskin is one of them?"

"I do," I replied. "If he's an old R&D guy, he's had access to all the company's toys, their laboratories, materials, and resources. With the other Wrigley-Boes locations shut down and up for sale, the corporate office might be his one safe harbor. He's there. I can feel it."

"I hope you're right, Doc," Leyla said.

"Me too," I said, sighing. "I promise to call when it's all over, okay?"

"You better," she admonished in a scathing tone. "And try not to get killed."

"Gee, thanks Mom," I said with a wry smile, and hung up.

The SMART gun was fully charged. I set the last bullet inside the transparent clip, reloaded the weapon, and returned it to my shoulder rig. Settling myself more comfortably in the chair, I leaned back and stared out the rain-streaked window as Empire City rushed along in a blur of white and grey.

"You haven't told me what you uncovered after examining Patricia Sullinger," I said.

Besim regarded me, head tilted to the side.

"I am uncertain of your meaning, Detective."

"Don't play coy with me," I countered, folding my hands behind my head. "You know exactly what I mean."

"She is in perfect health, if that is what you are wondering. Aside from the trauma inflicted upon her by the *golem*, of course. Miss Sullinger and I spoke at great length about her life, upbringing, family, and medical history. As was the case with Vanessa Mallery, she too had never experienced any instances requiring medical attention. That is, until yesterday's encounter."

"That's all well and good," I acknowledged, eyes narrowing. "But you've had ample opportunity to run a battery of tests, including her blood work. And I'm sure you've already compared it to Vanessa's tissue samples. Tell me what you know."

Besim closed her eyes, and for a second there, I thought she stopped breathing.

When she regarded me, I saw uncertainty reflected in them.

"Patricia Sullinger is not entirely human."

"Explain."

"What do you know of genetic resequencing and engineering?" Besim asked.

"About as much as the next guy," I replied. "Meaning, nothing."

"Resequencing is a key step in detecting mutations associated with a wide variety of human congenital diseases," the consultant explained. "Engineering is a deliberate modification of the characteristics of any organism through the manipulation of its genetic material. Without boring you with the finer details, suffice it to say Miss Sullinger's DNA was tampered with at a very early stage of her life. A new enzyme was introduced into her system, something manufactured, of a kind I have never encountered before. Her extensive good health, the lack of any blemish on her skin, no scarring, no history of illness or broken bones, could be one result of this substance."

"We've presumed the experimentation could've been an attempt to create some kind of new super health pill," I said. "Both Wrigely-Boes and Orpheus would reap the massive financial windfall by claiming a monopoly on the finished product."

Besim hesitated, then said, "This is troubling to me, Detective. I do not believe that is its intent."

"What does that mean, exactly?" I asked.

"It suggests whatever Rumpelstiltskin has done to these women is not something I can readily identify or duplicate," she replied. "Something external was introduced into Miss Sullinger's system to replenish it and maintain whatever levels necessary to ensure a continuous chemical reaction catalyzed by that enzyme."

"That's what's in the wine," I snapped my fingers as the thought hit me. "Orpheus mentioned something about this too. That's why those bottles were replaced. The wine contains both elements of goldjoy and the genetic milkshake you're missing. What's your theory?"

"I do not have one," she replied, her frustration evident. "Its application eludes me. However, when I discovered this, I was already too late. The substances degraded before I could properly isolate them. Miss Sullinger had been without her infusion long enough that the enzymes evaporated from her bloodstream."

"That I can understand. It's like going without medication that regulates blood pressure for several days, right?"

She nodded, but a sudden premonition made me shudder.

"How does that make her not entirely human?"

"It is my belief Miss Sullinger's DNA was intermingled with another's whose genetic sequence is similar in scope." Besim regarded me with such sadness, I felt my throat constrict in response.

As she spoke, the case took form in my mind, each clue we'd uncovered sliding into place one piece at a time. Even the smallest details, from her height and build, down to the vibrant color and luxuriant texture of Vanessa's hair. It all came together, as fine a picture as one of the murdered girl's own seascapes, painstakingly clear and real.

"She's Vellan," I breathed in awe. "How is that possible? Humans and Vellans can't breed."

"I do not know," Besim replied. "Yet, Rumpelstiltskin has devised a means of combining both human and Vellan DNA to create a hybrid, presumably containing the best of both species. The only plausible explanation is he employed magic to accomplish this feat. As with the cloaked signal Leyla has been tracking, to create something possible from the impossible, only magic has the power to do such a thing. However, I fear there is something far worse."

"What's that?" I asked, dreading the answer.

"Patricia Sullinger is dying," Besim said, tears in her eyes. "And there is nothing I can do to prevent it."

CHAPTER 37

$\mathcal{T}$he Wrigley-Boes Tower was located along Wall Street in one of the mammoth skyscrapers dominating the skyline of New Manhattan. Like all mega-corporations with more credits than sense, their philosophy of "bigger is better" was taken to the extreme. Most of the buildings on the block vied to top the other in height, style, and complexity. The result was a mishmash of bridges, towers, odd color schemes, and the occasional murderer's row of concrete gargoyles. Our destination was covered with glossy reflective glass all the way to its zenith at the 101st floor. Their holo-techies had installed dozens of projectors along its length. The odds were good you could see Wrigley-Boes advertisements from the moon.

We parked at one of the designated ECPD platforms several stories above street level. The enclosed parking and walkways offered welcome protection from the elements. In this part of town, the *'ways* ran up high, curving around the massive buildings to accommodate greater traffic. That meant additional pod hubs and stops. Most of these corporations had their main entrances above the mess and stench of the traffic beneath them. It was less about convenience, and more a means of reminding mortal pedestrians where their financial betters lived.

An enclosed walkway crossed a gaping chasm of space separating the hub from Wrigley-Boes. Despite the insulation, the frenzied howl of the October wind buffeted against the thick glass and spell-forged steel. Some architectural genius had come up with the brilliant idea of installing a reinforced glass floor, providing a stomach-turning view. Although I hadn't heard of any ever collapsing, there was always a first time.

Don't get me wrong: I wasn't afraid of heights, but I did maintain a healthy respect for anything that might have gotten me killed, like angry ex-boyfriends, or falling from a hundred-plus-story building.

Foot traffic here was as heavy as down below. The morning workforce flowed along, and we melted into the burgeoning crowd, maintaining a brisk pace. We passed through the large sliding glass doors embossed with the Wrigley-Boes logo and into the corporate headquarters of the pharmaceutical giant. I paused a few feet inside, took a moment to straighten my collar, and raked my fingers through my tangled hair. Buttoning my blazer, I left the SCU badge secure on my belt. Although we were here on official ECPD business, I didn't want to draw attention just yet.

"How do I look?" I asked Besim.

Her face betrayed nothing.

"Nervous," she replied.

Two uniformed security guards with stun batons at their hips sidled by, appraising the Vellan curiously before moving along. Dozens of people occupied the open floor, standing in small groups talking or wandering through numerous portals leading to who-knew-where. At the center of it all squatted an enormous circular kiosk, complete with the largest indoor holo-screen I'd ever seen. A constant stream of Wrigley-Boes advertisements played on it, along with the morning news from all the major enclave feeds, a side bar for sports scores, entertainment, trivia, and even the Nikkei, New London, and Azyrim-Dow indexes.

I stared at the numbers and symbols as they rolled along the screen.

"What is it?" Besim asked.

"I never noticed it before." I pointed at the screen. "Azyrim is part of the Empire City stock exchange."

"Indeed," she replied. "His influence reaches far and wide."

"His?" I raised an inquiring eyebrow.

She was about to respond when another advertisement caught my attention.

An attractive young couple dressed in casual attire embraced in front of an idyllic seascape backdrop. Seagulls wheeled in the sky, while soft waves crashed against the sandy shore. Romantic music swelled as the scene cut to the two walking barefoot, hands entwined.

"Live life the way you've always wanted," a man's deep, calm voice announced.

The full battery of Wrigely-Boes health products scrolled alongside the image of the two strolling into the sunset. Anxiety settled into my gut.

"Let's get going," I said, and headed toward the kiosk.

I stepped up to the first available agent.

"Good morning," greeted a fair-haired woman with a bright smile. "Welcome to Wrigley-Boes, the world's leader in personal healthcare! How can I help you?"

She wore a white blouse beneath a slate gray jacket. All the men and women occupying the chest-high kiosk wore the same uniform, and each manned an individual virtual workstation. None of them appeared to be over the age of thirty. A holo-plate with the name Jennifer Mathis hovering above it rested on the lip of the counter.

"Hello there, Jenny," I returned her smile with a bland one of my own.

Three alert security guards were stationed inside the ring behind her. I kept my eyes on Jenny. She smelled of lavender and artless youth.

"I'm Mr. Holmes, this is Dr. Watson, and we're from the Baker Street Consortium. We have an appointment with the R&D department at ten o'clock. Could you please tell me which floor they're on?"

"Let me see." Jenny swiped her hand across the colored screen. "Oh, I'm very sorry Mr. Holmes, but they were located at our Long Island facility, which was recently closed."

I frowned in consternation.

"Then why would I have been directed here?" I wheeled on Besim without waiting for Jenny. "Watson, I thought you confirmed the time and place of our meeting with R&D?"

Besim's demeanor went from placid to alarmed in an instant.

"I truly apologize, Mr. Holmes," Besim said, her posture bent, almost groveling. "The message I received was from James Solomon himself specifically stating we should arrive no later than ten o'clock, and to bring our proposal to him, and not the R&D team. I thought you already knew?"

I had no idea who Solomon was, but at the mention of his name, Jenny sat up straight.

"Something you failed to mention earlier." I glared at Besim. "I don't know why I keep you around."

I turned back to Jenny and forced a friendly smile. "It appears my plans have changed. Which way to Solomon's office, then?"

"Mister Solomon's office is on the ninety-ninth floor," the young woman answered. "Head around the kiosk, fourth elevator on the right. You will need to pass through security first. Mr. Holmes, I sincerely apologize for any inconvenience."

I thanked her, grabbed Besim's elbow, and led her away from the kiosk.

"Who is Solomon?" I asked in a low voice.

"The Director of Wrigley-Boes," Besim replied calmly,

belying the worried expression she maintained for appearance's sake. "The information Leyla provided us indicated their facilities were under corporate assault. While you were speaking with Father Davis, I contacted an associate of mine who confirmed all the Wrigley-Boes facilities have been closed. Their resources have been redirected to the corporate headquarters here."

"So, name dropping the head honcho of Wrigley-Boes was a good idea?" I grumbled, flicking away an invisible speck of dust from Besim's coat lapel. "That was a helluva gamble."

"This building has one hundred and one floors," Besim explained. "We presume Rumpelstiltskin is occupying one of them. The executive elevator grants us unfettered access to the entire complex. Once inside, we can visit any floor we desire."

"What about Solomon?" I countered. "Won't someone be expecting us?"

"Unlikely," she tilted her head to regard the kiosk. "Miss Mathis is responsible for providing the correct floors for visitors, among other menial tasks. She would have no direct communication with that level of management without first elevating any situation to her superiors. In addition, James receives a steady supply of daily visitors. We are not as uncommon as you initially believe. The security checkpoint, on the other hand, will be the greater challenge."

I felt the weight of the SMART gun in its shoulder rig.

"Good point."

Glancing ahead, I took note of the four-person security team guarding an enclosed archway leading to a series of glass and steel elevators.

"It will be impossible for you to go beyond them without assistance," Besim continued. "By now, our images have been added to the visitor registry. I calculate we have a few moments longer before our data is uploaded, and our identities revealed to Wrigley-Boes security."

"Lovely," I grimaced in frustration. "How are we supposed to get through?"

"Follow my lead, Detective," Besim asserted, and strode purposefully toward the checkpoint.

A small stack of plastic bins was arranged beneath a rectangular table before the archway. One uniformed guard spoke with an attractive woman wearing a white lab coat. A second watched the crowd with practiced disinterest. I wasn't fooled. I'd seen that expression a hundred times on trained professionals who could go from bored to ball-breaking at the drop of a hat. The remaining two conversed on the other side of the archway.

Besim walked up to the second man.

"I am Doctor Besim Saranda," she announced with authority, emphasizing her accent. "And this is my personal bodyguard, Deacon Kole. We have business with the director."

I felt the persuasive force of her voice, and the air around her quivered. The guard's eyes glazed over, then cleared. I maintained a neutral front, straightening my back, and glared at everyone with the same tough guy disgust I'd seen on Deacon's face dozens of times since we first met.

"I don't remember seeing your name on the list, Doctor Saranda," the security guard said.

"That is because James requested a private meeting, Mr. Sebastian." Besim's frosty smile was full of disdain as she stared down her nose at his nametag. "I do not believe someone of your... station...should be informed of such things."

"Well, like I said, your name isn't on the list," Sebastian responded with grit in his voice. "I'll need to verify it."

Besim dismissed the comment with a haughty wave of her hand.

"Of course. I'll be certain to inform James of how you delayed my arrival and wasted my time," she said loftily, adding more emphasis. The guard's eyes glazed again. "If you feel verifying my appointment with James' executive assistant Diana will save you from a formal reprimand, then do as you must."

She withdrew her phone from her coat and manipulated its controls. A heartbeat later, the image of a handsome middle-aged man with a mustache and goatee hovered above the screen.

"Or perhaps you could inform James yourself."

That gave the guard pause, and he hesitated, doubt reflected in his eyes. He glanced at her phone, then nodded.

"Please, step on through, Doctor Saranda," Sebastian smiled as if he'd swallowed moldy cheese. "You too, Mr. Kole."

"Thank you," Besim moved forward, beaming at him, her smile laced with contempt. She paused before the archway and gave Sebastian a pointed look. "You will disregard the sidearm my man carries. The weapon is for my protection, and I do not travel anywhere without it or him."

"Of course, Doctor Saranda," he replied, nodding to the others. One of them waved his hand over a control panel on the other side of the archway. "They're clear. Let 'em through."

We passed beneath the archway. I hunched my shoulders expecting the alarms to sound, but nothing happened.

"One final thing, Mr. Sebastian," Besim instructed in an off-hand manner as we entered the elevator. "Please erase our arrival from all your security footage, including the archives. This is a private meeting, and I suspect James will take it poorly if he discovered my presence was recorded. We would not want that now, would we?"

"Of course, ma'am."

The elevator door slid closed.

"How may I direct you?" a soft, feminine voice asked.

Ignoring it, I confronted Besim.

"What the hell was that?"

"Simple subterfuge was not going to be effective," she explained quietly. "I opted for a different approach."

"Sure," I said. "And Solomon?"

"James and I have known each other for several years. I mentioned to you when we first met that I consult with a variety of interests in Empire City. James held previous employment with the Tyrell Corporation, a developer and manufacturer of labor machinery. It was through my recommendation James received the offer of employment to join Wrigley-Boes. When I am engaged in Empire City, it is not uncommon for the two of us to meet and discuss business of one kind or another. It was James to whom I spoke with earlier regarding Wrigley-Boes, and the attempted takeover by Azyrim."

"So now we're expected to go upstairs and meet with him?" I threw up my hands, exasperated. "That's just great. How much does he know? Need I remind you, this is an official investigation, and he's a civilian! By telling him why we're here, you've jeopardized everything. Christ, Besim, what the hell were you thinking?"

"James is on holiday in the Caribbean Conclave with his family," Besim asserted calmly. "He will not return for another week. I merely explained to James I wished to drop off a personal gift, something I did not wish for his wife to know about. Naturally, he understood discretion was required."

I shot her a look. "I don't want to know."

"By instructing Mr. Sebastian in the manner that I did, there will be no official record of our visit," Besim continued unperturbed. "Thus, if Rumpelstiltskin maintains surveillance on anyone who enters the complex, he will have no idea of our arrival."

"Presuming he hasn't hacked into their security feed," I pointed out, unconvinced. "Hell, he's probably watching us right now."

"This elevator, and the accompanying executive floors above, is on a series of surveillance separate from the rest of the facility," Besim said. "I had Deacon oversee its installation when James was brought on board as the director. Unless Rumpelstiltskin is a member of the executive staff, he would not be aware of this."

"How convenient," I rolled my eyes. "Well, once I arrest the bastard, there will be an official record."

"You have probable cause, do you not, Detective?" the consultant asked, tilting her head to the side. "The evidence, albeit circumstantial, has directed you here."

"Fine. We'll leave that little problem for Mahoney and the DA's office. Let's track down Rumpelstiltskin."

Besim nodded her agreement.

"Have you ascertained his whereabouts?"

The interior of the elevator contained a miniature version of the holo-screen above the information kiosk. Waving my hand before it, I brought up a directory, and cycled through the different departments, looking for "Research and Development" without success.

"The transition is too new," I ground my teeth in frustration. "They haven't updated their intranet yet."

I searched for sister departments, but none of them contained what I was looking for.

And then I had a thought, because I was brilliant like that.

"Hey, um, Miss Elevator, I actually do need some direction."

"How may I direct you?" the elevator repeated.

"Where would I find the Research and Development team recently transferred from Long Island?" I asked.

"The Research and Development team has been relocated to the twenty-fifth floor. They now share workspace with Creative Design. Doctor Bartleman is in the conference room. Shall I contact him?"

The image of Bartleman floated on the screen, an amiable-looking man in his fifties.

"Uh, no, thanks, we'll just surprise him. Would you please take us there?"

The elevator hummed into motion, its smooth transition almost imperceptible.

A moment later, the door opened onto a small foyer ending at

a receptionist's desk. Tall glass walls wrapped around both hall-
ways revealing dozens of short cubicles. These were occupied by
men and women in white lab coats huddled around virtual workstations. Space appeared to be at a premium. I noticed a few
heated exchanges between several of the employees. Wrigley-Boes
must've installed noise-dampening ceiling tiles and walls, because
all I heard was a low murmur.

A skinny young man with watery eyes worked the front desk.

"Hi," he said, offering us a hesitant smile.

"Hello there." I held out my ID, placed the SCU badge on the
counter, and made with the introductions. "Now don't be
alarmed, but where can I find the R&D team? One of your scientists is a person of interest in an ongoing investigation."

"Oh my," he gulped, his face turning beet red. "I thought you
were here about my...um...never mind. I'll need to let Miss Chew,
the floor manager, know."

"Son, don't," I held up a hand, giving him a stern look. "There's
not a lot of time. Just take us to them."

"Now?"

"Now."

I'll give the kid credit. For a second, I thought he was going to
dig in his heels. But then his shoulders sagged as if I'd just stolen
his girlfriend.

"Follow me," he said.

We walked along the cubicle farm. Besim generated a few
curious stares, but most were intent on their work. Turning left,
we came across a glass-walled conference room occupied by over
a dozen men and women of various ages. As we approached, two
men wearing white lab coats stood at the head of the table by the
door. One was Bartleman. He spoke to the others, gesturing at
times to the second man, followed by a round of muted applause.
The second man nodded and bowed, then shook hands with
Bartleman.

"We'll take it from here," I said.

The young man tripped over himself as he doubled-timed it back toward his desk.

"Ready?" I asked Besim.

Without preamble, I stepped into the conference room.

I locked eyes with the second man who turned to face me the moment we entered. I didn't need the Insight to tell me who he was. His image decorated the Wrigley-Boes pamphlets at Tony's apartment and Ettelman's office.

"Rumpelstiltskin," I announced in a loud, clear voice. "By the authority vested in me by the enclave of Empire City, you are hereby under arrest."

CHAPTER 38

"What is the meaning of this?" Bartleman demanded. In his hand, he held a plastic knife. "And who the hell are you? You have no right barging in here!"

The men and women around the conference table regarded me with apprehension. Set on the table were plates, plastic forks, and a rectangular white cake with the caption "Happy Retirement Dr. Blakely" drawn in blue frosting. The cake sported three golden flowers on its upper right corner.

"My name is Detective Tom Holliday with the Empire City Special Crimes Unit," I stated with authority, holding my silver badge while jabbing a finger at Blakely. "I have a warrant for the arrest of this man. Now step aside please so I can do my job."

"I will do no such thing," Bartleman bristled. He positioned himself in front of Blakely. "This is obviously some kind of mistake. I'll need to see that warrant."

"Whatever you say, pal," I replied calmly, and withdrew my holo-phone, hoping my anxiety didn't show.

Oh, I had a warrant.

Just not the right one.

I flashed Bartleman the official ECPD search warrant for

Ettelman's office on my phone before he or anyone else could get a good look at it.

Mahoney had finally sent it to me an hour after I arrived at the deli. Better late than never, I thought at the time. Storing it on my phone, I went back to drowning my misery in Mortie's rugelach and hadn't given it much thought until we were on our way here.

Once I'd gone through the Wrigley-Boes personnel directory, I had narrowed down the suspect list to three: Bartleman, Doctor Robert O. Blakely, and Doctor Klaus J. Muller. All three fit the profile—they were over the age of fifty, worked in R&D, and had decades of experience in the fields of immunology, metabolic diseases, and microbiology. The problem was, none of the images in the personnel directory resembled the old scientist on the cover of the pamphlet I'd seen. It was a gross assumption on my part, but Orpheus wouldn't have left that out in the open for me to find if it didn't mean something more than just aiming me at Wrigley-Boes.

At some point, Rumpelstiltskin must've discovered his actual likeness on the pamphlet, and altered his directory image to stay a step ahead of any unwanted admirers.

That meant visual confirmation was needed. I couldn't ask Mahoney to get me an arrest warrant for all three men based on a hunch after he'd already gotten the search warrant from the DA. And we didn't have the luxury of time. To catch Rumpelstiltskin required some good ole fashioned chicanery. Fassendale and his legal eagles could sort it all out later.

I hoped.

My instincts said it wasn't Bartleman. He was the head of R&D, which didn't fit with Rumpel's MO of staying under the radar. That left two.

Since I didn't have a lot to go on, my credits were on Muller. He was of German descent, and a resident of Empire City for more than thirty years. The Brothers Grimm fairy tale of Rumpel-stiltskin, the most popular literary adaptation of the character, also originated from that country. Two plus two usually made four. However, when I spied Blakely in the conference room, I realized I had bet on the wrong holo-horse.

"Satisfied?" I growled with the appropriate amount of police angst reserved for bad guys and stubborn citizenry.

I kept my hand away from my gun, relying on the badge and my detective's scowl to act as a deterrent.

Bartleman wilted like a stale fart. He exchanged a confused look with Blakely.

"Oliver?" he asked uncertainly.

That cinched it. Another clever affectation by Rumpel, going by his middle name instead of his first. My body tensed, expecting a desperate Blakely to bull his way past me, since I blocked the only exit from the conference room.

The old scientist wore a mysterious smile.

"Congratulations, Detective," he said in a smooth, cultured voice, winking at me. He grabbed the handle of a steel briefcase lying on the credenza next to him. "It seems I have finally been caught. The devil must have told you that, eh?"

"Actually," I replied coldly. "Vanessa Mallery's cat did."

Blakely narrowed his eyes, then gave himself up.

The next few minutes were a blur. I explained his rights while cuffing him in front of his astonished co-workers. Besim and I led Blakely from the conference room. The cube jockeys watched in stunned silence, their little tiffs momentarily forgotten. On the way, I made the call to Mahoney, filled him in on the collar, and requested a prisoner transport. The sound of jubilation and relief in his voice should've made me smile, but it didn't. The hair on the back of my neck stood on end the moment Blakely winked at me.

There was something rotten in Denmark.

This was going too well, and I was never that lucky.

Worse still, the Insight lay dormant. As we retraced our steps, I was reminded of our trip to Kraze, the fight with David Crain and his vampire goons, and all the unpleasantness that followed.

It made me nervous as hell.

We were met at the elevator by John Kilcullen, the head of Wrigley-Boes security, and two of his men. After an explanation of the situation, Kilcullen ordered his men to escort us down to the main floor. I didn't mind the extra company. We filed into the executive elevator without a word.

Blakely broke the silence after the doors closed.

"The Guardian of Empire City," Blakely remarked with amusement, sizing me up as if I was a frozen dinner. "Protector of the innocent and downtrodden, or some such rubbish. From the glowing way Orpheus spoke of you, I had expected so much more than, well, you. She is rarely impressed by anything, let alone a strung-out police detective with an acute infatuation with coffee."

"Sorry to disappoint you," I replied. "My cape is still at the laundromat."

His knowledge of me didn't come as a surprise. With Flanagan as his rat inside ECPD, Blakeley probably knew how many times I wiped my ass. The Guardian part, on the other hand, was something else.

"So, Guardian, or do you still prefer 'Detective?'" he asked lightly. Blakely was a slight man, bent at the shoulders, with wispy gray hair and liver spots on his hands.

Both beefy security guards bookending him stared ahead. One held Blakely's briefcase.

"'Detective is fine," I replied. His use of the title and the smug way he said it bothered the shit out of me.

I glanced at Besim. Her head was bowed. She held that leather flask again, the one from the nightclub.

A victory drink now? I usually reserved mine until after the perp had been processed—that whole cart and horse thing. Besim frowned in consternation. Perhaps it was a Vellan custom?

"As you wish," Blakely continued smoothly. "Do you truly believe you've beaten me?"

He was at ease, holding a conversation as if we were two co-workers discussing the weather. At one point, he winked at Besim, who ignored him.

"I'd call this a win," came my cold reply. "You're in custody. Once I hand your ass over to the uniforms waiting downstairs, I'm going home to pour myself a cup of hot coffee, then I'll cuddle up with a nice book. You, on the other hand, will just be a distant memory until the arraignment."

"Ah yes, the former addict and doctoral detective." Blakely nodded sagely. "An ill-spent education studying long-dead wind-bags with a propensity for prosaic nonsense. No wonder you drowned yourself in narcotics, no doubt to wash away the tedium of all that useless reading."

"The joy of study has its perks, Blakely," I said. "For instance, I get a free membership at the Empire City University Library. You can't go wrong with that. And I also get to laugh at jerks like you who think adopting fairytale names gives you a myste-rious mojo to frighten little kids. Remember how that one ended?"

"Perish the thought, Detective," the old man chuckled. His eyes glittered with malice. "I must say, you were an interesting study. Once I learned it was you leading the investigation, I felt certain you would fall flat on your face. Imagine my surprise when you didn't."

"Sorry to disappoint you," I returned, flicking my middle finger off my forehead in a mock salute. "Now, if you would shut up, there's a prisoner transport downstairs with your name on it. I'd hate to keep them waiting. Miss Elevator, please take us to the lobby."

I felt a tremor, and then we were in motion.

The smile left his face.

"You have no idea what you've done."

My unease grew, but I hid it behind my customary bravado when dealing with scumbags.

"Oh, I've got a pretty good idea, Blakely," I said, fixing him with a grim stare. "Your goldjoy lab is gone, Crain and his crew are all dead, Patricia Sullinger is safe, and Orpheus has severed your relationship. Performance issues, or so I heard. Doesn't Wrigley-Boes have a pill for that? Anyway, a jury of your peers is going to send you to New Riker's for a very long time. I'd say you're pretty fucked."

"Perhaps," he conceded. "But not today."

The sweet scent of honey and springtime suddenly permeating the elevator car was all the warning I got. One breath of it, and my thoughts scattered into fragments, whisked away by the goldjoy that Blakely had somehow introduced into the air. My vision swam as my muscles took on the familiar, languid lethargy brought about by the narcotic entering my bloodstream.

Both security guards slumped to the floor, blissful smiles plastered on their vacant faces. I wasn't far behind, although I still had my marbles for the moment. Besim leaned against the wall, eyes closed, brow furrowed in an expression of intense concentration.

"A pity," Blakely lamented, bending over to regard me with twinkling, gold-flecked eyes. Somehow, he was free of the handcuffs. "To be so close to your goal, yet thwarted in the end. However, not all is lost, at least not for me. Your Vellan will make an excellent replacement, since my laboratory and notes have all gone up in flames. Thankfully, my mind is as sharp as ever, and while the hard copy is gone, none of it was truly lost."

"You'll," I struggled, but my tongue was muddy and didn't want to work. "You'll...never...get away...with this."

"How very droll!" Blakely capered with a flourish of his hands. The cuffs were broken at the chain. "But I already have. Now then, where were we?"

He turned toward Besim, studying her with pursed lips.

"A curious and quite unexpected aspect of goldjoy is not its effect on humans, but on Vellans," he said. "While the substance is a powerful euphoric to you, the opposite is true for our interdimensional friends. It attacks their sensory nervous system, causing intense stimulation of their nociceptors. In layman's terms: she now suffers from a great amount of pain, so much so she is barely able to function. Isn't that right, my dear?"

Blakely stroked the side of her face with a gentle hand. Besim groaned, muttering something unintelligible under breath.

"Unfortunately, your companion failed to inoculate herself with whatever is in that flask of hers," he explained with false regret. "How very thoughtless of you! But no matter. Where we're going, that will be the least of your concerns."

"What," I faltered, slipping deeper into the thick wool blanket consuming my senses. "What...you...going...to...do?"

"Once we take our leave of you, I shall continue my experiments elsewhere," he replied. "Gateway City, or perhaps New Hollywood. I've already established new identities in both enclaves. Exorbitant, but necessary in my line of work."

Blakely manipulated the elevator screen, selecting a different destination. The vibration created by the elevator's sudden shift in speeds sent shivers of ecstasy throughout my body.

"There's still so much to be done," he continued with a sly smile. "Despite what Orpheus thinks, the applications of the genetic synthesis I perfected are endless! Poor David and his lost boys were only a small sampling of the possibilities, and I considered them failures at first. But my, my, my, how they evolved! Biogenetically engineered vampirism! A far cry from Stoker, eh Detective?"

Blakely glanced at the chainless cuffs around his wrists. With a twist of his thumb and forefinger, he snapped each as if the metal was paper.

"Quite frankly, what happened to them was pure serendipity," he remarked casually. "But their misfortune led to the discovery of goldjoy. From genetic waste to the most addictive narcotic on the streets! Naturally, I saved the very best for myself. And from there, Rumpelstiltskin was born!"

The elevator slowed to a halt.

Blakely knelt next to me with a crackle of his old knees. Now that we were up close and personal, I saw the faint sheen of sweat coating his brow. A musky aura surrounded him, thick and pungent. With a sluggish start, I realized he was the source of the goldjoy in the elevator, the highly concentrated substance oozing from his very pores.

"And the twins!" he exclaimed.

His eyes took on a feverish cast, the irises engorged by liquid gold. But behind them lurked something else, a twisted and all-too familiar thing full of malice and hunger. Whatever held the Insight back suddenly vanished. It blazed before my vision, revealing the master *fetch* to me, larger and more fully realized than any of the others I'd seen before it. The creature was wrapped around the shriveled dregs of Blakely's soul, two lovers embroiled in a dance of sex and death. Twin pinpoints of golden light regarded me with an awful cunning. Its profound hatred for all things living was palpable. Despite the 'joy's hold on my body, I trembled with fear.

"The females were the pinnacle of our achievements!" hissed the master *fetch* occupying the shell that was Blakley. "Once Orpheus revealed the secret to unlocking the Vellan genetic code, and provided us the necessary samples, we spliced and synthesized human and Vellan genetic material together, a feat your modern science believed impossible! Finally, a suitable host could be fashioned, and we would be rid of this wretched flesh prison once and for all!"

The Insight informed all my senses of what was before me. I could no longer hear the man. Instead, Blakeley's voice was replaced by the monster manipulating his strings.

"Or they should have been," it grumbled, bearing shadowy fangs. "Twenty-five years we worked on them, watching them grow and develop. No sickness. No disease. Perfect. Pure. And then the wasting began, like all the others that had come before. But we were ready this time. Yes, we were ready! The enzyme saved them! The enzyme was proof against the wasting! It made the females better. Stronger. But more aware. Yes, yes, yes. It unlocked their memories. Vanessa remembered. She *knew*. The sleeping pills were not enough. They could not bury the memories. Something had to be done. We needed more time!

"But we were too late. Orpheus intervened, tricking that fool Flanagan, and stealing the body that was rightfully ours! And then the other. Its creature replaced poor, poor Marko, who had stolen Vanessa's blood from us. An exact copy Marko was, and for years, we none the wiser. But you, your fell cold witch and your pet Protector destroyed that dear little poppet. We should thank you for that, but we won't."

The master *fetch* recovered its briefcase from the floor, then turned back to me.

"Yet none of them know what we know!" it continued as if speaking to itself. "Not Orpheus. Not the other. None! They cannot replicate what we have done. And without the twins, Orpheus and the other shall wither and die. For Time is their enemy, and she cannot be denied! But not us! We have your Vellan, and we shall endure!"

The revelations were stunning. If I had any control of my body, I would've punched the goddamn thing through the wall. Instead, I stared at the master *fetch*, slack-jawed and unmoving.

"For decades, we have been moored here, bound to this weakling," it said in a hollow voice that reminded me of twilight's fall, of fading echoes and false promises. "Yet, without his mind, all would be for naught."

Through the Insight, the rotten core that was Blakely was exposed. His body was a ruin of disease and decay, the bits held together by the controlling creature's malicious will. Yet there was little remaining to sustain it. The master *fetch* had been grafted to

Blakely for so long, it couldn't escape. Whatever humanity remained of Blakely was a mask to the outside world obscuring the mad wraith within.

And it was dying.

"Willing test subjects were impossible," it acknowledged. "However, this human's work with addicts to develop a better method of detoxification opened the door to an unlimited number of fresh possibilities. There were hundreds of the pathetic fools, suckling upon the teat of welfare, and too stupid to die. We instructed Crain to secure unattached women with infants. Oh yes! You see, the procedure was more efficacious on the female of your species. Two hundred infants were sacrificed so that we may be saved! As if they were straw we had spun into gold!"

The jarring sound of the creature's madness swirled within my mind, cutting through the goldjoy. I clung to it with what little resolve I had left. But my thoughts drifted away. The world swam before me in pretty, iridescent waves.

"How tragic Patricia Sullinger will die now that she no longer has the enzyme to sustain her," it snickered, mocking me. "All compliments of you, Guardian. Had you not stolen our girl, she might yet live. But alas, 'tis time to go."

The creature lifted Besim under her shoulder, bringing her upright. Besim groaned, the fingers of her hands frozen and bent, as if she were trying to claw her way to freedom. The master *fetch* dragged her through the open elevator door. I caught a glimpse of an unlit office floor, and the stale taste of dust. The brief influx of air diffused the 'joy briefly, and my body twitched in response.

"Goodbye Detective, or Guardian, or whatever name you'll take to your grave," it whispered with delight. "Your death is inevitable. It shall be a pleasant one, unlike what is in store for your Vellan doll here."

The master *fetch* cackled with glee as the elevator doors closed.

CHAPTER 39

I drifted, weightless.
    There was nothing.
And I felt nothing.

Was I dead?

I had touched Death when I tried to pay her a visit with that broken piece of glass to both wrists. What I was experiencing now wasn't the same.

Back then, someone had called my name from far away, echoing throughout a gray expanse as dense as the morning fog on the Hudson. The weightlessness was the same, but there was something else, a presence both familiar and not, and a light touch on my brow. Who had that been? What had happened to me?

Afterward, whenever I'd focus on those memories, they'd slip from my mind like air through a cloud.

Now, I felt shut off from everything, confined to a prison of boundless nothing. I was somewhere in-between, and the silence was deafening.

I was isolated.

Alone.

Something flickered at the edge of my vision, unfolding like an iris, and suddenly I was somewhere else.

My mother sat at the counter of the bookstore with Abner and my grandfather, her eyes glued to some trashy romance novel. I stood beside her. Harry and Abner were arguing. They always got into it, whatever the subject, and it ended with both agreeing to disagree. Things stayed civil that way, except when they played cribbage. Then things got nasty.

The two stood, and as my grandfather limped past, he clapped me on the shoulder with a wink and a sly grin. They wandered to the back where Abner kept his office, then shut the door.

"Hello there, Tommy," greeted my mother with a soft smile, the kind that warmed a heart faster than a cup of Uncle Mortie's hot chocolate. "Why don't you sit with me and stay awhile?"

"That sounds good, Ma. I'd like that."

I plopped down next to her with a lopsided grin. She handed me an old hardcover and went back to reading. I brought the book's spine to my nose. The smell was divine, of worn leather, dried ink, and old paper. It reminded me of the dusty stacks in the classical collection at the university library.

I glanced at the title.

Paradise Lost.

Milton was a favorite. I flipped open the cover.

"You look so tired, honey," she said with that frown every mother owns.

"I know, Ma. The job takes a lot out of me. Can I just stay here with you?"

"Why of course you can, my sweet, sweet boy," she replied. She smelled of honeysuckle, homemade cookies, and endless dreams. "You can stay with me for as long as you'd like."

The bell jingled behind me, its sound carving my calm with the sharp edge of despair.

"Guardian," she called out. "You must rise. You must save her."

My heart froze.

"Kate?"

"Guardian," she urged again. "You must fight this. The drug is killing you, and time is short."

"What are you doing here? You're dead."

"She shall be, if you do not act," Kate stated, her voice drawing near.

"Ignore her, honey," my mother's warm, comforting hand covered my own. "She's just a dream. Kate can't hurt you anymore. She's not real. She's gone."

I stared at the words on the page.

The mind is its own place, and in itself can make a heaven of hell, a hell of heaven.

"Trust in the words," Kate implored.

She stood behind me, but I was rooted to the spot, unable to face her.

"All that you see is an illusion of your dying mind. If you allow this to continue, you will never awaken from it."

"But I'm finally happy. I'm content. And you left me, Kate. You died."

"That's right, honey," my mother urged. "Believe in me. In us. We're finally together. Lay down your burdens, my sweet boy. Life has been so hard on you. So very hard. But that is over now. Rest, Tommy. Be at peace."

She pressed my hand with a reassuring squeeze. I laid my head in her lap as her gentle fingers stroked my hair, just like when I was little.

Before she died.

Before everything went to hell.

It all came back.

The image of her in the plain casket, lying in state, pale and empty.

The hollow ache of a boy's broken heart. My heart.

The emptiness, the loneliness and the despair.

Awake, arise or be for ever fall'n, the open page read.

"What is happening to me?"

"You are dying," Kate said, her voice fading. "And so is she."

"Ma, this isn't right."

"It is, honey," she said. "Just let go. Let it all go."

Abner, my grandfather, and the bookstore vanished. There was only my mother and me.

"I'm here now. Lie here and rest. There's nothing to fear. I'll watch over you. The world has hurt you long enough. Close your eyes like a good boy. Sleep. Sleep, and dream."

"No, no this isn't right," I murmured, eyes half-shuttered. "You would never tell me to give up. This isn't real. It isn't real!"

A sickening rush, and I was on the floor of the elevator. The bodies of the two security guards lay in a heap across from me.

Milton's poem called to me a final time.

All is not lost, the unconquerable will, and the study of revenge, immortal hate, and the courage never to submit or yield.

I drew strength from the words, marshaling my thoughts. The Insight coursed through me, but was distant, as if it were in another room. I clawed toward it, summoning the rage I felt for the victims of the master *fetch*, David Crain, Julie DeGrassi, and Orpheus. Hundreds of helpless, forgotten women and children, enslaved and murdered. Their lifeless bodies, the twisted remnants of the creature's failed experiments, dumped down that shithole, never to be seen again. I relived the moment when we discovered the pit, visceral emotions carrying me on a seething current. The raw force of my feelings flowered, intensified. They sharpened my senses and inched me inexorably away from sweet oblivion.

Suddenly, Nine was there.

"Save her," the little girl whispered, pleading eyes locking with mine. "Save us all."

The Insight roared, infusing my body with renewed vigor. I levered myself off the floor and over to the control panel. The elevator hadn't moved. By the looks of things, I'd only been down for a couple of minutes. An alarm had sounded, alerting security that the elevator had stopped on the thirtieth floor. His voice shouted over the intercom, but I didn't respond.

I waved my hand over the panel to open the doors, then stepped into a darkened foyer, gun in hand.

"Tactical," I whispered.

Nothing happened.

"EVI?" I called in my mind, but the AI was silent.

Scuffling sounds further in caught my attention. I crept forward, maintaining a low profile. The floor was similar in layout to Research and Development, minus the people. I came to a break in the cubicle farm to peer around the corner, gun at the ready. One of the offices along the perimeter wall was lit by the glow of a holo-phone.

The creature was inside. I heard the familiar rise and fall of its sibilant rasp.

It was singing.

Today I bake, tomorrow brew
The next I'll have the young queen's child.
Ha, glad am I that no one knew
That Rumpelstiltskin I am styled.

I shook my head. "Misty Mountain Hop" it wasn't.

The master *fetch* danced with an object twirling in its hands, and triumphant joy on its face. It took me a second to register what it was—the last pinot bottle that had been in Tony's wine rack. Crain's cleaners must've gotten to it before Julie.

Besim lay on the floor of the office. As I watched, parts of her body twitched, as if charged with electrical current. An opaque cloud clung to her, something the Insight was unable to penetrate. Whatever lay underneath was insulated by that cloud.

"You see, my sweetling?" the creature chortled. "The last of the serum! No one, not even Orpheus, knows of its existence! Trick the police into finding our laboratory, will you? *Feh.* Destroy our equipment, our notes, our samples? *Feh.* The knowledge of the experiments resides within us! Once we are free, we shall find Orpheus and her bitch and make them suffer for their betrayal!"

It placed the bottle on the credenza next to the open briefcase with a loud thump, then knelt by Besim.

"A shame no one ever discovered *your* secret, my sweetling," the master *fetch* purred, tracing the angles of her face with its fingers. "The truth of why you became embroiled in this game. After all, you are the mirror image of them both, are you not?"

That caught my attention. I leaned in a little closer.

"How amusing that your disguise distracted everyone, even your precious Guardian," it continued. "To hide those markings, so integral to your identity, the very essence of Vellan culture! And then you adopted a human mask. Such a deliberate affront to your people! Oh ho, we know a little something-something about you, *Besim Saranda!* Self-imposed exile, was it not?"

Besim groaned in agony. I couldn't imagine the pain she suffered from the 'joy saturating her bloodstream.

"Still, how did Orpheus manage it?" the creature asked with genuine curiosity. "Few are allowed into your holy city, and only at the written invitation of the Circle of Adepts. For Orpheus to have smuggled the corpse of your very own daughter out from one of the most remote places on this miserable Earth is quite a feat! Orpheus had someone on the inside, no doubt. The Adepts must have believed the traitor to be you! No wonder you fled."

Besim didn't respond. Her face contorted while her body shook.

"For years you've scoured the enclaves, so desperate to find her, without any hint of her whereabouts," it burbled with malice. "And then one day, she appears, the ghost of your daughter reflected on the face of a murdered girl with red hair. Red, for the *Al-Aquibas*, the Vellan aristocracy. *Your* caste!"

I stared, enthralled by the story unfolding before me. Besim had said she was one of the *Nabira-Shas*, the caste of administrators and business. What the fuck was going on?

"Dyeing and cutting your hair to hide the truth," the master *fetch* gibbered. "Such a simple thing, really. To the average human, you are nothing more than a curiosity, a member of the Vellan middle class. But to your own people, to those who know who you *truly* are, why, you are considered royalty, yes? And your dead daughter, the very progeny of Besim Saranda of the *Al-Aquibas*, reduced to a laboratory rat! Her genetic essence culled to create the perfect vessel for us! Do not fret, my sweetling. You shall make a suitable replacement, and your suffering shall be delicious!"

Besim's eyes flickered open to glare at the creature with undisguised hatred. She said something, but I couldn't hear it. The master *fetch's* scornful laughter followed.

I leaned against the cubicle wall, stunned. The implications of what I'd learned raced through my mind. I wanted to pull the trigger now, end Blakely and take Besim to safety, but the angle wasn't right, even if I had the assistance of the gun's tactical. Looking around, I spied open floor off to the right. Somehow, I had to move the creature from the office for a cleaner shot and stay far enough away from it to avoid the goldjoy. Even at this distance, I tasted its foul bouquet.

"But now, we must escape," it murmured. "As we anticipated, the facility's security has been alerted. The contingency plan is required."

It picked up the holo-phone, manipulated the display, and placed a call. Almost immediately, I sensed EVI's return. The gun's tactical activated in my eye, and I braced myself as a host of sensory data filled my vision.

"Mr. Kilkullen?" the walking shamble that was once a human being said, mimicking the cultured voice of Oliver Blakely.

As it spoke, I skulked over to the open space.

"Oh yes, there has been a gross mistake," it said. "It appears Doctor Bartleman and my colleagues played a parting trick on me. And good for them, I say! Even the staff was fooled. Oh yes, the alarm in the elevator? I'm afraid a vial I carried fell from my pocket when I was jostled in the elevator. It broke, and a toxin was released. Detective Holliday and both of your men succumbed to its effects before I redirected the elevator to a different floor and escaped. I locked the elevator car here. Fortunately, none of the toxin spilled on myself or Doctor Saranda. Hmm? Oh, she's fine, although incapacitated. Would you please inform the Environmental Safety Department? Thank you, Mr. Kilkullen. We'll be here waiting."

It killed the call and returned the phone to its pocket. The holo-tech dampening field didn't reactivate.

"Come along, my dear," it said, and secured the bottle inside the briefcase.

The master *fetch* bent over and hauled Besim to her feet with a strength belying its skinny frame. She hung from its wrapped arm like a deflated sex toy, arms and legs splayed and loose.

I considered my options. Kilkullen and the environmental guys were on their way, but the creature was on the move. Not a lot of time to come up with a brilliant plan.

And let's face it, I was not that smart.

That left only one option.

"Blakely!"

The gun's tactical showed me distances and trajectories, but the cubicle walls afforded him some cover. I could blow a hole through one, but couldn't chance hitting Besim, either. Luring it out to me was my only choice.

"My, my, my," the creature crowed with delight. "The Guardian lives! How extraordinary!"

"You'll have to do better than that shitty head candy of yours if you want to take me out," I taunted, heart pounding in my chest.

"I don't need to," it replied. "I have nothing to fear. You are merely human, scraps of flesh, blood, and bone. You cannot harm me."

It moved down the aisle of cubicles, and away from the office.

"You think you're so all-powerful, huh?" I sneered, lacing each word with contempt. "I kicked the shit out of your little toys, blew the fuck out of your goddamn laboratory, and flushed your drug operation down the toilet. I'd say I'm more formidable than you think. You don't believe me? Then why don't you come over here and find out!"

The master *fetch* paused.

"I guess that makes two of us who've outsmarted you," I continued, stepping backward. "Orpheus left you to blow in the breeze. She called your experiments worthless. Flawed. And when you had Crain fix things, she knew you'd fuck it all up. So, she cut her losses, and distanced herself as far from you as she could. You're a fucking failure, pal."

The creature was livid but continued to move away.

"As for me, I'm just some ordinary cop," I pressed, sudden anger making my hands shake. "But even I got the best of you. So much for being three steps ahead of everyone else, asshole! You still think you'll get away with this? I don't give a damn what you are, or where you're from, but if you believe that then you're just another stupid fuck like all the other jerks I've busted over the years."

Finally, I struck a nerve. It turned back toward me, bearing Besim and the briefcase.

"We are no failure!" it spat, hatred plain on its twisted face. "We are the pinnacle of scientific and magical achievement! And we shall deal with Orpheus in time."

It moved into the open space with its arm wrapped around Besim's waist, then lowered the briefcase to the floor.

"But you?" it hissed. "Experimenting on humans taught us a great deal about your physiology. We will take you with us, so you may enjoy a long life of suffering before you die."

"We'll see about that," I grated, brandishing the gun. "Let her go."

"As you wish," it said, releasing Besim from its grasp.

I waited a breath, then fired.

And missed.

The moment my muscles tensed on the trigger, the master *fetch* blurred, moving faster than Crain or Marko. It flowed through the air, quicker than thought, its preternatural speed awful to behold. The bullet smashed the wall where it had been half a second before. Using the gun's tactical, I redirected the gun and fired five more shots.

They all missed.

The master *fetch* laughed.

A blow to the side of my head sent the world spinning. A second punch to my gut knocked the wind out of me. The gun fell to the floor as I collapsed to one knee. Concentrated goldjoy surrounded me, filling my eyes, nose and mouth, seeping into the pores of my skin, drowning me. The lethargy deadened my body. It stood over me, shivering with delight, relishing its victory. I stared up into its soulless eyes, slack and helpless.

I'd been beaten.

The creature grabbed me by my collar, drawing me close. Fangs the color of midnight glistened with an awful darkness. Its fetid breath held the memories of other lives, drawn from helpless victims too weak to fight.

"We have changed our mind, Guardian," it whispered seductively. Its tongue kissed my cheek, and my flesh crawled. "Now you will die."

A scream pierced the room then, a primal sound that evoked anguish and grief on an unimaginable scale. The creature's grasp loosened. I crumpled to the floor.

Head tilted back and eyes wild and unseeing, Besim knelt with both arms flung wide. She poured out her damaged soul in that scream. The very air vibrated with its power. I heard the craft and talent of her voice back at Armin's, the passion of its duality and the strength of its conviction, but this was far different. Now it was a weapon, an outlet from which she attacked using the anger, bitterness, and pain that imprisoned her.

Reinforced windows shattered into deadly fragments. Glass erupted all around. The wind and rain swept in, churning the shards in glittering swirls, like flying daggers. As the gale crashed into us, several cut my face and hands. I cried out, rolling to the side, and covered my head. Freed from the creature, the goldjoy dissipated, wiped away by the fresh rush of wind. I found a pocket of clear air and took several gulps, scouring my body and mind.

The master *fetch* clamped both hands to its ears. It shrieked, although its sound was drowned by Besim's own. The creature stood at the center of the maelstrom, glass shredding its clothing and flesh, rendering it a scarred and hideous monster, a reflection of its true self.

I gathered up my gun and moved to Besim's side, then placed a steady hand on her shoulder. Besim's body relaxed when she realized it was me. Her mouth closed.

"It's all right. I'm here now. Let me finish this."

She nodded.

I faced the master *fetch*. It hadn't moved, hands still clutched to its head. Blood flowed freely from dozens of wounds, saturating the carpet.

I narrowed my eyes, raised the gun, and fired.

The bullet that burst forth blazed with white fire. It caught the creature in the chest, burning a hole the size of a coffee mug. Aghast and unbelieving, it stared at the flaming wound.

"How?" it wailed, clutching at the hole, but its hands caught on fire, engulfing the flesh. "How is this possible?"

"A friend once told me all you need is a little faith," I responded, then put a second bullet in its left leg. "So I found another way."

More of the fire raced along its body, devouring the shadowy thing underneath. It backed away from me, fear and madness riding in its eyes.

"This isn't over, Guardian!" it screamed, spittle flying from its lips. "We shall return!"

"No, you won't," I said, the silver fire of the Insight burning in my eyes. "But even if you do, I'll still be here. And I'll be waiting."

I fired.

The impact propelled the creature through the yawning opening behind it, and out into the wind.

As Rumpelstiltskin spiraled into the swirling darkness below, it tore in two, consumed by white fire.

CHAPTER 40

*B*ill Mahoney took charge the moment he arrived. A light drizzle patterned everything, so without missing a beat, Mahoney set up a covered command center. It even boasted a beverage station. Mahoney had thought of everything, bless his crotchety soul. Nobody came in or out without his approving glare. The linked pavilions encompassed half a city block, centered around the spot where Blakely's remains lay. Two stone-faced officers kept watch over the corpse. Blakely had hit the ground with such force his body had fissured the pavement. The lingering stench of charred flesh, hair, and bone made my stomach turn. I looked away before I added new evidence to the crime scene.

The memory of the master *fetch's* fangs about to end my life before Besim's *deus ex clamo* saved us all sickened me. I'd be having nightmares about that one for a long time.

I swirled the coffee cup one of the uniforms had handed me. The CSI guys combed the area, collecting evidence, asking questions and taking images. It was nice to see them. I'd almost forgotten what they looked like.

Off to our left was the ground floor entrance to Wrigley-Boes

Pharmaceuticals, filled with dozens of officers, first responders, gawkers, and reporters. I even saw Rena Somethingorother from *The Daily Dose.*

The pharmaceutical giant's legion of lawyers performed damage control, well-groomed men and women in designer suits speaking with anyone with a recording device. Several gestured in our direction, but I ignored them.

I guess that's what happens when one of their employees plummets thirty stories to splatter on the pavement. Just like Frederick Murray. I thought about him for a minute. Poor guy. With Rumpelstiltskin pavement candy, at least goldjoy was off the streets. But there'd be other jumpers, high on the next drug du jour, falling off some rooftop because they were too jacked to care.

Empire City was like that. Some things never changed.

"And then you shot him?" Mahoney asked, rubbing his jaw. He lowered his voice, glancing around to make certain no one was within earshot. "With consecrated bullets?"

"Yeah," I answered with a weak smile, tugging at the heavy blanket a nice paramedic had given me. "I went to see an old friend. Thought the bullets might help."

"Is that right?" Mahoney murmured.

At the time, I had thought I was being clever, dipping six regular rounds in the font back at the Holy Redeemer while Besim dazzled me with her pep talk. I had no idea what we'd be up against when we confronted Rumpelstiltskin. The fight at Kraze had opened my eyes to a very different type of warfare. I had no plans on getting caught flat-footed like that again. Since Father Jack refused, I'd have to help myself.

When I checked the gun after our showdown, the ammo meter read nine shots discharged. The troubling thing was, I knew I had missed with the first six.

"Said a couple 'Hail Marys' for good measure, then came here," I added quickly, not meeting his eyes. "Deacon said the only things that could hurt a *fetch* were consecrated weapons. Since he and his magic baseball bat got benched, I needed to upgrade the old arsenal."

"Right," he responded, drawing the word out. "I remember. Thought you were Jewish, though. Why not go to your rabbi?"

"Uh, yeah, well someone once told me that sometimes, you just need faith," I replied, echoing my words to Rumpelstiltskin before he burned. "He didn't say which flavor. And I was in a hurry. Let's stick with that, ok?"

"Fair enough." Mahoney studied me with a solemn expression. "What about Besim?"

"What about her?" I said harshly, then took a long draw from the cup. I didn't blame Mahoney for hiding anything from me. My gut told me she'd probably kept him in the dark too. "Her people arrived before ours and escorted her back to the hotel. She was pretty shaken up by the whole thing."

I explained goldjoy's debilitating effect on Vellans. Bill didn't press me for more.

"I'm heading over there to pick up Leyla, and check in on Deacon," I finished. "Speaking of which, I don't expect you to pay Leyla any consultant's fee. Since I brought her in, I'll handle that out of my own pocket. She's definitely earned it."

"That's not necessary," the captain said. "When you file the report, make sure you mention her involvement, minus any illegal holo-activity. Maybe we can scrounge up a few credits for a job well done."

I nodded my thanks. A sudden thought hit me.

"Wait, does that mean I'm going to get paid too?" I asked hopefully.

"You're still a part of Special Crimes, Detective," he admonished in a stern voice, before his expression softened. "The mayor signed off on our funding about an hour ago, so no one's firing you just yet. Take a few days off, Tom. You've been through hell.

And go see a doctor about those cuts and bruises. When you're feeling better, report to me Monday at 0800."

"Monday?" I blinked, the excitement growing in my stomach. "There's another case?"

"There's always another case, son," he said with a grimace. "SCU is front page news, thanks to you. All the feeds are eating this up. People like Sam Gaffney may not be fans, but you did good, Tom. The mayor has high expectations for us."

It's hard to glow with pride when your face is a crossword puzzle of razor thin, angry cuts, but I tried anyway.

"Thank you, sir."

I resisted the urge to hug him. Instead, I finished the last of my coffee, said my goodbyes, and went in search of a refill.

A few minutes later, EVI picked me up for the trip to L'Hotel Internacional. Along the way, I called Abner to let him know I'd be bringing Leyla home soon. He asked if I would stay for dinner, as well as a few hands of cribbage. It was an offer I couldn't refuse.

The hotel lobby hummed with activity. A few people gave me curious looks, but I just kept walking. Mamika met me by the elevator, ushering me into the car with a courteous gesture. As soon as we arrived, a flash of white hair and intense cold greeted me with a crushing bear hug.

"Doc!" Leyla cried, releasing me after the third squeeze. She gave me a critical look. "You look awful!"

"You should see the other guy," I said with a weary smile.

"No shit," drawled Deacon, stepping in to shake my hand. His right arm glimmered with the zero-gravity cast, while thick bandages wrapped his shoulder down to his forearm. His nose was crooked and purple. "'Cause you sure don't look pretty."

"You're looking better," I commented dryly, nodding at the cast.

"I haven't had a goddamn cigarette in nearly twenty-four fucking hours," he complained. "Stupid, goddamn antibiotics and painkillers. As if that shit'll help. It's liable to kill me before it cures a goddamn thing."

"Yet you're still taking them," I observed.

"Fuck you, Holliday," he growled, although I caught the ghost of a smile.

We matriculated to the living room. Besim stood by the window speaking with Mamika in hushed tones.

The curtains had been drawn away from the window. As I stared out the clear glass, something dark shifted in the gray gloom. For a moment, it resembled the silhouette of a man. I blinked, rubbed my eyes, and the shadow was gone. Must've been a trick of the light. Damn, I was tired.

I reached into my blazer pocket and wrapped my fingers around the twisted metal fragment. It felt warm to the touch but cooled as if I'd caught it stealing from the cookie jar. Releasing it, I shook my head with a wry smile. My imagination was really getting the better of me. A hot shower and a two-day nap would do the trick. And a lot more rugelach.

Someone had left a mug of black coffee, cream, and sugar on the table, but I wasn't interested. Leaning deeper into the cushions, I filled Deacon and Leyla in on my encounter with Julie and Orpheus at Ettelman's office. The part about the Guardian, her brother, and the Game I'd leave for another day.

"Wow," Leyla whistled. "Do you have any idea why Orpheus was involved in all this?"

"No," I lied with a straight face. "We figured Orpheus wasn't in it for the credits, and I still think that's true. She said they'd been partners for a long time, but she never told me why, or what she gained from it. Honestly, I think she did it because she thought it was fun."

"Well, while you were busy playing hero, I tried backtracking Marko's dual signal," Leyla yawned, sprawling in a comfortable chair by the workstation. "After a while, I got bored with that, so I tuned into the Wrigley-Boes feed. Right about the time Rumpel-stiltskin tried to kill you."

"You saw that?" I asked. Chills crawled down my spine.

"Most of it," she grinned, but my discomfort went unnoticed. "I slipped a tracker onto your jacket before you left. It was Deacon's idea. We wanted to keep tabs on you."

"Gee, thanks," I made a sour face.

"You're welcome," Leyla replied brightly. "Anyway, the tracker showed you were at the deli. I figured you stopped for coffee while planning your next move. But then it went dark, as if it got fried or something. I knew something was wrong. That's when Mamika got the call from Besim. She told us what happened. We both wanted to come to you, but Mamika wouldn't let us. Right after that, the tracker reactivated, and you were on the move again. Then you called us from the pod on your way to Wrigley-Boes. Since I had already hacked into their network, picking up their internal feed was easy."

"You were damn lucky getting past their security," Deacon added. "I'd forgotten about Saranda's relationship with Solomon. I sent a team to the building across the street in case you needed a quick evac. By that time, though, you'd already taken Blakely into custody."

"Yeah, and then the shit hit the fan," I said, shuddering at the memory. "The moment the elevator doors closed he activated the same dampening device in his phone that Flanagan had used. It shut down everything except the local elevator controls."

"It's real useful, whatever it is. Wish I had one," Leyla sighed wistfully. "Deacon was about to give the order to storm the building when the feed popped back on. We watched what happened after that, but there was no audio. Jesus, Doc, that was some scary shit!"

"You don't know the half of it," I muttered, shifting my weight on the couch.

"Saranda filled us in on most of the details," Deacon said,

nodding at Besim. "There's a special kind of hell for that piece of shit. Burning it was a kindness. You'll have to tell me how you killed the damn thing with that peashooter of yours, Holliday. I didn't think consecrated bullets were standard issue for Empire cops."

"Maybe not ECPD, but they should be for SCU." I gave him a tight-lipped smile.

Mamika strode from the room, but not before inquiring if any of us needed anything. I declined, offering my thanks. Besim hadn't moved. Her back was to us, hands clasped before her.

"Did you learn anything more about Marko's signal?" I asked, changing the subject.

The cushions did their best to swallow me, and I almost obliged them. I was beat, both physically and otherwise, but I wasn't ready to give in to my fatigue yet. There was still something I had to do.

"Nope," Leyla sighed. "Whoever built him, they're damn good at staying hidden. They severed the connection the moment you blew up Marko. With Rumpelstiltskin dead, and both Julie and Orpheus gone, I guess we'll never know who was behind Marko."

"I wouldn't be too sure about that, girl," Deacon said. "An outfit like that ain't none too happy with how everything went down the past few days. Payback's a bitch, and she'll always get her pound of flesh. I bet we'll run into them again."

"Maybe," I conceded, lacing my fingers behind my head. "Where's Patricia?"

"Haven't talked to her since we brought her here," Deacon replied. "Last I checked, she was still in her room."

"That is incorrect," Besim announced quietly. "Patricia Sullinger has been sent to Vellas."

She turned to regard me. Pale and drawn, Besim hadn't reapplied any of her makeup or dye. Darker splotches of deep auburn, like liver spots, bled throughout her short-cropped hair.

"What?" I sputtered. "Why? When did this happen? She's the

only witness to the case the DA's putting together. How are they supposed to implicate Wrigley-Boes in anything with her a continent away?"

"I have already made arrangements with your district attorney," she explained. "Her testimony will be provided via holotransfer, under the auspices of my personal law firm and the blessing of Mayor Samson. However, I do not expect Wrigley-Boes to survive the matter regardless of the outcome in your courts of law. The corporation was financially unstable as it was, and this blemish to their public persona will no doubt finish them, of that I am certain."

"Then why send Patricia to Vellas?" Leyla asked.

"Because she is Vellan, of course," Besim replied simply. "Her newfound citizenship affords her the protection of the Vellan people. She will be well-cared for there."

Deacon's head whipped toward Besim. "The fuck?"

"She's also dying," I pointed out. "The hospitals here are perfectly—"

"Your medical science is inadequate," Besim interrupted me, the color rising in her cheeks.

"Maybe," I said, staking an angry finger at her. "But your people have no idea how to save her, either. Whatever Blakely did, all his research died with him. His notes, his theories, everything. Your people will be just as clueless as any doctor here."

"Perhaps," Besim replied, desperation edging her voice. "But I must try. The die has already been cast. She and most of my security team left not two hours ago. They should arrive in Vellas later this evening."

"Why wasn't I consulted?" Deacon demanded. "What the fuck's going on?"

"You were not needed in this," she answered, turning to him. "Her safety is paramount, and time was of the essence. I made the necessary arrangements. It is done."

Deacon's eyes flashed with anger, and it appeared as if he would respond. Instead, he exhaled, then shook his head.

"You have no right to do that!" I pressed. "She's an innocent girl who's been abused in ways we can't even begin to imagine!"

"Hey now, Holliday," Deacon warned, taking a step toward me. "Simmer down before things get ugly."

I looked at Besim as the realization dawned on me.

"He doesn't know."

"Know what?" the former Protector asked.

"No one does," Besim whispered. A single tear bled down her cheek.

"Can someone please tell me what's going on?" Leyla cried.

"Do you want to tell them," I said. "Or should I?"

"Very well," Besim sighed, glancing from Leyla back to Deacon.

She recounted to them her theory regarding the enzyme and the wine, the results of her examination of all the tissue samples, and her discovery of both Vanessa and Patricia's unique genetic code.

"Without this formula, Patricia will die," Besim finished in forlorn tones.

"How long does she have?" Leyla asked in desperation. "Months? Weeks?"

Besim's eyes lowered.

"Days."

Leyla stifled a sob.

"You're saying we saved her from that monster just to find out she's still going to die," she cried through angry tears. "And there's nothing we can do about it? What the fuck is wrong with this fucked-up world?"

"As I said, the healers in Vellas possess skills your human doctors do not," Besim explained patiently. "It is possible they will discover a cure in time."

"How can we trust them not to turn Patricia into someone

else's goddamn science project?!" Leyla shouted, surging from her chair. "Jesus Christ, Besim! Why didn't you tell us?"

"You have my word, that will not happen," Besim responded in a firm tone. "And I did not tell you because I did not feel it was relevant that you knew. With Doctor Blakely dead, the murder investigation is over. Your involvement has come to an end. I thank you for your timely assistance. It is now a Vellan matter."

Leyla's mouth hung open as she glared at Besim. She grabbed her things.

"I gotta go," she addressed me with red-rimmed eyes. "Meet you down at the pod?"

"Sure thing, kiddo," I replied gently as she stormed out. "See you in a few minutes."

Deacon's mouth worked. Outrage flickered in his eyes. Besim returned his flinty stare. Not for the first time, something unspoken passed between them.

Deacon stomped from the room.

Silence filled the vacuum, broken only by the faint howling of the wind outside, a dying echo harboring its secrets, and revealing nothing.

"Why not tell them the whole truth?" I stood, straightening my pants.

Besim glided to the chair opposite me but didn't sit.

"Because I do not require their sympathy, Guardian," she replied. "My daughter is dead. The pain is something I live with every waking moment. She haunts my dreams, and is both my greatest loss, and greatest shame. I do not wish to share it. With anyone. Surely you, of all people, must understand this."

We stood across from one another, a human and a Vellan. Despite her greater height, she looked diminished, a fragment of the vibrant creature I'd come to know over the past few days. What the future held for her, I had no idea.

And right now, I really didn't care.

"Then I guess this is goodbye."

"Indeed," the Vellan said. She walked back to the window, hands behind her.

Conflicting emotions warred in my chest. There were so many things I wanted to say, but each one of them led to a different kind of madness. And I was just too damn tired. Instead, I removed the wine bottle I had kept inside my blazer. I studied it, noting the dark liquid inside, and the secrets it contained. Placing it carefully on the table, I made my way to the elevator without another word.

The door opened at my approach, spilling soft white light into the foyer.

"Guardian," Besim called out.

I didn't answer.

"Tom?"

Her voice was hollow and distant, bereft of its customary resonance and depth. About as far apart as our two worlds.

I hesitated, then stepped into the elevator.

"Thank you," she said.

The door closed behind me.

THE END

EPILOGUE

*A*lan Arthur Azyrim pondered his reflection in the window. He was an imposing man, with thick, dark hair and a double widow's peak flecked with silver. However, it was to Azyrim's eyes that most were drawn. One blue patterned with gold, and the other amber rimmed in gray, his heterochromia was unique to anywhere, and not just Empire City. The blue called to mind the deep oceans of the world, an unclaimed vastness the depths of which had never been fully explored. The amber was savage, the feral light of an unbound predator, its iris refracting the light.

Some claimed each eye bore a mind of its own. One brightened while the other dimmed in response to Azyrim when he laughed or grew angry. And some whispered of a third eye, hidden from the waking world, possessed of an unnatural sorcery, which might explain his company's unprecedented success. Financial pundits always bet on Azyrim Technologies. When Azyrim bought, the market followed. And where Azyrim sold, unemployment lines swelled.

His was the tallest building in Empire City, dominating two blocks of the most sought-after real estate in the enclave. Azyrim

Technologies employed thousands, maintaining satellite offices in all the major enclaves around the globe. The man himself was a fixture in the news, attending or hosting enclave fundraisers and upper crust social gatherings. He dated fashion models, athletes, and holo-stars. Whether cutting ribbons at the newest medical center he built or advocating support for the enclave's war against drugs and child prostitution, Azyrim had secured himself a place as one of the most influential people in Empire City.

"Orders, my Lord," Reaper One stated, static accompanying the words.

"Patience," Azyrim replied in a voice deep and rich, full of a resonance and timbre that some found musical, and others intoxicating. Tall and strong, Azyrim's broad, tanned face was accentuated by a full mouth accustomed to laughter.

He wasn't laughing now.

"Truthseeker," Azyrim called.

A sleek, black table made of glass sprawled behind him. Light bled into its surface swallowed by the darkness. The piece was large enough to seat two dozen, yet only thirteen chairs surrounded it. It was an antique by all standards, lacking any of the puritan lines and rounded edges of modern technology. To the casual observer, the table bore neither blemish nor scar, and seemed perfect in every way.

But Azyrim knew better. He had discovered its weak point. A gossamer, thin thread, the faintest of cracks, that ran through its center.

An imperfection.

A flaw.

His lips curled in a tight sneer at the memory of how the crack came to be.

Something on its surface flared to life. Sapphire lettering skittered across in straight lines. He didn't turn from the window.

What is it that you desire?

"Reveal to me their words," he commanded.

As you wish.

"Do you have any idea why Orpheus was involved in all this?" a girl asked, her youthful voice projecting into the room as if she were standing in the office with him.

"Not this," Azyrim growled, irritated. "Forward."

"Patricia Sullinger has been sent to Vellas," a woman said.

Her voice contained an intricate tonal quality and complex inflection intimating layers of meaning that would be lost on most human ears.

But not his.

"Forward," Azyrim scowled, crossing his arms while raising a hand to stroke his chin.

"Without this formula, Patricia will die," the same voice said. "And thus far, I have been unable to replicate it."

"Pause," he said.

Azyrim's blue eye glittered as his mind worked. A search of the Wrigley-Boes warehouse in Hoboken had revealed nothing. Blakely's other safeholds were much the same. The wretch had cleaned house. Azyrim held little doubt that his people dispatched to recover the data had been thorough. Their lives depended on such things. Blakely had either kept the research on his person or destroyed it. With nothing of value gained, and nowhere else to search, the warehouse and Blakely's other nests had burned.

As had Blakely himself, although not by Azyrim's hand.

"Why not tell them the whole truth?" a new voice asked. This time, a man, the one he had seen through the *golem's* eyes before it was destroyed. His was all-too-human, but within the weft of his voice, something else.

Something old, and familiar.

"Forward," he ordered again.

A memory niggled at the edge of his consciousness, a fragment from a distant sun he had buried long ago.

"She haunts my dreams, and is my greatest loss, and greatest shame," the woman's voice said. "I do not wish to share it. With anyone."

"End," he said, the words laced with contempt.

As you wish.

His blue eye closed. Angry amber glared at his reflection. Suffused with fury, this eye imagined a world ravaged by fire. He suppressed the desire, crushing it behind a will that would not be denied. The amber eye closed, reluctant, like a stubborn child.

"She is lost, then," Azyrim muttered. "Another solution must be found."

He exhaled, resisting the urge to shatter the window with a glance. He laced his fingers behind his back.

The blue eye opened.

"Reaper One, status," he said.

"We are in position, my Lord," Reaper One replied. The faint hum of rushing air interrupted the transmission. "Terminate?"

"Withdraw," Azyrim growled.

He was unaccustomed to the bitter taste in his mouth. For a moment, he imagined another place, on a different world. There, those who opposed him had met their fiery end, but not before allowing others to escape his wrath. Something splintered in his mind's eye, the cracking of sapphire, the glitter of emerald, the sparkle of ruby, the depthless swirl of onyx.

"My Lord?" Reaper One asked.

There would be a reckoning.

But not today.

"Withdraw," Azyrim repeated, his calm restored. "The Guardian has returned, and with it, the Game has changed."

He turned away from the window.

"Well played, sister. Well played."

SAVE AN AUTHOR, WRITE A REVIEW

Now that you've finished BLOODLINES, what's next?

How about leaving a rating and/or write a review?

Independent authors like me live and die through aggregated Amazon and Goodreads ratings and reviews. The more we get, the greater the chance other readers looking for the right blend of science fiction, urban fantasy and crime thriller will find stories like BLOODLINES.

You, fearless reader, wield great power! And with great power...well, you know the rest. By leaving a rating or a review, you directly influence the story's exposure worldwide.

So what are you waiting for?

Thank you so much for taking the time to read and review my work!

(Kindle and Paperback) Amazon US: mybook.to/BloodlinesEBook

(Kindle and Paperback) Amazon UK: mybook.to/BloodlinesUK

Goodreads: https://www.goodreads.com/author/show/18373280.Peter_Hartog

ACKNOWLEDGMENTS

The long and winding road has finally reached its end. It took a village, and I'm very fortunate mine tolerated its idiot. From Arlen, Christopher (the real Deacon), Dan, Derek, Michele (the real Leyla), Nigel and Thomas, who were my beta readers, and provided me with essential feedback while I shaped the story and characters into something that made sense. To Mook, for his first round of copy and line edits of the manuscript. To the incomparable Liz Heijkoop at ARC Editing, who did a tremendous job pointing out all the major flaws in story, characters and structure, and transformed BLOODLINES into the story it is today. To the Brandeis Connection of Jon and Scott, for educating me about dialysis, Latin phrases and the other religion. To Lance Buckley for his incredible re-imagining of the book cover. So many thanks go to Christopher, Michelle, Sean, Scott and Wendy, who allowed me to breathe life into our role-playing misadventures, something that has spanned the decades, and without whom I wouldn't have had the inspiration to write this novel today. And last, but never least, to my wife Traci, who still puts up with my constant soul-searching, and the long days of doubt and self-pity. She reminded me I do have talent, and that Tom Holliday's story needed to be told.

ALSO BY PETER HARTOG

Detective Tom "Doc" Holliday and the Special Crimes Unit will return in

PIECES OF EIGHT (Book Two of the Guardian of Empire City Series)

Find it here: Mybook.to/PiecesOfEight

In the UK: my book.to/PiecesOfEightUK

Read on for a preview.

And available NOW!

PIECES OF EIGHT

The red and blue flare of emergency and law enforcement illuminated the scene as the pod settled to a stop. EVI fed the chatter of the onsite personnel through the internal comm system, but it was background noise to me.

I stared out the window at a massive stone edifice, its tall walls alit with the scurrying shadows from the activity below. The Holy Redeemer Church hunkered along Brighton Beach Avenue within a few blocks of the waterfront. Made of thick wood and solid stone, its origin hearkened back to the late nineteenth century, and held a storied reputation in the surrounding community for its educational, social and religious outreach programs.

I'd grown up several blocks from the church. Despite my mixed religious heritage, the Redeemer had been a safe harbor for me, one of the few places where I'd felt welcome. Back then, my education choices were limited. There were no active synagogues in Brighton Beach, or many other neighborhoods throughout Empire City for that matter. Those had shut down decades ago from rampant antisemitism and both the half-hearted and futile attempts by local authorities to combat it. Eventually, a lack of funds coupled with disinterest from a dwindling and fearful

Jewish population made any brick-and-mortar institution a thing of the past.

But thanks to my grandfather's job as the Redeemer's gardener and custodian, I had attended the church's parochial school. The church was also the home of Father John Davis, a man who had helped shape the paths of hundreds of families over the years, including my own. I'd always known him as Father Jack. To me, he wasn't just a teacher. He was family, something that I'd had in short supply throughout my life.

I shrugged on my blazer and stormed from the hatchway into the brittle morning, making a beeline for the main entrance. Despite the cold and the early hour, several uniformed officers had created a cordon to keep the gawkers and media swarm at bay. EVI registered me with the attendance log, but I flashed my silver SCU badge at one of the officers. The strange, ambient glow it produced shrouded me in an argent nimbus as I passed through the translucent yellow holo-tape ringing the perimeter.

"Captain Mahoney is awaiting you," EVI announced.

She provided me his location as well as a layout of the church, although I didn't need the latter. Heart racing, I crossed the entrance broad steps and through the double doors.

A small command center had been established in the vestibule, but I veered sharply to the right, then moved along a broad pillared aisle past the nave toward a flight of steps leading into the basement. The air down here smelled musty and warm, mingled with the sickly-sweet metallic tang of blood. The sounds of activity above were muted by the dense stone of the church.

Mahoney stood in the hallway conversing with a tall, thin man wearing a heavy winter coat. My heart unclenched at the sight of them.

"Detective," Mahoney said in his gravelly voice. The captain resembled everyone's grandfather everywhere. He was medium height, with close-cropped white hair and deep crow's feet around the eyes. A twin to the badge I carried rode on his breast pocket. I nodded at him, then turned my attention to the other man.

"You okay?" I asked.

Father Jack had a widow's peak at both temples, and salty gray hair. His brown eyes, normally brimming with good-natured humor, were wide and apprehensive.

"No," he replied. "But I am better than poor Gus in there. He—"

"You should go upstairs," I interrupted gently. "I'll be along in a bit."

I wanted to reach out, provide some sign that everything would be all right. But I couldn't. Not in front of the captain. Not while I was on the job.

The old pastor was about to protest, then thought better of it, and excused himself. I watched him go, crushing my roiling emotions in favor of the need to be dispassionate and professional.

"What do we have?" I asked.

"The room's clean," Mahoney began. "Dispatch contacted me after Father Davis made the nine-one-one. The description was, well, you'll see for yourself. I've appropriated it, Tom. I knew you'd want to be here."

Mahoney's voice faded as I moved past him to study the room beyond.

I hadn't noticed the Insight's presence until now. The magic seethed around my eyes, its effect tingeing everything I saw with its silver haze. I'd been told the fickle clairvoyance was a living magic of an ancient order, but I still had no idea where it came from. It also represented a destiny I refused to accept. Because I kept telling myself that I lived in the real world, and not some fairytale where the concepts of good and evil were living, tangible things.

Then I joined SCU, uncovered an ancient magical conspiracy orchestrated by a mysterious woman named Orpheus, and destroyed a shadow parasite with consecrated bullets that had never been consecrated. I tried not to dwell on that, or Besim, the individual who had clued me in on my unwanted destiny in the first place.

Grinding my teeth, I focused on the present. My vision responded to the Insight's magic, sharpening with intensity. Everything around me had slowed to a crawl. Dust motes clung to the air, suspended between time. I saw the current of heated air propelled through the vent high on the far wall opposite me, undulating in rhythmic waves. I knew the thread count on the old sheets of the twin bed just by glancing at them.

The room was simple—bed, footlocker, closet, virtual workstation, chair. One thin window ran horizontally along the upper wall, barred and secured from the outside. Nothing adorned the walls, other than an eggshell coat that had been applied within the past six months.

"Jesus Christ," I swore quietly.

The body slumped in the chair, arms and legs splayed wide. Blood stained the floor, covering the walls, the ceiling, the workstation, behind the open door and the bed. I couldn't get too close without stepping in any of it, although my preternatural senses were already swimming in the stuff.

"Stentstrom's arrived," Mahoney announced, breaking me from my trance.

"Good," I said absently. My eyes shifted from the corpse back to the desk.

The workstation was active. A darkened holo-window floated dormant above it. An open book lay atop the desk, but no holo-picture frames or other personal items.

I needed to get in there.

"Who's our vic?" I asked.

"Gustavo Sanarov," the captain replied. The name meant nothing to me, but something in the captain's voice drew my attention. "He was the soup kitchen super for the church. Father

Davis said he'd only been staying with them until he could get back on his feet."

I nodded, and as I did so, the Insight evacuated from me in a rush. I staggered against the doorframe. Bill stepped forward, but I waved him away. He watched me with wintry eyes. I was about to ask him a question when a sing-song voice greeted me.

"Ah, Detective Holliday!" gushed Doctor Gilbert Stentstrom, chief medical examiner for Empire City.

The skinny little man was covered head to foot in a bulky white overcoat, gloves and matching *ushanka* with the earflaps down. He carried a steel briefcase. A sticker was affixed at an angle on one side displaying a symbol of two poodle heads back-to-back, one black and the other white, with the tagline "Loud and proud member of the PC of EC".

Stentstrom was the only other person inside ECPD that knew the specifics about Special Crimes. I'd known him years before when I was a cadet at the academy. He was one of the good guys, brilliant with just the right dose of crazy.

I filled him in on what little I knew. His bulbous eyes widened with interest.

"Good," the medical examiner enthused. "With all the garden-variety murders that have come through my office lately, it will be refreshing to work on something with meat on the bone! No pun intended, of course."

"Um, sure," I remarked, my smile faltering.

"Will Mr. Kole and Doctor Saranda be joining us?" he asked, looking around hopefully.

"No," I exchanged a glance with Mahoney, who raised his eyebrows in silent question. "At least, not for the moment," I added hurriedly. "It'll depend on what we find."

Stentstrom set his briefcase on the floor. He removed his coat, folded it neatly, followed by his hat and gloves. He placed them carefully next to the briefcase. Popping the top, he opened the case. Inside lay plastic clothing, shoe covers and gloves, as well as a variety of forensic tools.

"Please help yourselves," he gestured.

Moments later, Stentstrom and I were bedecked in clear plastic from head to toe. We entered the room, stepping lightly around the blood splatter. Mahoney remained behind, an inscrutable look on his worn face.

The Insight returned, simmering on the edge of my senses, present, yet aloof. I sensed its hesitation, as if held back by apprehension, or fear.

That was a new experience, the Insight afraid of something. Because that didn't bother me at all. Nope, not one bit. Now wasn't the time to analyze the Insight's feelings. Or the fact it might have any.

"EVI, calculate the bloodstain pattern following my POV, and share the results with Detective Holliday and Captain Mahoney," Stentstrom stated, making a slow, wide circuit around the body in the chair.

Three-dimensional graphs and figures appeared in my visual center, revealing angles, points and areas of convergence as well as the area of origin. As the images cycled, EVI included expected trajectories, and projected heights and distances.

"Extraordinary," Stentstrom remarked. He shuffled up beside me with a hop to his step. "Do you see it?"

"It looks like our vic was shot by dozens of small-caliber bullets," I replied slowly as I assimilated the data stream. "But I don't see any stippling or powder burns around the wounds. And the angles are all wrong. No shell casings, and no bullet holes or scoring in the wall or ceiling."

"What do you think it means?" Stentstrom asked, his voice quivering with barely suppressed excitement.

"He wasn't shot," I answered, feeling like a trainee back at the Academy attending my first forensic science class. "At least, not in the traditional sense. So, what killed him?"

"An excellent question. Look closer at the blood stains. Notice the lengths, and the direction of travel. Do you see anything now?"

I turned toward the wall near the door to study the stains. The Insight continued to roil behind its self-imposed exile.

"I don't get it," I frowned. "This is all wrong."

"Indeed, Detective Holliday." Stentstrom came up next to me and pointed at several splotches with his plastic finger. "Here, and here. Note how these stains are inverted because of the force which caused them. Now, look at the body. Tell me what you see."

I moved toward the chair to study the corpse.

Sanarov had been in his late sixties or early seventies, judging from his sallow skin, gray hair and liver spots on his hands, neck and head. He was tall, an inch or two over six feet, and his body was muscular despite his age. I caught an old, faded tattoo on the upper bicep of his left arm around the short sleeve. It was a spider web, with the spider climbing out. Three small bell tattoos were arrayed on the back of his left hand, starting at the pinkie finger, one along each consecutive knuckle. However, his body was covered in thumbnail-size wounds. Even his clothes had holes in them, as if he'd been perforated by a high-powered nail gun. As I looked more closely, I realized the fleshy wounds resembled boils that had burst outward, rather than skin that had been punctured or cut.

"He exploded," I said.

The Insight eased into me as if inhaling, like a cup filling with water. My senses swelled, and I was drawn to the open book on the desk. Even at this distance, I recognized the unmistakable structure and style of the Bible. I couldn't see which passage, but the pages were marked with crib notes and other scribblings. When my eyes raked across the desk, the holo-screen flickered. Instinctively, I waved my hand at the screen, expecting nothing since I stood beyond its standard activation radius, and didn't have Sanarov's password to reactivate it.

The screen flared to life. One line of text appeared in big, bold letters. I focused on the text.

"Why do the righteous suffer?" I recited. As I uttered the words, the holo-screen shimmered, and the verse changed. *"He repays everyone for what they have done. He brings on them what their conduct deserves."*

I became dimly aware of Mahoney behind me in the doorway. I smelled his body wash and sharp cologne, and beneath that, stark and painful memories of his past coming back to roost. The Insight gave them life and depth, and a distinct bouquet of frustration and loss. Mahoney knew something about the victim. Their paths had intersected at some point.

"Detective?" Stentstrom asked, his voice quivering. "What is happening?"

Before I could answer, the words faded to be replaced by a new passage.

"And no creature is hidden from His sight," I continued. *"But all are naked and exposed to the eyes of Him to whom we must give account."*

"How are you doing this?" the medical examiner whispered.

I shook my head and said, "I don't know."

More text appeared. My heartbeat accelerated.

"For your sins will always find you," I read, my eyes captured by the words scrolling across the holo-screen. My breathing quickened. Sweat gathered on my brow. *"Your sins will never forget you. Your sins can never forgive you."*

The screen went dark.

With the last vestiges of the magic dissipating, I turned to Mahoney, only to face a youthful version of the man wearing a fresh-pressed suit and tie. He stood in a dank, dark room that was not the church basement, but somewhere else. The stench of blood and gore filled my nostrils. A small body lay at Young Mahoney's feet. Whoever this had been, the head and face had been crushed by a tremendous force. The face was a pulpy mess.

Suddenly, an unbridled hatred and despair permeated the

room in which I stood, and I nearly choked on its intensity. I tried clearing my throat several times hoping to wash the feeling away without success.

The Insight vanished, enervating me further. My breathing grew shallow. Sweat ran down my face in cold rivulets. The image of the captain and that room dissolved, and with it, the raw emotion I'd just experienced. Something very bad had happened both here, and in that place from Mahoney's past.

But of one thing I was certain: Gustavo Sanarov had been killed in an unnatural manner. Not by a gunshot or stab wound, but by something far more profound, primal, and sinister.

I also realized whoever or whatever had done this didn't just want Sanarov dead. They had wanted him to suffer until the very end

ABOUT THE AUTHOR

A native son of Massachusetts, Peter has been living in the Deep South for over 25 years. By day, he's an insurance professional, saving the world one policy at a time. But at night, well, no one really wants to see him fighting crime in his Spider-Man onesie. Instead, Peter develops new worlds of adventure, influenced by his love of science fiction, mysteries, music and fantasy. Whether it's running role-playing games for his long-time friends, watching his beloved New England sporting teams, or just chilling with a movie, his wife, two boys, three cats and a puppy, Peter's imagination is always on the move. It's the reason why his stories are an eclectic blend of intrigue, excitement, humor and magic, all drawn from four decade's worth of television, film, novels, and comic books. You can learn more about Peter and his writing projects at peterhartog.com, or send him a tweet @althazyr.

twitter.com/althazyr
instagram.com/althazyr
goodreads.com/peter_hartog

Made in United States
North Haven, CT
31 October 2022

26156630R00245